THE NO KISS CONTRACT

What Reviewers Say About
Nan Campbell's Work

The Rules of Forever

"This is one of those books where silence fills the air when you put it down because your brain is saturated with the characters' voices while reading. I loved it. Beautifully written with tons of interesting tidbits about art, literature, New York, and life. The characters were so well developed and I loved following both of their journeys. The tension that typically comes wasn't overly dramatic though it was gut-wrenching. I was totally rooting for these too and would be so happy to have just kept on reading about them."—*Queer Media Review*

"I needed this book. I won't say I have been in a slump, but it's been a while since I really liked and related to the main characters. Nan Campbell's debut book gives us two complex, well developed women. In a terrific balance of romantic chemistry, angst, and humor. I can't wait to read whatever she writes next."—*Odd Girls Media*

"I bought into *The Rules of Forever* hook, line and sinker. This is mainly because the characters are so likable. …Besides well-developed characters, Campbell uses sound literary devices that give readers a romance they can count on but not find overly predictable. She charms readers with her delightful dialogue, entertaining subplots and engaging secondary characters. In addition to that, her use of conflict and sexual tension is masterfully done. Readers quickly become engrossed as well as captivated. The romance flourishes because of it."—*Women Using Words*

"This was such a fun story to read. Aside from the whole second chance arc, there's also the rich girl / poor girl storyline and while you think you know where the narrative is heading you'll be in for an interesting ride that seriously keeps the pages turning. …This is an amazing debut for new author Nan Campbell and I can't wait to read her next."—*Bookista*

By the Author

The Rules of Forever

The No Kiss Contract

THE NO KISS CONTRACT

by

Nan Campbell

2023

THE NO KISS CONTRACT

ISBN 13: 978-1-63679-372-6

THIS TRADE PAPERBACK ORIGINAL IS PUBLISHED BY
BOLD STROKES BOOKS, INC.
P.O. BOX 249
VALLEY FALLS, NY 12185

FIRST EDITION: APRIL 2023

CREDITS
EDITORS: JENNY HARMON AND CINDY CRESAP
PRODUCTION DESIGN: SUSAN RAMUNDO
COVER DESIGN BY TAMMY SEIDICK

Acknowledgments

My childhood could almost be called idyllic. I had a mom and dad and three sisters. Our suburban New Jersey life had the usual ups and downs, but I never knew how good I had it until much later. My family surrounded me with love, respect, and support. I was blessed in an untold number of ways.

So when I began writing, years ago, my topic of choice was a bit of a head-scratcher. Instead of writing from my experience, I was drawn to telling stories of fractured families. Deceased parents, decaying marriages, and clashing stepchildren became the conflict-rich fodder for the stories I liked to tell. It was satisfying to give my characters some hard-won happiness in new, found families. *The No Kiss Contract* is a holdover from my early writing days, where a family doesn't necessarily adhere to a typical nuclear configuration and requires only large amounts of love to fuse it together.

Thank you to everyone at Bold Strokes Books—Rad and Sandy for keeping the BSB machine well oiled and singing. Thanks to Cindy, Ruth, Toni, and everyone who helps me get my book in front of readers. Thank you to Jenny, who has made editing my favorite part of the publishing process. Thanks to my beta readers, Michele, Cade, and Rita—it would've been a very different book without your helpful input.

My family deserves all of my gratitude. Not only for providing the template of what familial love looks like, but also for the unfettered support they have shown the last few years over this new endeavor I've undertaken. They are my biggest fans—and I couldn't ask for better!

My wife, June, knew my writing before she knew me. She was one of my very early readers and continues to encourage me in all that I do. I couldn't do this without her.

Finally, to the readers who reached out with a review, a social media post or comment, an email, or in person to tell me what they thought about my first book. I'm honored and gratified that you decided to take the journey with my characters. That you chose to share your opinion with me about my work is even more meaningful, and I thank you most sincerely.

Dedication

To June
For sending that first feedback email

PROLOGUE

Summer 2007

Davy Dugan snuck into the living room and opened the cabinet where Anna's mom kept the liquor. Weeks ago, she had spotted a dusty bottle of peach schnapps she'd bet wouldn't be missed and today was their last chance to drink it. She had just shoved it in her backpack when she heard Anna behind her.

"What's taking you so long? Let's get out of here." Anna stood there, glorious in her summer uniform of black Docs, a sleeveless, paint-spattered T-shirt, and faded denim cut-off shorts. "It's your last day. We can't spend it sitting around here." The smile she directed at Davy was like warm sunshine, and Davy soaked it up like she was seriously Vitamin D deprived.

Davy took a look around the comfy room where she had spent a lot of time with Anna these last few months, the remains of late-night popcorn and Netflix DVD sleeves scattered on the coffee table. She couldn't believe summer was just about over. When her father picked her up at boarding school in June and informed her she would be spending the summer with his new girlfriend and her daughter, Davy never thought she would be sorry to leave at the end of August. But she was. And sorry this was the last time she would be following Anna out into another hot and humid New Jersey day.

Anna flicked her tied-back blond hair and shouldered her art bag before she and Davy trooped through the kitchen. "Bye, Mom. We'll be gone all day."

"Bye, Dad," Davy said to her father. The two of them sat at the fully set breakfast table, but neither was eating. The look on her dad's face caused Davy's hackles to rise. Something weird was going on.

"Wait," Anna's mom, Pam, said. Anna stopped mid-stride, and Davy bumped into her. "Where are you going?"

"I told you we were leaving first thing for the set strike."

"Right." Pam seemed distracted. "Have a seat, girls. We want to tell you something."

Anna resisted. "We gotta go, Mom. Can it wait?"

Davy's dad put his Blackberry down. "No, it can't wait. Sit."

She immediately planted her ass in the chair across from him and Pam. His dealing-with-Davy expression, the downturned eyebrows and mouth, as if he smelled something gross like heated up old tuna fish or something, now seemed to extend to Anna too. Davy was very familiar with it, although she'd seen it a lot less this summer since he'd been with Pam. But he was still bossy and brusque with Davy. And now his eyes twitched with irritation, which Pam allayed with a quick touch on his arm.

"Please, Anna." Pam patted the chair next to her. "It's important, and it will only take a moment."

Davy darted a look and saw Anna's aggrieved look at Davy's quick capitulation, but Davy knew her dad. The sooner they heard their respective 'rents out, the sooner they could be on their way.

Anna's blue eyes flashed as she plopped into the chair. "Okay. What is it?"

Pam took a big breath and gripped his hand. Now that Davy was paying attention, Pam didn't look too good—pale and sweaty and maybe about to blow her breakfast.

But her smile grew wider as she looked into his eyes and said, "We're pregnant."

"We are?" Davy blurted.

"Don't be impertinent." Her dad frowned at her.

"I mean, *you* are?" *What the fuck?* This was the absolute last thing Davy expected. Her dad wanted to be a dad again? She had no idea how to react right now. Davy shot another look at Anna, who looked wholly confused.

"You're what?" Anna's entire face was scrunched up in incomprehension.

"Gregory and I are going to have a baby." Pam sort of looked pleased, dazed, and overwhelmed all at once. "It's very early days, but we wanted you girls to know right away."

Anna still appeared to be struggling to understand. "Aren't you too old to have a baby?"

"Apparently not," Davy's dad said, pinning her with a glare. He didn't even bother to look Davy's way to gauge how she felt about it.

"Thirty-eight isn't that old, Anna." Pam laughed.

"Are you going to get married?" Davy asked her father. She thought it was a pertinent question.

Pam glanced at him. "We haven't really disc—"

"Not right away," he interrupted. "But eventually, yes. Give me a chance to propose, girls." He smiled, but it looked more like a pit bull baring its teeth. "We'll also find a bigger, better house." He surveyed the slightly rundown kitchen with its aging appliances.

He turned back to Pam and gazed at her in a way that Davy didn't recognize, a way that was prideful and possessive and a little bit creepy. "We'll be a family, and I expect you both to assist Pam and your new sibling in whatever ways they require." The conversation, as far as he was concerned, was over, and he reached across the table for his copy of the *Wall Street Journal*.

Davy was used to her dad laying down his pronouncements like he was managing subordinates. He had been doing it since her mother died when she was three. And now he wanted to start doing it to another kid? What the fuck was he even smoking?

Pam looked as if she wanted to say more, and reached out to Anna, but Anna pushed her chair back from the table.

"Can we go now? Announcement is over?"

Pam tilted her head and silently gazed into Anna's eyes. Anna responded with a short, seemingly irritated nod. Their nonverbal communication wasn't easily translatable, but if Davy had to guess, Pam had just promised to answer Anna's unasked questions. Both seemed to know that now was not the time for it.

"Where did you say you were going?"

"Striking the set," Anna said through gritted teeth. "It's what we always do the day after the last performance."

Pam took a twenty from her purse. "Here. So you can contribute to the pizza. Have fun, girls."

Anna plucked the bill from her hand and gave her a quick, one-armed hug. "Thanks, Mom. Sorry I called you old. See you later."

"Davina." They had almost made good their escape when his voice forced her to turn around. He took his time lowering his newspaper and skewered her with his eyes. "I trust you will be packed and ready by seven tomorrow morning and not a minute later."

"Yes, Dad." Davy stood stock-still and waited until his attention returned to his newspaper, but Pam was out of her chair and across the room before the paper rose to his eye level.

"Your last day with us, Davy. I can't believe the summer has gone so fast." Pam wrapped Davy in an affectionate hug. "We're really going to miss you around here, but it won't be long until you're back for the holidays, right? I'll be showing by then."

"Right," Davy mumbled into Pam's shoulder. She did not want to think about Pam and her dad procreating for another goddamn second.

An impatient groan from Anna. "Mom, you can hug her later. We have to *go*."

"Bye, Pam," Davy said before following Anna out the front door toward freedom. They cut across the front lawn and avoided the sprinklers in the neighbor's yard. It was already hot but the leafy canopy provided by the oak trees that lined Anna's street offered a bit of relief. By some unspoken agreement, neither of them brought up their parents' announcement.

"What does *striking the set* mean?" Davy asked, walking beside Anna as she shortcutted and trespassed her way to the main road. They walked on the sidewalk-less strip next to the street and tried not to be in the way of sporadic Sunday morning traffic.

Anna seemed to shake off her gray mood as she slung an arm around Davy's shoulder even though she was a few inches shorter. Davy stooped a little as she walked to make it easier for her.

"Your first season as a stage crew member in the Southfield Summer Community Theater is almost at an end, Day. We have only one more task before *Cats* is officially closed."

Davy tried to ignore the blaze of pleasure the nickname gave her. Nobody but Anna had ever called her Day. "Do we dismantle the set and throw it into a huge pile and set it on fire?"

"Yes to the first part, no to the second, pyro." Anna removed her arm and bumped Davy with her hip.

They crossed into the J&B Market parking lot. Outside the market was a community bulletin board. SSCT's poster for *Cats* had disappeared yet again.

Anna heaved a dramatic sigh when she saw it. "Hang on." From her bag she took three rolled up posters and a staple gun. She attached all three to the board with about fifty staples each. "Let's see them take those down."

Davy watched her. "Why? Last night was closing night."

Anna turned to her, her expression sheepish. "Oh, yeah." She gazed at all the staples she had just wasted. "Doesn't matter. I don't want to give those poster-rippers the satisfaction."

The posters were of Anna's design and were totally clever and cute. But Davy snorted at the musical's tagline. "*Cats: Now and Forever*? More like *now and for five performances only*."

"Yeah. I'm always a little sad when it's over." Anna tilted her head and surveyed her handiwork.

"Maybe they'd attract a bigger crowd if they called it *Pussies*." Davy made her voice like a commercial announcer. "*Pussies*: Meow and Furrr-ever."

"Ha. That's funny. Hey, I have to make a stop." She headed for the market entrance. "It'll only take a minute."

Davy followed Anna inside. The market was small and rundown, but she appreciated the blast of refrigerated air nonetheless. Anna made a beeline for the small case of prearranged flowers wrapped in cellophane bunches next to the shelves of produce. They all looked a little past their prime to Davy, but Anna confidently chose a bouquet that was mostly yellow and pink carnations with a few already half-opened red roses thrown in.

"Oh, no, Anna, you're not."

"I am." Anna's jaw was set, but her voice wavered while she inspected the blooms and avoided her gaze. "Sure, she got tons of flowers last night, but will she get any the day *after* closing night? If I'm the last one to give her flowers for this show, I'm the one who gets remembered."

Davy had already heard every possible angle in the flowers vs. no flowers for Winnie Bowerchuck debate in the lead up to closing night. "If you say so. I'm going to get some orange juice."

It was pointless to argue. Winnie Bowerchuck did not deserve flowers from Anna. Or anyone, really, in Davy's admittedly meaningless opinion. Her Grizabella was a lifeless lump with a thin and reedy belt. She could concede that Winnie was conventionally pretty with her curvy figure and dark curly hair, but Davy thought Anna was a knockout, and her carefree, blond-haired, blue-eyed boho look was heaps more attractive. And Winnie was only about three years older than Anna and Davy, but she acted like they were peons privileged to witness her onstage brilliance. If she was so great, why was she performing in suburban community theater?

But Davy didn't say any of this to Anna, who had gazed at Winnie with heart eyes all summer. She had come out to Davy and disclosed her feelings for Winnie, and Davy, the supportive new friend, had been the unfortunate recipient of every excruciating thought and feeling Anna experienced about her first same-sex crush.

Davy had only known Anna since June, but already felt closer to her in the brief time she'd known her than to her boarding school friends. With Anna, she felt seen and understood, not to mention that clenchy feeling in her chest when Anna directed her attention solely on her. For the first time in her life, Davy was experiencing the wild and uncontainable feelings of her budding attraction to another person, even if she didn't have the guts to tell Anna about it. If only Anna hadn't arrived in her life with all the extra baggage of being the daughter of the woman her father was now having a child with. So fucking inconvenient.

The fact was, Davy cared too much about Anna to destroy her dreamy fantasy of kissing the leading lady and riding off into the sunset with her. Even though it was hard, she would keep her mouth shut.

❖

"Careful, this one's heavy."

They were all heavy. Davy accepted the barrel light from Toby, the lighting designer, and laid it gently on the platform. She had volunteered to help dismantle the rented stage lights because she thought it might be fun to be up on the scissor lift. And it was. It was kind of godlike to be suspended forty feet in the air and observe everyone else participating in the strike with varying levels of enthusiasm. Industrious stage crew types, like Anna, got shit done while cast members arrived late, sat around eating snacks and shooting the breeze, and then flitted from one task to another without really helping at all.

And she noticed everyone, both cast and crew, took a moment to tag the upstage wall, pausing with a Sharpie or some paint to commemorate their involvement in this summer's production. This wall was always camouflaged with curtains and scenery during a show, so it didn't matter that it was covered in years of graffiti, a monument to a small New Jersey town's dedication to live theater.

She watched Anna take a quick photo of the scrim before they brought the ladders out to remove it. The scrim was a heavy canvas curtain that spanned the length and width of the stage, onto which Anna had singlehandedly painted the urban night sky, a melding of deep purples, blues and black with a few dim stars and a bright yellow harvest moon right in the middle. Anna had worked long and hard on it. Davy had tried to help, but she hadn't an artistic bone in her body, and Anna had found easier tasks for her to do.

The auditorium door slammed open, drawing everyone's attention. Of course, it was Winnie fucking Bowerchuck making her fashionably late entrance. Just the sight of her made Davy's skin heat in annoyance. Winnie ignored the stage crew peasants and made the rounds of her castmates, spending a few moments chatting with everyone before she settled in the fourth row for a natter with the actors who played Skimbleshanks and Jennyanydots.

Anna approached with her sad bouquet and waited until Skimble-shanks nudged Winnie and gestured at Anna. Winnie stood and got right into Anna's space, her giant knockers thrust toward Anna's chin. Davy crossed her arms over her own concave chest as she sourly watched the pair chat for a moment. Winnie bent to whisper something in Anna's ear and Davy could swear she saw Anna's face turn red even from this height. Then Winnie kissed Anna's forehead in a move that was indulgent, condescending, and dismissive all at the same time.

"Davy, are you going to take this, or what?" Toby asked, his frustration clear.

"Yeah, sorry." She reached for the light. By the time she was free to watch again, she saw Winnie toss the flowers to Jennyanydots, saying something that made them all laugh loudly. Anna's back was turned and she paused as she mounted the steps to the stage, but she didn't turn around. It was obvious that many others besides Davy had observed the exchange, and Davy's heart ached for Anna.

❖

Late in the afternoon, most of the cast and crew were leaving or had left, but Anna didn't seem to be in a hurry to go. Davy stepped to the edge of the stage and watched Anna, quiet and morose, as she pushed a broom over its hardwood boards.

Davy fetched the dustpan and placed it near the pile of debris Anna had accumulated, holding it steady while Anna brushed the pile toward it. Davy broke the silence with the completely inane, "You okay?" She moved the pan backward so Anna could brush the remaining dirt into it.

"No, I'm not okay. I am experiencing a deep, abiding hatred for this line of dust that will not go into the dustpan."

Davy drew the dustpan back and smeared the little bit left with her shoe. "What line of dust?" She caught Anna's eye and grinned at her, but Anna didn't smile back. "Give me that." She reached for the broom. "I'll put these away."

"Okay. I just have to close up the prop room. Be right back."

On Davy's way back from the janitor's closet, someone hit the house lights and the auditorium was plunged into artificial twilight, the ghost light at center stage their only source to see by. Coming back down the left aisle, Davy spied Anna's flowers from earlier, right there on the floor in the fourth row, where Jennyanydots had probably dropped them. She retrieved her backpack and Anna's stuff and detoured to kick the flowers farther away so Anna wouldn't see them.

Davy sat on the lip of the stage and took from her bag two plastic cups, a bottle of warm orange juice, and the illicit peach schnapps. Someone from school had raved about fuzzy navels, and Davy had filed away the recipe for just such an occasion as this. She poured out two cocktails and smiled at Anna as she joined her.

"Nice. You came prepared," Anna said.

"I knew we'd be thirsty." She handed Anna her cup.

Anna spied the bottle. "Wise choice. My mother will never know it's gone. She used it in a punch recipe once years ago and promptly forgot about it."

"I figured. It had a neglected look about it."

She took a sip and grimaced. "Hoo. Warm and sweet. Just the way I like it."

"Here's to *Cats*. My introduction to the world of stagecraft."

"Seems appropriate to start—"

"And end..."

"—your career with one of the classics of eighties musical theater." Anna downed her drink and peered at Davy. "Seriously? It's over already? What about next summer?"

Davy chugged instead of answering. She picked up the bottle. "Another?"

Anna held up her empty cup and sang, "Look, a new drink will begin." She grinned and waited for a reaction.

"No. Stop. Show's over and so are your lyrical references." Davy poured out two more and thought about Anna's previous question. She had been kidding, but musical theater was Anna's thing, not hers. She only did it this summer because she had nothing better to do and she liked hanging out with Anna. "I guess if I'm around next summer it wouldn't be awful to spend more time backstage with you."

"If you're around?" Anna frowned. "Where will you be?"

"I don't know." Their parents' little announcement notwithstanding, who knew what the year would bring? She had enjoyed living in the Resnicks' home this summer. Maybe a little too much. Pam was sweet, and a great cook, and she really liked Anna. Definitely a little too much. It felt safest to hedge. "We're graduating next year. Not sure if I'll have time for this next summer."

"You don't have to let me down easy. It's okay if you have big plans for next year. I know you have it all figured out."

"I don't have it all figured out."

"Sure. UPenn business degree, then Harvard Law, just like dear old dad."

That was the plan. They were his alma maters. He told her when he dropped her off at boarding school in seventh grade that those were the degrees and schools he was willing to pay for, so she'd better get accepted to both. "I've been working my ass off. I have to get in."

"I don't get it, though," Anna said. "Why do you want to be like him so bad?"

"I don't want that. I'm not anything like him."

"Except you'll have the same degrees and the same job. Do you even want to be a lawyer?"

Davy didn't know. She'd never been a lawyer so how could she know if she would be good at it or even like it? She would do it for her father. Yes, he was cold, and mean sometimes, and she'd seen him more this summer than the last several years put together, but he was the only family she had, and she wanted to make him proud. "Yeah, I do," was all she said to Anna. "What about you? Don't you want to pursue your art?"

Anna shrugged. "I guess."

"You're good, Anna. If I were you, I'd be going to art school."

"Ah, I learned most of it from books at the library."

Davy shook her head in wonder. "Un-fucking-believable. You have more talent in your left ass cheek than I do in my entire body, and you get your technique for free at the library. Jesus titty-fucking Christ."

Anna laughed. "The mouth on you. I'm going to miss you and your way with words."

Davy was going to miss Anna too, but she didn't say it. Some of her more unseemly feelings might sneak out at the same time. She drank her overly sweet cocktail. "I'm sorry about Winnie. If that bitch had another brain, it'd be lonely." And she couldn't act. Or sing.

Anna's lingering smile disappeared. "Thanks. And thanks for listening to me go and on about her all summer. I don't know what I would've done without you. You're really easy to talk to about…things."

Davy felt her cheeks get warm. It was probably the schnapps. Should she come out to Anna now? Here they were, all alone, having a quiet chat. It seemed like the perfect moment. She'd wanted to tell her, but how could she yank the spotlight onto herself when Anna still needed her support? She didn't want to be selfish.

"I'm giving up on her. Cutting her loose. Throwing her back in the sea."

"Oh. Okay. She doesn't deserve you anyway." That was good, but how could she tell Anna now? It would look like she was trying to scoop up Anna for herself. *But you kind of are.* This was impossible.

"I guess I thought since I finally accepted who I am—"

"And had the guts to tell me about it." *Unlike me.*

Anna nodded. "That too. I thought I should take it out for a spin. My, um…inclination, you know? I thought I might at least get to kiss a girl this summer. See if it gave me the feels. And I chose Winnie because, well, she's hot, first of all, and I know she's been with girls and guys—"

"It's no reflection on you that she's too much of a fucking idiot to see how great you are, Anna! And you're super-hot too! Hotter than her, anyway." *Cool it, you dope.* "Let's have another drink." Davy sloshed more schnapps into their cups.

"Look at you, leaping to my defense." Anna looked pleased and surprised. "You'll be a great lawyer."

"Thanks." Davy gulped at her drink and gazed ahead at the shadowy sea of empty seats. She exhaled slowly, trying to get her heart to slow. If Anna wanted to kiss a girl this summer, Davy would enthusiastically volunteer. But she knew Anna didn't see her that way. Friend zone: population Davy.

A silence opened up between them. She could feel Anna's gaze upon her, but she refused to meet her eyes.

Anna put her drink down and spread her hands wide behind her on the stage floor. "A baby," she said.

Davy tossed a look at her, but Anna's face was in shadow. It was hard to tell how Anna felt about it from those two uninflected words. "Yeah. Weird."

"We'll be eighteen by the time she's born."

"She?"

"I have a feeling. And I guess it'll mean we're related."

"No, it fucking won't." That really felt weird. And wrong, when Davy thought about the belly full of lit M-80s that started to go off whenever Anna's eyes held her own. That wasn't a we're-going-to-be-stepsisters-when-our-folks-get-married kind of feeling. "We'll share a half-sibling. That does *not* make us related."

"All right, simmer down. You don't want to be related to me. I get it. I'm not even offended by your violent denial."

"Fuck, Anna. That's not what—"

"You say the word *fuck* a lot."

Davy paused to consider where this was coming from. Anna had never judged Davy's method of expressing herself before. She had been reprimanded from time to time at school for cursing, so she knew how to control it, but with Anna she felt comfortable enough to express herself freely.

Anna didn't look offended, more curious about how Davy would respond. Maybe Anna didn't want to talk about their impending familial bond any more than Davy did and was merely changing the subject. "You're just noticing? We've known each other three fucking months."

Anna grinned and seemed relieved that Davy had picked up her conversational ball and run with it. "I don't think lawyers swear. They use big, sexy words like"—Anna's voice went all breathy—"*allegation* and *continuance* and *habeas corpus.*"

"Ooh, Latin. So hot." Davy laughed even though Anna's sexy voice had those M-80s in her belly popping off one after the other. She dropped her voice an octave and said, "Hey baby, I'm in love with your *prima facie*. You wanna *ipso facto* with me? I'm *in loco* for your *parentis.*"

Anna wheezed with laughter. "Did you just say you're crazy for my mom?"

"Shit, did I? That's not what I meant." She knew that wasn't what the phrase meant, but she didn't want to correct Anna.

Who was still chuckling. "Words matter, especially if you want to be a lawyer." Anna banged her fist on the stage like it was a gavel. "I hereby order you to remove *fuck* from your vocabulary."

"Well, your honor, I'm not a lawyer yet. And I submit that *fuck* is like the Swiss army knife of words. It has a million uses. Also, I don't think I'm hurting anybody by using the occasional offensive word. It's a victimless crime." She drained her drink. "May it please the court."

Anna twisted her lips like she was trying not to smile. She set her cup down on the stage. "Did you sign the wall?"

"No, did you?"

"Not yet." She reached for her bag. "Come on, let's find a spot."

Davy followed Anna as she slowly inspected the back wall, looking for a space to put her name. It was obvious that there wasn't an inch of space at eye level, and although there were some open areas near the floor, Davy didn't think Anna would want to commemorate her name down there. She had an idea.

The scissor lift beeped when Davy turned it on. After watching Toby operate it all day, she knew exactly what to do, and slowly positioned it so it was parallel to the backstage wall. "Hop in."

Anna scrambled up into the basket with a fistful of magic markers and Davy raised them up about ten feet where there was free wall space.

"Higher," Anna said, and Davy brought them up another five feet or so. There was no graffiti up here, and it was also pretty dark. Anna surveyed the concrete expanse like it was a blank canvas. Then she uncapped her thickest black marker and got to work.

Davy lowered herself onto the floor of the platform and watched. Anna drew a foreshortened cartoon mini-replica of the Southfield Community Playhouse stage with billowing side curtains and shiny footlights that pointed at stylized writing which said *A & Day: Now and Forever*.

Anna stepped back as far as the narrow platform would allow to consider her work, and Davy groaned at the wording. "Really? Now and forever? You're consigning me to live in your memory alongside this craptastic musical?"

"Yeah, in my *memory*." Anna sang the last word and laughed. "But seriously, it's where we were established. It makes sense."

Did it? What exactly had been established, Davy wondered. Their friendship? Their complicated and tenuous family relationship? Their knowledge of each other as people living on planet Earth? Should she make the move that would establish them as more than friends? Davy's heart thumped so loudly she feared Anna would hear it.

Anna sank down and leaned against the safety bars of the basket, her shoulder pressed against Davy's. Had Anna done that on purpose? Should Davy make a move? For fuck's sake, they were confined in this tiny space high above the stage, enshrouded in shadows, all alone, with a sugary buzz coursing through their veins. It seemed like a moment with a capital M.

They both sat and gazed at the graffito.

"Not to be dumb, or maybe I am, but what have we established?" Davy turned. Anna's profile was knife sharp against the faint ghost light below, but she couldn't decipher any meaning from Anna's veiled expression.

"Well…" Anna carefully shifted next to her, the scissor lift quaking as her hips pivoted and one knee butted against Davy's thigh. And Davy suddenly didn't want to know what Anna was going to say. Not until she knew the answer to an entirely different kind of question.

She slowly closed the distance between them, ready to pull back at a word, a look, a gesture from Anna, but Anna's eyes were wide with comprehension of what Davy was about to do. Then her eyelids fluttered closed and the shape of her mouth changed, her lips looking soft and ready. Davy's last coherent thought was to accept this as permission before she tilted her head slightly and pressed her lips against Anna's.

And Anna's lips were as soft as they looked—softer. And warm. Blood rushed to Davy's ears of all places, and it sounded like waves pounding on a beach as she absorbed new information from being this close to Anna: the heat of her sweet orange breath, the faint scent of shampoo overlaid with sweat and dust from the day's labor, the featherlight touch of her fingers on Davy's forearm, the little hairs there standing upright at the completion of their electric circuit.

Davy broke it off sooner than she wanted because it felt like she hadn't taken a breath in approximately a year, and she dragged air audibly and embarrassingly through her nose. But then Anna gripped her shoulder and drew Davy close again, and her heart swooped down into an unknown place. When she felt Anna's tongue push tentatively against her lower lip, she gasped, and touched it with her own. Anna made a noise in her throat that Davy instinctively knew was positive. Eventually, minutes or hours later, when Davy finally found the lever that returned them to terra firma, she felt some ownership over Anna's dazed smile, just visible at the edge of the locus of light created by the bare bulb on the stage.

❖

"Do you have to leave tomorrow?" Anna asked, kicking a stone down the road as they walked home.

"Yeah, school starts the day after." Davy felt exposed as they walked beneath the fluorescent pool of the streetlight. Once they had passed through it and into the darkness, she wondered if it would be weird if she pulled Anna close and licked her neck. It was all she could think about right now.

"Southfield doesn't start until Thursday. Where's your school? Is it far away?"

"Not that far. An hour? It's still in New Jersey, just out toward Pennsylvania."

"What's it called? Do they allow visitors?"

"Perry Bidwell School for Girls. And believe me, you don't want to come visit. It's a pus-filled zit on the hairy ass of fucking nowhere."

"Sounds charming."

"It's not that bad, really. I like it. There just wouldn't be much to do if you came."

"You want to come back and visit me then? How about this weekend?" Anna grasped her hand and swung it in a way that Davy guessed was supposed to show that she was joking. "You could come back for Halloween. My school usually has a dance that weekend. Or maybe Thanksgiving?"

Davy looked down at their entwined fingers and gripped them harder. Why had she waited until their last night to kiss her? She stopped walking and faced Anna. "I know I'll be back at Christmas. I go to my grandparents in Palm Beach for Thanksgiving every year. My mom's parents. It's the only time I see them."

"Oh." Anna's disappointment came through clearly in that one syllable, and Davy was secretly pleased by it.

"I'll try to visit before. I'll ask my dad."

Anna nodded.

This had to be an advantage to her father's pronouncement that they were to become a family. Families didn't go four months without seeing each other, did they? But she and her dad often went that long, and longer, without contact. The truth was she didn't really know how families operated. She and her father didn't count as one.

All Davy knew was that she couldn't wait four months to see Anna again. "And we'll keep in touch. We'll text and email and call. It'll be like I never left." She gave Anna a reassuring smile. They fit together—tight and seamless—and nothing was going to break them apart.

CHAPTER ONE

Fifteen Years Later

"Your father is on the line."

Davy raised her head from the legal brief she was reading, and it was as if she were surfacing from the murky depths of the deepest, darkest ocean. She stared at her assistant until the world snapped back into focus and what she said made sense. Through the glass walls of her office, she could see there were still a few associates at their desks, but the overhead lights had dimmed, and the distant sound of a vacuum cleaner signaled the workday was long over. "Shit, Halima. What are you still doing here? I thought you left hours ago."

"I have a paper due tomorrow. It's quieter to work here." She shouldered her workbag. "But I've finished and I'm leaving now. And you should too."

"What's the paper on?"

"Nope, you're not going to delay speaking to your father by faking a sudden interest in Behavioral Psych. I'm going home."

"I'm not faking. I really want to know."

Halima lifted a hand in farewell. "Right. See you tomorrow."

Unable to avoid it any longer, she stood and stretched as she picked up the handset. "Hey, Dad."

"Davina."

"Where are you?"

"Wanaka."

Had the European skiing season ended already? She guessed the month of May certainly meant very little snow in the northern hemisphere.

"How's Middle Earth?" Nine p.m. New York time would have to be lunchtime tomorrow in New Zealand.

"Gorgeous. Seven inches of fresh powder at the highest elevations. Early this year."

And that concluded the small talk. Their phone calls usually centered around any business they had to discuss, but there was nothing pressing, and she hadn't heard from him in months. Davy brought up the only other thing he could be calling about. "I have our appointment arranged with Tally in June. I just have to confirm."

"I'm not going to make it. I'll be in Bariloche."

Davy gazed out the south-facing windows toward lower Manhattan. Somehow, she was always caught by surprise when he demonstrated his callous indifference to his family. "Do you want me to reschedule?" *Sure, Dad, let's reschedule your daughter's fourteenth birthday.*

"No need. Pam informed me that Tally doesn't want to see us anymore. That's why I'm not bothering to return to the States."

"What? Why?" The news was a surprise, but truthfully, she couldn't blame Tally. What teenager wants to drink tea in a stuffy hotel on the one day of the year her father deigns to spend with her? Still, it hurt that Tally had turned her back on her. "She doesn't want to see us at all?"

"Will you meet with Pam to discuss it?"

The fuck? It was all becoming clearer. An innocuous sounding request, but it was really shifting his responsibility onto her.

"If Tally doesn't want to meet anymore, you tell Pam that I'll withdraw support when she turns eighteen," he said. "She can forget about me paying for college."

Davy gripped the phone hard. He was not going to put Tally through this bullshit too if she could help it. "Hell, no. I'm not telling her that. And even if we never see Tally again, you will not hold her education over her head. You can afford it."

Even as a teenager, Davy couldn't fathom why her father had attempted a domestic life that included a baby. He had stuck it out with Pam until Tally had been about six months old, when their relationship had disintegrated, and he had departed the New Jersey suburbs with undue haste. She had been away at school for most of that little hiccup in her dad's life, but still, she remembered Pam fondly. Unlike her father, Pam knew how to be a parent.

And then there was Tally. Or Tallulah, as her father had pretentiously named her. Nobody called her that. Tallulah Dugan was what you'd name a prize-winning pig at a state fair, or a silent era film star—not a sweet little girl who liked to talk about what unicorns might eat. Her half-sister was the collateral damage in her father's midlife folly, and her own guilt about her absence from Tally's life grew most acute around her birthday, the only time they spent together.

Her father ignored what she said. "Pam said she'll come to you. Tomorrow at seven p.m. I told her you would meet her in that tavern in your office building."

Davy let a pointed silence linger between them. She sensed there was a deal to be made here. Ironically, it was a skill she had inherited from him. If her father was transferring responsibility of Tally's birthday to her, perhaps it was time for a restructure of terms. It was an opportunity to press the advantage for something she really wanted—for both herself and Tally.

He cleared his throat. "Bionational. I'm hearing rumblings that the board is not happy with their counsel."

His proffer. As she rose through the ranks at Archer, Conant & Spar, Davy's father had begun to show the tiniest amount of respect for her achievements by discussing legal scuttlebutt with her, but this was new: a tip that was designed to force her to do his bidding and make her beholden to him. A quid pro quo arrangement the likes of which she was sure he had built his career on back in the day. That he still thought himself privy to the New York legal world's grapevine—after leaving the profession years earlier under a cloud—was laughable.

And that was not how Davy operated anyway. She avoided at all costs having her name and reputation in any way associated with her father and his gelatinous ethics and slippery business practices. There was a clearly drawn line between business and their pitiful familial relationship; she always made sure of that. And did he really want to trade the well-being of one of his daughters for business gossip?

"Rumblings? Is that all they are on the peaceful shores of New Zealand's south island? Bionational's already a goddamn feeding frenzy. I've thrown a few elbows to get closer to the head of the line, but I haven't had my shot yet. It's coming, though."

"Bully for you." He sounded miffed.

Here was the moment when she usually bowed to her father's wishes. It was what she had always done. Not this time. Not when he was casually making threats about Tally's future.

"Will you meet with Pam?" he said again. It was the closest he could come to asking a favor.

Her counteroffer. Sort of. "I'll do it on two conditions. One—You will put in writing that you will fund Tally's education. This document is not for Pam. It's for me. Any institution, any course of study. You will not do to her what you did to me."

"Did to you? Only make it poss—"

Davy overrode what she was sure would be his revisionist history. "And two—I'm going to try to fix what's wrong in my relationship with Tally. I'll give her whatever she wants for her birthday, and then I'm going to spend more time with her, be more present in her life. Enough of this once-a-year bullshit. And you don't get to say anything about it."

She knew she surprised him because he didn't immediately launch into further negotiations. The only sound on the line was his breathing.

"Davina, are you implying that I've prevented you from seeing your sister?"

"Yup, I am." Of course he had. What the fuck?

"I did no such thing. You're a grown woman. Whatever stopped you?"

Only the fear of losing his love and acceptance if she wasn't the most dutiful of daughters. But she was thirty-two fucking years old and if she hadn't received his love and acceptance yet, she doubted she ever would. It was time to grow the hell up and be the adult in her relationship with her younger sister—if it wasn't already too late. There was nothing to be gained by furthering the argument. "You're right. I should have done more than accompany you and Tally to the Plaza once a year. I'm going to fix this. I'm going to be a better sister."

"So you've got this handled?"

Jesus, he was cold. Not even a *tell Tally I'm sorry*. Now that he got what he wanted, he was in a hurry to end the call. The slopes must be calling.

"Yes."

"Good. Thank you. Good-bye, Davina." Transaction complete.

❖

Davy had been sitting with her scotch at a high table in the bar area for fifteen minutes with no sign of Pam. Sure, the rain was really coming down, and Pam probably had to catch a taxi from Penn Station, but she was only going to give her another three minutes before she went back upstairs to her desk. She gazed at her phone and flicked a finger over her brimming inbox, looking for something she could take care of quickly.

"Day. It's been a long time."

Davy froze. Only one person in her whole life called her that. She lifted her head. Anna Resnick stood before her, absolutely sopping from the rain. Her dirty blond hair fell around her face in lank wet strands and she was wearing a ridiculously long heavy woolen sweater—in May—with alpacas marching across the chest, upon which beads of water clung and glistened in the bar lights. Had the woman never heard of an umbrella?

"Anna. Still too lazy to utter more than one syllable of my name."

"Sorry," Anna said, not sounding sorry at all. "Davina."

Davy looked past her. "Where's your mom?"

"Where she should be. At home on a night like this. I told her I'd do this for her." Anna fished what looked like fast food napkins out of her gargantuan tote bag and dabbed at her face. "I'm going to the ladies' for a second. Be right back."

"Can I get you a drink?"

Anna observed her lowball of scotch and wrinkled her nose. "Sure, but not that. Something a bit more girly, please."

Davy thought about ordering her a fuzzy navel. Anna probably didn't remember that summer night all those years ago, but Davy definitely did. But what if Anna did remember it? Having to awkwardly talk about it all these years later was worse, so she decided against it. Instead, a frosty pale pink cocktail in a curvy coupe arrived at the table at the same time as Anna returned, now slightly less waterlogged.

"Thanks. What is it?" She held it up and gazed at the large sphere of ice that floated in the glass, which had a purple flower encased within it.

"Not sure. I asked for something girly."

"Mission accomplished."

Davy stared as Anna took a sip and closed her eyes in apparent enjoyment. From the first day they had met as teenagers, there was something indefinable that had attracted her to Anna, to the way she moved through the world with a sureness about herself that Davy had to work hard to project. Even now, with her sopping sweater and matted hair, she seemed completely at home in a midtown lawyer hangout bar. She'd always seemed to have that ability to be comfortable anywhere. And even in her bedraggled state, she was probably more beautiful than the last time

Davy had seen her. God, how long had it been? When Anna opened her eyes, Davy looked away.

"Delish, but it packs a punch. Nice choice."

Davy shrugged. The bartender deserved the credit, not her. "You're right. It has been a long time."

Anna's smile didn't reach her eyes. "While I was on the train, I tried to remember when we had last seen each other. I think it was Tally's kindergarten graduation."

"That was a really nice day." It had been a nice day until Anna had said something spiteful and Davy couldn't help biting back with something equally mean. She had left shortly thereafter, not wanting to ruin Tally's day. Had it really been that long? And now Tally was turning fourteen. How could that much time have gone by when every day seemed at least eighty-nine hours long.

"Why don't we just get to it?" Anna set her glass down with a click.

Davy had fond memories of Anna, and of the summer she had spent in Pam's house, but the foundation of friendship they had begun to build that summer had been abandoned and allowed to become derelict. That graduation ceremony was one of the only times they had seen each other in the intervening years, and they hadn't been nice to each other. But they were both mature enough to move past it now, weren't they?

"Tally doesn't want a birthday afternoon at the Plaza with you and Gregory anymore. She hasn't wanted it for years. My mother forces her to go."

Davy tried to remain expressionless. Hearing Anna baldly state the facts was a bit galling, but she'd be damned if she'd show it. Even if their once-yearly date on Tally's birthday was a pretty pathetic showing, she enjoyed their brief moments as the Dugan family. Tally's birthday tea date was the only occasion she spent with the people she was related to by blood, and it hurt to know Tally didn't want it anymore. At least Anna hadn't said that Tally was rejecting her completely. Yet. Maybe she should figure out how to change up the status quo. "Is there something else she wants?"

"A party. With all her classmates—not just the girls." Anna's smile could only be categorized as a my-little-sis-is-growing-up kind of smile, but then she got serious. "It's going to be expensive. We'll need a venue, and probably a DJ. Oh, and she wants it to be a costume party."

"Costumes? In June?"

"Yeah, she's kind of theatrical these days."

"Like you were." Still was? Davy had no idea.

"I was theatrical-adjacent. Tally is an all-caps thespian. In her mind, she's already won an EGOT." Anna's gaze shifted to over Davy's shoulder, her expression turning grim. "Don't look now—hetero assholes in three, two, one."

"Hey, ladies." A tall, besuited man invaded their space, his elbows on their table and Jägermeister stank breath wafting over them.

Davy leaned back. Anna seemed to be the object of his attention anyway.

"Care for some company?" he said, leering. His colleague stood next to him, shirt unbuttoned to his pecs and copious chest hair spilling out.

"No, thanks," Anna said, her voice cold. "You're interrupting our conversation."

"Aw, come on," Jäger-Breath said to her. "I can conversate with you."

Anna's hands curled into fists on the tabletop. "Really? We were just trying to decide which one of us was going to carry our baby. How could you possibly contribute to that?" Her anger had gone to eleven alarmingly fast.

"Sorry," Chest Hair said, pulling his friend away. "We'll stop bothering you."

"They're dykes, Larry," Jäger-Breath whisper-yelled so loud they could hear it in Canarsie.

"I know, buddy. Keep your voice down."

Anna watched them go, shaking her head in disgust.

"I have a bad back," Davy said.

Anna frowned in confusion. "Um, okay?"

"There's no way I can carry our baby. It'll have to be you, I'm afraid." She tried to hide her grin behind a sip of scotch.

Anna threw back her head and laughed. It was a sound so joyous and carefree, Davy was instantly hurtled back to a summer when she had heard it often.

"Good one, Day. When did you buy that sense of humor?"

And then she had to ruin it.

"Thanks for pulling me out of my extreme irritation at those two guys," Anna continued. "And I wasn't trying to suggest anything. Your sexuality is your business."

What was that supposed to mean? Davy didn't want to know. "Let's get back to this party for Tally. I can take care of the venue and the catering. How many kids are we talking about?"

"That's generous of you. The guilt finally must be kicking in. Probably thirty to forty teenagers. Maybe we could rent the Elks Lodge. It's probably cheapest."

Davy ignored the dig. She'd felt guilty for years, but it was an intermittent kind of guilt, which was probably worse than steadfast, ever-present guilt. At any rate, she wasn't about to give Anna the satisfaction. "I was thinking we could have it at my house."

Anna gave her a look. "You want forty teenagers to trek into Manhattan and trash your Tribeca loft?"

"How did you know I lived in Tribeca?"

Anna gazed at her like she was stupid. "Tally and I talk. A lot. I get the debrief after her yearly tea parties with you and your amazing invisible daddy."

"I don't live there anymore. I moved. I bought a house in Elmdale."

"Elmdale?" The incredulity in Anna's tone could've registered on a Geiger counter.

"I closed about a month ago. The house is still pretty empty so we wouldn't have to worry about guests trashing it, as you say."

"You live ten minutes from me?" The anger was back at eleven, edging toward twelve.

Davy felt her own anger rising. She didn't appreciate the accusatory tone. "I don't fucking know. Where do you live?"

"Southfield."

Anna still lived in Southfield?

Her rage didn't seem to have an upper limit. "Why the hell did I come into the city in the pouring rain when we could have met at your place, or my place, or a fucking coffee shop, or anywhere that doesn't require a train and a subway to get there? Or here's a thought—why didn't we just do this over the phone?"

This was an Anna Davy knew from their more recent encounter, although still eight years ago: argumentative, overly dramatic, and immature, with the ability to drive Davy around the bend with frustration in seconds. "I didn't arrange this meeting," Davy said from between clenched teeth.

"That's right. Your out-of-touch, entitled father and my people-pleasing, backboneless mother left us to deal with their enormous pile of bullshit."

"Are you referring to Tally as an enormous pile of bullshit?"

Anna gave her a withering glare and drained her cocktail in two gulps. "I'm outta here. Thanks for the drink." She picked up her giant tote bag and began walking away.

Good fucking riddance. See you in another eight years, or better yet, never. But the reason for their meeting was still unresolved. "Wait, Anna, what about Tally?"

Anna turned. "Now you're worried about Tally? After no-showing for three-hundred sixty-four days a year?" The gaze she leveled at Davy was as filled with disgust as it had been for their two gentlemen visitors. "Call my mom. Work it out with her."

Anna squelched away in her battered combat boots, and in spite of the anger she had once again inspired, Davy couldn't help notice how her wet jeans clung to her thighs. And she cursed that damn alpaca sweater for ruining her view of Anna's perfect ass as she walked away.

CHAPTER TWO

Anna left her soggy boots on the mat and pulled her drenched sweater over her head, hanging it on a hook next to her dry and unused raincoat. If raincoats could talk, hers seemed to say *I told you so* as it hung there all smug and judgmental. She padded through the kitchen and found her mom asleep in front of the TV with a very awake Louis in her lap. He was watching an octopus unscrew a jelly jar on the screen, but smiled at her when she came closer.

"Hi, Ma. Octopuses are smart."

Anna bent over his small frame and pressed the back of her hand to his cheek and forehead before running her fingers through his sweaty dark curls. "Hey, Louis. Feeling any better?"

"Grammie let me have green Jell-O. It felt good in my throat." He didn't take his eyes from the antics of the octopus.

Anna's mother woke up and the recliner snapped to an upright position. "You're back. How did it go?"

"How are you feeling, Mom?"

"No more fever, thank goodness. For either of us. I gave Lou the children's Tylenol at six, and I think he's feeling a little better, but I'm still pretty wiped."

"Why don't you go to bed? We'll stay tonight since it's so late. Can I put Lou in with you and I'll take the couch?"

"Sure." She sat up. "I notice you didn't answer my question."

Anna slouched in the doorway. "We didn't accomplish much. She'll call and finish the arrangements with you."

She gave Anna a despairing look. "I don't understand why you can't be adults and get along. For Tally's sake, at least."

"It doesn't matter. She's not a part of our lives." Time to change the subject. "What do you think, Lou? You up for going to school tomorrow?"

"I think I'm still too sick."

She grinned. "Somehow I thought you would say that. Why don't we see how you feel in the morning?"

"Come on, Louie. Let's go to bed. We can watch the octopus tomorrow."

"Okay, Grammie." Instead of negotiating for five more minutes, he went docilely with his grandmother, and that's how Anna knew he really was still ill.

The tinny sound of music leaking from headphones was all Anna could hear when she put her ear to Tally's bedroom door. She quietly opened it to see her sister sitting on the floor watching a YouTube video on her laptop while typing on her phone. Anna nudged her with her foot and Tally reacted violently, tearing her headphones off and clutching at her chest simultaneously.

"Crap! Knock much, Anna?" she said and slapped the spacebar on her laptop.

"Sorry." Anna plopped down on the floor beside her. "What are you watching?"

"Joanna Gleason as the Baker's Wife. Her phrasing is sublime. Rumor has it SSCT is doing *Into the Woods* this summer. I'm brushing up."

"And you're going for the Baker's Wife?" There was no way Tally, at almost-fourteen, would be cast as the Baker's Wife.

"Hardly. I'll audition for Little Red."

A much better fit, but still a reach. "You'd be perfect." She hoped the set wouldn't be very elaborate. She didn't have a lot of time to give the Southfield Summer Community Theater this year.

Tally picked up her pencil and twirled it around her fingers. "Did you see Davy?"

"I did. There's still some details to work out, but you're going to get your party."

Tally clapped with excitement. "Yay. When?"

"That falls under the aforementioned details yet to be arranged. Did you know she moved to Elmdale?"

"No. She did? That's so close. But I bet she doesn't know Mom sold the house and we live in this trashy condo now either. You're lucky you live in your own place."

Anna ignored that. Her space was barely livable, and really not suitable for raising a kid. "Elmdale is full of snobby rich people. Perfect for Davy. And that's where you're having your party. At her new house."

"Really?" Tally was quiet for a moment. "I know you don't like her, but I don't think she's a snob. She's always pretty nice to me on my birthday."

An immediate spike of anger made Anna's voice loud and harsh. "If she's so nice, why can't she spare any more time for you? Why does she only see you once a year?"

Tally looked at the floor and shrugged.

This was all Davy's fault. "I'm sorry, Tal. I'm annoyed at her on your behalf. She should be a better sister to you."

Tally put her headphones back on. "Whatever. I'm kind of busy."

Anna took the hint and left her alone. She returned to the living room and threw herself down on the couch, punching up a throw pillow and pulling an afghan over herself. As soon as she closed her eyes, a vision of Davy popped into her head, with her business lady haircut and fancy lawyer pantsuit. And the chunky silver men's watch she wore and looked at repeatedly during their date—not date! Meeting!

Seeing Davy—even just thinking about her—always did this to Anna. She spiraled into a seething, humiliated, defensive mess, and behaved in a way that made her embarrassed for herself. She exhaled violently and threw the afghan to the side. Her mom's freezer yielded no ice cream. The pantry was devoid of cookies, candy, canned frosting, or anything else that might constitute a good side dish for the feelings she was about to eat. In a high cabinet, hidden in the aluminum bowl for the stand mixer her mother never used, Anna found a Ziploc bag of what had to be Halloween candy, but it was May and she couldn't even be certain this was from *last* Halloween. It would do.

She returned to the couch and gnawed on a very stale mini Three Musketeers, then threw it down in disgust when its overabundance of taste-free nougat reminded her why it was still left in the bag. She rummaged for something edible with a citric-acidic punch.

Davy looked good. She had to admit. To Anna, she had looked good as a foul-mouthed, sad-eyed, underfed teenager, her chestnut hair scraped back into a ponytail most of the time. And she looked good now— polished, still with that deep brown hair but now styled into something shoulder-length and sleek. She had filled out at the curves somewhat but still bordered on too slim, with that ever-present thin veneer of disdain toward Anna and everything about her. But her eyes. Above the shadowy smudges that marked what had to be fatigue, they still seemed sad.

Jackpot! She unearthed a tiny box of Nerds, which barely met the definition of actual food. It probably had a use-by date sometime in the next century. She poured the contents into her wide-open mouth, taste buds already singing in anticipation of high fructose corn syrup and carnauba wax. Her teeth ground the gravelly pellets into a paste as she thought about that summer, when she had initially been annoyed by her mother's request to be nice to her boyfriend's daughter. But then she met Davy—sweet, loyal, willing-to-try-anything Davy—who had instantly become her best friend and sounding board, protector and keeper of Anna's secrets and dreams.

She remembered dragging Davy to a matinee of the movie *Once* a few days after they'd met, at a shabby, second-run theater a few towns over where they were among only a handful of patrons at the screening. How Davy had sat there, with quiet compassion, two fingers resting on Anna's wrist long after the lights had come up and Anna had lost the battle to control her sobbing reaction to that beautiful, heartbreaking movie.

And when Davy, who possessed very little artistic skill and zero interest in musical theater, accompanied Anna without complaint to every set building session, technical run-through, dress rehearsal, and performance of *Cats*, even though she claimed she might become a cloistered nun to avoid hearing "Memory" ever again.

Davy, who in an act of kindness, kissed Anna so she would forget the rejection she had suffered by another, but then with equal cruelty, had ceased all communication after promising to keep in touch.

Anna still didn't know why Davy never contacted her after their summer together ended and she left for school. And then she had reappeared for twenty-four hours on Christmas Eve and the way they treated each other during her brief stay became the template for future occasions when their orbits collided. Anna's hurt, manifesting as biting sarcasm and passive-aggression, provoked Davy out of her sullen, wary silence and into lashing back at her. It only got worse when Anna witnessed over the years how little commitment Davy had to their sister, and any remaining amiability between them had long since eroded into a sharp nub of animosity.

Anna sat back on the couch and let regret wash over her. Regret for the Nerds, which left an unpleasant residue in her mouth in a way she didn't remember from her youth, and regret about Davy, who always managed to get under her skin like no one in her entire life ever had.

But regret was uncomfortable, and action would help her banish it. Anna went to her mom's bathroom in search of a toothbrush. She wanted indifference to be her baseline reaction to Davy, and most of the time she achieved it since Davy's presence was so infrequent. She only had to get through Tally's birthday party before Davy would once more retreat to the outer reaches of Tally's life, and could be dismissed altogether from Anna's.

❖

Anna was early for a meeting with Louis's kindergarten teacher a few days later. From down the hallway she could hear the din that accompanied thirty rambunctious children eager for the school day to end. A peek through the window in the door revealed exactly what she didn't want to see. The teacher was nowhere to be seen, but two aides were present. One sat on a mat in the corner with a group of four students, their heads bent over their books. Another aide perched on the windowsill, gazing at her phone. The remaining students were running amok. A few had piled on to the teacher's wheeled desk chair while two boys pushed them across the room. A group by the bookshelves stacked readers into precarious towers and then launched their best haymakers to send the stacks flying. Louis sat alone at a desk with his treasured marine life encyclopedia open in front of him, his hands clapped over his ears as he tried to concentrate on the pages.

"Ms. Resnick?"

Anna turned to find Louis's teacher approaching. "Hello, Mrs. Albee. I'm a little early." She hoped her expression conveyed *what the hell is going on here* even if she refrained from saying it.

"So I see. I was just making some copies of a letter the students need to take home today."

Anna nodded and tried to stifle her anger. Why couldn't the phone-using aide do that? "I'll wait out here until the bell rings." She leaned against the wall and heard Mrs. Albee bring order to the room. The students became quiet, and a few minutes later when the bell rang, they burst into the hallway. Louis slowed when he saw her.

"What are you doing here?" He tilted his head and looked at her as if she were a duck in mountaineering attire.

"I have a meeting with Mrs. Albee. I told you this morning, remember? Let's go back inside."

"I forgot." Louis frowned but marched back to his desk and retrieved his book from his backpack.

Anna sat on one of the small desks in front of Mrs. Albee's teacher desk.

"We have a good news-bad news situation today, Ms. Resnick."

"Okay." *Uh-oh.* Why did people think that was ever a good way to open a conversation?

"The good news is that Louis qualifies for the district's accelerated learning program. He's reading at a third-grade level and his math skills are strong. His socialization is not quite where we want it to be, but he has definitely made progress over the course of the year."

"That is good news." This is what Anna wanted to hear. Louis needed a different environment in order to keep thriving. He already disliked school. Something like this could help him find the fun in learning.

"The bad news is the accelerated learning program has been cut due to budgetary constraints."

She dug her nails into the wooden desktop and counted to five. Why even tell her he qualified for it? This was a blow. Anna turned to Louis and saw him from moments ago, hands over his ears, trying to read in peace. She faced Mrs. Albee, again trying not to show how upset she was. "What can we do? Are there any schools that are continuing the program?"

"I'm afraid this is a district-wide decision."

She took a slow breath and tamped down the anger that threatened to erupt. "What will Louis do next year while his classmates are learning to read? I don't want him to stagnate."

"I'm sure his first-grade teacher will be able to address any concerns you may have."

Like you did? Anna knew Louis's teachers worked hard, but there were too many kids in Louis's class for him to get the attention he needed. It was too easy for a quiet kid like him to get lost in the shuffle. "This is disappointing." That was putting it mildly.

"I know you were counting on this. You can always explore other options like private schools, parochial schools."

No, I can't. Anything that cost money was not going to work. "Thank you, Mrs. Albee." *For nothing.* Anna called to Louis. "Let's go, buddy. We're leaving."

She gripped the steering wheel hard and half-listened while Louis told her about whale sharks on the way home. Maybe she could talk to the principal about skipping a grade, but she didn't want Louis to feel out of his depth socially. The accelerated learning program had really offered the best solution. How could the school district just pull the plug like that? She would start researching private schools and scholarships tonight. Perhaps they could get lucky.

Louis prattled on about gill rakers and plankton as they climbed the two flights to their apartment above Hunan Lee's. As they approached the front door, she could see something posted to it, and a dark foreboding settled in her gut.

"What's that, Ma?" Louis pointed to the official-looking document taped just below the peephole.

Anna sighed. And the hits just kept on coming. "It's a letter from the landlord, Lou."

CHAPTER THREE

There's a Pam Resnick on the line?"

"Thanks, Halima." Davy picked it up. "Hello, Pam."

"Hi, Davy. I hope you're not too busy. I thought I'd call later in the afternoon in case you were in court today." The warmth that Davy always associated with Pam was audible in her voice.

"That's thoughtful of you, but I wasn't in court." She hadn't seen the inside of a courtroom in a while. Ever since she'd been made head of litigation, she spent all her time overseeing others' cases instead of chairing her own.

"I still remember a few things from working for your father."

"I suppose you're calling about Tally's party?"

"Yes, but before we talk about that, I just want to explain about Anna. She's got a lot on her plate, and Louis and I were a little under the weather the other night, which was why she had to come instead of me. She was worried about us, that's all."

"I see." Who was Louis? Pam's husband? Boyfriend?

"Anyway, it's so good to hear your voice. It's lovely that you've moved nearby, and that you've offered to host the party. Tally is really looking forward to it."

"I want her to have whatever she wants. I want to fix things." She brought her calendar onto the screen. "Let's talk dates."

It took about ten minutes to hammer out most of the details. Pam suggested a caterer and a DJ, and Davy offered to pay for it all. As they were wrapping up the conversation, Pam said, "I'm sorry to ask you this, but do you know anything about evictions?"

"It's not really my area, no. Why? Are you having a problem with your landlord? But I thought you owned a house?"

"Oh no, not me, honey. Anna got an eviction notice, but I know for a fact that she always pays her rent on time."

"Without knowing the details, there's not much I can do. Tell her to call me and maybe I can help—either answer some questions or refer her to someone who knows more than I do." Davy doubted she would be getting a call from Anna, but there was something about Pam that made her want to be helpful.

"You're so kind, Davy, thank you. I know you girls didn't always see eye to eye, but now that you're living close by, maybe you can be friends?"

"We'll see." She doubted it. "I'm glad Tally's excited about the party. I heard she wants us to wear costumes. What are you going to wear? What costume should I wear?"

"Oh, I wasn't going to wear a costume, but you should. Be a princess or a superhero or something. Whatever strikes your fancy."

Davy would put Halima on that task. Or maybe she could get advice from Tally. It would be a good way to open up the lines of communication. "Does Tally have a phone? I could ask her."

"Of course. She got one for Christmas. Here's her number." Pam sounded almost overjoyed that Davy was asking for it, and that made her feel terrible. She jotted down the number and said good-bye just as her boss gave a cursory knock on her open glass door and breezed in.

Roland Spar—leonine and graying—sank into the chair opposite her desk, looking ready for a chat. "Howdy, neighbor. I haven't seen you around the block. How's the new house?"

Davy flushed, still somewhat ambivalent about her new house. A five-bedroom behemoth in suburban Elmdale, three houses down from her boss's home, purchased primarily because he mentioned it in passing one day. She had figured that emulating the lifestyles of the senior partners was the quickest way to a place among their offices on the thirty-seventh floor, but some gossip around the proverbial watercooler now had her thinking she had acted in haste. "Never mind that. Is it true about Conant? He's getting de-equitized?"

Roland had a good poker face, but Davy could tell he was surprised that she had already heard the news. Leonard Conant hadn't contributed to Archer, Conant & Spar in any meaningful way in years. If he was on his way out, a name equity partnership would become available. And Davy wanted it.

"Not de-equitized." Roland stood and wandered to the wall of barrister bookcases that lined the only nontransparent wall of her glass office, then fiddled with the gold scales of justice her father had given her when she passed the bar. "Retirement."

Retirement, her growing-larger-by-the-year ass. He was getting the boot. The fact that Roland didn't meet her eyes told her that much. An opportunity like this was unexpected, to say the least. "How do I get on the short list for consideration?"

Roland turned to her, not bothering to hide the surprise this time. "Davy, come on. You only just made partner. Not even you can make the leap that far, that fast."

Who the hell said so? Davy had been hearing no all her professional life and still managed to become the youngest partner at the firm, and they both knew why. She was a motherfucking rainmaker, with a more robust book of business than practically every other lawyer in the shop.

"I'm sure I'd become even better at landing the big fish with my name on the door." She was making bank for these old men. They'd better keep her sweet.

"Duly noted. What's happening with Bionational?"

Davy clenched her jaw at the blatant change of topic, but went with it. She had made her point. "Lunch on Tuesday. First step is setting the snare."

"Good. Do you need any support?"

"Do I ever?"

"All right, hot shot." Roland laughed. "Keep me posted." He made for the door.

"Hey, I'm serious about taking Conant's seat."

"I hear you. Let me get the lay of the land." He turned back. "Oh, you have a guest pass waiting for you at the club. If you're going to live in Elmdale, you'll have to go where the action is. I have a magic putter if you need one."

Davy shot daggers with her eyes at his retreating back. It wasn't enough that she was excellent at her job, worked insane hours, and brought in a ton of business. She had to play the game. Move to a ritzy suburb, buy a house, and keep her membership at the Elmdale Country Club in good standing. Nobody expected her to play golf and glad-hand her neighbors when she lived in Tribeca. Who had time for golf? The goddamn commute was already eating into her productivity, and she hadn't even thought about furnishing that fucking Overlook Hotel of a house she had bought yet.

She swiveled so she was looking out at the city and took several deep breaths. This is what you want, she reminded herself. *Once your name is on the letterhead, you won't be beholden to any of these men. You could play golf every damn day like Roland, or you could chase the ski season like your father, or whatever the hell you want.* All her drive and ambition were aimed at reaching the top spot at this firm, and once she got there, she would have lots of time to decide how to fill her leisure hours while those on the lower rungs lined her pockets. One thing was certain: she wouldn't be filling those hours with fucking golf.

CHAPTER FOUR

The Hoboken Art and Music Festival was blessed with a day that was sunny and warm. A beautiful June Saturday meant more business for Anna. It was a good thing Tally agreed to help out today with the massive number of people attending: strolling by her stall, eating street fair food, and listening to local music. For every fifteen or twenty looky-loos, she usually got one sale, which was a tremendous return on her vendor fees. She loved the citizens of Hoboken and their perpetual need to put paintings on walls.

Tally was usually great at chatting up potential buyers. She had told Anna she viewed it as an acting challenge. "My sister is so talented," Tally said to a thirty-something woman who lingered over a large watercolor of Sandy Hook at sunrise. "She's been particularly inspired since she lost her foot. And you could be the proud owner of this one of a kind original by a footless artist. Isn't it gorgeous?"

Anna stepped in and offered the woman her card. "Still have both my feet, thanks. Tally loves to embellish. If you're interested in beach landscapes, I can do them any size, in watercolors, acrylics, or oils. You name the beach—I can paint it." She smiled at the woman as she drifted on to the next booth. "The link to my Etsy store is on there too."

Tally flopped into a lawn chair behind the bins of pre-matted eight-by-tens. Anna followed, pulling two cold waters from her cooler, and handed one to her sister.

"Try to keep the outright lies to a minimum. That's not going to get me many sales."

"You don't know that." All her attention was on her phone as her thumbs flew over the screen. "I'm pushing the big canvases since Mom told me you're getting evicted. I figured you'd need the money."

"It's none of your or Mom's business. And I'm not getting evicted."

Tally looked up for a millisecond. "She told me you're getting kicked out of your place."

"It's not an eviction," she grumbled. "The landlord wants to raise the rent, so he's renovating."

"So you don't have to move?"

She looked away for a moment before admitting, "No, I do. I am getting kicked out."

"Eviction has reentered the chat."

Anna stuck her tongue out at her.

Tally remained impassive. "So where are you and Lou going to live?"

"I don't know. I have until the end of the month to figure it out."

"That's, like, two weeks. If you're in a jam, Louie can stay with me. On the floor. Not you, though. You snore."

Anna nudged Tally's thigh with her foot. "I do not."

The corner of Tally's mouth lifted in a sly grin, but she didn't look up from her phone.

She nudged her again. "Who are you texting?"

"Nobody."

Anna made her voice all sing-songy and suggestive. "Is it Brandon?" Tally had paired with them in a tap routine for her school's spring revue.

"No, nosy, and for the last time, I'm not interested in them."

"Okay, if not Brandon, then who has all your attention when I'm paying you to be here?"

Her fingers paused in their typing. "You're paying me in pizza."

"Well, it ain't Bitcoin, but I would've thought it was an acceptable currency for someone your age. So who?"

Tally gave her a mulish look but relented, putting the phone in her lap. "If you must know, it's Davy."

Anna's neck recoiled. "Davy Dugan? What does she want?"

Tally sighed. "We're texting about the party."

"What about the party?"

"She wants my opinion on the menu for the caterers and I'm giving her suggestions for a costume."

"Huh." Anna stood when she saw a couple with a stroller pause in front of the oil of the New York City night skyline, but they quickly moved on. She sat back down. "How long have you been texting with her?"

Tally hunched her shoulders. "Not long. She's nice. I like her."

Her defensiveness made Anna give her all her attention. If Davy was making a sincere effort to connect with Tally, Anna didn't want to get in the way of it. "I'm glad you're in touch with her. Maybe her new place will mean you'll get to see each other more."

"Yeah." Tally gave her an uncertain look. "Do you think a birthday cake and an ice cream sundae bar is too much?"

"You only turn fourteen once, kid. Can't hurt to ask." Suddenly, Anna's present of a portrait of Tally and all her friends seemed pretty paltry in the face of Davy's generosity with this party. "What did you suggest for her costume?"

"Well, I told her I was going as Dorothy from *The Wizard of Oz*. She asked if anyone was going to be the Scarecrow."

Pretty presumptuous of her to assume that one of Tally's friends wouldn't take that costume. Anna was about to say Davy should be the Wicked Witch of the West but held her tongue.

"But Su-Jin is going to be the Scarecrow and Brandon wants to be the Cowardly Lion."

"She's not going to be the Tin Man, is she?" Anna would love to see Davy decked out in metal with silver face paint. And pretending to be someone without a heart would be pretty accurate too.

"I don't think so. It sounded like she was going to leave the whole *Wizard of Oz* theme to me and my friends."

Anna nodded approvingly. "So she's not going to be a flying monkey or the mayor of Munchkinland?"

"Probably not. What about you? What are you going to be?"

"I haven't come up with anything yet." Mostly Anna just wanted a costume that would keep her cool. It was supposed to be hot next weekend. She didn't envy Brandon and their lion costume.

"Can I ask you something?" Tally sounded hesitant.

"Sure."

"Why don't you like Davy?"

Anna didn't want to go into the drama from before Tally was born when they were teenagers, but if it was even a possibility that Davy was going to be around more often, then Anna was going to have to watch her behavior. She would never get in the way of Tally's relationship with Davy, and she resolved to try to be as mature as her thirty-two years suggested she should be. "I'm really sorry if I gave you the impression that I don't like her. The truth is, I don't know her that well, and all I have to go on is her relationship with you. I've always had a problem with the way you've been treated by her and your dad, but if she's trying to improve on that now, all I can say is I wholeheartedly approve."

"But didn't you live together when Mom and my dad were together? Didn't you know her then?"

"Mom and Gregory moved pretty fast. She was his assistant for a little while, but he found her a new position when she wouldn't go out with him. Then he moved in only a couple of months later. Davy showed up in June after she finished her semester at boarding school. We got along great from the jump. I thought we had become friends. Then she went back to school in September, just after Mom told us she was pregnant with you. She promised to keep in touch, but I never heard from her. When she came back over Christmas, she was a totally different person."

"Different how?"

Cold, stiff, standoffish. Anna had been ready to forgive Davy's radio silence and could barely stand the wait to see her again. She remembered a chilly, windswept December day, standing on the platform with Gregory, waiting for Davy's train to arrive. That fluttery feeling in her chest that day came back to her now, as she had watched Davy, lanky and a bit disheveled with her long dark hair swirling in the wind, descend the steps of the train. Anna could've sworn Davy's eyes had lit up when she saw her on the platform, but then she turned to her father, and that light had dimmed to a watchful resentment that Anna couldn't break through. After a Christmas dinner where Davy radiated hostility toward everyone, she left. The next time Anna saw her was years later at Tally's kindergarten graduation. "She didn't seem very happy," she said, and left it at that.

"Was she mad because Mom got pregnant with me?"

Anna frowned. "Why would you think that?"

"You just said she left after Mom announced she was pregnant."

"She had to go back to school, Tal. It had nothing to do with you. And look, now she's trying to make things right." Anna hoped this was true. "Whatever you're thinking, cut it out. Her absence was never your fault."

"Then what happened? What changed?"

She had asked herself that question many times. "I really don't know. You'll have to ask her."

"Okay, I will." Tally gazed at a man who stood before the oil of the lifeguard stand at sunset, but she made no move to help him. "Are you still going to make my ruby slippers?"

"Sure." Anna got up to greet the potential customer. "You provide the shoes, and I'll make them sparkly."

CHAPTER FIVE

A nna parked at the curb and double-checked the address on the invite before getting out: 14 Darling Drive. She was in an unfamiliar part of Elmdale, on a street populated by enormous houses with vast, verdant front lawns. *So this is where Davy lives now.* She gathered her bags—costume, camera, and tote—and surveyed the house, weighing her options for gaining entry.

The house was clad in light gray shingles with handsome white trim, kind of a country cottage style but on steroids, with wings extending from either side of the front facade and what looked like three levels. People and activity surrounded a catering truck in the driveway, so she dragged her belongings in that direction.

Anna followed a caterer through a spacious mudroom and into an immense kitchen, a hive of activity, but no Davy. She wandered through empty rooms until she found her, on her phone, pacing and harried, in what Anna guessed was the living room. It, too, was empty except for an Eames lounge chair and ottoman positioned next to a large fireplace.

She hadn't been noticed yet, so Anna stood in the doorway with all her bags and watched. Davy stopped pacing and rattled off names of cases with her eyes closed and her fingers pressed against her forehead, as if she were pulling them out of her brain. "And ARCOA v. Colorado, try that one too. Find the fucking precedent. Why do I have to help you with this? This is your job. I want the brief on my desk by eight a.m. Monday." She ended the call without saying good-bye and lifted her head when she heard Anna's garment bag slide off her shoulder. "Anna?"

"Yeah, hi." She sketched a tiny wave down around her waist. The bags in her arms made her unable to lift her arms any higher.

Davy shifted her weight to her other foot. "Moving in?"

"God, no," Anna said. "This is my costume."

"What are you doing here? The party doesn't start for another three hours."

"I thought I'd come early and see if there was anything I could do to help. There always seems to be a ton of things to do just before a party."

"Right." She still looked vaguely put out. "That's nice of you. Why don't you leave your bags here and follow me."

They stepped through the sliding glass door and out onto a multi-level terrace, surfaced in slate pavers and framed around its edges by a low stone wall. Round banquet-style tables were positioned throughout the first two levels, and people were setting chairs and unfurling white tablecloths with snappy precision. The lowest level, which abutted the lawn, was clear of all furniture.

Far from the terrace at the rear of the property, in front of a tall, dense hedge of cherry laurels, two burly men were setting up a giant rectangular trampoline. This wasn't your regular backyard Wal-Mart trampoline; it looked like it belonged in a gymnastics training facility. It was so huge, about half the size of a tennis court, it looked like fifteen people could jump around on it at the same time. Anna put a hand on her hip. "That is some trampoline."

"I wasn't sure if Tally and her guests would enjoy it, but I thought it couldn't hurt."

"If they don't use it, I will." Anna knew Louis would love it. She was grudgingly impressed by the effort Davy had expended, despite the tiny voice in her head reminding her of all the years she had been a ghost in Tally's life.

"Maybe you could take over for me with the catering crew? They need to know where the mobile pizza oven should go and where to set up the taco bar. I have a few more calls to make and then I can be fully present." She looked past Anna. "If you'll excuse me, I have it on good authority that the balloon guy has arrived."

Davy walked toward a man holding two enormous bunches of helium-filled balloons of blue and green, Tally's favorite colors. Anna looked around at the preparations for a dream party that any fourteen-year-old girl would love. It looked like Tally's sister Davy had finally shown up.

❖

"Halima," Davy whispered into her phone ten minutes before guests were supposed to arrive. "What the fuck is this costume you got me?"

"It's Glinda the Good Witch, just like we decided. Actually, movie Glinda's dress is pink but the pink one was unavailable. I didn't think you'd mind white. It's really blingy. Super good-witchy."

"But it has this giant hoop skirt. How am I supposed to move around?"

"Boss…did you even look at a picture of Glinda? This one is toned down."

Halima was the one to suggest the good witch. Davy hadn't seen *The Wizard of Oz* since she was a kid, and barely remembered that there even was a Glinda. "Ugh. Can't do anything about it now anyway. This is my fault, not yours. Go back to enjoying your weekend."

"Oh, I will. A rare Saturday off? You know it. Have a good time. Take pictures. Bye!"

She clomped down the stairs sideways, carrying her starry scepter and the most ostentatious crown she'd ever seen, and was met by stifled laughter. Anna waited at the bottom of the steps, a hand covering her mouth. She stood in a gauzy, sheath-like, halter-top white gown, dissimilar to Davy's costume in every way except color. The neckline was appropriate for a teenager's party, but Davy couldn't help noticing her graceful neck and shoulders and how the fabric hugged her at the bodice and hips. A wig of complicated platinum braids and a tiny toy dragon held in her hands completed her costume.

Davy refused to let her eyes wander and gave her a preemptive, sullen, "Shut up." She was a frowsy baked Alaska next to a svelte coconut cupcake.

"Hey, Bo-Peep. Where are the sheep? Are they hiding beneath your yurt of a skirt?" Anna unstifled her laughter, letting loose a hearty guffaw.

"I'm not Bo-Peep, I'm—"

"I know who you are." Her eyes twinkled as she stepped closer and fingered the layers of tulle that covered the hoop. "I have to hand it to you, Day. You do nothing by halves. Are you Glinda from the movie or Galinda from *Wicked*?"

"The movie. I've never seen *Wicked.*"

"So you jumped on *The Wizard of Oz* bandwagon."

She rested her hands on the shelf that jutted out from her waist. At least she'd always have a place to put her drink. "I thought Tally might appreciate it. Who are you supposed to be?"

Anna posed, assuming a regal look. "You can't guess?"

"No idea. An R-rated Disney princess of some sort?" The dress was perfectly chaste. Davy didn't know why she said that. Well, she did, but she refused to let her mind wander too.

"R-rated?" Anna looked confused, then offended. "No."

The muffled thuds of car doors closing sent both of them scurrying to the front window. The Joker, a ninja, and what was either a unicorn or a narwhale were making their way up the driveway.

"I gotta get my camera." Anna turned toward her bags.

"Not necessary. I hired two photographers to be the paparazzi."

"Well, I guess it'll be two paparazzi and one Mother of Dragons," she said as she maneuvered around Davy's skirt and dashed toward the kitchen.

What the fuck was a Mother of Dragons?

❖

Anna sensed trouble brewing by the dance floor.

It had all been going so well. It helped that Tally's classmates were well behaved and also seemed a little awed by the extravagance of the party. The trampoline had been a big hit, the taco bar had been pillaged and scores of pizzas consumed, and everyone was raving about the fruit smoothies waiters delivered to each table in plastic cocktail glasses. When her mom and Tally and Louis arrived, a little late, a cheer went up from Tally's friends and the curious parents who had decided to stick around. Tally was a picture-perfect, dirty-blond Judy Garland with her curly braids and blue gingham. And she looked so happy. Anna took loads of pictures of Tally and her friends, loving her sister's wide smile and obvious enjoyment.

But now the DJ was attempting to lure party guests to the dance floor with zero success, and Tally, whom Anna knew really wanted to dance, stood at the edge of the patio-dance floor looking uncertain. Her starched blue gingham dress had withered in the heat, and the flush in her cheeks matched her ruby slippers, but she wasn't smiling now.

Anna hustled over to her. "Let's dance. Once we're out there, your friends will join us," she said.

The obligatory eye roll. "Dance with my sister? Hard pass."

"Where's Su-Jin?" This was a job for a best friend.

"She went to the bathroom with Allie and Mona."

"Go grab Brandon. You know they like to dance."

Her mom joined them, pulling Louis, in last Halloween's shark costume, by the hand. "What's happening? Why isn't anyone dancing?"

Anna put her hand on Tally's shoulder. "Maybe they're too full from eating. Give them some time."

"I'll dance with you, Tally," Louis said, shuffling his feet and swinging his shoulders.

Tally smiled and tugged on his shark nose. "Thanks, Baby Shark. Maybe later."

"It's this awful music," her mom said, already moving toward the DJ. "Who wants to dance to those computer noises? I'll tell him to put something better on."

"No," Tally quickly said.

"Wait, Mom," Anna said. "That's not going to fix it."

Davy glided over, smooth and serene and seemingly without the use of her feet. Did she have a hover board underneath that skirt? "What's going on?"

"Anna, stop her," Tally pleaded. "You know what song she's going to request."

"Yeah, I do." She turned to follow her, but the first few notes of the pounding piano intro already boomed out of the speakers, and it seemed louder than before.

Tally turned her back on her guests, cringing with embarrassment, but most of them were still seated at the tables on the terrace, gazing at their phones.

Davy's eyes darted between Tally and Anna, her confusion clear.

"My mom just asked the DJ to play her favorite song," Anna said.

Davy said to Tally, "'Build Me Up, Buttercup' is your favorite song?"

"No," Tally moaned. "My mother's."

Their mother rejoined them, looking smug. "Just wait. They're about to pour onto the dance floor."

Tally's groan contained all the disdain a fourteen-year-old could muster. "They're not fifty. They don't even know this song."

"It's a pretty good song, though," Davy said.

Her mom patted Davy's arm. "Thank you, Davy."

"It's ruining the party!"

"Don't be dramatic, Tally," Anna said. Once somebody started dancing, everyone would start dancing. Even though she was a terrible dancer, Anna designated herself as that somebody. She wandered out into the middle of the patio, bopping her head as she listened to the organ and the horns, and surrendered to the undeniable catchiness of this cheery bop. She kicked and hopped and shot finger guns at her little sister, making as much of a spectacle of herself as she could. Her mom and Davy laughed, but Tally was still sullen. Anna rocked her hips to and fro to the joyous chorus, and smiled with relief as Davy pointed at her and danced over to her in a comically seductive manner, her ridiculous giant skirt bouncing to the beat. At least she wouldn't be out here alone anymore.

Apparently caught up in the music, Davy pulled her close and Anna froze in her arms. Davy didn't seem to notice as her grip tightened, and she waltzed them across the dance floor like they were in an extremely unrehearsed production of *The King and I.* The steps were an unlikely match to the quick pace of a sixties pop song, but Anna couldn't help but relax into Davy's arms, feeling the press of Davy's enormous skirt against her legs. She grasped Davy's hand and shoulder more tightly as they hurtled around the patio, giving in to her confident lead so completely that she didn't bother looking down at her feet, ensnared as she was by the keen expression on Davy's animated face.

No sooner was she comfortable with the rhythm of the steps, than Davy masterfully steered them back to the center of the floor and raised Anna's arm, twirling her before bringing her close again. Somehow, their steps mutated into something like a jitterbug and Anna found herself dramatically unfurled away from Davy. Then with a tug of Davy's hand, Anna was furled back into her arms and plunged into a dip.

Suddenly, Anna couldn't get enough breath in her lungs. She was suspended in Davy's arms, their torsos pressed together above the frame of Davy's hoop skirt, now bowed and twisted by Anna's legs. All she could see was Davy, her mouth lifting in an enigmatic smile. And even if their pose was precarious, Anna felt entirely safe in Davy's arms. *Nope. This is too much.*

In the following moment, Anna was pulled upright and unfurled again, and this time she let go and spun out toward the small crowd of teens that had gathered at the edge of the patio. She radiated back toward Davy, but returned to her dorky moves, which had the added benefit of keeping the touching to a minimum—an eight count from the "Thriller" dance, some spanking-looking move Tally had shown her on TikTok, even a combination she remembered from an old 'NSYNC video—which Davy copied gamely. As the last bars of the song played, it seemed Tally couldn't bear it any longer and raced over to join them.

The three of them joined hands—ring-around-the-rosy style—circling with their arms raised in triumph, and as the DJ transitioned from their mom's favorite song to something that met with youthful approval, many of Tally's friends now charged the dance floor. Mission accomplished.

She and Davy ceded the floor to the teens. They stood at the edge of the patio and surveyed their success. Tally was smiling once again, and the party was back on track. The moment needed to be remarked upon somehow, their joint effort commemorated, but Anna didn't know what to say. "You're a great dancer," was all she could come up with.

"Oh, I'm sweating. That was so fun." Davy mopped her face with a cocktail napkin. Anna couldn't help staring at the pleasure in her expression, but then it completely changed. Davy looked like she had seen someone licking dog poo off the sole of their shoe. "What. The. Fuck."

Anna turned to follow Davy's gaze and saw two older, gray-haired men standing just inside the gate.

"Excuse me." Davy walked toward them without a backward glance.

❖

"Roland, what are you doing here?" Davy tried to compose her features into bland disinterest, but doubted she succeeded.

"Congratulations, Davy. I'm so happy for you." He enveloped her in a hug, and his usual cologne was masked by the scents of grass clippings and scotch. "This is Jim Sanders. We just finished a round at the club."

"A round of drinks?" They obviously had been celebrating for a while, and she had no idea why she was being congratulated.

"Ha! No, golf," Roland said.

Jim went in for a hug too, but she put her hand out for him to shake instead. "Hello, Jim. I didn't know people golfed in the dark."

Jim swayed a bit as he said, "We spent some time at the nineteenth hole after."

"Right. So"—she directed her gaze back at Roland—"why are you here?"

"I saw all these cars in front of your house and I figured you must be having a party. You're new here on Darling Drive, so you probably don't know what a close and convivial community we are. Neighbors are always invited to parties."

"Is that so? Nobody told me that rule when I closed on the house." She tried to make her delivery drier than Prohibition.

"Well, it's an unofficial rule, really. But neighbor or not, I'm a bit hurt that I wasn't invited. I had no idea you were getting married."

Davy took a step back. "What?"

"What do you mean, what?"

"I'm not getting married. Jesus, fuck."

He looked momentarily taken aback. "But I saw you. Dancing. Here come the brides, all dressed in white," he sang, gesturing to her outfit and breaking into giggles. "I like that your dresses are both white, but contrasting. Yours is definitely a special occasion dress." He gave Davy double thumbs up for the fashions. "Your first dance song was a bit peculiar for a wedding, though. But then, I always imagined you to have a touch of whimsy in your personal life. And now there's proof of—" He was obviously about to say more but stopped.

"Proof of what?"

"Nothing," he said, miming locking his lips.

She put her hands on her hips. "Proof of what, Roland?"

"That you swing that way. We always thought maybe, since you never bring anyone to work events." His eyes brightened. "Ah, look who it is—the bride." He elbowed his friend and snorted. "The other one, I mean."

Davy whirled around to see Anna approaching. This was all Davy needed right now.

"Is everything okay?" she called.

"Hello! I'm Roland. What's your name?" Roland tried to get past Davy, but she sidestepped and got right in his face.

"Time to go. I'll see you Monday."

"Come on, let us stay. I want to celebrate your blessed event. I've never been to a lesb—"

"Roland!" Davy took him by the shoulders, giving him a little shake. "This is my sister's birthday party. I'm sure you don't want to party with a bunch of fourteen-year-olds."

"You don't have a sister." He gave her a can't-fool-me look, then gazed at Anna, who was now standing right behind Davy. "My heartiest felicitations. Let's toast."

"We're not toasting." Davy chanced a look at Anna and saw her utter confusion. "I don't need you," she barked. "Go back to the party."

Anna's face became expressionless, and Davy watched as she turned and walked away.

Roland had his flask out and offered it to her. She took it from him. "You're drunk. I have a feeling you're going to regret this tomorrow, if you even remember it." She motioned the two tipsy men toward the driveway with swooping arms, like they were lost sheep. Anna was wrong. She was the anti-Bo-Peep. *Get these fucking sheep away from me.* "Go home, Roland. Good-bye, Jack."

"Jim."

"Whatever." She made sure they actually exited the yard before turning toward the party. She looked for Anna's white dress and platinum braids among the throng of guests on the dance floor, but they had disappeared.

❖

Anna was on her knees in Davy's powder room, consoling a crying shark. "Lou, it's okay. We can throw this in the wash and it'll be good as new." She dabbed at him with a hand towel where fruit smoothie had stained his white fleece shark belly. "You can't really be upset about this admittedly very large stain. What's wrong?"

His tearful, woeful expression broke her heart and secretly amused her at the same time. He'd been adopted as sort of a mascot by a few of Tally's friends, running around and whipping himself into a frenzy. Then he'd eaten his body weight in pizza and ice cream and guzzled probably three fruit smoothies. He was overstimulated and exhausted.

He sniffed loudly and tried to pull himself together. "Tally wouldn't let me go on the jumpy thing. She said it was only for her and her friends."

"This is Tally's party, so she gets to be the boss, but she and her friends are dancing now. I don't think she'll mind if we use it."

"Really?" He used a fist to wipe the tears from his cheeks.

She gave his belly one last swipe. "Let's go."

They weaved through the crowd and crossed the dewy lawn, the patio lights lengthening their shadows until they passed through their radius and into the darkness. Louis reached for her hand and pulled her toward the trampoline.

After discarding their shoes on the grass, they shinnied up the aluminum ladder and galumphed to the middle of the mesh. Louis gasped and giggled as he adapted to the shifting surface beneath their feet.

She didn't intend to jump at first, her feet not leaving the surface as his bounces gained height and confidence. But soon, she had pulled her dress up and she and Louis were leaping as high into the air as they could go. Endorphins surged through her with the rush of weightlessness. After a while, her wig began to slip and she sat off to the side to remove the bobby pins that held it to her head as she watched Louis.

He jumped around, laughing madly, for about ten more minutes before he lay on his back, breathing heavily and smiling. "Can we get one of these, Ma?"

"Where would we put it?"

"In our new backyard."

Anna sighed. "It sure would be nice to have a backyard, wouldn't it?"

Louis knew she was looking for a new place for them to live, but her priority was space for the two of them plus room for all her supplies. Her price range would most likely not stretch to include a backyard. Maybe she could find somewhere within walking distance to a park. With swings. He would love that. It wasn't a trampoline as big as a football field, but it would be something fun for him.

She gazed back at the party, reluctant to admit to herself that she was searching for Davy, but that telltale giant skirt was nowhere in sight. She had to give Davy credit for tonight's success. Davy had continually surprised her today with the extravagance of her party planning and willingness to embrace Tally's love of costumes and theatricality.

And their dance. When Davy joined her on the dance floor and encircled her in her arms, Anna's heart rate had tripled. That seemed to happen around Davy, but usually it was because she got under her skin so fast and so fiercely that Anna's anger spiraled out of control. Being tossed about in Davy's arms reminded her of the last night of that long ago summer, when Anna's friendly feelings had been upended and transmuted into instantaneous yearning when they had kissed. But the curt dismissal she had received when Davy had been dealing with those interlopers reminded her of everything that had happened after that. She would be nice for Tally's sake, but she wouldn't let her guard down.

❖

The Glinda dress defeated her. After getting rid of Roland, Davy couldn't bear the thought of flouncing around in it any longer and went inside to quickly change. When she returned to the terrace, most of the guests were on the dance floor, stomping their way through the "Cha-Cha Slide."

Tally raced up to her as she passed along the perimeter of the dance floor. "Davy! Come dance."

Seeing Tally so obviously excited made it clear exactly why she and Halima—well, mostly Halima—had put so much effort into planning this party. But when she did a mental check-in with herself, she realized she didn't want to dance anymore. Her dancing highlight had already happened, and she wanted to tuck it away and savor it a little later when she was alone. She shook her head. "You have fun with your friends."

Tally was already inching back toward the floor. "Okay. Thank you for everything. This party is fire."

In a moment, Tally's friends had surrounded her. Davy wandered around, seeking some task that needed to be done, but everything was handled. She turned and saw a figure in white sitting on the trampoline and realized who she sought. She went back inside and grabbed a couple of beers from the fridge and then strolled over the dark lawn to join her.

Each step on the trampoline was a feat of balance, but she awkwardly made her way to where Anna was sitting with her matted hair and her wig beside her. There was a little boy in a shark costume lying on his belly a short distance away, his fist pressed up against his chin, dead asleep. She had seen him at various moments throughout the evening and wondered who he belonged to.

Anna accepted the beer she held out. "Thanks, Glinda. You truly are a good witch."

"Happy to help. Something to wash down the pizzas and tacos."

Anna clinked her bottle with Davy's. "Pizzas and tacos and beers, oh my."

"Oh my is right. I'm exhausted."

"You've put together a great party. Tally will never forget it."

"But you saved the day. Your moves on the dance floor are singlehandedly responsible for the stampede that followed."

"Ha. Right. You're too kind."

They sat in silence for a few moments, watching the antics of the dancers.

"Who were those men?" Anna asked.

"Oh, ah, I'm sorry I was short with you." Davy took a sip before continuing. "Neighbors. Apparently, they expected to be invited."

"To a private party?"

"Well, one of them is my neighbor and my boss." She didn't tell Anna about Roland's misinterpretation of the event. She wasn't sure how Anna would react, and she just wanted to sit in the darkness with her and spectate the party from afar.

"Your boss gate-crashed and you didn't let him stay? You're not worried about any work ramifications?"

"He was drunk. No way should he be allowed into a child's party in that state. I'll go over and smooth it over tomorrow."

"Over where?"

"To his house. He lives down the street."

Anna's eyes bugged. "That's a little close for comfort. Did you know that when you bought the place?"

She turned and gazed at her mammoth house. What had she gotten herself into? "Yeah."

"It's quite the hacienda."

Davy glanced at Anna, not sure if she was being sarcastic, but couldn't glean any meaning from her composed features. "I guess it is." She didn't want to talk about her house. "I still don't know who you're supposed to be."

Anna scooped up her wig and plopped it back on her head. It was now officially a rat's nest. "I had a toy dragon I meant to clip onto my shoulder, but I put it down somewhere and have no idea where it went. Does that help?"

"Nope."

"*Game of Thrones*? The Khaleesi? The Breaker of Chains? The Mother of Dragons?"

Davy shook her head. "I've heard of that show, but I never watched it. She's a character on it?"

"Daenerys Targaryen—dress from season one, hair from season six! Only the most iconic queen in all Westeros and Essos." She tried to arrange the braids back into some order, but it was hopeless.

Davy grinned. "Are you even still speaking English? You have to admit, it's a little obscure."

"It's so not obscure. Get with the times. Everyone but you knew who I was right away—even without the dragon. And it was a really good show, at least until the last season." She pulled the wig off and flung it in Davy's direction.

Anna's indignation was cute. Davy liked seeing her riled up. And she didn't know why, but there seemed to be a suspension of the usual antagonism Anna was so good at flinging at her. Davy just wanted to coast on it for however long it lasted, because there was no doubt she would do something to piss Anna off again, and they'd be right back where they started. "Is it as good as *Big Brother*?"

Anna opened her mouth in mock shock. "How dare you bring up my terrible teenage viewing habits?"

During that summer she had spent in the Resnick house, she had suffered through countless hours of *Big Brother* and Anna's addiction to it. "What? You don't still watch it?"

"It's not still on, is it?"

"I have no idea."

"I forgot you were never much of a TV watcher."

"Or a movie fan, or a theater goer. I believe you once told me I was stuck in a hermetically sealed mayonnaise jar and that I should live a little."

"I was an opinionated little brat, wasn't I?"

Davy laughed. She sat back and sipped her beer, alternating her gaze between the party and Anna. The silence between them was comfortable for once. After a while she said, "Should we tell the parents of this little boy that he's here? I wouldn't want them to worry."

Anna gave her a funny look. "She's not worried."

Okay. How could she know that?

"I thought you knew. I should have introduced you when he arrived. That's my son, Louis."

Davy was speechless for a moment. "Y-your son? I had no idea you had a kid."

"I didn't actually have him, but he's mine. Well, as good as."

Anna had a child? One who was as big as that little boy? Who was the other parent? If Anna didn't have him, her partner must have. Was this other person still in the picture? In the jumble of her memories, Davy had always pictured Anna in a solitary pose. She was overcome with the need to know, but didn't want to seem nosy. "I'm glad he was here to celebrate with Tally. You came early. Did your partner bring him?"

Anna directed her gaze at the little boy. "My mom brought him with Tally. I don't have a partner. I'm a single mom, like my mother before me."

Davy released all the breath in her lungs. She realized she had been bracing herself for whatever Anna was going to say, and now she suddenly felt a lot less tense, but she still couldn't get over it. Not that she expected Anna to be suspended in amber in between the occasions when they saw each other, but she was bewildered by this news. And why hadn't Tal—

"Tally never mentioned Louis at your yearly teatime get-togethers?"

"She never did." Davy reflected on their last few birthday celebrations. "She hasn't talked much the past few years. We'd ask lots of questions and she would answer with as few syllables as possible. It drove my father crazy, and he'd end up lecturing her about her future for forty-five minutes. It was miserable for everyone." She picked out Tally from the crowd of dancers, her happiness visible even from this distance. "We've talked more by text over the past two weeks than we have in the last three years combined. It's been great to get to know her a little better."

Anna nodded. "She's becoming a fantastic human."

"I'm glad she forced this change in tradition. I should've done it years ago."

Anna blew out a breath. "Why didn't you? We both know your father isn't going to win any prizes for parenting, but you could've done better."

Davy bristled but made an effort to answer civilly. She wanted to keep the peace. "I'm not her parent, but I know what you mean." It was hard not to get defensive. She supposed Anna, who had been there for Tally the whole time, had a right to ask. She had absolutely no desire to talk about her father right now, but she couldn't see a way around it. "You may remember my relationship with my father is complicated—and difficult. He was barely present but still managed to control my behavior pretty well. He always had some leverage to hold over me, some way of forcing me to obey his rules. And there were always consequences I knew would somehow come down on me if I stepped out of line, so I never challenged him about how he dealt with Tally because I knew if I did, I would have to pay for it."

"How?" Anna asked, her voice laced with dread. "He didn't—"

"No. He wasn't violent. That's not his style. He's a master of the mind games. And I honestly believe, even if you might think it's convenient for me to say, Tally is better off for having such limited contact with him."

Anna was quiet.

She tried to explain further. "I'm at a place now where he can't do much to exact those consequences anymore. And I think he understands that I'm going to pursue a relationship with Tally whether he likes it or not. I know I haven't been good to her, but this party is the first step in changing that."

Anna's expression was solemn. "Tally really likes you, and you seem to be making some implied promises here with this party and the texting and everything. What happens when you get bored and withdraw from her? Or your work gets too busy and suddenly it's been six months since she's heard from you? Please don't insert yourself into her life if you're just going to blow her off and leave when the novelty wears off."

"I hope that won't happen, but I'm not going to lie. My work keeps me busy *always*. I work like a fiend, usually twelve to sixteen hours a day." She wanted to say that the reason she bought this house was for Tally's sake, but while it was a convincing argument, it wasn't the truth. "Tally will just have to trust that I'm going to stick around."

"I'm going to hold you to your promise, Day," Anna said.

After a moment of silence, it seemed Anna had let the subject drop. Davy was relieved. But now she was curious about Anna's life, and the choices that led to the little boy in the shark costume sleeping nearby.

CHAPTER SIX

One of the things Davy liked about her new home was that it was within walking distance to Elmdale's charming main street. Lined with cute little shops and boutiques, it was one of the features that made the town so attractive. Since the early summer weather was nice, she had gotten into the habit of walking to and from the train station for her daily commute. It had made her transition from the city not quite as jarring.

And now, on Sunday morning, she had bought a box of fresh pastries from a cute bakery called Grigsby's before walking back, past her own house, to Roland's.

She rang the bell and didn't have to wait long before Roland came to the door, looking fresh from the shower. He opened the door wide for her, looking chagrined. "Hello, Davy."

"Roland. Good morning. How are you feeling?" She handed him the flask she had confiscated the night before and entered. "Do I smell coffee?"

He hastily shoved the flask into the drawer of a console table in the foyer. "You do. I'm hosting brunch before our tee time."

"And I wasn't invited? Not very neighborly of you." She offered her box of baked goods to him, which he accepted in an abstracted way.

"Of course, you're welcome to stay. I'm sorry for barging into your party last night. It was unforgivably rude."

"The last time I saw you that drunk was at the holiday party two years ago. I believe it was scotch that did you in that time as well."

Roland's eyes darted back toward the rear of the house. "Could you keep your voice down? Leanne doesn't know how soused I got last night.

She was already in bed when I got home. I know you don't want to get me in Dutch with the missus." He waited for her to nod, then led her into the kitchen, where Leanne was taking some muffins out of the oven.

"Well, hello, Davy. I didn't know you were golfing today," Leanne said. "Gosh, how long has it been since I've seen you? Last August's Summit?"

Every year Melvin Archer, one of the senior partners, held a gathering at his Hamptons home for key personnel. He called it the Summit because he liked to believe it was a meeting of great legal minds. Mostly it was a bunch of male lawyers smoking Mel's Cuban cigars and puffing up their accomplishments in front of the name partners while their wives talked about…whatever wives talked about. Davy had gone the first time she was invited and then blown it off ever since. Her time was better spent working rather than talking about work. "Must have been the year before. I was running point on a big case last summer and couldn't make it." She accepted a hug from Leanne, one of the nicest women Davy had ever met.

"You work entirely too hard. I'm glad you've moved into the neighborhood. I wanted to bring over some goodies when you moved in, but Roland insisted I let you be. How are you adjusting to Elmdale life? Quite a change of pace I would imagine."

"I'm slowly getting used to it. I've discovered the pain au chocolat at Grigsby's. That's helping me get over my city withdrawal."

"Aren't they divine?"

With one hand, Roland offered the opened box of pastries to Davy and his wife while he shoved one in his mouth. "You shouldn't have, Davy," he said around a mouthful. "Good thing I'll be able to walk it off later."

She refused the croissant but accepted a mug of coffee from Leanne as the doorbell rang. Melvin Archer arrived with a man that Davy had absolutely no love for, Kevin Keeley. While Leanne welcomed them in the foyer, Davy turned to Roland. "What is Keeley doing here?"

"I invited Mel to play today, and he brought Kevin. What? What's wrong with him?"

The two name partners who mattered were meeting to play golf today and they invited Keeley to play with them? This was not good. Couldn't Roland see that Mel was positioning Keeley for Conant's spot? And of course, they were doing it on the fucking golf course. She'd have to stay for brunch now and suss out the undertones here.

Bull-necked, bushy-browed Melvin Archer entered the kitchen and greeted Davy with surprise. "Are you joining us today, Ms. Dugan?"

"Just here for some breakfast. I live down the street."

"Right. I heard you moved out of the city. That's usually the sign that one is settling down. True?"

"Perhaps. It certainly takes some adjustment."

"Davy! I didn't know you'd be here." Kevin Keeley approached with his sun-touched brown locks and movie-star caliber veneers. Davy bet he played a mean game of golf.

"Keeley," she said. "How're things in Greenwich?"

"Great! But I've been hearing so much about this Elmdale course from Roland here, I had to try it out. Are you coming?"

"I don't golf. I have plans later anyway."

"Too bad. I would've liked the chance to bend your ear about a regulations issue Wax Corp is having. We could've discussed it on the course."

Of course he would. When it came to creative solutions to their clients' legal problems, he had all the acumen of a sea slug. But she could sense Archer listening to their conversation and knew she'd have to play nice. "Call Halima. She'll put you on my schedule tomorrow. It might be early or late, though. My day is packed."

They all moved into the dining room where a buffet was laid out on the sideboard. Davy helped herself to some fruit and nursed her coffee and considered who she now believed to be her competition for Conant's chair. Keeley was older, mid-forties, and had joined the firm about five years ago; his lateral move from a prestigious Boston firm was supposed to lift the tone of their wannabe white shoe operation. He was seen as a real up-and-comer, but Davy couldn't understand why. He was all style and no substance. His father was a former senator, but even with all his connections, he didn't bring in much business.

"...have plenty of time. Len's retirement will become official within the next few months. At any rate, we'll have to be careful about who we choose to succeed him."

They were talking about Conant. Davy was now alert and listening to Roland.

"Where do we see the firm in ten to twenty years? We're the old guard"—he gestured to Melvin and himself—"and we need someone with vision to help maintain our hold on current business while generating relationships in new industries."

She saw Keeley sit up straight, so she sat up straighter too.

"Of course, Roland." Melvin placed his mug on the table with extreme care as he gathered his thoughts. "But we also need someone who believes in good old-fashioned American family values. Someone who recognizes that family and community are as important as making money. I hope I can count on everyone's discretion here. Len let us down in that regard. His after-hours behavior did not represent our ideals. No, we're going to need a pillar of society whose public profile is above reproach."

This was a bit rich coming from Mel, who'd mow down his own mother if it helped him make the deal. But it was typical for old white men to start rewriting history once they started getting a little long in the tooth. And it didn't bode well for Davy—steadfastly single, sexually ambiguous, and religious about keeping her personal life out of the office. It could be an automatic strike against her, at least in Mel's eyes.

"I'm in total agreement with you, Mel," Keeley said.

Who asked for your opinion, you pustulant preppy fuckweasel?

"My wife and kids are my everything," he continued. "Ainsley is the reason I get up in the morning, and knowing I have to pass on this world to my girls informs every decision I make."

Was anyone buying this horseshit? The addition of a wife and children had absolutely no bearing on a person's ability to effectively practice law, and she would argue that their presence was a deterrent to one's productivity.

But Davy gazed around the table to see Mel nodding soberly and Leanne getting misty. Fuck. She couldn't compete with this. She glanced at Roland, who appeared to be discreetly administering himself a couple of pain relievers and washing them down with coffee. It was unbelievable what he had thought he saw last night. Two white dresses and a drunk man's erroneous assumptions were about as close as she would ever get to wedded bliss. But then a plan began to form. Maybe she *could* compete with this. She took a deep breath.

"I couldn't agree more, Kevin. I know I don't usually share much regarding my personal life, and at work I'm all about the work."

"Oh, we know that about you, Davy. You're a machine," Mel said. He was smiling, but in the context of this conversation, it didn't sound like a good thing.

"But I'm making changes in my life. Moving out of the city, buying a new house. Family values are important to me too. My fiancée and I want to build something lasting, something that represents our values in

all the communities we are members of—this firm, Elmdale, America…
and our LGBTQ+ community." She couldn't get around that last one, and
her breath left her in a rush. Trepidation made her spine stiff, but she was
intensely curious about how the partners would react to her coming out to
them. Did she work for a bunch of homophobes or not?

"Fiancée?" Leanne gasped. "You're getting married?"

"I am. Roland met her last night."

Leanne turned to her husband. "You did? You didn't tell me. But
wait, you were with Jim?"

"They stopped in last night at a party I threw for my sister. Roland
offered his congratulations and then swiftly departed before I could even
offer him a drink." She eyed him and nodded, and he quickly began
nodding too.

"Yes. I'm ashamed to say, Davy, that I don't recall your lovely
fiancée's name."

"It's Anna. She and her son are thrilled that I finally moved out of the
city. They live in Southfield." She took in the faces around the table. All
of them looked like they were waiting for the fifth card to be revealed in a
high stakes round of Texas hold 'em. All except for Leanne, who reached
out and grasped Davy's hand.

"Oh, Davy, you've got yourself a family! I'm so happy for you."

"I'm really happy too, Leanne." Now she had to finesse the optics a
little further. "Part of the reason I didn't disclose much about my personal
life was because I didn't have one until recently. Work was my life. And
why bother coming out to any of you when there was no reason to? But I
knew that when I did share my story, Archer, Conant & Spar would be as
welcoming to me as to any heterosexual person. And I also knew that the
firm that I give my blood and sweat to would support me wholeheartedly.
After all, the firm is forward thinking and enlightened and inclusive—it
is now and will continue to be in the future." The firm was not especially
enlightened or inclusive, but it could be if they chose a queer woman to
help run it.

There was silence at the table for a moment. Keeley didn't look up
from his plate, Mel gazed at her speculatively, and Roland sat back and
crossed his legs, seemingly in no hurry to say anything. Then Mel cleared
his throat and said, "It gratifies me to hear that, Davy. And of course, may
I wish you the heartiest of congratulations on your upcoming wedding."

Take that, Keeley. I'm back in the game.

"Have you set a date?" he added.

Shit. Now that she'd made this big pronouncement, she had created an untold number of problems for herself—the least of which was acting like she was a joyous bride-to-be. "Not yet. We're in no hurry."

Leanne reached out and grasped her hand. "I simply must meet them. You said her name is Anna? And what is the child's name?"

She felt the blood leave her face. What was his name? Dammit. They all looked at her expectantly. She plucked it from her memory just before it got awkward. "Louis. His name is Louis."

"Roland and I will host a dinner for you all as a welcome to the neighborhood. Does next Saturday work for you?" Leanne glanced at her husband. His blank face was all the approval she needed. "Of course you'll have to clear it with them. Why don't you check and confirm with Roland tomorrow." She squeezed the hand she was still gripping. "Oh, this will be wonderful. We'll keep it casual. A barbeque in the backyard."

"I'll do that, Leanne. Thank you. But now, I should be going and let everyone get on with their golf outing." She stood and made a quick getaway, the consequences of her words just beginning to sink in.

CHAPTER SEVEN

Anna and Louis had just returned from a scavenging trip to find boxes for her move. The liquor store and the independent bookstore had produced a bonanza. She surveyed her apartment, overwhelmed by the task ahead of her. How had she and Louis accumulated so much stuff since she'd brought him here as a one-year-old? And how could she begin to pack up their lives when she had no idea where they were going yet?

Their large loft above Hunan Lee's had served them well. There were no walls, just open space, so she'd set up her studio at one end where the large plate glass windows looked over the street and got the benefit of eastern exposure. Their beds and the bathroom were in the rear of the space, and a living area and kitchen broke up the living and working zones. It had been perfect, and cheap, even if the lingering aroma of General Tso's chicken permeated everything they owned.

Packing and moving her art supplies was going to be the biggest headache, and she still had a few unfinished projects that needed to be wrapped up, but she had to start somewhere. And Louis needed to start somewhere too.

"Lou, where'd you go?"

"I'm right here." He took a seat at the kitchen table and slapped the book she had just bought for him onto it. "I was getting crayons." The book was called *The Deep Dive* and featured coloring and activities on the topic of sea life—he already called it his favorite thing ever.

"I'm glad you like your new book, but remember I said we would have to do some packing today?"

"Yeah. Do you mean now?" he asked, selecting what looked like, to Anna's practiced eye, the periwinkle crayon from his sixty-four pack.

Whatever she was going to say was halted by a brisk knock from the hallway. Louis ran to the door.

"Ask who it is first," Anna said.

He halted at the door and asked, turning back to her in confusion at the muffled response. "It's baby?"

"You can open it. It's Davy. Remember, from last night? We were at her house." *What in the world could she want?*

Louis pulled the door open, and Davy stood there, a sober expression on her face.

"Hi." Anna's welcome was cautious.

Davy didn't wait for an invitation. She strode past Louis and into the apartment like she owned the place. "I have to talk to you."

Anna gripped the back of the chair where she stood. "How do you even know where I live?"

"Tally gave me your address. I need to talk to you." The urgency on Davy's face put Anna on edge.

"So you said."

She gazed wildly around the loft. "Nice place."

"Don't lie. You'd never want to live here."

"You don't know that." Her eyes were drawn to the half-finished canvases leaning against the wall.

"Um, I kind of do. You just bought a property that's the opposite of this place in every way."

Davy sighed. "You've got me there." She slowly spun three hundred sixty degrees. "But it's very you. I like it."

So did Anna. Too bad she had to leave it. "Lou, say hi to Davy."

"Hi." Presumably picking up on her anxious energy, he gave her a wide berth as he returned to the table and picked up his crayons.

Davy gazed at him like she was trying to solve a complicated algebraic equation in her head. Her hands went into her pockets, and she pulled out her car keys and a few crumpled bills. "I'm sorry. I don't have anything for him. I should have brought something." She smoothed out a five-dollar bill, and it looked for a moment like she was going to offer it to him.

Anna was grudgingly amused by this business. "Put that away, weirdo. You don't need to give him anything."

She hastily stuffed the money back into her pocket. "Can we talk?"

"Sure. Would you like something to drink?"

"No, thanks. In private?"

"You want some music, Lou?" she asked, retrieving his headphones from a shelf. She plugged them into her phone and set them on his head. She turned back to Davy. "You were saying?"

"What's he listening to?"

"Right now, he likes the *Les Miserables* Broadway cast album." She led them toward the studio area of the apartment, pulling out stools for them at her worktable.

"Training him early to like musical theater, I see." Davy smiled. "And Tally loves theater too."

"Yeah." They both knew this.

Davy rested her forearms on the table and really looked at Anna for the first time since entering her apartment. It was as if she had pressed the pause button on whatever mission she was on and allowed herself to be in the moment. "I have really good memories of that summer, you dragging me to the theater and working on the sets all day long. What show was that?"

"*Cats*." It was hard for Anna to think about how great that summer had been, knowing their friendship hadn't been able to survive until Christmas. Davy's detour into nostalgia made Anna hoist her guard up a little higher. She crossed her arms and waited for her to say something.

"Jesus. How could I forget that?" Davy stood and drifted over to the unfinished canvases, squatting to get a better look at them. They were a series of landscapes in oil of the Hudson River from some photos Anna had taken from a lookout off the Palisades Parkway. The watercolors of the same view had sold well so she was doing larger canvases in oil, but waiting for the layers to dry always took longer than she anticipated.

"These are fantastic. Is this how you make a living?"

"Yes."

"I'm impressed. You were always so talented." She got up and continued to wander past the open shelves of brushes and chemicals and colors and all the other tools of her business that Anna wasn't very good at keeping tidy. The longer Davy kept silent the more curious Anna became, but it seemed like Davy either was reluctant to talk or didn't know what to say.

"You said you wanted to talk to me about something?"

Davy returned to the table. "I need a favor. A big one."

"From me?"

"Yes, from you. It's going to sound a bit crazy so just bear with me while I try to explain. Remember my boss who crashed the party last night?"

Anna nodded.

"His name is Roland Spar. He's a senior partner, an equity partner, at my firm. There are three of them, Archer, Conant, and Spar, the name partners. And Conant is retiring. I want to take his place, get my name on the door."

"Wow. Ambitious. Isn't that for people who are further along in their career?"

"Usually yes, but my firm is smaller than the big-name white shoe firms. We pride ourselves on our ability to compete with the larger, less nimble shops, and in the past few years we've developed a reputation for winning business away from them. And that's because of me. I'm really good at exploiting our competitors' weaknesses, finding opportunities for new business, and getting them to sign with us."

It didn't surprise Anna that Davy was good at her job, but the person she was describing—this brash, go-getting, Machiavellian manipulator— seemed so different from the Davy she used to know. Teenage Davy had been super smart, but she was also quiet, amiable, and not the most confident person in the world. When had the girl she used to know changed? "Why do they want to sign with you?"

"Because when it comes to the law, I'm a goddamn savant. If everyone has a talent, then mine is figuring out legal ways for my clients to overcome any obstacles in their paths. And so far I've been rewarded for it. I'm head of litigation and I'm already a partner."

"Okay, now I'm impressed. But that's different from what these three men are?"

"Yes. A name partnership doesn't come up very often. It's a chance to become part of the leadership team, to develop a vision for the firm that would carry us into the future. And I think I've earned it more than anyone else."

"And to make some money too, I'll bet."

"Yes, of course, it means a lot more money, eventually. First, I would have to buy in."

"You have to pay to become one of these name partners?"

"That's why it's called equity. I put my money in, but also get a bigger share of the profits."

All very interesting, but Anna was no more enlightened as to what Davy wanted. "Well, good luck with that. I hope you get what you want."

"Thanks." Davy took a breath. It seemed like the preamble was over, and she was finally preparing to say what she'd come to say. "This morning I went to Roland's house to talk to him about what happened last night. He was getting ready to go golfing with another senior partner and one other lawyer from my firm. He comes from a political family and looks like a Kennedy, but he's a shitty lawyer. Still, it was pretty clear to me that they were vetting him for the job."

"Oh, bummer."

"Right?" Davy rubbed her hands on her jeans. "Anyway, we're sitting around having brunch and the partners start talking about Conant—he's the one who's retiring—and basically how he didn't live up to their values because he was a swinging bachelor who drank all the time and fucked a lot of women and never settled down. And Keeley—the guy who's gunning for the job—starts in about his beloved wife and saintly kids and how they're the fucking wind beneath his wings, and everybody's eating this shit up with a spoon, and I see my chances going up in smoke."

"Why? Do you fuck a lot of women and drink all the time?"

"I pretty much do the opposite. I'm a goddamn workaholic, opening a vein and bleeding on the daily for my firm. They made me the head of litigation, so I have a hand in every case that goes before a judge. I never go to court anymore, but my fingerprints are all over every brief, every motion, and every defense strategy. I'm the one actually producing value for our clients. But in that moment, they weren't seeing that. I'm too young, and I'm a woman. They're not even seeing me as name partner material. And they certainly don't see me as married with kids and an upstanding member of society, either, like Keeley is positioning himself. So I had to change their image of me."

"Okay. How did you do that?"

"I told them I moved to Elmdale because you and I are getting married."

Anna stared at Davy. She didn't understand.

Davy leaned in. "Did you hear me?"

"Yes, I heard you, but it makes no sense."

She put her hands up. "Let me back up a little. Roland, drunk Roland, thought Tally's party was our wedding. He saw the two of us in white, dancing all by ourselves out on the patio and thought we were brides dancing to our first song."

"But it was 'Build Me Up, Buttercup.' That's not a wedding song."

Davy gave a short bark of laughter. "That's the part you take issue with?"

She took issue with all of it. She had never heard of anything more preposterous. But there was still a matter of this favor Davy spoke of. "All right. Let's put to the side the absurd notion that you and I would ever get married." She decided to ignore the way Davy's brows scrunched in injury. "I still don't understand what you need from me."

"I need you to be my fiancée, just for a little while." Before Anna could say anything, Davy threw her hands up. "I told you it was crazy."

"It's not crazy."

Davy's shoulders relaxed in apparent relief.

"It's psychotic."

And there those shoulders went, back up around her ears, tension radiating out of her. "Look, I wouldn't ask you to do this if it weren't important. And I realize it's completely outside of how we normally interact with each other. I'm willing to compensate you for this."

Compensate her? So Davy perceived her as for hire? Bile rose in her throat. "You'll have to find someone else." Her words came out serrated. "I don't want to get involved in whatever this is."

"But, don't you see? It has to be you. Roland saw you last night and I already told him and the partners about you and Louis."

"You brought my son into your psycho scenario?" Anger shot through her so fast she stood and took several steps back.

Davy rounded the worktable and followed her. "Wait, Anna. There has to be some way to work this out. I need you for this. What do *you* need? Money? I will pay literally anything you ask."

She whirled around to face her. "Fifty-seven million dollars."

Davy stopped in her tracks. "I don't think—"

"So we're not really talking literal, are we," Anna cut in. "I was kidding. I don't want your money. I think you should go."

"I would only need your presence at a few work-related events."

"What you need is a prostitute."

"Whoa. Wait. You have the wrong idea. We wouldn't actually be together."

Did Davy realize how hurtful she was being? "Do you even prefer women?"

She drew herself up to her full height. "Yes, I do."

"See? I didn't even know that. I came out to you that summer. You were one of the first people I told. And then you…"

Davy looked like she was bracing herself for whatever Anna was about to say. And suddenly she didn't want to bring up the kiss. She didn't want to hear Davy disavow it, or deny it. It felt important to protect that moment from Davy.

"But I guess you didn't care enough—trust me enough—to do the same," Anna said instead. "You should find someone else for this. Someone who either doesn't know you at all and will take your cash, or knows you better and wants to help you."

Davy stared at her with eyes that were dark pools of desperation. "There is no one like that."

"Well, then I'm sorry for you." Anna crossed her arms over her chest. They stood staring at each other, and the tinny melody of "Master of the House" leaking out of Louis's headphones seemed deafening.

Davy's eyes dropped first. She gazed at the flattened boxes near the kitchen counter, and comprehension stole over her features. "You're getting evicted. Your mother told me."

A flare of frustration shot through her. "I was not evicted. The landlord wants to renovate this space."

"And your lease allows him to do that while you're a tenant?" Her disbelief was clear.

"I was month to month."

"So he could eject you with only a month's notice. Where are you moving to?"

She glowered at Davy but didn't answer. Didn't have an answer.

"I could find you a place. I could cover the rent for a year."

"No."

Davy took a step closer. "Or you could stay in my house? It's huge. Maybe Elmdale isn't your style. It's not as funky and cool as what you've got here, but there would be plenty of space for you and Louis and all your art stuff."

"No, Davy."

"Please. It's a perfect solution."

"To a problem that is not of my making. Would you be there?"

"Ouch, Anna." She rubbed her butt as if Anna had kicked her there. "Yes, that's where I live. We'd be roommates. I'm hardly ever home, if that makes it more attractive to you."

"What about Tally?"

She frowned. "What about her?"

"How do you think she would feel about you and me shacking up— poor choice of words—*coexisting* in your house?"

Davy looked stumped.

"You know what? Don't bother answering. This is not happening. I really want you to go now."

"Okay, I'll go. Will you please think about it?" She left her card on the kitchen counter. "I'll wait for your call."

"Then you'll be waiting a long time. Use that magic wand from your Glinda costume and conjure up a fiancée for yourself. Because it's not me."

CHAPTER EIGHT

"And you would have access to the pool and the community room."

Anna listened to her Realtor, Janet, while she examined the third apartment they'd visited, keeping one eye on Louis, sitting on the step that led to the sunken living room with its expanse of grubby harvest gold carpeting. Since school was out, she had no choice but to bring him with her as she house-hunted. He had been perfectly behaved after she set him up with her phone and a YouTube video entitled *One Hour of Amazing Ocean Moments*. She looked around the uninspiring unit. It was okay—two bedrooms, an aging but clean kitchen, but nowhere to really set up a studio.

"The rent doesn't include parking, which is an additional monthly fee."

Of course it was. The pros: it was close to her mother's place and Louis would remain in the same school district. The cons: it was barely enough room for them, at the top of her price range, and Louis would remain in the same school district. Anna was running out of time. It was time to poo or get off the pot.

"What do you think, Louis? You'd finally have a real room with walls, all to yourself."

No response from Louis, headphones on, and intently gazing at the small screen.

"Aw, he's a good little boy," her Realtor said.

"He is. He can get a little preoccupied if he's indulging his obsession with anything that lives in the ocean."

"My daughter is the same way, except it's trains. It started with Thomas the Tank Engine when she was three, and now she's nine and just built a steam locomotive as a science project for school."

"That's incredible."

"We encourage her hobby, but her first grade teacher really developed her interest and applied it to all her subjects, from reading to math to history. And all her other teachers since then have done the same." Janet seemed to remember where she was and tempered her effusiveness. "Sorry. I'm just really glad her school keeps her so stimulated and eager to learn." She gestured to the empty space around them. "So what do you think?"

Stimulated. That's what she wanted for Louis. "That's terrific that her teachers foster her learning through her interests. Does she go to school here in Southfield?"

That had certainly not been Louis's experience at his Southfield school. Probably a private school, which Anna could not afford.

"Elmdale Elementary. We used to live in Southfield, but we moved when my daughter started kindergarten."

It figured. Elmdale Elementary. Just when free accommodation in the very same town had been dangled in front of her. Of course, Elmdale had a well-known reputation for academic excellence. It had one of the best school districts in the state, but its high prices had precluded her from considering it as a reasonable possibility. Still, it wouldn't hurt to ask. "I don't suppose you have any rental listings in Elmdale."

Janet shook her head. "Elmdale has almost no inventory in the rental market, but when you're looking to buy, there are a few properties I would love to show you."

"Maybe someday." Anna surveyed the unimpressive apartment while Davy's beautiful home materialized in her mind. Then she remembered the melancholy look on Davy's face as she gazed at her home while they sat on the trampoline at the party. Why was it there instead of an expression of satisfaction, or pride, or triumph? No. Now was not the time to be distracted by Davy, and before her brain could even go there, she shut down any thoughts of Davy's cockamamie scheme. There was no way she was moving her son into a living situation with someone she barely trusted, even if it could mean he might have an exponentially better experience in school come September.

Wait. Anna excused herself from Janet and stood by the window. What was she thinking? She would do anything for Louis. If his enjoyment of school could increase in the slightest, didn't she owe it to him to at least consider Davy's ridiculous idea? And what would it really cost her if she set aside her dignity?

She didn't know anything about Elmdale Elementary. Before she ruled it out completely, she would have to see what the school offered. The term had only ended a week ago. Maybe she could talk to someone about Louis. Maybe they should go right now.

"Would you like to move on to the next apartment on my list?" Janet asked.

Anna turned from her spot by the window. "You've already given me a lot to think about. Can I get back to you?" She had to at least consider this option for Louis's sake. She would go check out Elmdale Elementary and put this apartment on the back burner for now.

CHAPTER NINE

One of the benefits of Davy's office, besides its southern views of Manhattan, was that it looked out over many buildings of lesser height. One of the adjacent buildings had a helipad, which occasionally made for interesting viewing, but another had a restaurant on its top floor with an outdoor space that catered to a brisk lunch business. At the moment, she watched two miniscule people greet each other with a hug she could tell was filled with affection even from this distance.

It was ridiculous that the emotions of two complete strangers as they ate a meal together would fill her with loneliness.

Three days had come and gone, and she hadn't heard from Anna. It had been a long shot, but Davy had really hoped Anna would come through for her. Okay, it was more than a long shot. It was definitely crazy for her to think Anna would agree to such a harebrained idea, but she couldn't believe how wounded she felt at the rejection. Now she had to figure out how to gracefully extricate herself from Leanne and Roland's barbeque even though it was in her honor.

"I'm going out for some lunch. Do you want me to pick you up anything? A salad? Some soup?"

Davy swiveled her chair back around to her desk and answered Halima, who stood in the doorway. "No, thanks. I've been woolgathering. I need to get some work done."

"Are you sure? You haven't eaten anything yet today."

Davy gave her the smile she reserved for the times when Halima, six years her junior, tried to mother her.

"Okay, I'm going." The tone sounded on Halima's desk phone that meant she was being hailed from the reception desk. "Wait, hang on."

Davy sighed and maximized her email window. Time to start plowing through the recent onslaught.

Her hand over the receiver, Halima leaned back toward Davy's office. "You have a visitor. Anna Resnick?"

Davy gripped the edge of her desk with both hands, and Halima noticed, but came to the wrong conclusion.

"She doesn't have an appointment. Shall I tell them to turn her away?"

"No!" She was probably coming to reject her some more, but Davy had to know for sure.

Halima put her purse on her desk, probably assuming Davy would want her to fetch Anna from reception.

"Go to lunch. Whatever she's here for, it's personal. I'll go get her."

Davy ignored the curious eye Halima gave her as she collected her purse and left. She took a few cleansing breaths and went to greet Anna.

She was gazing at the art in the reception lobby, art that Davy had never once stopped to look at in the eight years she had worked there. The calf-length peasant skirt paired with a simple camp blouse and Birkenstocks was maybe her attempt to look professional, or what Anna the artist imagined professional to be. Whatever her rationale, Davy liked the look and appreciated the effort. "Anna?"

"Hi, Davy." She crossed the lobby, her expression tentative.

Before she could say anything, Davy gestured for her to follow her back to her office. She closed the door and moved behind her desk. "Have a seat." She pointed to one of the chairs that faced her desk and tried to quell the nervous energy that roiled through her belly. "What brings you into the city?"

Anna's ruefulness was apparent. "Let's open the negotiations."

"Negotiations for…" She waited, her nerves at the edge of their seats.

"Don't try to lawyer me, Day. I know you haven't found a new fake fiancée since Sunday. Do you want to do this or not?"

Davy's breath left her in a whoosh, and she couldn't hold back her smile of relief. "Yes, I do."

Anna leaned forward. "Before we really get into it, how long do you think it's going to take them to choose you?"

Much as Davy wanted to excuse herself to the bathroom and jump up and down for about six hours first, she tried to pull herself together and act like she was in control of herself. "Allow me to thank you for your positivity in thinking they're going to choose me, but I don't think it's going to be that easy. To answer your question, Conant's departure date hasn't been announced yet, but these kinds of decisions usually take between three and six months. I would think a new name partner would have to be decided by October, the latest."

"Oh." She sat back, deep in thought.

"Why?"

Anna didn't say anything but looked into Davy's eyes, and it seemed like she was trying to measure something of tremendous importance, and it made Davy's knuckles whiten as she clenched the arms of her chair and waited for her to speak.

"Getting this position, or promotion, or whatever you call it, is obviously very important to you. I understand that. What's most important to me is Louis."

Davy nodded.

"He just finished kindergarten. He had his graduation last week. Do you remember Tally's kindergarten graduation?"

She nodded again.

Anna's expression changed to one of fondness and remembrance. "Her whole class was up on the stage singing 'The Circle Game,' and Tally was in the front row, and she was so into it, closing her eyes and swaying and doing her little dance moves, and everyone loved it, and she loved it, and I love that memory."

"So do I."

"Lou's class sang a song too. 'Brave' by Sara Bareilles. Do you know it?"

"Yeah, it's great."

"It is, it is. Perfect for kids at a graduation." Anna paused. "And Louis was as brave as he could be. He was in the back row, half-hidden behind a taller girl, and I could tell it was painful for him to be up there, and he probably mouthed the words, but he did it, and I was proud of him."

Davy's heart went out to that little boy coloring at the table from the other day.

"Lou had a tough year. He's very bright, but he likes quiet and order and figuring things out on his own. His kindergarten classroom was a pretty boisterous place and he's already starting to not like school."

"Poor guy." Davy leaned in and rested both elbows on her desk, listening closely. She thought she knew what was coming.

Anna took a breath before continuing. "Lou and I visited Elmdale Elementary yesterday and we met the first-grade teacher, Ms. Mobley. Summer vacation has just started, but she was there, inventorying her class library and getting a book order ready for the fall. She has a whole section on marine life. He was enchanted by her and her library."

"Enroll him. That can be his new school."

Anna seemed not to hear her. "Elmdale has one of the best school districts in the state and—"

Davy couldn't help interjecting. "With the property taxes that go along with that."

Anna was thrown from what must have been a carefully planned monologue. "Well, yes—"

"Property taxes I'm paying whether I have a kid in school or not. Anna, enroll him. Move into my house. We both can get what we want."

"But don't you see the problem?"

All Davy could see was the solution right in front of them.

"What happens after you get your new job and we end this farce? Do we go back to Southfield and Louis's shitty school after he's had better? I can't do that to him."

Right. "Lay your cards on the table. What do you want?"

"Whether you get your partnership or not, I want us to live in your house for the entire school year. It's possible that the rent I save while living with you would increase my savings enough for a deposit on a small place in Elmdale so he can continue there."

Davy gazed at her while she considered her proposal. Anna sagged in her chair, seeming to become boneless after she had gotten out the words. It was really not asking that much, but it still gave her a moment of unease. Davy had been prepared to pay Anna a large sum of money for her help, but money was easy. Yes, she had offered her home at the start, but the reality of it was now sinking in. She hadn't shared her space with anyone since college, and living with a child would be an adjustment, but this is what she wanted, wasn't it? And she spent hardly any time at home. They'd be like ships passing in the night.

Anna cleared her throat. "And in return I'll help you in any way I can to get your partnership, but I think there should be some parameters. And a contract."

"A contract?"

Her backbone seemed to reassert itself and Anna sat up straight in her chair. "Yes, Ms. Attorney-at-Law, I assume you're familiar. A contract that spells out the terms of our agreement and exactly what is expected of each of us. For instance, if I'm to pretend to be your fiancée, exactly how much *affection* am I to show you?"

"I think the normal amount if we're in public."

"Define normal."

Davy threw up her hands. "I don't know. It's not like I expect you to throw me down on a picnic table and fuck me in front of everyone at my boss's barbeque on Saturday."

"So you want me to go to that with you?"

"Yes, obviously. It's being thrown in our honor. And Louis's."

"Whoa. Wait." She held up a hand. "I'm agreeing to lie for you, but I will not involve Louis. He stays out of it. And furthermore, to Louis, you are our roommate, not someone I'm pretending to marry. This is nonnegotiable."

"But—"

"I'm serious. If you can't agree to that, the deal is off. It'll be confusing for him and he's already been through enough."

"What do you mean?"

Anna started to speak but then closed her mouth with a click. The way she regarded Davy made it seem like she was weighing what—or how much—to tell her. Finally, she said, "The way he became mine is a pretty messy story, and I'm trying to keep things simple for him. But this is already way too complicated. You know what? This is a mistake. Let's forget the whole thing. I'm going to go."

"No! I agree. Louis stays out of it. Whatever you want. I'll draw up a contract."

Davy waited for her to say something, but Anna turned in her chair and stared into space. It was another few moments before she directed somber eyes back to her.

"There's one more thing."

Davy was back to clenching the arms of her chair. "What?"

"Tally. We have to get her blessing for this. I won't do it if she doesn't want us to."

"Well, let's ask her." Davy reached for the phone.

Anna stretched across the desk and put her hand on Davy's, preventing her from picking up the handset. "We need to ask her in person."

Out of the corner of her eye, Davy saw Roland out in the hallway. She made eye contact with him at the same moment she grasped Anna's hand. It had the intended effect of drawing him directly into her office.

"Hello, lovebirds." He stood in her doorway with a big fat smile on his face. "You're not going to deny me an introduction again, are you, Davy?"

She and Anna stood, and Davy gripped Anna's hand hard even as she could feel her trying to withdraw it. And there they were awkwardly holding hands across her desk while Roland beamed.

"I'm Roland."

Anna wrenched her hand free and stuck it out for him to shake.

"This is Anna, Roland. You almost met the other night."

"Yes! Please forgive my boorish behavior. Too much sun and not enough hydration makes Roland a very inebriated boy, I'm afraid." He took her hand in both of his and stepped closer. "But enough about me. I'm so happy to meet Davy's intended. We just love her here. The place can't run without her."

Anna took a deep breath and smiled like a lovestruck paramour. "That doesn't surprise me at all. She puts her heart and soul into everything she does."

"Yes, indeed. You know, I scooped her up right out of law school. The best hiring decision I ever made. I tried to take her under my wing, but she didn't need me. She was flying in no time."

"Everything I know about the law, I learned from you," Davy said to Roland. No harm buttering up her mentor. "Okay, not that I don't like hearing all this praise, but—"

"So modest, am I right, Roland?" Anna said.

Before Roland could say anything, Davy said, "I'm leaving early today. I'll have Halima move my afternoon meetings." She grabbed her briefcase and her suit jacket, then extended her hand toward Anna. "Shall we go, dearest?"

Davy felt her heart lift when Anna reached out and took it, but then tried not to cringe as she heard her reply.

"Lead the way, Sugar Butt."

They left Roland standing by her office door. "Sugar Butt! Oh Davy, I think you've got a live one, here. So may I tell Leanne you'll be coming to the barbeque on Saturday?"

Anna turned back and waved, her smile at Davy's boss blinding. "Wouldn't miss it for the world. A pleasure to meet you, Roland." She entwined her arm with Davy's as they walked toward reception, and the smile dropped from her face.

"So we're doing this?" Davy just wanted to be sure.

Anna nodded grimly. "As long as Tally is okay with it, we're doing this."

CHAPTER TEN

Their New Jersey Transit train was quiet in the midafternoon, and Anna sat at the window of a three-seater while Davy took the aisle. If Anna thought they would be hashing out the terms of their contract on the ride from the city, she was wrong. Davy took out her laptop before they'd even left Penn Station, explaining that she needed to get a few things done before their meeting with Tally.

While Davy was preoccupied, Anna had the chance to watch her unobserved—how she scowled at the screen as if it owed her money. And the way she reached up to tuck a disobedient lock of her dark hair behind her ear every fifteen seconds was certainly more entertaining than gazing out at the swamps of North Jersey.

Now that they had come to a tentative agreement, Anna thought about what came next, which was sharing a home with Davy, something that made her unaccountably nervous. She wanted their arrangement to work. They were both getting something important out of it, so it behooved Anna to adjust her habitual dislike of Davy. When she thought about why she disliked her, it all stemmed from that Christmas when Davy gave her the cold shoulder. She had felt embarrassed by her admiration and enthusiasm for Davy when the feelings clearly weren't mutual. Anna thought they were going to be friends, and for a tiny window of time she had thought they might be something more, but she had been wrong, and all these years later, she still couldn't let it go.

And now Davy needed her.

She had to let it go. Louis needed this. Tally deserved this. She resolved right there to make every attempt to wipe the slate clean, to absolve Davy of her long-ago adolescent sins and make this outlandish situation work.

They rode the train one past the Elmdale stop to Southfield where they took Anna's aging minivan to Tally's friend Su-Jin's house, where the two of them sat on the porch giggling over their phones when Anna and Davy arrived.

Tally sauntered over to the car and rested her elbows on the driver's side window. "Hey. Why are you here instead of Mom? Where are we going? Can we get something to eat? Can Su-Jin come? Her mom's making something gross. Su-Jin's words, not mine." She finally noticed Davy sitting in the passenger seat and broke out into a grin. "Hi, Davy. What are you doing here?"

"I'm here to see you." Davy grinned back at her, then said to Anna, "Can we get something to eat? I'm starving."

She turned to Tally. "Yes, we can get some food, but say good-bye to Su-Jin. She'll have to eat whatever her mom made her."

"But she—"

Anna interrupted. "We have things to talk about. Family things."

"We do?" Tally's gaze swung from Anna to Davy, who gave her a solemn nod. "Okay. Be right back."

Anna watched her amble back over to her friend. "She always argues me to death. One nod from you and she's as obedient as a dolphin."

"Are dolphins obedient?"

"So Lou tells me."

"I think it was the way you said *family things*, all ominous and scary."

Had she been ominous and scary? She could admit she was a little anxious about throwing her lot in with Davy, but she wasn't scared, and she certainly didn't want to project that onto Tally.

Tally got in the back seat and stuck her head between them. "What are we eating? Can we go to Dougie's Dogs?"

"Dougie's Dogs?" Davy asked. "Hot dogs?"

Tally grabbed the back of the front seat with both hands. "Yeah. Only the best in the whole fucking world."

"Tally." Anna threw her a warning look. "Language."

"Sorry."

Anna sensed Tally directing her rolling eyes to Davy.

Davy grinned back at Tally and leaned against the door so she could see her properly. "The world is an awfully big place, and hot dogs are my absolute favorite."

"They are?" Tally and Anna said in unison.

"I've eaten some of the best hot dogs in the world and I've never heard of Dougie's Dogs. I'm going to have to put your claim to the test."

Anna put the car in gear. "I guess we're going to eat some hot dogs."

❖

Davy had to admit it was one fine hot dog.

She sat on one side of a picnic table and Anna and Tally sat on the other, in an area that had been cordoned off in the restaurant's spacious parking lot, serenaded by the sonorous strains of traffic from Route Three. It was strangely engrossing to see how Anna and Tally dressed their dogs. Both of them had loaded up on toppings: Tally the sweet ones like ketchup and pickle relish, and Anna just everything. Her now extra girthy hot dog bun was crammed with every condiment on offer, plus what appeared to be a double helping of hot peppers.

"You're really only going to put that gross mustard on your dog?" Tally asked her as ketchup dripped from her bun, directing a pointed gaze at the thin yellow strip on Davy's otherwise naked hot dog.

"Rude, Tally," Anna scolded her.

"Sorry, but mustard is nasty."

Davy wanted to taste hot dog, not Heinz. "That's the way I like it."

"Huh. I never knew that about you." Tally's disapproval was still evident.

Anna picked up her laden dog with two hands. "Why would you? They don't serve hot dogs during high tea at the Plaza." Her eyes held a hint of mischief as she chomped, diced onion and banana peppers flying everywhere.

"Rude, Anna." Tally's expression seemed to say *neener*!

After Anna swallowed she said, "Was it? Or was it just factual?"

Davy passed Anna a napkin to wipe the mustard from her chin, refusing to be drawn in. "You two would probably like Chicago-style hot dogs. They add a bunch of things too—*dragged through the garden* they call it."

Tally made a face as she thoroughly coated a fry with ketchup. It was possible that all her food was merely a ketchup delivery system. "That sounds kind of yuck. Like a dirty dog. How does this one compare to all the others you've had?"

"One of the best."

"Toldja." Tally managed to appear smug even while she chewed with her mouth open. This was altogether different behavior than on her birthdays, more genuine, less best Sunday manners, and Davy liked it.

"You did."

Tally put her hot dog down. "Hey, I think this is the first time I've been with both my sisters together."

"We were all at your birthday party last weekend," Anna pointed out.

"Yeah, but it's never been just the three of us."

Davy thought it an observation worth celebrating. She lifted her soft drink. "To sisters."

Anna raised her cup. "Sisters."

"My sisters!" Tally bumped her cup with theirs. Her smile was bracketed with smudges of ketchup at its corners. "So, what's the reason we're here, all together?"

A spike of regret radiated through Davy, that Tally knew there was an ulterior reason for their hot dog date. "I want you to know that I plan to be around a lot more. I want to hang out with you, get to know you better. No more once-a-year-at-the-Plaza on your birthday."

Tally leveled a considering gaze at her.

"Now that I live nearby, we can see each other more often."

"Cool."

"You know that I've been looking for a new place, right?" Anna took over. "Not only do I have to find somewhere that's got space for all my art stuff, but I've also been looking for a better school for Lou."

"You should move to Davy's town. Su-Jin's cousin goes to Elmdale High and it's a really good public school. Not as good as mine, but it could be better for Louie, since you can't pay the tuition." Tally had been in private schools all her life, courtesy of her father.

"Don't be a jerk, Tally," Anna said, fixing her with a glare.

"What? I'm only being *factual*." She held up her ketchup-covered fingers in air quotes and glared back at her.

Davy tried to head off the impending argument. "If Louis could have an opportunity to go to a better school, you'd want that for him, right?"

"Yeah."

"I want that for him too, even though I just met him. You never mentioned him during our birthday teas."

"Oh. Was I supposed to?" Tally brushed some crumbs from the table. "He's really cute. He's into fish and sea life and stuff."

"Davy has offered her home to Lou and me so he can go to school in Elmdale." Anna obviously wanted to get on with it.

"Really?" Tally directed her gaze at Davy. "Where are you going to live then?"

"I'll be living there too, with them."

"But I thought you guys didn't like each other."

Davy snuck a look at Anna and saw the way she gave Tally a sidelong look of exasperation. It seemed like confirmation of Anna's negative opinion of Davy.

She was already completely aware of this, but it hurt a little bit to have Tally corroborate it. It was true that their infrequent meetings in the more recent past were marked by irritation and impatience, but it felt wrong to dwell on that when they were going to try to help each other out. Davy could only speak for herself, and something inside her wanted to smooth over the rough edges of the past and prepare a frictionless future for them all. If that was even possible. She looked down at the table and said, "Anna and I have known each other longer than we've known you. We haven't been close lately, but we were good friends once. I really want to be friends again."

She could feel both Anna's and Tally's eyes on her, and even though she wanted to see the effect her words had on Anna, when she raised her head she didn't have the courage to look at her. Tally gazed at her thoughtfully, but Anna replied.

"We had some fun times, didn't we, Davy?"

"We did." She finally met those blue eyes and saw nothing but warmth and amiability. Perhaps they really could forget their animosity and be friends.

"You know," Anna said to Tally, "Davy worked on the sets with me one summer for SSCT when we did *Cats*."

"No way. Really?"

Anna nodded, that mischievous look back. "And I can tell you she was about as artistic as a chunk of concrete."

"Hey, wait a minute. How much artistic talent does it take to staple garbage onto wood?"

"That was about all you could handle. We couldn't trust you with anything more complicated than that."

"You were so bossy and such a perfectionist, who'd want to handle any more than that?" She balled up a napkin and tossed it in Anna's direction.

"Do you want to help this summer?" Tally started tapping the table with both hands, her eyes shining with excitement. "We're doing *Into the Woods*. I'm going to try out for Little Red Riding Hood. Auditions are this weekend."

Davy didn't want to say no, but when would she possibly have time for this? Anna watched her, waiting for her answer.

"Come on," Tally urged her. "We always need volunteers to help with stuff. Anna does the set design every year, and I'll be practically living there all summer. You said you wanted to spend more time with me."

She knew not to fight it. "Okay, I'll help. But like Anna says, I have no artistic talent so I'm not sure how I'll be useful. And work keeps me really busy, so I'll have to squeeze it in with that."

"Yay!" Tally raised her fists above her head in triumph.

"So you're good with me and Lou moving in with Davy?" Anna asked.

"Sure, as long as I can come over and use the trampoline sometimes."

"Oh, Tal, I think that was just a rental." Anna looked to Davy for confirmation.

"No, it'll be there. Come over anytime you like." Davy smiled and reached over to grasp Tally's sticky fingers. If her home now had an attraction that would lure her long neglected half-sister to visit, it was a small price to pay. Good thing they hadn't come to dismantle it yet. It looked like she had just bought an enormous trampoline.

CHAPTER ELEVEN

Anna pulled into Davy's driveway on Friday night; the house was dark and unwelcoming. She approached the front door and rang the bell but there was no answer. She checked the time on her phone. Davy had said to meet her at nine p.m., and it was ten past.

The smooth granite of the top step of the porch looked inviting, so Anna eased herself down onto the cool stone and let it soothe her after a long, sweaty, dusty day indoors. She couldn't even be annoyed by Davy's absence, so happy was she to be off her feet. Moving day was tomorrow and the past two days had been nonstop packing and tying up a thousand loose ends. Her to-do list was still a mile long, but Davy wouldn't be around tomorrow, so she needed to pick up keys.

It was heavenly to be sitting on the shadowy porch with nothing to do but wait. Her mind settled from the endless rejiggering of priorities and tasks to complete, and as she sat in the dark she became aware of the chorus of cicadas and the wafting scent of honeysuckle. Darling Drive was tranquil, unlike the constant sound of activity that accompanied her soon-to-be-former apartment. She would miss the morning light and the space to work, but was glad to leave behind the regular thump of a cleaver from the restaurant kitchen downstairs, the clang and clatter of pots and dishware, and the Cantonese cursing when the dishwasher had broken down yet again.

A black sedan rolled up to the curb and Davy appeared from the back seat. She hurried up the front path with her head down while fumbling in her briefcase and had almost reached the door when Anna quietly said, "Hi."

Davy dropped her bag and clutched at her heart with both hands. "Anna! You scared the living shit out of me. I didn't see you."

"Maybe put your porch lights on a timer?" She stood. "You didn't see my car in the driveway? Did you forget I was coming?"

Davy gazed at Anna's car in the driveway, and then turned back. "No, I didn't forget. I didn't see your car." She picked up her bag and rummaged again, quickly producing her house keys. "Sorry. I was congratulating myself for getting here before you. I was going to pretend to be mad at you for being late and everything."

Anna put her hands in her pockets. "You can still be pretend mad if you want. I *was* ten minutes late."

The side of Davy's mouth curled up in an alluring way. "I pretend forgive you. Come on in."

She followed Davy through the foyer and into the kitchen, where Davy headed straight for the fridge. "Something to drink? I'm having wine. It's Friday, and it's been a fucking day."

"I hear that. Wine sounds good."

Davy's kitchen was large and very white. It was exceptionally clean, with all the fancy appliances that were in vogue right now, but it seemed vacant, unlived in. There were two stools tucked under the island in a space that looked like it could accommodate at least four more, but the large adjacent nook where a sizable table and chairs could go was empty. Anna recalled from the party that most of the other rooms were empty as well.

"When did you move in here?" she asked.

Davy retrieved delicate stemmed glasses from the cupboard and poured from a bottle of white. "Beginning of May. Sauvignon blanc okay?"

"Sure." That was two months ago. "Don't you have furniture?"

"Not much." Davy took a sip and sank onto one of the stools. She pulled the other one out for Anna to sit on. "The buyer of my place in the city liked my stuff so he made me an offer that included the furniture. It was all pretty modern—lots of chrome and glass and leather. It wouldn't really fit here, and I had kind of outgrown that look. I brought a few things—my bed, my favorite chair, books, kitchen stuff. I got these stools online, but I haven't had time to shop for anything else."

No wonder she was never here. It was barely a home.

"But now you're bringing furniture, so yay for me." Davy took another sip and propped her head up with her hand. She looked absolutely exhausted.

"Don't get your hopes up about my interior design style. It could generously be called early post-collegiate, with aspects of Ikea, and smudges of paint everywhere."

"Do you have a couch? You don't really miss a couch until you don't have one."

"I do. You probably even saw it when you came to my place."

"Oh, yeah. I don't remember." She stifled a yawn. "Nothing beats lying on a couch and zoning out in front of the TV when you're down."

Was Davy feeling down? *Should I ask her?*

But she kept talking. "How's Louis?"

"He's great. He's having a sleepover with Tally and my mom tonight."

"Is he okay with coming here?"

"Once I mentioned the trampoline, he had his bags packed. Don't be offended if he calls you the trampoline lady, okay? He means it with affection."

Davy chuckled. "I've been called worse. By adults. In court." She reached into her briefcase and pulled out a manila file folder, which she then slid toward Anna. "The contract."

Right. In all the upheaval of packing up her life, she had forgotten she had asked for it. This was why she was here, and to get the keys. It didn't matter that she was feeling the lassitude that comes with a glass of wine and a high degree of comfort sitting here with Davy in her kitchen— soon to be their kitchen. Strangely, she wanted to continue this relaxed conversation instead of getting down to business, but Davy honestly looked like she was ready to drop and probably couldn't wait for Anna to leave. Still, she couldn't bring herself to open the folder. "Before we do that, maybe you could show me around a little? We could discuss where you want the bigger pieces to go. And you could tell me where you want Lou and me to sleep? Where I can put my art stuff? I was thinking the garage. I could easily work out of there."

Davy looked appalled by the suggestion. "You're not working in the garage. It's stifling in there right now, and what about when it gets cold? No way. Besides, there's a much better place. Come on, let me give you a quick tour."

❖

Davy couldn't seem to catch her breath. This was the first time she was showing her new house to anyone, and she was both proud and self-conscious. It was an ostentatious empty shell, but Anna was cooing and admiring over everything. Davy couldn't tell if it was sincere.

After traversing the downstairs rooms, they toured the upstairs, and Davy hastily closed the door to the primary bedroom before her unmade bed and the week's worth of discarded clothing on the floor could be seen. Anna chose two bedrooms next door to each other for her and Louis, and marveled at the adjacent laundry room, calling it the height of luxury.

She realized it really mattered to her whether Anna liked her home. As they had sat with their wine, Davy imagined other such nights when they would chat and laugh and wind down their respective days. But at the same time she had to keep in mind that this was artificial. She could never forget that. This wasn't real.

When the tour ended up back in the kitchen, Anna said, "The basement? Is that where I'll be working?"

"No." Davy snagged the file folder from the counter and held the side door open for Anna. "This way." She led her across the driveway to the detached three-car garage, and mounted an exterior staircase attached to the side of the building. At the top of the stairs, she again held the door open and gestured for Anna to come through. She closed the door behind them and flicked on the lights.

Anna stood still. "Incredible. It's bigger than my apartment."

Above the garage was a large, mostly empty space with three enormous skylights. There was a long, saloon-style wet bar along one wall in the midpoint of the room and an equally long tobacco-colored leather sofa opposite it. The sofa had probably remained in the space because getting it in there to begin with was probably akin to an act of God. The floors were a dark hardwood and the walls were coated in a hideous shade of muddy brown, but Davy thought it would suit this new purpose. "AC in the summer and heat in the winter. Would this suit for a workspace?"

"It's perfect. What was it for?"

"It used to be the former owner's man cave. There was a pool table and some pinball machines, but he took all that with him. We could paint it a different color. What color are art studios usually?"

Anna drifted toward the middle of the room. "Something lighter than this." She poked around behind the bar. "You have a kegerator."

"I know. I'll need it for my annual Super Bowl blowout."

Anna turned toward her with an expression of disbelief.

"That was a joke. I've been to an occasional game with clients and can usually camouflage my gross ignorance by plying them with expensive snacks and alcohol."

"I feel like you've changed a lot since when we were teenagers, but it can't have been that much."

"Nope. Still uncoordinated, inartistic, and utterly uninterested in sports."

"You're not uncoordinated on the dance floor."

"But you think I've changed?" Davy asked.

Anna came from behind the bar. "It's been a long time, but I remember you pretty well from that summer. You were mostly quiet and sweet when we first met—you kept your cards close to your chest. Now you're a hard-charging business lady who gets what she wants. But the then-you and the now-you both have a sort of impenetrable quality, like you're always holding something back. You're kind of enigmatic."

"I just got older, Anna. I grew up. And I promise you—" Davy took a few steps closer. "I'm not an enigma. I'll tell you anything you want to know."

She nodded but didn't continue the conversation. Maybe there wasn't anything she cared to know. Her eyes lingered on the floor below her feet. "I don't think this will work. It's too nice. No matter how hard I try, I know I'll get shit all over the floor, and this looks like real mahogany. I'm pretty hard on my workspace. What if you wanted to use it as something else after I'm gone? Set up a screening room? Make it a wo-man cave?"

"Don't you think I have enough unused rooms in my house that I can afford to let this one go? Please use it and don't be precious about the floors or anything else. It's perfect for what you need. It even has a sink."

Anna checked out the bar sink and scoffed. "That tiny thing? I would destroy it."

"Look at the skylights. Wait'll you see its amazing morning sunlight. It's ideal for your purpose. It's not a man cave anymore. It's an Ann...a cave!"

"Wow. That was astoundingly terrible." Anna's voice was deadpan, but her smile was big and her eyes were warm. "I'd almost forgotten how much of a dork you can be. Glad to see that hasn't changed."

When Anna directed the power of that high-wattage smile at her, it was all Davy could do to remember to breathe. It felt so good to be the cause of it. This was exactly the way she felt that summer before things turned bad. How could Anna still affect her this way? She turned her back and focused on breathing.

"Hey, are you okay? I'm sorry. That was mean. You're not a dork."

Davy could hear her approaching. She whirled around, and Anna was nearer than she expected. At close range she could see the concern in Anna's azure eyes. Her nostrils were filled with the scent of…was that orange blossoms? She held up the file folder between them with both hands, like a shield. "It's okay. It's true. Total dork. The defense rests on that very fact."

"No—"

"Let's look at the contract, shall we?" She walked past Anna and stood at the bar, opening the folder and fishing a pen from her pocket. "It's a pretty standard boilerplate agreement, but I've left room if you want to add any clauses." She felt Anna's presence beside her, but she didn't look at her, pretending to pore over the contract that she had written earlier that day. "It outlines what you get—the one year rent-free tenancy for the purpose of maintaining Louis's enrollment at Elmdale Elementary. In return, you do everything in your power to assist me in attaining a name equity partnership at Archer, Conant & Spar." She handed a copy of the contract to Anna and placed a pen in front of her. "If you agree, sign where the yellow arrows indicate."

Anna stood with one hand on her hip while the other flipped the pages, her brows drawn downward. "What does *everything in my power* mean?"

"Well, what does it mean to you? Here's your chance to add amendments and clauses."

She chewed on her lip for a moment. "I'll talk you up. I'll tell everyone how great you are. I'll lie for you. Is that okay to say in a contract?" She picked up the pen.

Davy tried to remain expressionless. Was Anna going to lie about how great she was? *Semantics. Keep going.* "It's fine because it's between us, but I don't need you to do that. I'm sorry, but your opinion of me as a lawyer has no bearing in the legal community. My ability and reputation are not the issue. What I need from you is to present yourself as my partner and fiancée, exhibiting the pretense of a loving, committed relationship with me so I can appear to be dedicated to preserving and supporting the ideas of family, community, country, and democratic society."

"Appear to be? Don't you support those ideas anyway?"

"It doesn't matter what I personally think as long as the partners believe it."

Anna put the pen down. "But do you?"

"Yes, hypothetically, I do." She didn't bother saying she didn't believe she would marry or have a family of her own. Her relationship rehab with Tally notwithstanding, she couldn't imagine ever needing people in her life like that, or being needed. "What are you willing to do to make it look believable? I won't ask you to do anything you don't want to."

"I can do believable. I'm not an actor, but I can act like I like you."

Davy sighed. "Great." This conversation wasn't doing much for her ego.

"And I—I do like you…"

Ugh. Moving on. "What about physical demonstrations of affection?"

"Um…I'll hold your hand?"

"Are you asking me or telling me?"

"Telling you." Anna's voice became more certain. "I'll link arms with you. Put my arm around your shoulder or waist. Hugs are okay. I'll gaze adoringly into your eyes. I'll dance with you. That was fun when we danced at the party. You're a great dancer."

Davy didn't look at her, couldn't look at her. She grabbed the pen and started writing.

"We can kiss."

Davy jerked her head up. "We can?"

"Tasteful public kisses. That's all. I'm not going to make out with you."

She couldn't help a tiny grin as she wrote. "Tasteful public kisses, got it."

"Wait," Anna said.

Davy waited, her pen poised. Anna's eyes were downcast, and she was still as a statue, caught up in her thoughts. Then she licked her lips. Was she thinking about kissing Davy right now? Because merely the idea of it had pushed every single other thought out of Davy's head.

"On second thought, I don't think we should kiss." She cut her eyes over to Davy as if to gauge her reaction.

"You don't?" She tried to keep all inflection out of her voice.

"I've changed my mind. It's not a good idea. We can get around it anyway with the hugging and touching."

Davy scratched out the lines she had just written, the pen digging in harder than she intended. "No kiss." She wrote instead. The word probably should have included the -*ing* to make it sound more like an across-the-board thing, but Davy could barely bring herself to write what she had. She couldn't believe how disappointed she felt. For some fake, meaningless kisses that might or might not have happened anyway.

Then Anna mumbled something.

"What?"

She cleared her throat and spoke louder. "No sex. If it's not real, there won't be any sex."

Davy stared at her, but Anna wouldn't meet her eyes. If there was no kissing, there absolutely would be no sex. What kind of person has sex with someone but doesn't kiss them? Did Anna think she was a monster?

Anna seemed to grow more uncomfortable as the silent seconds ticked by, crossing her arms over her chest and looking down.

"Of course," Davy said. "That should go without saying, but I'm writing it in."

"Thank you."

It was quiet while she added the language to one of the copies. The fraught atmosphere lessened by degrees after the negotiating was done, and by the time Davy finished writing everything into the second copy, things felt calmer in the man cave. Her hand only gave the slightest tremor before she signed both copies. Anna took the pen as soon as she was finished and quickly added her signature to both of them.

"It's late. I have to go."

She accompanied Anna to the door. "What time are the movers coming?"

"Nine. And I'm not finished packing yet."

"Well, good luck." Davy held out one of the copies. "Did you want to take this? Or I have a safe. I could put them both in there."

"Thanks. I'd only lose it in all the hubbub tomorrow. What will you be doing while a bunch of burly men and I are moving house and home?"

"I'll be at the office." Where she always was on Saturdays. Should she be home for Anna's move? "Do you want me to be here?"

"No. Please don't change your plans."

She followed Anna down the stairs and to her car. "Roland's barbeque will start around five or six, but we don't have to go that early."

Anna faced her. "Oh, right. I completely forgot about that."

"I know it'll be a really long day for you."

"No, it's fine. I'll have to ask Mom if she's okay with keeping Lou another night."

"You can bring him if you want." Davy knew she'd refuse.

"No, she loves having him, and he loves being spoiled rotten." She regarded Davy for a moment and then reached out her right hand, higher than a handshake, lower than a high-five. "And so it begins. As of tomorrow, you're the love of my life."

"Lucky me." Davy awkwardly grasped it and for a moment it looked like they were arm wrestling without a table. She took another cleansing breath. In less than twenty-four hours, Anna was going to be living with her. She hoped she knew what she was doing. "See you tomorrow."

CHAPTER TWELVE

Anna heard footsteps in the hallway as she sat on the floor in Louis's new room, unpacking his clothes and organizing them into piles.

"Anna?" Davy's voice was hesitant.

"In here." It was sometime in the late afternoon, and the slanting sunlight had softened to a golden glow as it imperceptibly crept across the wooden floorboards. The movers had dispatched her belongings to the various corners of Davy's house with deadly efficiency and departed hours ago.

Davy appeared in the doorway. "Hi. How did it go?"

"Very smoothly. If you don't like where I placed any of the bigger pieces, we can switch it around. And I put my kitchen stuff where I thought it should logically go, but if it interferes with yours, I can move it."

Davy sat on Louis's mattress, yet to be covered with his favorite undersea sheets, which Anna hoped would reveal themselves sooner rather than later. "No, everything looks good downstairs. Your sofa looks really comfortable. And it'll be nice to have a table to sit at in the kitchen."

"Okay, good. But you can still let me know if anything bothers you. How was your day?" Anna abandoned the clothes and maneuvered herself so her back rested against Louis's dresser.

Davy blew a raspberry and flicked her hand in a way that said *don't want to talk about it*. "What can I do to help?"

"You can sit here and keep me company while I take a break. I've been at it all day."

She moved a few stacks of clothes and stretched out on her side, propping her head on her hand. "I guess this is when I congratulate myself for my impeccable timing."

Anna laughed. "I was thinking. Tonight's going to be like a first date for us. We have the cliché beat big time. The moving van arrived before even our first date."

"The cliché?"

"Or joke, maybe."

Davy raised her eyebrows in inquiry.

"What does a lesbian bring on a second date?"

"Right. A U-Haul." She gave Anna a wry smile. "We'll have to get our stories straight, like how we met and that sort of thing."

Anna directed her gaze at the floor. Even though it was a necessary request, something about manufacturing their courtship rankled. "I'll agree to whatever tale you want to tell. Might as well make it something that advances your cause."

"Like what?"

"I don't know. You want to be seen as someone who cares about family and community, right? Maybe we met at the women's march or a local protest of some sort? No, too political, probably. How about you asked me out when you were helping me with a legal matter?"

"Nope. Unethical."

"Really? What if I was a former client at the time?" At Davy's forbidding expression, Anna changed tacks. "How about we ran into each other on the street and you spilled orange juice on me? Or you gave me a few bucks when I was short at the supermarket checkout?"

"Those scenarios sound vaguely familiar."

"Yeah, maybe I saw them in a movie." She thought for a moment, but the only ideas coming to her were from rom com meet cutes. "Maybe it's Louis you helped. You helped him find me when he got lost in that supermarket. Or got him down when he climbed up a tree too high?"

"Anna, he's not a cat. And nobody would believe I climbed a tree for any reason."

"That did happen once, when my mom was watching him, but he was only a couple of feet off the ground. How about you pulled him from a burning car?" Anna knew that one was ridiculous.

"So I'm a superhero now?"

"Well, how could they give the job to that other guy when you've saved a child from a burning car?"

Davy laughed and shook her head. "I like the way you think, but let's leave him out of it. I thought that's the way you wanted it. And what if someone asks him about it?"

"You have a point." She was quiet, thinking, and she could feel Davy's eyes on her. The silence lengthened. She twisted to face the dresser and opened the bottom drawer. "Break time's over. I'm sure you'll come up with something, and I'll back you up, whatever it is." She began transferring piles of clothing into the dresser and heard Davy stand behind her.

"Okay. I'm going to grab a shower. Want to head over to Roland's around seven?"

"Sounds good. I'll be ready."

When the sound of Davy's footsteps faded, Anna paused in her labor. Getting ready meant becoming more comfortable with this, because their public debut was about to happen despite her ambivalence about it.

❖

Davy walked around the side of Roland's house with Anna by her side. She was a little nervous, but not nearly as nervous as she thought she would be on the inaugural outing of their propagation of a large-scale deception. Maybe it was Anna who was keeping her calm, looking like a Nordic fairy in her diaphanous, pink sundress. She had made an obvious effort in her appearance, more of an effort than Davy had. Could she be feeling nervous too?

She took Anna's hand before they reached the gate that led to the backyard, then gazed down at their two hands. She couldn't remember the last time she had held someone's hand, and it instilled in her both comfort and confidence. "Is this okay?" she asked, gripping tighter.

Anna nodded as she eyed the tall timber gate in front of them. "I guess once we walk through there, it's show time."

"Did I mention how great you look tonight? If I didn't, I'm saying it now. You look really pretty."

"Thank you. It's a miracle I was able to find the exact outfit I wanted, and the iron, and the ironing board, considering roughly eighty percent of my possessions are still in boxes." She darted a look into Davy's eyes before looking down. "You look nice too. I don't think I've ever seen sneakers so blindingly white."

"Oh." Davy stopped walking and gazed at her feet. "They're new. I thought they would be okay with the pants. Too much?" She thought her white linen trousers and vibrant aqua top were a tad dressy and the sneakers toned them down. "If it's not my office uniform, I'm usually a fashion don't. Or on a good day, a fashion go-ahead-and-do-it-but-don't-say-I-didn't-warn-you."

"Don't sell yourself short. You look good." Anna squeezed her hand and smiled at her. "Perfect for a backyard summer barbeque—cool and classy and casual." She was being so encouraging. It was nice.

"Thanks." Davy lifted Anna's hand and grasped it with both of hers in an oddly formal way. "And thank you for doing this. I know it's weird and a little crazy, but I trust you."

Anna withdrew her hand. "You're welcome. Shall we go in?"

Too serious, Davy. She opened the gate and allowed Anna to precede her. The backyard was aglow with tiki torches and strung lights, and some subdued jazz could be heard from somewhere.

Leanne spotted them right away and hurried over. "Our guests of honor! Welcome."

"Leanne, this is Anna, my fiancée." Davy felt a bit dizzy saying it out loud.

Leanne ignored Anna's outstretched hand and pulled her into an effusive hug. "I'm so happy to meet you, Anna. I can't tell you how much I adore Davy, and I'm so excited for you both. I saw the moving truck earlier. You two must be exhausted after a day of moving furniture and boxes around. Thanks for coming to our little backyard shindig instead of falling straight into bed. But aren't we missing someone?"

"Anna's son, Louis, is with his grandmother this weekend," Davy said.

"Very sensible for moving day," Leanne agreed. "And nice to have a bit of private time too, right?" She elbowed Anna in a friendly way.

Davy glanced at Anna, hoping she was okay with Leanne's implication.

"Yes, exactly," Anna said with a laugh. "Thanks for this. It's wonderful to meet new people already."

"I've invited most of your neighbors. Darling Drive is a friendly place. There are a few ACS people here too, but we won't let them talk too much business tonight. Come, let me get you something to drink." Leanne led them further into the backyard.

ACS? Anna mouthed.

"My firm," Davy murmured. She scanned the crowd and saw Roland in discussion with a few people from work. Most were unfamiliar and likely her new neighbors. Leanne was a perfect host and introduced them around. It seemed like the majority of the neighbors were families with older children, but Leanne took care to connect them with one family with young children around Louis's age. Anna was quickly drawn into a conversation with this couple about the school and their twin sons' experience there.

Davy went to get more rum punch for them and met Roland at the bar. "Roland. The punch is delicious."

"Hey, Davy. You and Anna having a good time?"

"Yes, of course. Thanks for doing this. It's a nice welcome for Anna."

"And you." He jostled her while he filled his highball with ice. "We've got to get you settled in here too. Don't forget about the club. I'll show you around if you like."

"Thanks, but I don't play golf. You know that."

"You can start to learn. I'd say it's good for business, but not playing hasn't slowed you down. And there's tennis and a fabulous pool area, great restaurant." He cleared his throat in a way that she guessed was supposed to be funny. "And I can definitely vouch for the quality of the booze at the bar."

Davy smiled. She was glad she had been assigned to Roland's research team when she first started at the firm. He was more than a work mentor. Not quite a friend, and not a father figure. Uncle Roland, maybe. He was the rare man who seemed to care about her beyond career success. Certainly more than her own father. She watched him put a tiny splash of bourbon in his glass and fill the rest with seltzer.

He caught her looking. "Can't overdo it when I'm hosting. Leanne would kill me."

"This is quite a bit fancier than a backyard barbecue." She nodded toward the long table set for twenty under a leafy elm with candle-lit lanterns hung from its branches. "I can't thank you enough for the warm welcome."

"Oh, this is nothing. You know Leanne has the caterer on speed-dial and this is what she can throw together in a few days." He clutched her around the shoulder and led her away from the bar. "We're both excited for you and happy to have you as a neighbor. You're one of the good ones."

Davy felt herself get a little misty. She was lucky to have a mentor like Roland.

"But I didn't get a chance to tell you about Kevin Keeley."

She stopped in her tracks. "What?"

"You were right. He's fired off his own starting pistol in his race for Len's spot—with Mel's blessing. He mostly pussyfooted around it last weekend, but his intention is clear. He's positioning himself."

"I knew it."

"Now, there may be others who will throw their hats in the ring, so we have to be ready."

"We?"

"I'm officially backing you. You can run circles around Keeley, Davy, and I don't think he's got the fire like you do. Or the talent."

"Roland, thank—"

"First thing I want you to put on your to-do list is to total up all the business you've brought in. Do both dollars and yearly billable hours. Make it a pretty little spreadsheet and I'll get it into the right hands. Next, I want you to meet Joel Kleinman, that guy in the maroon polo and legs too hairy for shorts. He lives across the road and is the CEO at Teltech. Can you imagine the billing we could do with them? They're constantly battling for free speech and whatnot with that hot social media platform they launched. I've been trying to convince him to come over for about two years. Start working your magic on him."

"You got it." Davy strode over to the group that included Joel Kleinman, Roland right behind her.

❖

Anna stood by herself near a table of hors d'oeuvres, pretending to be interested in the deviled eggs. The couple she had been talking to had taken a call from their babysitter and suddenly departed. Davy had never returned with her drink, and when Anna spotted her in the crowd, she was talking animatedly amidst a group of people, offering Anna's punch to a man with very hairy legs. She had debated with herself about whether to join Davy but decided that gazing at finger food was the easier option.

"It's something you'll probably have to get used to."

Anna turned and Leanne was there, a glass of punch in her outstretched hand.

"Thank you," she said, and took a sip to mask her embarrassment. Leanne had noticed she'd been deserted by her brand-new fiancée at a party where Anna knew no one. "What will I have to get used to?"

"Lawyers gravitating toward their own kind. And also their prey."

"Their prey?"

"That would be anyone who has the potential to throw business their way."

"Like that person Davy's talking to?"

"Exactly. For people like Roland and Davy, who are in love with what they do, every business meeting is a party, and every party is a potential business meeting."

"I see."

"I blame my husband. He must've put a bug in Davy's ear. He's been trying to get Joel to sign with the firm for years. My guess is he's inflicting Davy on him now."

Yes, but Davy had a mind of her own, didn't she? Anna didn't want to talk about this with a woman she had met ten minutes ago. "Apparently, she's pretty good at drawing clients to the firm?"

"Oh yes, from what Roland says. He's happy she bought that house. He's so excited, he may start coming over unannounced." Leanne laughed. "You tell me if he becomes a nuisance. I'll put a stop to it."

"It sounds like they have a great working relationship."

"Davy delivers. And she works harder than anyone else. Roland admires that about her. I remember so clearly the day I met her. We always have a reception for the new hires at our pied-à-terre in the city and the year Davy started, she made quite an impression. She stood quietly on the outskirts of a group of her fellow first years and some of their more established colleagues. I remember I had her pegged as meek—can you believe that? Well, she's simply standing there, listening, until this one person said something smug and foolish, something she disagreed with. Well, she came to life! Her evisceration of that young man was total and complete, and he never recovered. He left the firm a year later, and Davy's reputation as a dynamo was born right there."

Anna gazed at Davy. Meek wasn't far off from who she had been when Anna first knew her.

"You should come," Leanne said.

"Sorry?"

"To the new hires party. It's next Thursday. We encourage the new hires to bring their spouses if they like, and Davy should bring you. This year's theme is December holidays in July—Christmas, Kwanzaa, Hanukah, Solstice, or any other celebration of your choice."

"A work event with a theme?"

"I'm the one who plans it every year. I have to keep it interesting for myself, don't I? Last summer was Luau on Mars. Not one of my better ideas. Nobody knew if they should wear a grass skirt or a space helmet."

"December holidays in July sounds much more straightforward. Thanks for the invite. I'll talk to Davy about it."

"Great! I hope to see you there." Leanne laid a friendly hand on her forearm. "What do you do, Anna?"

"I'm an artist. A painter. I specialize in natural landscapes, mostly."

"Wonderful! I must see some of your work. Do you show anywhere?"

"Oh, I'm not that kind of artist. My gallery is an Etsy page. I sell at festivals and street fairs. I do commissions too. I'm basically a paintbrush for hire."

"What materials do you work in?"

"I like acrylics best, and they sell well, but I can do whatever I'm asked to do."

Leanne looked her up and down like she was the most interesting person in the world. "I'm so curious. I'm going to look you up."

Anna grinned. This woman was so warm and endearing. "Go right ahead. If you see anything you like, I'll give you the three-doors-down discount."

"Marvelous. I'm going to keep that little bonus to myself."

"What do you do, Leanne?"

"A million years ago in another life I was an event planner. But with raising the girls it became too much, so I've been a professional wife and mother since. But our youngest starts at Brown this fall and I'm dreading the emptiness of this big old house. Maybe I should get back into it."

"Your skills are formidable if this party is anything to go by."

"This? This is nothing. You should have seen my Martian pig roast." Leanne linked arms with her and steered her away from the hors d'oeuvres. "Come with me. There's some people I think you should meet."

❖

Davy and Anna were among the last to leave, and Davy thought the evening had been a success. Leanne was a maestro of seating and had placed Anna and Davy side by side at the midpoint of the long table. Although they hadn't spoken much to each other, both she and Anna had never lacked for conversation. She'd made some inroads with Joel Kleinman and would follow up with him in a few days. In between her conversations with Joel and some other neighbors and associates, Davy overheard Anna speaking with a gallerist and an interior designer.

"Did you have fun?" She glanced at Anna, walking silently beside her as they made their way back to the house. As soon as they were alone, the engaged, attentive expression she had worn all evening fell away and was replaced by a solemnity that suggested something was less than okay.

Anna sighed. "Yes, but I'm exhausted. There were times tonight when I thought moving all my worldly possessions was not nearly as strenuous as casually socializing with new neighbors."

"You looked like you were enjoying yourself."

"I was. I'm just tired," Anna said.

"If we're ever out together and you're not feeling it, just tell me and we'll go."

"You mean I'll be able to pull you away from Mr. Hairy Legs and get your attention for five seconds?"

Davy stood still. Had Anna been trying to get her attention? Had she missed it? "Wait. What's happening here?"

"It's nothing. I just need to get some sleep. I'm cranky," Anna said over her shoulder as she kept walking.

Davy caught up. "Is this because I forgot to bring you your drink? I said I was sorry about that. But I made sure your glass was always full when we were at dinner. Your water glass *and* your wine glass."

"Yeah, you did," Anna said shortly. "But there's a lot you don't know. Just like Jon Snow."

"Who the Christ is Jon Snow?"

"He's from—" Anna groaned. "Never mind. He's nobody."

Davy was completely bewildered. "Anna, please stop. Obviously, I did something wrong. Tell me."

"I'm going to bed." Anna stomped away, leaving Davy by herself in the driveway.

CHAPTER THIRTEEN

Anna woke, discombobulated, the sun streaming through her uncovered windows. *Why is it so bright in here?* Her brain synced up with her surroundings. She was in Davy's house, now her house too. And the bratty way she acted last night came back to her in a rush.

She started a shopping list in her head. *Curtains. Garbage bags. Shampoo. Self-esteem.* Then she picked up her phone and saw the time. Her mom was bringing Louis in a few hours. Time to get moving.

Her old Mr. Coffee gave a phlegmatic gurgle as Anna watched liquid trickle into the pot. Davy's gleaming Italian espresso machine sat beside it. It looked like she would need a master's degree to operate the thing.

Anna realized her expectations for her first outing as Davy's fiancée had been wildly inappropriate. Did she think Davy was going to lead her around with a reassuring hand at her back and proudly introduce her to all her work colleagues? Hang on her every word like she actually cared about what Anna said? Remain by her side and be fascinated while Anna discussed Elmdale Elementary with some other parents? Yes, she had to admit. She kinda did.

But that wasn't what this was, and she had to recalibrate those expectations. And she should apologize to Davy. After a moment, she took a second mug out of the cupboard.

When she knocked on Davy's door, she thought she heard something—a grunt? She pushed it open to find Davy lying on her back in bed, limbs splayed like a starfish. The sheet was pulled up, but barely covered her breasts, and if she wasn't completely naked under there, she was something very close to it. Very little of Davy's skin was exposed, but Anna couldn't control where her mind went in that moment—a heavy, molten heat erupted in her solar plexus and the hand that held both mugs trembled slightly. "Oh. I'll come back later."

"Wait. Is that coffee?" Davy sounded like her vocal cords were made of sexy, seductive tree bark, and the lava flowed southward toward Anna's center.

She swallowed the sudden excess of saliva in her mouth. "Yes, but—"

"Can I have it, please?"

Anna entered and held a mug toward Davy, standing perpendicular to the bed and averting her eyes.

"Unless you want the show you're trying so hard to avoid, you're going to have to get that cup a little closer to my hand."

She glanced in Davy's general direction and saw a two-foot gap between the mug and her outstretched hand. After shuffling closer and achieving the handoff, she said, "Where do you keep your clothes? I can't talk to you like this."

"T-shirts are in the second drawer in the closet," Davy replied through a yawn.

The closet was almost as big as Anna's room, with a large amount of formal business attire, naturally, hanging on one side, and drawers and cubbies on the other. Anna stepped over yesterday's clothes, now in a heap on the floor. She threw a gray T-shirt emblazoned with the Notorious RBG's face toward the bed and gazed out the window while Davy put it on. She tried to scrub the last three minutes from her memory bank.

Ten seconds later, Davy said, "You can turn around now, prudie." She was sitting up, the sheet covering her lower half, and a big grin on her face. "And before you get mad, that was a joke. You're not a prude— probably. I've seen no evidence of it, anyway. And thanks for the coffee. How did you know I take it black?"

"I didn't. You don't have any milk in the fridge."

"Oops. I get groceries delivered. We'll put in an order."

"It's fine. I need the undiluted caffeine today. This is regular coffee from my drip coffee maker. I'm going to need lessons if you want it from your machine." She leaned against the windowsill and stole a quick look at Davy with her mussed hair and tired eyes before lowering her gaze. Even though she was now decently covered up, Anna was unnerved by how much she wanted to simply stare at her.

"Sign me up too. I don't know how to use it."

"You don't?"

"No, I just got it. It's a housewarming present I bought myself."

"What do you do in the mornings?"

"Behave like a beast until I get to the office and have my caffeine infusion there."

Anna thought she was joking but couldn't be sure.

"But seriously," Davy continued. "You don't have to make me coffee."

"Okay." Anna surveyed the room. Davy's king-sized bed was the only furniture that occupied it. The headboard was an enormous slab of tufted, brown, distressed leather—as if a Chesterfield sofa in a British gentleman's club unfolded itself into an upright position and now stood sentry against the wall. Besides that, there was nothing except a pile of plastic and paper and wire hangers from several days of dry-cleaning on the floor. *Waste basket*, she mentally added to her shopping list. "Listen, I wanted to apologize for the way the night ended. I'm sorry. I was really grouchy, and you didn't deserve my obnoxious behavior."

Davy gazed at her from over her coffee mug. "I meant what I said. You don't have to do anything that makes you uncomfortable."

"Come on, nights like that are why I'm here. It's fine. I'll hold up my end of the deal. It won't happen again." Anna wanted to move on from this. "My mom, and Louis, and probably Tally will be here in a little while. I thought it might be nice for you to be here too. Maybe you could give him a tour and show him his room? So he starts to get to know you?"

"Yeah, sure. When will they be here?"

"Not for a couple of hours, but I wanted to give you a heads up so you can, I don't know, put on some pants?" She tried to suppress a smile.

"Didn't I tell you? We're clothing optional here."

Anna studied her expression, again not sure if this was a joke.

"Fuck, Anna, lighten up. I'm kidding."

"I know, it's just…"

"What?"

"There's going to be a kid around, now. He's pretty good about honoring others' privacy, but mistakes might happen. Are you ready for that?"

Davy held up a hand like she was making a pledge. "I promise I will be decently attired from now on."

"Thank you." Anna's relief was for herself as well as for Lou. And as much as that flare up of lusty emotion might contradict her intentions, there could be no feelings of any kind toward Davy.

❖

Davy and Anna went outside to meet their guests. When Louis saw Anna, he ran across the grass to her. Anna sank to her knees.

"Ma, I'm here," he cried and launched himself into her arms.

"Thank goodness. I missed you so much." Anna pressed her face against his head, her eyes closed in contentment.

Davy looked away, their greeting seeming too private for her to witness. She suddenly wanted to touch someone too. She approached Tally and slung an arm around her shoulder even though they had never been very demonstrative with each other. "Hey, Tally. How're you doing?"

"Eh." Tally curled her body into Davy's and stood there, waiting to be hugged.

Davy wrapped her arms around her in surprise and smoothed her hand over Tally's hair. She directed a questioning glance over her head toward Pam, who rolled her lips inward and gave her head a little shake. Davy was mystified. She stepped back but kept her hands on Tally's shoulders. "What's up? You okay?"

Tally's eyes were teary. "I didn't get Little Red."

Davy didn't know what that meant.

Anna came over and put a hand on her arm. "Aw, Tal, I'm sorry."

"Madison Bathgate got it. She always gets the parts I want. I'm totally a better singer than her."

Oh. This was about that play.

Pam joined them. "But she still got a part and rehearsals start next week. She's going to get over her disappointment and be ready. Right, Tally?"

"I guess," Tally muttered.

"What part did you get?" Davy asked.

"One of the wicked stepsisters." Tally rolled her eyes so hard Davy thought she might hurt herself.

"That's great!" Anna said. "You've always been in the chorus. Now you've got an actual part. And you're only thirteen. It's an accomplishment!"

"Fourteen." Tally frowned.

"Right, sorry. I have to get used to you being a year older. I'm proud of you." Anna shook Tally's shoulder.

"I brought food. Where can we eat?" Pam held up a large shopping bag.

❖

After they had eaten their fill, Davy showed Louis the house. Everyone else followed and made encouraging noises as he cast an unimpressed eye over everything. There wasn't much to excite a five-year-old. When they got to his new bedroom, which was currently the most furnished room in the house thanks to Anna, he picked up the stuffed octopus from his bed and hugged it to his belly.

"What do you think, Lou buddy?" Anna asked. "Your own room, all to yourself. You're really a big boy now. And here are all your books and toys."

"Where's your bed, Ma?"

"It's in the room next to this one."

Louis shook his head and squeezed his octopus tighter.

Anna leaned across the bed and rapped on the wall. "My room is right on the other side. You can knock or yell and I'll hear you."

Tally sat on his bed. "And maybe you can invite me for a sleepover, Lou. I love your new room."

He looked skeptical at that.

"We also have to finish decorating it," Anna added. "We can paint it any color you like. Or we can paint a mural. What would you like to see on your wall?"

Louis looked at the empty wall. "We can paint stuff on the wall? Like a picture?"

"Yes. Maybe you'd like some fish? Or an underwater scene?"

He turned to Anna. "How did you know I would want that?" He seemed truly puzzled.

"Oh, Lou. Have you met you?" Anna gazed at him with so much love in her eyes, it filled Davy with an emotion that was less clear-cut, but somewhere between mournful and yearning.

"Could I have a whale shark? And an octopus?"

"Yes, you may," Anna said and sat cross-legged in front of him. "Nothing else is changing. We'll still do bedtime books. And I'll be right next door."

"Will I be able to see you from my bed?"

"No, buddy. But all you have to do is say my name and I'll come. Don't you want to at least try having your own room?"

Davy waited with bated breath for his answer. Anna sat and gazed at him with a serenity that made Davy calm too.

"Okay," he said.

Anna reached out and he and his octopus sank into the cradle of her lap. "That's my brave boy."

It seemed like everyone in the room exhaled at once.

"The last stop on our tour is the backyard," Davy said. "It has a big ol' trampoline back there. Do you remember it? But maybe you're not interested in that."

"I'm interested," Tally said.

"Me too. So is Jeff." Louis thrust out his octopus and made him nod.

Davy put her hands on her hips. "Well, you need at least two legs to jump on the trampoline. How many legs do you have?"

Louis inspected his lower half. "Two."

"Then you're good to go." Davy made a check mark in the air. "How many does Jeff have?"

"Eight." Louis giggled.

"Eight? That's so many! He'll probably be able to jump a lot longer than us. Let's go show him." Davy reached out her hand and Louis took it. She pulled him up from Anna's lap. Then she grasped Anna's hand and pulled her up too. They stood face to face and Davy smiled, ready to give her all the compliments for her parenting skills, but Anna lowered her eyes and quickly turned away.

"Come on, Lou. I'll race you to the backyard," Tally said, and the two of them were off.

Pam's gaze was appraising as she took in first Davy and then Anna, who busied herself straightening the bedcovers Tally had mussed. "You jumped that hurdle pretty easily. It's a good sign." She grinned and put a hand on Davy's back. "Welcome once again to the family, Davy."

"Thanks." The word came out high and thin, like a wheeze. Davy stood back and gestured for Anna and Pam to precede her out of the room. There were so many people in her lonely, empty house now. Shit had just gotten real.

❖

Anna stood with her mom a short distance from the trampoline, watching Tally, Louis, and Davy giggle breathlessly as they boinged all over the mat. She had been concerned about this new setup for Louis. He had slept all his life in their scrubby, open, Chinese-food-smelling home, essentially one extra-large room, where her bed was within sight of his. What it lacked in privacy it had made up in security, but Anna knew—hasty move or not—they wouldn't have been able to stay that way for much longer. Growing boys needed their space, and so did their moms. She was relieved he seemed willing to embrace a room of his own.

"I have to admit I'm a little surprised at this turn of events." Anna's mom watched the antics on the trampoline. "It's awfully generous of Davy to offer you a place to live, especially when you've not been quiet in voicing your opinions about her. I'm also surprised you accepted. What made you get off your high horse?"

She darted a quick look at her mom but refused to rise to the bait. She probably should tell her about their arrangement, but something in her was loath to do that. It's not that she was ashamed of it; they were both getting something of value out of it.

"How much rent is she charging you?"

"Not much," she hedged. "Very reasonable."

"Why do you think she's being so kind?"

Anna shrugged. "She has a big house?"

"That is a fact. Her house is big and empty. Perfect for you and Louis and all your belongings. Maybe she's lonely."

"She's too busy to be lonely," Anna scoffed. "She works like a maniac."

"There's that judgment. I was wondering when it would arrive."

"Is it judgment if it also happens to be true? We went to a party at her boss-slash-neighbor's last night and it was as if she was on the clock the whole night."

Her mom frowned. "Her boss is her neighbor too?"

Anna gave her mother a stiff nod. "She bought the house *because* it's close to her boss. There's not much daylight between work and rest for her."

"Lawyers don't seem to ever be off the clock. Gregory was the same." She sighed. "He was a workaholic too. It was part of the reason I ended it. There was no balance, and he valued things that held no importance to me."

Anna turned to her mom, shocked. "*You* ended it? He didn't leave?"

She nodded, and what looked like regret creased her features. "We were a mistake, and getting married would've compounded that mistake. It would have done more harm than good, especially for Tally. It was being around Davy and getting to know her that made me realize the way I raised you, and the way I wanted to raise Tally, wouldn't work if he were a daily presence in our lives."

"What does that mean?"

"We don't need to dredge up all that. The past is past."

"Mom, what are you talking about?"

But she ignored Anna's question. "Now that you've accepted Davy's generosity, you need to be generous to her too. I don't think she's had an easy time of it. So every time you want to sit in judgment, keep it to yourself. And make sure you and Louis are good housemates to her. That girl deserves some goodness in her life."

Anna's brain spewed about a thousand questions, but she knew better than to try to get more out of her mother right now. Her shuttered expression meant the subject was closed.

"And having a lawyer around could come in handy. You could ask Davy for advice about Louis's situation."

Anna's hackles rose. Her mother seemed to be going for nonchalant, but detonating this little land mine had probably been an action item on her agenda as soon as Davy had reentered the picture. "Doesn't seem very *generous* of me to immediately use her like that, does it? And don't you go asking her either. I know you're the one who told her about my housing problem."

"And look how that turned out for you." Her mom swept her arm to encompass the trampoline and Davy's house. "I'm just saying you can't keep your head buried in the sand on this. Louis needs for it to be settled. Davy is a good girl. I'm sure she'd want to help."

"Mom, I love you, but please stay out of this." Anna could shut down a conversation too. She'd learned at the feet of the master.

She turned her gaze to Davy, laughing heartily as her jumps sent a grinning Louis sprawling each time he attempted to stand. There was a lightness in her eyes and her hair flew every which way. Anna's eyes were drawn to the alluring strip of pale skin showing at her waist when her RBG T-shirt rose up every time she descended back to the rubber surface of the trampoline.

How was she supposed to do this? Now she had to ignore her inclination to stare hungrily at any of Davy's exposed skin, and keep her at an emotional distance, plus be kind and generous toward her, all while she figured out how to fulfill her end of the bargain and be an Academy Award-winning pretend fiancée to a woman who only cared about work.

The only way to accomplish this, as far as she could see, would be total distance—physical, mental, and emotional. She would maintain a buffer between herself and Davy in all ways possible, and that way she could focus on fulfilling her end of the bargain without getting sidetracked by a tangle of unnecessary emotions.

CHAPTER FOURTEEN

Davy was sitting at the bar chewing out a junior associate on the phone when she saw Anna through the bar's mirror as she pushed the door open and entered. She disconnected the call without another word and turned to watch Anna approach. The crimson red summer dress Anna was wearing made Davy's pulse pound. The only thing that marred her glamorous appearance was the huge canvas tote Anna seemed to carry everywhere. When Anna drew closer, Davy couldn't help blurting, "You look fantastic."

"Thanks." Anna smoothed her hands down the bodice. "It's not too much is it? I thought the color suited the theme. It's the only red dress I have."

"What theme?"

"The Christmas in July theme? Sorry—December holidays in July theme." Anna faltered. "Oh, no. Is this the kind of party where everyone ignores the theme?"

"You look stunning. The fact that your dress goes with one of Leanne's crazy themes is just a bonus." Davy hoped she wasn't too blatant as she eyed Anna's hotness, from the plunging neckline to the curve of her hips to her tanned and toned legs. Was it suddenly hot in here? "You're a far cry from wet woolen alpacas."

Anna frowned. "Is that supposed to be a compliment?"

"No, I just meant—" Davy gestured over to the high table where they had met to discuss Tally's party, now almost two months ago. "The last time we were here, you were soaked from the rain, and you were wearing…never mind. We should go."

Roland and Leanne's city apartment was in Midtown East, not far away, and the soft breeze and golden evening sunlight made the Manhattan evening so pretty it felt almost cinematic. They walked in stilted silence, and Davy slowed her pace so Anna could keep up in heels that were higher than Davy's. Anna looked amazing, but maybe a skosh too dressy for a weeknight work event. She probably should have given her some guidance.

But how was she supposed to guide her when they never saw each other? There was evidence of Anna's and Louis's existence around the house, more food in the fridge and toys and books scattered in a few places. The lights in Anna's studio had been on a few times when she arrived home, but it was like she was going out of her way to avoid Davy. One night she poked her head in Louis's room to see if he was awake and to say hi, but he wasn't there—at ten p.m. Where the hell was he? Maybe he was helping Anna in the studio or something, but it seemed really late for a kid his age.

In the elevator, Anna rummaged in her bag and pulled out a round, green and gold cookie tin and some colorful, furry cloth. "Should we wear these?" She held the cloth up for Davy to see. Two Santa hats, one red and the other one rainbow striped, both with a large white pom-pom at the tip. "Sorry about the pride hat. I don't even know where it came from, but it was in with my Christmas decorations. I knew exactly which box they were in."

"Uh, sure." It wouldn't hurt to embrace the theme. It might hurt to wear the rainbow hat, though. She chose the red one. Anna struggled to put the rainbow hat on with one hand. Davy stepped closer and helped her, getting a whiff of orange blossoms, baby shampoo, and a sharp underlying note of turpentine. She smelled great to Davy.

Anna reached up and adjusted the pom-pom on Davy's hat. "There. Very festive."

"Thanks."

Leanne greeted them wearing a complete Mrs. Claus costume that included a white chignon wig and tiny glasses perched on the end of her nose. "Hi, Davy. Anna, welcome."

"Hello, Mrs. Claus. You look fantastic for your age." Anna thrust the round tin into her hands. "My son and I made some holiday cookies today."

Leanne opened it and Davy saw beautifully iced sugar cookies in shapes of fir trees, wreaths, dreidels, and snowflakes. "I simply have to meet your son. Look at his fine work."

"Well, I decorated those. His were a little less than perfect, but he got to eat them, so he was happy."

Davy suddenly wished she could have been there to see the two of them making cookies today.

"We'll set them out over by the menorah. They'll go splendidly with the eggnog ice cream and frozen hot chocolate," Leanne said. "Come in, come in."

The gathering was in full swing, their apartment covered in decorations from every winter holiday on the calendar. It looked like the Spars had a supply of Santa hats in Hanukah blue or Christmas red, since most people were wearing them. Davy didn't know any of the first years yet, but one or two would be assigned to her over the next couple of months. She guessed she should start to get to know them, but all she wanted to do was pay Anna compliments all night—better ones than that travesty from earlier.

"Should we get a drink?" Anna asked, nodding toward the bar.

"Good idea." Once their drinks were secured, Davy clinked her tumbler of scotch against Anna's wine glass. "Thanks for coming."

"My pleasure." Anna scanned the room. "I'm going to let you get on with it." She started to walk away, but Davy grabbed her arm.

"Where are you going?"

Anna gently removed Davy's hand from her arm. "This is a work thing, right? Go and work. Do your business. I don't want to get in your way."

"But you don't know anyone here."

Something heated sparked in Anna's eye, but then she smiled. "Don't worry about me. I won't have a problem joining in any reindeer games." She slipped away, and Davy watched her cross the room to where Roland was holding court in a shirt and tie and Santa pants and boots. Anna gave him a quick hello and then began talking with a few people standing nearby.

Davy prowled the outskirts of the room, joining a conversation or two, but always aware of where Anna was and who she was speaking to. She had seemed to form a little gang with some women Davy didn't know—spouses probably—and they laughed a little more often than the other clumps of people. Then she caught a few words coming from her left.

"—that hottie in the red dress. Do you know who she is? I wouldn't mind getting the desk next to hers." One of the newbies, a young man in a suit so new the white threads from the removed label still clung to his sleeve.

"Bro, does she even work here? Somebody that hot is probably fucking one of the partners." Newbie number two was double-fisting with a beer in each hand.

Davy swiftly stepped between them and growled, "That's my fiancée." *So don't even look at her, dickbags.*

"I'm so sorry. I didn't know." New Suit Boy looked like he wanted to swallow his own tongue.

But Double-Fister didn't even have the sense to look ashamed. "You're Ms. Dugan, aren't you? I'm interested in litigation—"

"Not even if you were Clarence fucking Darrow risen from the dead." She strode away and headed for the bar. *Who the fuck was hiring these butt trumpets?* Davy insinuated herself into Anna's group and handed her a fresh wineglass. Anna widened the circle to make room for her and looped her arm around Davy's, and immediately her irritation at the two newbies was quelled.

Anna quickly introduced the klatch of women, who were indeed spouses of first years. They seemed to be looking to Anna as some kind of guide to the inner workings of ACS, which Davy found low-key hilarious.

"Honey, Lorna here just got back from her honeymoon—Belize."

It took Davy half a second to realize Anna was referring to her. "Oh, congratulations. How was it? I've never been to Belize."

"It was magical. The water was crystalline. Anna told us you're recently engaged. Any thoughts about your honeymoon?"

None whatsoever, Lorna. "I'm fine with wherever Anna wants to go. She can decide."

Anna turned to her, her gaze adoring, but underneath that, a twinkle of mischief. "Davy works so hard, I'm sure she just wants to sit on a beach somewhere, but she knows how much I like cold weather."

Their conversation suddenly felt like an improv workshop Davy took years ago in college. What was the rule again—*yes, and?* "Yes, and Anna's not talking the ski slopes of Colorado cold. I'd heard the winters get really cold way the hell up there in northern Canada, but we're getting married in the summer."

"Yes, and that means a honeymoon in the southern hemisphere." Anna was grinning widely now.

"Yes, so we're going south. I just heard from the travel agent today."

"Oh, honey, are we really going to—?"

"Antarctica!" Davy said triumphantly. "Turns out, McMurdo Station *does* have a honeymoon package."

Anna looked like she was two seconds away from busting out with laughter, but she kept it together. "You're the best, Sugar Butt. How will I be able to wait until next summer?"

"Just you, me, and twelve million penguins, babe. It's gonna be great." She wrapped her arm around Anna's shoulders and gave her a loving look. "We'll just have to take good care of your remaining toes after that last case of frostbite." Everyone looked down at Anna's feet.

Anna gave one of them a little kick, thankfully shod in a closed-toe red pump. "You'd be amazed at how much more comfortable high heels are when you only have three toes on each foot."

Davy could barely hold it in anymore. "There are some people I'd like you to meet, babe. Will you excuse us?" She pulled Anna across the room and away from the group, and ducked into an unoccupied hallway. They collapsed against the wall and gave in to their giggles, and Anna bent over with the effort of trying to catch her breath, her rainbow-striped hat falling to the floor.

"That was inspired," Anna said when she was upright again.

Davy picked up the hat and stood closer, entranced by the sight of Anna as she wiped a tear from her eye, her expression infused with elation and so, so beautiful. "I really chose the right fiancée."

Anna took a step backward, and the elation was replaced with guardedness. Davy checked herself and reestablished some space between them. They had been in sync for those few minutes, and it had felt like they were riding a two-person bobsled, each leaning into the curves of their conversation at the exact right moment. But the sled had jumped the track now, obviously. All she had wanted was to be near Anna, but that's not what this was.

Anna cleared her throat and said, "Who did you want me to meet? The partners?"

"No, the only partner here is Roland. That was just an excuse so that I didn't spew laughter all over those poor women." Davy took off her red Santa hat and handed it to Anna. "Here, you should be wearing this one. It matches your outfit better." She placed the rainbow hat on her own head and watched while Anna put on the red one. "Do you want to go? I think we're done here."

Anna nodded. "Let's just say thank you to Leanne and Roland."

Davy gestured for Anna to precede her out of the shadowy hallway.

As soon as they stepped back into the living room, Roland called out, "Mistletoe! Davy and Anna, you're standing under the mistletoe."

Davy looked upward, and sure enough, there was a bunch of green leaves studded with white berries attached to the ceiling with a red ribbon. God only knew how Leanne had procured it in July. All eyes turned toward them. A few people clapped, and there was a wolf whistle from somewhere. Davy glanced at Anna and saw how absolutely she did not want to be kissed, never mind their contractual agreement against this very thing.

"Come on, you know what that means!" Roland egged them on by tapping a spoon to his glass, as if they were at a wedding reception. More people looked over at them and they had become the center of attention. Davy didn't know how they could get out of it.

She turned around and faced Anna, shielding her from most of the crowd. Anna's eyes shied away from hers and toward the few people still in her line of vision.

"Hugs are allowed, right?" Davy murmured. "Follow my lead." She maneuvered them two steps back so they had returned to the semi-shelter of the hallway, but still within sight of the assembled guests. Anna now looked as skittish as a spooked horse, but Davy took her in her arms anyway and twisted them into a shallow dip, as if they were dancing, and Anna had no choice but to reach up and grasp Davy around the neck. Making sure that Anna was still protected by her body, Davy got as close to her face as she dared, her lips coming within a hair's breadth of Anna's, but stopping short of touching her. Anna's chest heaved, and hot panicky breaths came from her flared nostrils. Davy could see how the whites of Anna's eyes flashed her discomfort with their playacting. She pulled Anna upright and let her go, and it was then that she registered the sounds of more clapping and whistling. *I'm going to kill you, Roland.*

"Ladies and gentlemen, the newly engaged Davy and Anna!" Roland announced.

Davy tried to play it off with a stiff smile, but it faltered when she noticed Anna's pinched expression and beet red complexion. She stalked over to Roland, pulling Anna behind her. "We're leaving. Thanks for making us the entertainment portion of the evening. Don't fucking do that to anyone else. I'm serious."

"It's all in good fun, Davy. I didn't think you'd mind." Roland was immediately apologetic.

Leanne approached. "It was over the line, Roland, to make such a spectacle of it."

"Who doesn't want to kiss their fiancée just about every minute they're together?" He said to his wife. "We used to do that and more."

"Not everybody is us." Leanne turned to them. "Please accept our apology."

Anna stepped forward, her smile perfectly calibrated for ignoring a social faux pas, and Davy wondered if she had imagined Anna's extreme reaction from moments before. "There's no need for that, Leanne," Anna said. "It was a bit of harmless fun. Thank you for a lovely time tonight. Good night, Roland. Leanne."

And they left, with Davy hanging on the coattails of Anna's dignified exit.

CHAPTER FIFTEEN

Halima was already there when Davy arrived at the office on the next Monday.

Davy slowed as she approached her assistant's desk. "Morning. Good weekend?"

The stank face Halima unleashed on her was her first tiny clue that something was wrong. Her usually even-tempered assistant went back to glaring at her screen.

Davy continued into her office, set her briefcase down, sat, and then leaned over in her chair to observe Halima ignoring her. *The fuck?* Davy had never not gotten a greeting from her. It was totally out of character. Now that she thought about it, Halima had been moody all of last week, but whenever Davy had noticed how odd that sullenness was for her usually imperturbable assistant, another work crisis had come along to shove it out of her brain. She couldn't exactly remember when Halima's shoulder had started getting progressively colder—over a week now, she would guess.

She couldn't deal with this. Not Halima *and* Anna.

Davy whirled her chair around to gaze out the window. She'd think about how to deal with Halima in a minute, because from the moment she had sat down on the train this morning, all she could think about was her arrangement with Anna—which definitely wasn't working—and she wasn't done processing all the ways it was going wrong yet. After the new hires party at Roland's place, Anna had been quiet in the car service on the way home. She accepted Davy's apology with grace but shut down any attempts to discuss what had happened. She suggested Davy use the time to work, and then pulled out her phone and did something with an Etsy app all the way home.

Davy had hoped for a chance to clear the air over the weekend, but that opportunity hadn't arisen. Anna wasn't around when she had gotten home Saturday afternoon, and Davy had slept most of Sunday away before joining Anna and Louis while they watched a nature show in the early evening on that comfortable sofa. Anna had perched on the arm of the couch, about as far away from Davy as she could get. Davy had been so relaxed she had fallen asleep again, and woke hours later in the dark, curled up in a soft, sweet-smelling, throw blanket that had come from God knew where.

And now Halima's face looked like a puckered asshole, and Davy was probably responsible for it, yet she hadn't a clue what she had done. What the hell was going on? At least with Halima, Davy could order her subordinate to tell her what was wrong, not that that would count for effective management or anything. But she had to solve one of these two problems, and the one directly in front of her seemed the easier of the two.

Davy hit the coffee station and returned with two steaming cups. She held one out to Halima. "Can we talk?"

Halima gazed at the cup but made no move to take it. She sniffed and picked up her notepad, ready to work.

"Not work just yet. Come in. And take this cup, will you, please?"

Halima accepted the coffee and followed Davy into her office.

"I have to ask you this even if it sounds like I'm in junior high. Are you mad at me?"

Halima seemed to have been waiting for this and shot back, "Am I trustworthy?"

The fuck? "Of course. I wouldn't keep you around if I didn't trust you. What is going on?"

"Why did I have to hear about your engagement from Roland's assistant?"

Shit. "You heard about the mistletoe thing?"

"Yes." Halima's voice was pure venom. "But I heard about your engagement a week and a half ago when I got back from lunch, and you were gone. *Left for the day with her fiancée* was what I was told. And then you came in the next day and didn't say a word. I didn't even know you were seeing anyone. I know you play things close to the vest, but it hurt, Davy."

"I'm sorry." And Davy was, truly. She had fucked up royally. Halima was her secret weapon around here, and Halima took care of her, watched out for her. She was more than an assistant; she was an ally, maybe even a friend. "There's a reason I didn't tell you."

Halima waited.

Was Davy really going to tell her? Could she disclose this insanity to her assistant? And keep her self-respect? She took a cleansing breath. "You have to swear by the assistant's code, or no, whatever you value most in your life—your degree."

Halima gave her a look of supreme distaste. "That's not what I value most in life."

"Then what is?"

"Duh. My girlfriend."

"Right. That makes sense. Swear on your girlfriend's life that you will not tell a living soul—or a dead one even—no loose talk in cemeteries—what I'm about to tell you."

"Have I ever given out trade secrets?" Halima looked insulted.

"No, but I still need you to swear. And close the door."

Halima rolled her eyes but went to shut her office door. Davy got up and sat in the other visitor chair in front of her desk. This way, both her back and Halima's faced the glass wall and hallway beyond. She wasn't going down because someone could read lips. Davy gave her an *I'm waiting* look.

"All right, I swear. God."

"I didn't tell you because it's not real."

Halima looked as if Davy had suddenly started speaking Esperanto. "What's not real?"

"Any of it. Whatever you heard from Roland's assistant. It all started when you told me that Len Conant would be leaving the firm."

"What does he have to do with you getting married?"

"It's a long story, so I'm going to give you the bullet points." Davy proceeded to tell Halima everything. Sometime around when "Build Me Up, Buttercup" was mentioned, she wondered if she hadn't entirely lost her mind. When she was finished, she waited for Halima to say something.

"You seriously didn't know who Daenerys Targaryen is?"

"Halima! So not the point here." Davy sat back in her chair.

"So she's your sister's sister?"

"Yeah, we met when we were young, before Tally was born. We started out as friends, but it kind of fizzled out." She didn't add that the reason for that was completely her fault. "Before Tally's party I hadn't seen her in eight years. And we did not get along then."

"And now you do?"

"No, we still don't. I was just lucky there was something she needed that I could exploit—I mean, provide. I thought maybe since she and I agreed to do this, and we're living together now, we could get past our differences, but I don't think I can change her mind about me. Everything started off well when she moved in, and went mostly fine at Roland's barbeque last weekend. There were even some bright spots at the first years' reception the other night, but she's been really distant and detached. It kind of bothers me that she doesn't like me."

"Sorry, boss, but she doesn't have to like you. From what you said, liking you isn't part of the deal."

"I know." And Davy did know it, but she didn't like it. She had been drawn to Anna since the first day they had met, and all those old feelings from when they were teenagers were coming back again, with a vengeance.

"Wait. When did she move?"

"A week ago Saturday."

"But we were here at the office then."

"Yeah." Davy didn't understand. "And?"

Halima's eyes grew round. "You didn't help her move?"

"No, she told me not to. Was that wrong? Should I have been there?"

"Yes, you should have." Halima stared at her, apparently flummoxed. "And how did it go at Roland's barbeque?"

Davy shrugged. "Fine. Oh, shit, that reminds me, I need you to contact Joel Kleinman at Teltech and set up a lunch. I should've gotten back to him already."

Halima nodded like everything was becoming clear. "And where did you meet Joel Kleinman?"

"At Roland's barbeque."

"Ah. I can picture it now. Just a sweet, little ol' business conversation at a barbeque between Joel, you, and *the love of your life*?"

"First of all, she's not the love of my life—"

"But that's what you're telling the world, right? And whether it's true or not, you should be treating her as such, especially in public. No wonder she's distant. She's probably taking her cues about how to act from you. And you know what you are, boss?"

"What?" she asked warily.

"You're all business."

That was supposed to be a bad thing? Her confusion must have been plain as day to Halima.

"One thing I know from working for you, it's never boring." Halima gave her a shrewd look. "You're like the MacGyver of lawyering. You always find a way—you always figure it out. That's why your clients love you so much. I'm not surprised you've masterminded an edge in meeting this goal of yours. It just may work."

"Fuck yeah, it'll work." Whatever their personal relationship, Anna was delivering in the faux fiancée department.

"And you could talk the leaves down from the trees and have them march themselves into neat little piles in the height of summer if you wanted to, so I totally believe you've gotten her to agree to this." Halima raised her hands when Davy was about to interrupt. "Yes, I know, she gets something out of it as well. It's sad, though."

"What is?"

"It's ludicrous that you can't just rely on the work you've done, and the value you've brought, and the contacts you've made. You are far and away the biggest asset the firm has, but if they're entertaining the likes of Keeley-the-gold-plated-moron, it's no wonder you feel you have to resort to this kind of deception." Halima really understood, and it filled Davy with relief.

"I kind of love that you're so on board with this."

"Of course I am. I wouldn't bet against you. It could definitely work. I'm hearing the staccato strains of the *Mission: Impossible* theme right now. But you have to motivate her into playing her part competently. And it doesn't sound like you've gotten off to the best start." Halima tapped her chin. "You don't have much experience with relationships, do you?"

That got Davy's dander up. "What's that got to do with anything? And sure I do. I've had girlfriends." In college. And law school. Not very recently.

"Forgive me, boss, but your personal calendar is pretty bleak. And in the four years I've worked for you, I've never had to order birthday flowers, or make a Valentine's Day reservation, or—"

"I wouldn't ask you to do that anyway. It's personal."

"Keeley would, and he does. All the senior partners do too."

"Well, that will change if I get to start making the decisions around here."

"I have no doubt, and I didn't mean to insult you. I only meant that maybe expressing appreciation for a loved one isn't something you do very often."

Halima was right. She was a little out of her depth here. She had managed to get the plane in the air, but how the hell was she going to land it?

"Even if this isn't real, you have to convince her—what's her name again?"

"Anna."

"You have to convince Anna that you're thankful she's doing this for you. Maybe whenever you're supposed to act all lovey-dovey with her, replace that fake emotion with gratitude, because that's real, and you feel it. You're grateful she's doing this, right?"

"Absolutely." That master's in psychology Halima was working toward was coming in handy. "That's a great idea. So I should get flowers?"

"It couldn't hurt, but maybe you want to think bigger? What does she want? What's going to show her that you appreciate what she's doing for you?"

Davy was going to have to think about that. But at least it seemed like one crisis had been handled. "I'm sorry I didn't tell you. I really appreciate you. What kind of flowers do you like?"

Halima gave her a knowing grin. "You're a quick study. But flowers won't work on me. How about you think of something I want and then give it to me?"

Damn. This wasn't going to be easy.

❖

It was after nine p.m. and Anna was finally getting some work done. She had a watercolor production line going. Working from a gridded photo on her iPad, she repeated the same brushstrokes on five identical 8x10 beach scenes set before her of the Barnegat lighthouse on a bright summer day. People loved lighthouses. They scooped up anything she created that featured a lighthouse, so she tried to have a lot of variations on that theme. She heard footsteps on the stairs outside and moments later, Davy appeared at the door of the studio, still in her work clothes, a large, wrapped bouquet in her arms.

"Hi. May I come in?"

"Of course. It's your house." Anna had been wondering if Davy would ever make the climb and visit the studio. It had happened sooner than she had imagined.

"No, this is your domain now. I want to be mindful of your space. You can refuse me entry anytime if you're busy or you don't want to see me or whatever."

"Get in here, but please keep your voice down." She nodded toward the sofa, where Louis lay sleeping, wrapped in a blanket and the pillow from his bed.

"What happened? Why isn't he sleeping in his room?" Davy whispered while she tiptoed toward the worktable where Anna sat with her watercolors.

"He's having a hard time adjusting to sleeping on his own."

"Poor kid." Davy offered her the flowers. "These are for you."

"For me?" She peeked past the cellophane and paper to see a flash of blue. "Thanks, but why?"

Davy didn't answer; instead, she sat on an adjacent stool and watched while Anna unwrapped a gorgeous bunch of blue irises with little flames of yellow bursting from the base of each petal. They were absolutely magnificent. Anna buried her face in them and inhaled a subtle powdery scent.

"They're beautiful. Thank you." Anna reached for an empty coffee can that usually held brushes. She quickly trimmed the end of each stem and dropped them in, taking a moment to arrange them before she crossed to the bar sink and filled the can with water.

When she returned and set the can in the middle of the table, Davy said, "I see my other present arrived too. I thought it might be something you could use up here. There's a plumber coming tomorrow to connect it."

Anna glanced at the new utility sink that sat next to the bar, a gleaming stainless steel model that had been delivered in the afternoon by a big box home improvement store. "It's not my birthday, and Christmas is six months away. What have I done to deserve this?" She moved to a clear space at the table and placed a fresh sheet of card stock in front of her. She dabbed at the cakes of violet and cobalt pigment in her tray, and then with quick, sure brushstrokes, the bouquet started coming to life on the paper.

She could feel Davy watching, but besides the thank you she had already expressed, she didn't know what else to say. The flowers were lovely. The utility sink was even more thoughtful because she already knew the bar sink was not going to cut it. It was something she needed, and she appreciated Davy anticipating that need. Two considerate gestures, but she hesitated to ascribe meaning to them.

So far, she had stuck to her plan of avoidance, and it seemed to be working. Except for that party in the city last week. She had been a letter-perfect fiancée, and she had successfully recalibrated her expectations and allowed Davy the space to network or make deals or whatever it was she needed to do. But Davy hadn't seemed to want that, and it was confusing.

Davy cleared her throat before speaking. "You apologized to me last weekend, but I think I should have been the one apologizing. I should have been here to help you move. I should've been more attentive at the barbeque. And I'm more sorry than I can say about the mistletoe thing the other night. I should've handled it differently. I've been a jerk, but I'm going to try not to be from now on."

"You're not a jerk," Anna protested, realizing it was exactly how she would have described Davy only two months ago. "It'll just take some time for us to get used to this. And I don't know why you're apologizing about the mistletoe. We were able to keep the ruse going without breaking any of the clauses in the contract. I was fine with it." Her body, and its instantaneous reaction, was definitely not fine with it. She had been a millisecond away from pressing her lips against Davy's and making the fakery real. Her desire to turn the charade into a hot, steamy make-out session in full view of Davy's colleagues had been nearly overwhelming, but they were *not* going to discuss that. "So you don't need to buy me presents, but I do love the flowers, and the sink even more."

"Good. I took a chance you would be here for the sink delivery. Will you be around tomorrow for the plumber?"

"I'll be here. You can always call or text me to check, but as you can see"—Anna pointed to countless boxes that looked untouched—"I'll be around. I still have a lot of unpacking to do. Things have been a little tricky with Louis. My plan was to use the evenings after he goes to bed to get organized, but he's having some adjustment issues. I hope we haven't woken you at all."

"No, I haven't heard a thing. Is he okay?"

"He wakes up confused in the middle of the night. We've basically slept in the same room his entire life, so a bedroom of his own is taking some getting used to." Anna turned to gaze at him. "In the summers, I spend lots of time with Louis during the day, and I get my work done at night. I build up inventory for a couple of art fairs and festivals that I usually go to, plus keep my Etsy store stocked. I've been bringing him up here with me, thinking I could work, but I'm limited to quiet tasks for obvious reasons." She blew a breath toward her hairline. "I know it's not a good solution."

Davy seemed to think about it for a moment. "How about a baby monitor?"

"Yeah, maybe." They'd never needed one in their no-walls living situation. Anna wondered how Louis would take to it now that he was clearly not a baby.

"What did you two get up to today? It's summer. Does Louis go to camp or anything?"

Anna looked up from her work. "He's five. I can't send him to camp."

"Oh." Her brow furrowed. "I was pretty young when I started going to camp. Maybe a little older. Six or seven."

"Day camp?"

"No, sleepaway. I went to the same camp for years and years. Made some great friends. The summer I lived with you was the first time in forever that I didn't go to camp. I remember I was pissed because I was supposed to finally be a full-fledged counselor that summer after being a CIT."

"What's that?"

"Counselor-in-training. I was going to be a swimming counselor. Swimming was coveted." Davy stared into space, obviously remembering her summer days. "Anyway, I got over it."

"Is that what you did the summer after you stayed with us?" Anna had always been curious about where Davy had been. Things had been crazy with Tally's birth, but she had always thought it strange that Gregory never talked about his daughter at all. And when Anna would bug him with questions about what Davy was up to, he always brushed them aside.

"No. My dad sent me to Europe on this package tour with a bunch of other teenagers. He said it was my graduation present, but I think it was really because he didn't want me around when he was starting this new thing with your mom and Tally."

"He should've sent me along with you. He never came out and said it, but I think he thought I was in the way too." Anna chose a brush with a smaller tip and dabbed it in cadmium yellow, then softened the hue with water.

Davy scoffed. "He wasn't about to do that."

"Well, no. I wasn't his responsibility." She dabbed yellow onto the paper and allowed the rag of the paper to soak up the tint.

"That's not what I mean. Yeah, he probably wanted you out of the picture too, but he wanted you hanging out with me even less. The whole point was to keep us apart."

Anna frowned. "What are you talking about?"

"His thing with Pam, he really wanted it to work. I think he thought it was like a second chance after my mom died so young. I was on my way to college, grown in his eyes, and here was his opportunity for a do-over. Maybe he thought he could be present for Tally in a way he never was for me."

"But it fell apart before Tally was even six months old." Anna paused before applying more color to the paper. "My mother just told me the other day she was the one to end it with your dad. All this time, I thought he left her, but leaving wasn't his choice."

Davy nodded. "And it made what he did pointless." Her eyes were pinned to Anna's and that sadness that was so familiar when they were teenagers was back.

"What did he do?"

"He's the reason I didn't stay in touch. After that summer."

Anna put the brush down. "I don't understand."

"God. I've wanted to have this conversation for fifteen years. I can't believe we're finally about to have it." Davy put her elbows on the table and covered her face with her hands.

Anna stood. All her senses were on high alert, and she waited for Davy to say something. At last, she brought her hands down and stared at the table as she continued to talk.

"You know what he's like, Anna. He wasn't about to let anything get in the way of what he wanted, and he saw you and me as a threat to that."

"What does that even mean? How were we a threat?"

"When he drove me back to school at the end of that summer, I asked him if I could come back to visit. You probably don't even remember this, but you wanted me to."

Anna remembered. She remembered very well.

"I wasn't supposed to come back until my December break, and you asked me to visit before then, and I didn't want to wait that long to see you again either. We had gotten so close, and I liked you so much. And he wanted to know why. I didn't want to tell him specifics. I barely knew what the specifics were, but he demanded to know everything. It was as if the interior of the car had become an interrogation room. He even pulled into a rest stop so he could focus on extracting every last embarrassing detail out of me."

Davy paused, and flicked her eyes toward Anna, maybe deciding whether or not to say whatever came next. Anna needed to know it all. "It's okay. Tell me the rest."

She took in a breath and exhaled slowly first. "When I told him we kissed, he flipped out. I honestly thought he was going to kick me out of the car and leave me there. He said if I continued any kind of contact with you, I could forget about any financial help from him for school. He said he would disown me, Anna. My own father. And there wasn't a doubt in my mind he would do it." She paused before she whispered, "He called what we did incestuous. I didn't even know what that meant. I had to look it up."

"It wasn't," Anna interrupted, her fists clenching.

"Of course it wasn't. But it sure didn't fit in with whatever image he had in his head about his new happy family. He said no way were you and I going to ruin what he had with Pam. When he left me at school that day, I was kind of wondering if he would ever come back. I mean, he was a shitty fucking father up until that point, but after that I really thought I was going to be on my own."

Anna's nails dug crescents into her palms and her anger at Gregory felt uncontainable. She couldn't imagine putting conditions on her love for Louis.

"And when I came back at Christmas, I knew the whole thing was a test. He was making sure I toed the line. He was just waiting for me to try to talk to you. Believe me, I wanted to, but I couldn't. I wanted to think I was the kind of person who could say fuck him and his money, but I couldn't. Not then. I'm sorry. That's why I left so quickly."

"Davy—"

"I know what you're going to say."

She did? Anna didn't know herself.

"You're going to ask me why I didn't do anything after their relationship ended. But I was going to. I had it all worked out. I was almost finished with law school, the tuition was all paid up, when I saw you again for Tally's kindergarten graduation. I was hoping we could have some time to talk, and I could explain what had happened. But your anger was like a forest fire. Dense and fierce and raging. I couldn't get within miles of you, much less have a heart-to-heart about the old days."

Anna felt her neck get hot. It was true. Her attitude toward Davy had been scorched earth until very recently. "I was upset about Tally."

"Yeah, I got that. So I backed off. And I was going to try again, but I wasn't about to put myself in the path of another encounter with your accusing eyes and all that fury just...radiating off of you and directed at me."

Shame consumed her, and she found it hard to look Davy in the eye. But she listened as Davy kept talking.

"Then my job—busy wasn't even the word for it, and I let Tally stay on the back burner. It just became easier to let the status remain quo and leave the shit unstirred. To slide by with the barest of minimums—yearly teas at the Plaza. It was wrong. And I almost lost Tally completely. It took that for me to realize I needed to change things. But now Tally and I are starting something, and you're helping me. I had to clear the air." Davy's shoulders drooped. She looked over at Louis, sleeping on the sofa.

Anna stood where she was, a little bit frozen in place. "I'm sorry your father did that to you."

Davy nodded but didn't look at her.

"And I'm sorry I was such a bitch. I didn't know. I wanted Tally to know you. I didn't understand."

"I let it go too long. I really regret that."

Anna felt like she needed to expose some of herself in return for Davy's revelations. "If I'm being totally honest, my anger wasn't just about Tally. We were friends, and then I don't know what we were, and then you were just gone. The hurt I felt, it was hard for me to get over it."

Davy shut her eyes for a second. "I'm sorry. I broke something with you we'll probably never be able to mend. But I'm grateful to you, Anna, that you can see your way around all this and help me now. I've got my head screwed on properly now, and I'll show you how thankful I am."

Anna didn't know where the guilt came from, but it rose up in her all the same. "You don't have to buy me things. We made a deal."

"Okay." Davy sat up straighter. She seemed relieved. "Should we talk about something else now?"

"Yes, please." Anna expelled a breath and sat down again. Please let them talk about literally anything else. She chose another brush and resumed her work on the bouquet in front of her, and made a few vertical green slashes below the blooms.

Davy kept her eyes on Louis, and the silence lingered between them, but it wasn't uncomfortable. What had been said needed time to sink into the ground, to take root in both of their psyches. Eventually, Davy said, "What did you do with Louis today?"

"We spent a lot of time on the trampoline. It tired me out, but it didn't seem to have the same effect on Lou. I tried to get him to sketch out what he wants to put on his wall, but he wasn't into it." She stopped to think, then shrugged. "We did a whole bunch of stuff, but none of it very memorable, which is usually the case during summer."

"What does he usually do during summer?"

"He loves the water. We sometimes head out to the beach so I can take pictures and he can play in the sand, but usually we go to the Southfield pool. And we can't do that anymore since we don't live there."

"Hey." Davy snapped her finger. "You can go to the country club. I hear they have a nice pool. And other stuff too, I suppose, besides golf. I'll see about getting a membership for us."

"You don't have to do that." She sketched the can in a deep red. Just a few lines. The suggestion of a vessel.

"Of course I do. I was going to anyway. Roland makes it sound like a requirement for living here. And I think…" Davy stopped talking.

When Anna lifted her head, Davy was gazing at her, but she quickly looked away.

"What?"

"If it's not an imposition," she said, business-like, "we should probably share a calendar. I'd like to know the dates of your art stuff, and I'll put down the work events I'll need you to attend."

"Okay. My next art fair is in two weeks, and I really need to increase my stock." She nodded at the array of lighthouses beside her.

Davy got up and inspected her operation. "These are great. So this is how you do it? You batch them out? And work from a photograph?"

"Yup. Every bathroom on the Jersey shore should have one of my lighthouses in it." She spoke like an announcer on TV. "Put a Resnick watercolor above the toilet. Give the male members of your family something to look at when they go."

"Male members." Davy snickered and gave Anna a sly look. It was the Beavis-y cornball humor Davy had specialized in years ago.

Anna laughed. It felt good after the intensity of their previous conversation.

"What about females who live inland? Could I have one too?" Davy was just being kind.

"Sure." Anna put her brush down and bent toward her flower illustration, blowing on it gently. Then she pushed it toward Davy. "Look. Now I'll get to keep them forever." Unlike the lighthouses, the irises were more abstract, an impression of an arrangement done with as few lines as possible.

Davy reached for it, but Anna pulled her hand away and held onto it. "Don't touch it. It's still a little wet."

Davy's grip was strong, and her hand felt completely right in Anna's. "I love what you do, Anna. The colors are perfect. And how you can just get the essence of it down on the paper so quickly. I'm amazed by your talent."

Anna observed Davy as she examined the watercolor. She was wearing a slight smile, but her eyes squinted a bit as if they were feeling strain. Anna was still grasping Davy's warm palm. After a minute, she let go, before it got weird, and started clearing the table and cleaning up. Anna wanted to show gratitude to Davy too. When she returned from the bar sink with her clean, wet brushes, she said, "Have you eaten?"

"No, but thanks. I'm not hungry."

"Are you sure? There are leftovers from dinner. I could heat something up for you?"

"I'm sure. You're wrapping up for the night?"

"Might as well. The later it gets, the harder it will be to wake him and get him into his own bed."

"You're not going to carry him?"

"I don't think I can get him down one set and up another set of steps. He's heavier than he looks."

"Want me to try?" Davy was already up and walking toward the sofa.

Anna followed and stood next to her as they both gazed at Louis. He was all tucked up under his blue blanket, lying on his back, deeply asleep. His nearly black hair appeared damp at his hairline "He's heavy," she repeated. "You really don't have to."

"I think I can do it. May I try?" Davy waited for permission. She had a few inches in height over Anna, but she was wiry where Anna was more solid.

Against her better judgment, Anna acquiesced. She removed the blanket and Davy grinned at his shark pajamas.

"He certainly has a brand, doesn't he?" she whispered, and took a moment to decide how to lift him. Then she bent at the knees and scooped him into her arms like he was an infant, his head on her shoulder, and supported him around the back and under the bum. He sighed, but didn't wake.

Anna preceded Davy down the steps to the driveway, into the house, and up to Louis's room, where she peeled back the sheets in readiness. When Davy laid him in his bed, she was breathing heavily. Anna tucked him in and followed Davy to the doorway, where she waited and watched. "Told you he was heavy," Anna murmured.

"I'll never doubt you again."

She closed the door and the two of them faced each other in the hallway. "Thank you again for the gifts. Nobody's ever given me flowers before. Or a sink."

Davy raised her eyebrows. "You've never gotten flowers? From anyone?"

"I guess I'm usually the giver, not the receiver." Her memory flashed to a moment from their past. Davy trying to dissuade her from buying some bedraggled carnations in the old J&B Market.

Davy nodded in understanding. "I haven't had a lot of practice in giving or getting them either."

Anna was getting the sense that Davy hadn't had much experience with relationships, but how could that be? She was successful, smart, and good-looking. She could envision a day, probably sooner than she ever imagined, when she asked Davy to tell her about the years between their first meeting and now. But tonight was not that night. She stepped backward in the direction of her own bedroom. "Thanks again. Good night."

It wasn't until she had closed the door behind her that she heard Davy's footsteps retreat down the hall.

CHAPTER SIXTEEN

Davy caught the 4:38 out of Penn Station and stopped by Grigsby's Bakery before walking home in the golden Friday afternoon sunshine. She passed through the front door a little before six p.m. and marveled at being home so early. Was this how regular people lived? Coming home early enough to unwind and relax from the day? And not drop exhaustedly into bed moments after arriving? She'd have to catch up on her laptop later after Louis and Anna went to bed, but it sure was a nice change.

"Got your text," Anna called from the kitchen. "We're almost ready to go."

"Hi, you two." Davy placed the bakery box on the counter and saw Anna sitting in a chair with Louis standing between her knees as she put a comb through his disheveled hair. Two rosy cheeks, flushed from exertion, were lifted by his wide grin.

"What's in the box?" Louis tried to wiggle free, but Anna yanked him back and clamped her hand around his chin and continued to wrestle with his cowlick.

"I went to the bakery and got"—Davy counted off on her fingers—"dolphin doughnuts, tuna tiramisu, barracuda buns, puffer fish pie, whale waffles—"

"Oh my God. Please stop," Anna groaned. "I bet you were coming up with all of those on the walk home."

Anna was right. Davy had thoroughly enjoyed herself thinking up her fish-themed jokes. She couldn't help chortling. "And crab cakes. Geddit? Cakes!"

Louis's smile turned upside down. "I won't eat any of that. I told you I don't eat fish." He looked so upset, Davy felt bad for teasing him.

"Right, you told me you're a carnitarian."

"Tally said that's what I am," he said with a surprising amount of dignity for a child.

Davy opened the box and bent toward where Anna was still trying to tame his locks into some kind of order and showed him six cupcakes with frosting in a variety of hues. "Oh, snap. They must have mixed up my order. These look like regular, non-fishy cupcakes."

Louis's dramatic sigh of relief made Davy grin.

"Why's your hair so crazy?" She put the cupcakes down.

Anna rolled her eyes. "Someone wanted to spend the time waiting for you out on the trampoline, and now he's a sweaty, unkempt mess."

Davy grasped the sides of her suit jacket and flapped them to encourage the air conditioning closer to her body. "The walk home has done the same to me. Give me a minute to get kempt, will you?"

Louis, finally free from his mother's clutches, followed her to the stairs. "Where are we going? Ma said you said it's a surprise."

Davy tousled his hair and smiled naughtily at Anna's squawk of outrage. "It is, kid. You'll find out soon. Be right back."

She entered her bathroom and looked longingly at the shower before deciding against it. She was in too much of a hurry. If someone had told her two months ago how excited she would be for an outing with a five-year-old boy, she would have laughed their ass out the door. But the snatches of time she'd spent with him—and Anna—had been the highlight of her week. She had lately begun making an effort to wrap up her workday earlier. When she returned home at eight or nine o'clock, she'd come up to the studio when she saw the lights still on, and a couple of times Louis had still been awake even though it was way past his bedtime. She and Lou hung out for a little while and chatted about his day, or he showed her the books and toys he had with him.

On the days when Louis was already asleep, Davy visited with Anna while she worked, always in her artist's uniform of an old, paint-spattered, plaid, flannel shirt with the sleeves torn off and faded jean shorts. Davy could barely stop herself from salivating over this version of Anna. To her, it was just as sexy as Red Dress Anna.

One evening, Davy brought out her laptop and got a few things done while Anna packed orders from her Etsy store. Two hours went by as they worked in companionable silence, and Davy found she didn't feel as exhausted as she usually did at the end of a long day. Sharing space, even in silence, made the work feel like less of a grind.

She didn't offer to carry Louis to his bed again. He was really heavy, especially climbing the second set of stairs. But the night when she had, she couldn't get over how he had felt in her arms. He was a little ball of heat with sweet smelling baby shampoo hair, and Davy liked it. He still refused to sleep in his room if Anna wasn't with him, so his bedtime got later and later, and Anna's concern was starting to show. Davy had an idea for that, one she hoped would solve the problem, but she was cautious about overstepping.

These microdoses of Louis's company the past few days had her jonesing for more, and the prospect of several hours with him and Anna filled her with energy. The three of them drove in Davy's car to an immense white clapboard-covered building with hunter green awnings protecting the windows from the evening sun. It had a wide front porch littered with white Adirondack chairs where a few folks sat with cocktails in hand. As they passed through the heavy oak doors into the Elmdale Country Club, the lobby revealed groupings of white rattan furniture with that same hunter green color for the cushions, as well as a grand stone fireplace, where Anna and Louis retreated while Davy stood at the concierge desk.

As soon as Davy gave her name, the receptionist's smile became even friendlier. "You're Mr. Spar's neighbor. Welcome. He left us instructions to roll out the red carpet for you."

"That's very kind, but we just wanted to get a bit of a tour."

"Of course, and you'll be his guests for dinner in the Lodge this evening?"

She looked around in surprise. "Is he here?"

"Not that I'm aware of." The receptionist's smile was sweet. "Just something else he told us he wanted to do for you. Let me get someone for that tour."

Davy joined Anna and Louis. "Want to see what they offer here? I know they have a pool."

"A pool, Ma!" Louis said.

"I guess we should have a look, huh?"

"Ms. Dugan?" A tanned, fit young man whose nametag read Noah approached. "If you'll follow me, I can show you around."

The club had a pro shop, two restaurants—the aforementioned Lodge and a casual eatery poolside—and a bar called the Nineteenth Hole. There were six pristine tennis courts, the majority still in use at the moment. The golf amenities seemed top of the line and plentiful and included a practice putting green, a driving range, and a small parking lot filled with golf carts.

When they rounded the bend that led to the pool complex, Louis shouted, "Ma! Look!"

Three pools—a splash pool for little kids, a medium-sized pool, and an Olympic-sized pool with several diving boards of varying heights— were set among a shady landscape populated with trees and umbrellas. Many club members were still making use of the plentiful chairs and chaise lounges that rimmed the pool deck. Anna asked Noah if the club offered swim lessons, but Louis interrupted.

"I don't need lessons. I did them last year." He pleaded his case to Noah. "I swim real good. Like a shark." As if Noah was in charge of letting him in the pool.

"Yes, but you still wear your floaty vest. Maybe just a few more lessons? Last summer was a long time ago. Just to practice," Anna said.

"Okay." Louis must have known a losing battle when he saw one. "Do you like to swim, Davy?"

"Yes, but it's been a long time since I've been in a pool. Maybe you could give me a few pointers."

"Sure. It's easy. Except when you can't touch the bottom. Then it's a little harder," he warned her, turning grave. "Don't worry. I'll show you."

"Thanks, Lou. I appreciate it," she answered him with equal seriousness.

Louis turned to his mother. "Can we go in now?"

She held up her hands. "How're you going to swim? You don't have a bathing suit on."

He looked down at his T-shirt and shorts and cast an accusing glare at Davy. "You should have told me to wear a bathing suit."

"Lou, take it down several notches," Anna warned him.

"Then it wouldn't have been a surprise." Davy put a hand on his shoulder. "Why don't we have some dinner instead? Maybe we can come back tomorrow to swim if your mom says it's okay."

"Can we, Ma?"

"We have to go with Tally to play rehearsal tomorrow, but maybe we can swim for a few hours on Sunday."

Davy raised her palm down low and Louis high-fived it. "I'll have to go shopping for a new bathing suit tomorrow. I'm gonna need it."

Anna said, "You don't have a bathing suit?"

"I probably do, but it's old. I haven't needed one in a while."

"And you're not working tomorrow? I thought you worked on Saturdays."

"I wanted to do something nice for my assistant, so I gave her all the Saturdays in July off. It's not going to kill me to take one off too." Davy paused at the thought that she might be intruding on their time. She had assumed she would be part of the plan. "Am I included? Do you mind if I come along?"

"Of course not. We'd love it, right, Lou? Besides, you're the member, not us."

"We'll all be members, and Tally and your mom too."

"Thank you. It's very generous of you." Something about Anna's sincere smile, how it took over her whole face, and how the appreciative look in her eyes seemed to penetrate deep into Davy's body, made her cheeks feel hot.

Noah still hovered in the background. He stepped forward. "Would you like to see the changing rooms and showers?"

Davy extended her hand, and Louis gave one hand to her and one to Anna on his other side. "I think we'll head back to the restaurant, Noah. Thanks for the tour." She glanced at Anna over Louis's head. "Maybe they have shark-cuterie on the menu."

Anna's snort of disgust warmed her heart.

❖

At the end of their meal, Anna and Louis headed to the restroom while Davy returned to the concierge in the lobby to complete the paperwork for their membership. She was busy signing things in triplicate when she heard a voice behind her.

"Fancy meeting you here." Joel Kleinman approached in rumpled tennis whites and a racquet under his arm. "Are you becoming a member?"

"That's right. Roland made it seem like terrible things would befall me if I didn't."

"Yeah, probably." He laughed. "Do you play tennis? Or are you a golfer?"

"A little tennis, but not since high school. Hoping to play again."

"Great. I'm terrible. Maybe we can play sometime."

"Sure. Sorry we never connected for that lunch. I know Teltech's board is happy with its in-house counsel, but I was hoping to talk a little more about your litigation needs."

"Yeah." Joel looked down at his shoes.

Wrong approach. She had met his friendliness with a hard sell, and that wasn't going to work here. What was wrong with her? The right strategy for attracting business was something she always instinctively knew, but she had read his affable overture incorrectly. Hopefully it wasn't too late to undo the damage. "But I should probably get some advice about a new racquet first. What brand do you suggest?"

He handed over his racquet for her to inspect. "Oh, I love this. Got it at the pro shop here. Ask for Dennis. He'll set you up."

"Thanks. And listen, I appreciate getting to know you as a neighbor. I won't mention business again."

He smiled at her. "Great. Would you tell Roland that too? The guy's relentless."

"You're on your own there. I can't tell the boss anything."

Joel laughed and then looked past her. "Here's Becca. You remember my wife? And these are our girls, Shayna and Alana." Two little girls in matching dresses and sandals smiled shyly. Their wet heads revealed they had come from the pool.

"Did you have a good time swimming?" Davy asked the girls.

Anna and Louis arrived and made their little group larger. Louis pressed into Anna's side, soberly eyeing the girls from behind her skirt.

"Anna, it's Joel and his wife, Becca, from the other night?"

"Nice to see you again so soon. This is Louis, but he's being shy." She squatted and brought Lou forward a bit. "Hi, girls. I love your sparkly sandals."

One of them, Alana, maybe, extended her foot so Anna could admire her footwear. She was clearly in love with them too. "They're new."

"They're really pretty. Don't you think, Lou?"

Louis turned to Davy with a get-me-out-of-here expression.

"Do you like trampolines? Would you like to come over and try ours out?" Anna darted a glance at Davy before extending an invitation to Becca. "We could do a casual dinner out on the patio, maybe sometime next week? I'm dying to get the lowdown on Elmdale."

Anna didn't need the lowdown. She'd lived in the next town over all her life. But gratitude filled Davy as she gazed at Anna, who didn't even realize she had just salvaged the situation. Her friendliness to Joel's family was the exact right response. She and Anna were supposed to be new in town, and Anna was reaching out, making connections.

For the first time in her life, Davy saw the advantage to having a partner, someone who was working toward the same goal as she was. Was this what couples did? Fill in where there was a need and make the pair stronger? She had never been this close to a supportive, functioning relationship before. It was getting harder to heed the insistent voice in the back of her head that reminded her that this was temporary—and fraudulent.

CHAPTER SEVENTEEN

Davy was already in the kitchen when Anna shuffled in looking for coffee. She was bent over her espresso machine, a bag of coffee beans in one hand and an instruction manual in the other. The frustration seemed to clear from her face when she saw Anna. "Morning. You want espresso?"

"That depends," Anna grunted. "How long do I have to wait for it?"

"Not long. I think I got it."

Louis came in from the living room and sat at the table. "I'm hungry. Can I have cereal?"

"I didn't know you were up already." She yawned. "What were you doing in there?"

"Watching a show. Davy couldn't get the goddamn TV to work, so I'm watching it on the iPad."

Anna thought she might have heard wrong. "What did you say?"

Davy was by his side in less than three seconds. "Hey, Louis, I didn't think you were listening to me. I shouldn't have said that word. It's not polite." Her face was tinted pink as she looked between Louis and Anna and tried to fix the damage.

Louis's eyebrows scrunched in confusion. "What word? TV?"

"No, the one before that one. The one that started with God."

"Oh. Okay." Louis looked at Anna and shrugged.

Anna tried not to roll her eyes. *It's too early for this.* "It's not a nice word. Don't say it again. I'll get your cereal."

Davy slunk back to her espresso machine and soon the high-pitched whine of grinding beans filled the air. After fixing Louis's Cheerios, Anna was returning the milk to the fridge when she heard the hissing and gargling of the espresso machine. Then she heard Davy.

"Ow! Mother*fuck*er!" Davy brought her hand close to her chest and whirled away from the machine as her eyes welled up with tears.

Anna's heart leapt into her throat. She dropped the milk on the counter and hustled over to her. "What happened?" She drew Davy's arm down to see an angry red welt along her lower index finger.

"I burned myself on that fucking thing."

Anna dragged Davy to the sink, then she thrust her hand under the tap and let cold water gush over it.

"Fuck, I'm sorry. I said another—and I just said it again. What the hell is wrong with me? God, it hurts."

"You're okay," Anna soothed her. "It doesn't look too bad. It's going to be fine."

"Ma?" Louis said, his voice wavering.

"Everything's okay, Lou. Davy got an ouchie, but she's going to be fine," she called to him without looking away from Davy's hand.

"I'm okay," Davy repeated. "It's not that bad."

"You stay here. Keep it under the cool water. I'll be right back." On her way out of the kitchen for some first aid supplies, Anna stopped by the table to run a hand through Louis's hair. "She's really fine. Eat your cereal. Don't let it get soggy."

When she returned, she turned off the water, gently wrapped Davy's hand in a clean dishtowel, and led her to the table. She sat Davy down and showed Louis. "See? She's fine, but she burned herself. Davy's finger must have touched something very hot, and now she's going to have a blister. This will make it feel better and help it heal." She smoothed antibiotic cream over Davy's hand and secured some gauze over it with medical tape.

Davy gave Louis a weak smile. "I'm a dum-dum."

Anna tsked and shot her a look.

"No, you're not," he replied, and laid a hand on her uninjured arm. "It was an accident. And Ma made it better. She can make anything better."

"Not anything," Anna muttered. Her heart rate was returning to normal. Even though she tried to remain calm in situations like this, she was always spooked for a long while after.

"I think you're right, Louis." Davy gazed at Anna like she had burst into a burning building and carried Davy to safety. "How did you know what to do?"

"It was nothing. Just a little first aid." Anna busied herself with recapping the ointment. The doorbell rang and Louis ran to get it. "Ask who it is."

"It's a delivery man," he called. "He left a big brown box on the porch. Should I get it?"

"Yeah," Davy called back, then said to Anna, "That's something I ordered for Louis."

Anna huffed out a breath. "I thought I told you. You don't have to keep buying us things."

"I know, but this is different. It's not a present, really. I think it might help with—" Davy broke off as Louis reentered the kitchen, pushing a large box ahead of him.

"With what?" Anna prompted her.

"Who's this for? Can I open it?" Louis asked.

They both looked to Anna for permission. She surrendered and picked up a butter knife from the table. "I'll open it and you can see what's inside."

In a minute, Louis had pulled four professional-looking walkie-talkies out of the box. "Look, Ma! These are so cool."

"Here's my idea, Lou," Davy said. "We can all have one of these. When it's bedtime, we can leave them on so you can press a button and talk to your mom if you need her. That way, she can be in the studio, and you can be in bed, and she'll hear you. Or you can talk to me, because I'll have one too. We can even give one to Tally and your grandma because they have a range of ten miles."

Anna gazed at Davy, astounded by her thoughtfulness. She hadn't said anything about her worries about Louis not adjusting to a new bedtime routine, but Davy obviously had picked up on them. She really needed to be more gracious. She spoke to Louis. "What do you say to Davy?"

"Thank you," he said automatically as he pulled one unit out of its box.

"We can charge them up and try it tonight." Davy looked almost as excited as Louis.

"Thank you, Davy. You're very thoughtful." Anna got up from the table. "Now, who wants coffee?"

❖

They ended up spending a leisurely Saturday morning at home. After breakfast, Davy put aside her files and watched Louis play with Lego bricks at the kitchen table while Anna retreated to the studio for a bit. He narrated every part of the aquarium he was building, which was helpful since it looked like a mishmash of multicolored bricks to Davy.

He kicked his legs as he chattered and chose bricks, and it soothed Davy to listen to his quirky ideas.

The doorbell rang and Louis ran to get it. Davy followed him, not believing how lively her house had become. Two doorbells in the space of an hour.

Pam and Tally stood on the porch.

"Hi, Grammie," Louis said. "We got walkie-talkies!"

"Terrific," Pam said, as Davy ushered them both inside.

"Hey, Tally, how're you doing?" Davy asked.

Tally dropped her backpack where she stood and walked right past Davy. "Good. You have any snacks?"

"Tally. Move your bag from the middle of the floor." Pam's voice was heated, but it downgraded to terse when she spoke to Davy. "She just ate. She's driving me a little nuts today, and I'm sure I'm doing the same to her."

Without a backward glance, Tally kicked her bag off to the side and stalked into the kitchen. Louis followed her.

"She can hang out here. Doesn't she have play practice or something today?"

"Yes, at one, and Anna has to go too, so I was hoping I could leave her here until then."

"Sure. You don't need to ask. If I'm here, Tally's welcome."

Pam gave her shoulder a distracted pat. "You're a good girl. You may regret saying that, though. I think the teen years are about to get rough for our Tally."

"What do you mean? Here, would you like to sit?" She stepped outside and left the front door open so the residual air conditioning could be felt and sat on the top step of the porch. The granite was still shaded and felt cool.

Pam lowered herself next to her. "I don't know. Anna always knew exactly who she was. She had principles—and an innate sense of right and wrong from a pretty early age. With Tally, it seems like she's waiting to see which way the wind blows."

Davy chuckled. "You think there's a chance Tally could break bad?" She thought it pretty unlikely considering Tally had benefited from Pam's example all her life, but then again there was her father and the wildcard Dugan genes to be accounted for.

"I hope not. She's got a good group of friends right now, and wholesome interests, thanks to Anna." She gave Davy a sly grin. "Looks like there's going to be more musical theater in your future. How we suffer for the ones we love."

Davy opened her mouth in pretend shock. "Are you trying to say, after all these years of supporting Anna and Tally, that you *don't like musicals?*"

"Some are better than others, but personally, I could take them or leave them. I thought I had a kindred spirit in you. I seem to remember you not appreciating whatever show you got roped into enough for Anna's satisfaction."

"It was *Cats*, and I think she was pretty done with it by the time that last curtain came down too."

"Yikes, *Cats*." Pam made a face. "And I notice you didn't answer the question. You have a little of your father in you. He did that all the time."

Davy's lips turned downward. She knew Pam wasn't trying to insult her, but it wasn't something she wanted to own.

It got quiet for a moment, and then Pam asked, "What happened to your hand?"

"I burned myself on the espresso machine. It still hurts a little, but Anna was like a paramedic. She took care of it with zero fuss."

"Yes, she's like that. Unflappable. I honestly wonder where she came from sometimes. Always there when you need her, backing you up when it comes to the crunch. She took on quite a bit of Tally-rearing when she wasn't that much more than a child herself. It's why I'll never say no to looking after Louis when she needs me. I don't know how I could've made it through Tally's childhood without her."

Guilt pressed down on Davy—strong, heavy, and suffocating. She pulled a blade of grass from where it had sprouted between blocks of granite and focused all her attention on it.

She felt Pam's hand on her shoulder again. "I'm sorry, honey. I keep saying the wrong thing. I didn't mean to make you feel bad."

"I'm trying to make it right," she said to the single strip of grass.

"I know. I'm glad. And you were going through your own stuff. I can only imagine how it was for you, trying so hard to earn the approval of a man who can't love."

Davy gazed into Pam's eyes. "Is that what's wrong with him?"

"I think so. To me, it felt like he didn't understand the definition, like his dictionary had switched the words *love* and *ownership*. But it's not really my place to say."

Davy considered that for a moment. It would certainly explain a lot of things.

Pam kept talking. "I regret I couldn't do more for you. I really wanted Tally, but spending that summer with you and your dad, I realized I didn't want him. And I knew your adolescence could have potentially improved with Anna and me in it, but I had to cut him—and by extension, you—out of our lives. I'm so sorry for that."

Davy drew her knees up to her chest and wrapped her arms around them. "I would've done the same thing if I were in your place."

"He made some reckless decisions, didn't he? I certainly felt bad for you when he got in all that mess with the authorities. That couldn't have been easy, you just starting your professional life."

"Yeah." Davy didn't know what to say, so she stayed quiet.

"But life's a circle I guess, because here we all are again, minus your dad. I almost can't believe it. I'm getting a second chance with you, and Anna's getting a second chance with you, and Tally's getting to know you properly. We're getting a do-over. Let's all make it better this time."

Davy couldn't look at her. She felt like a teenager again. "Okay."

"I still can't understand how you and Anna came to be sharing the same home. I mean, we all love Anna, but sometimes she can be a real pill."

Davy snuck a peek at Pam and saw the fondness and exasperation in her expression.

Pam caught her looking and grinned at her. "It's true. She'll fixate on the wrong thing, and cling with a deathlike grip to those principles of hers."

"The wrong thing?"

"Sure. She hasn't been kind to you. I know her heart was in the right place. She was thinking of Tally. But she spent too much energy fuming over the fact that you weren't around instead of the reason *why* you weren't around. That should have pissed her off more."

"It should've?" Davy could've stayed there all day listening to the world according to Pam.

"I'm sure those aspersions she cast your way must have hurt you. You two were attached at the hip once." Pam scooted over and put an arm around Davy. "But I'm glad you're figuring things out about your dad. His shadow looms pretty large, and I'm sure it hasn't been easy to step away from it."

"No, but I'm working on it."

"Hey, who left the front door open?" Anna bellowed from inside the house. Her voice grew louder as she approached the porch. "You're letting all the air condit—oh, Mom, hi. What are you two doing out here?"

Davy turned to see Anna framed in the doorway, a smudge of dirt on her forehead.

Pam stood up. "I hope you don't mind I dropped off Tally a little early. I have some errands I need to do. But be advised—she's in a mood."

Anna and her mother shared a look. "Thanks for the heads up."

"She can stay over tonight if you want—and if she wants," Davy said.

They both swung their heads in Davy's direction.

"Just, you know, if it would be easier."

Pam started to make her getaway, as if she thought Davy would change her mind, and raised her hand in farewell. "Sounds great. See you later."

Anna continued to gaze at Davy, her brows lowered in wariness.

"What? I want to spend time with her." She headed back inside and waited for Anna to come through before closing the door.

Anna headed up the stairs. "I'm going to take a quick shower before we go. You'll have a nice quiet afternoon without us."

"Oh, can't I tag along? I thought Tally wanted me to help out with the play."

She turned back in surprise. "You can come if you want, but there's not much to do yet."

What sounded like a thousand Lego bricks hitting the floor at once came from the kitchen, and then the wounded wail of a five-year-old. "Tally! It's ruined!"

She and Anna sped into the kitchen, and it was exactly what it sounded like. Louis stood sobbing dramatically, giant tears suspended from his lashes and ropes of mucous inching toward his lower lip. Lego bricks were scattered around him while Tally sat sullenly at the table.

"What happened?" Anna said through gritted teeth.

"There was kind of a tug-of-war over the Legos," Tally said in a monotone. "Nobody won."

Anna stepped into the debris field. "Lou, I want you to stop crying. Nothing is broken here." She gave him a quick hug before she bent and started retrieving bricks from the floor. "It's okay. You can build one that's even better."

Louis made an effort to pull himself together, and sniffed snot back up his nostrils. Davy knelt and scooped bricks onto the table. Tally just sat there.

"Tally, help us," Anna said.

She folded her arms. "I didn't do anything. He was being a little asshole and wouldn't show me."

Oh shit. Davy had the presence of mind not to say that out loud, and glanced wide-eyed at Anna for her reaction. Anna's stare at Tally was so hot it was like her eyes were lasers and their target was teenage impertinence. She would never want to encounter that face in a courtroom.

Tally shifted her eyes toward Davy and appeared visibly unnerved by the solemn shaking head Davy gave her. *You're in deep doo-doo,* she tried to communicate telepathically.

But Anna's ire seemed to subside almost instantly. "I guess you're walking to rehearsal, aren't you?" She said it quietly, almost offhand, and continued to clean up. Louis picked up on her dangerous mood and dropped to his knees, and grasped from the floor as many bricks as his little hands could hold. Tally seemed to realize the error of her ways and began to help as well.

Davy put a hand on Anna's arm. "Why don't you take that shower? We'll finish up here."

Anna left the room without a word, and they finished transferring Lego bricks to Louis's plastic bin. The three of them sat at the kitchen table in silence, and Davy tried to figure out a way to adjust the atmosphere.

"Can I have chocolate milk?" Louis asked.

"Can you bring me to rehearsal?" Tally asked at the same time.

Tackling the easier question first, Davy said, "Sorry, I don't have any chocolate milk."

"Yes, you do. Ma got chocolate syrup and we have milk."

"Really?" At Louis's nod, Davy banged her fist on the table. "Then let's have chocolate milk. Tally, you in?" At Tally's grudging nod, Davy produced the ingredients and squeezed syrup into three generous pours of milk. For a while, the clinking of spoons against glasses was all that was heard. At the first sip, Davy was transported back to tiny cartons and school lunches. She couldn't remember when she last had chocolate milk. Louis and Tally both sported brown milk mustaches, so Davy gave herself one, and the three of them giggled at each other. How had she not known about the redemptive power of chocolate milk?

"So, can you give me a ride?" Tally repeated.

"You have to understand—"

"So it's a no? Fine. Unsubscribe." Tally punched her finger in the air as if she really could just delete Davy.

Annoying little shit. Davy stayed silent and counted to ten. Tally was putting her in a difficult position. The situation with Anna felt unresolved.

But Davy had to take some ownership for Anna's frustration too. She leaned in with both elbows on the table. "Look, you picked the wrong day to call Louis an asshole." She jerked a thumb toward Louis. "He already said goddamn—my fault, I admit—and I lobbed about six f-bombs just this morning. Anna has had it up to here with the foul language." She waited a moment for that to sink in. "Plus, who was really the asshole? You've acted bitchy since the moment you walked in."

Tally lowered her eyes but didn't say anything. Louis looked between them like he was watching a tennis match.

"What's the matter, anyway? I've never seen you like this."

Tally looked up, her eyes fiery. "That's because you've never been around. Don't act like you all of a sudden know me."

"Whoa." Davy sat back. "Okay, fair. I don't get to make blanket statements about your behavior, but you don't get to be rude to everybody with no consequences."

"Whatever. I just won't go. I'm going to suck anyway. I don't even want to be in the stupid play anymore." She put her arms on the table and rested her head on them.

And then it all became clear.

"Louis," Davy stage-whispered. "I think Tally fell asleep. Can you poke her for me? Gently? I want to tell her something, and I want to make sure she's listening, but I can't reach her."

Louis prodded Tally's tricep with his forefinger. Tally didn't respond.

"Again," she whispered. "Maybe tap her very lightly, and keep doing it so it gets annoying."

Louis grinned and tapped. Tally didn't move, and Louis and Davy began snickering.

"This appears to be a very challenging case, Lou. Now while you're tapping, say that you're tapping."

"Tap, tap, tap," Louis said, with every poke of his finger. Then Davy joined him, and their *taps* became a low monotonous mantra interspersed with giggles.

Finally, Tally whirled upward, her hair flying out behind her, exclaiming, "What? God," in that teenage way of stretching small words to at least three syllables each. She pretended to be irritated, but Davy could see the smile she was trying to hide.

"Listen to me, Tally. You're going to be a part of that play, and you're going to work at it, and try your hardest, and come opening night, you're going to kick ass all over the stage. Hear me?"

Louis pointed at Davy. "You said a bad word again."

"I did? Shit."

Louis and Tally cracked up.

Davy pointed back at Louis. "Don't tell your mom."

"Too late," Anna said, breezing into the kitchen with her hair damp and her skin dewy. "She already heard you."

"I'm sorry," Davy said to Anna as she sat at the table with them. "My name is Davy and I'm a swearaholic. I know I have a problem."

"So what are we going to do about it?" Anna looked at all of them.

"Swear jar?" Davy said in a tentative voice. She could drop a twenty in and be covered for at least a day or so.

"What's the big deal anyway? Everybody curses. Freedom of speech," Tally said, reverting back to surly adolescent. "I've heard all the words, even the really bad ones. You'd have to be living under a rock not to."

"Do you think Lou has?" Anna asked.

"He will by the time he hits fourth grade."

"Is that a reason to use them? Because everyone else does?" Anna asked Tally.

"No, but—"

"How would you feel if a curse word was directed at you?"

Tally shrugged. "Bad, but most times I only curse when I'm frustrated. I don't call anybody bad names. And why aren't you yelling at Davy? She curses all the time."

"I do," Davy said. "Nobody ever gave a sh—I mean—nobody cared what I had to say when I was younger. It got me attention—now it's just a bad habit. Usually, I use foul language to give what I'm saying a bigger impact, a little jolt, you know? Or yeah, when I'm frustrated or upset, like this morning when I burned myself. But I wouldn't call anybody a bad word either—at least not out loud. That's inappropriate and hurtful."

Anna took over. "You can talk any way you like, Tally. So can Davy. Nobody's going to stop you from using offensive language whenever you want, but you have to think about how it reflects on you. What kind of person do you want to be? Do you want to be the kind of person who calls Louis an a-hole? Or do you want to be kinder than that?"

Her words were directed at Tally, but Davy knew Anna was talking to her as well. She sank a little lower in her seat and kept quiet. Davy could see Tally was thinking about it, but maybe it was best to leave the question rhetorical for Tally. And not rhetorical for her. "Well, I want to change. I want to break this bad habit. So about that swear jar?"

Anna gave her a shrewd look. "Do you really think a swear jar would work?"

"No way," Tally said. "You've got lots of money."

"And could you really quit cold turkey?" Anna continued, the hint of a twinkle in her eye. "You've been swearing like a trucker since we met when we were seventeen. How will you be able to stop?"

"I don't know." Davy felt her face getting hot. It was possible that Anna had been the last person to call her out about her filthy mouth, and that had been when they were teenagers. "Well, what do you experts suggest then?"

"If it's going to work, the price has to be something you put a lot of value on." Tally said, and Anna nodded. Louis was content to spectate.

Davy waited to hear what they would come up with.

"Time," Anna finally said.

Shit. That was a good one. She was already stretched so thin.

"Wow. Look what her mouth just did," Tally said to Anna. "It got all tight and turn-downy."

Anna actually rubbed her hands together. "Hmm. How about this? For every time Davy uses an offensive word, which will include any word that makes someone feel bad about themselves—like when she said dum-dum earlier—"

"Wait, dum-dum isn't a swear," Tally said.

"I called myself a dum-dum," Davy said. "That wasn't hurting anyone but me."

"I think we should include any words that hurt no matter who they're directed toward. No putting ourselves down. Don't you think that's a good idea, Louis?"

Louis nodded.

"Can everyone agree to that?"

Nods all around.

"So, every time Davy uses an offensive word, she has to trade ten minutes of her time for it."

"What is she going to do during those ten minutes, just sit around?" Tally asked.

"Like a time out?" Louis said.

"I absolutely cannot just sit around." Davy was deeply disturbed by the thought of it. "That's an obscene waste. Do you know how much people pay me for my time?"

"This time you'll be the one paying." Tally grinned. "For your curses. I'm going to keep count."

"But what will you do with that time? I agree that you're a bit beyond a ten-minute trip to the naughty step," Anna said.

"Collect trash on the side of the highway?" Davy couldn't keep the sarcasm out of her voice.

"You can play with me!" Louis said.

They all looked at him. Anna turned to Tally, who nodded and gave her unspoken blessing. Davy couldn't believe it. Tally's conversion from bratty insolence to mature kindness was whiplash inducing. She reached out and grasped Tally's forearm and gave her a look that she hoped conveyed how proud she was of her. Davy didn't mind spending time with Louis; she enjoyed it, if she was honest with herself, but she wouldn't let this development cut into her Tally time. And she'd really have to watch her language. She suddenly felt pulled in about sixteen different directions.

Anna was gazing at her, waiting for her to reply.

"Okay. I can agree to that. For every swear, I'll play with Louis for ten minutes."

"But we'll add them up and Louis can redeem his time on Sundays when you're not at work." Anna made sure Louis understood. "If Davy slips up right before bedtime, you don't get to stay up later playing with her."

Louis yanked his fist back toward his chest. "Yes! We're going to play for hours!"

Davy was chagrined by his lack of faith in her. "Hold up, Lou. What if I don't curse at all? Then we won't get to play together."

He gazed at her with guileless eyes. "Have you met you?"

Tally cackled at that. Anna smiled, and then she rescued Davy from having to answer Lou's embarrassing question. "All right, who has to use the bathroom? We're leaving for rehearsal in ten minutes."

CHAPTER EIGHTEEN

M a?"
   "Yes, Lou?" Anna paused at the dresser where she pulled a set of pajamas from the drawer.

"I like it here." He flung his towel away and spun in place naked in the middle of the room until he flopped on the floor, giggling crazily. His comfort level had definitely improved.

"What do you like about it?" She helped him into his pj's. She knew he was old enough to do it himself, but she couldn't help it.

"I like the tub in our bathroom. It's really big. I like the trampoline. I like the room where you do your work and the bar. And I like Davy. She's funny. We had fun at the playground."

"Good. I'm glad."

As predicted, there wasn't a lot for Davy to do at the playhouse today while Tally and the rest of the cast lounged on the stage and did a dry read of Act I. Anna met with the director to get a sense of what she wanted for the set. Thankfully, she was a minimalist and planned to use mostly lighting effects to convey mood and tone. Anna's job was to design a few tall flats that suggested trees and greenery, so she got started right away and made some sketches for her to approve. The sooner Anna was done with it, the sooner it was off her plate.

Davy volunteered to hang with Louis at the park next to the theater, and they both seemed tired and happy when Anna and Tally met up with them. Anna appreciated how easy Davy was making their transition to life in Elmdale. Davy was trying really hard. Harder than Anna had initially thought she would. It couldn't be easy for a busy, single woman to adjust to a ready-made family, but Davy didn't seem bothered by the intrusion in her personal space that two additional people—plus Tally—had made.

It would be so nice for Anna to relax into the comfort of having another adult around, sharing the load, giving her a break. But she couldn't allow herself to succumb to the illusion of what her life was at the moment. For now, it was enough that they were settling in without too many problems. Now if she could get Louis to stay in bed, she could finally get some work done. "Do you like your bedroom?"

"Yeah. I like that Jeff is on the wall now. When are you going to color him in?"

In an effort to make Louis more comfortable, she had sketched out the beginnings of the mural for his wall. There was now a charcoal outline of a friendly-looking octopus lounging along the baseboard trim.

"I have to get some different paint first, but soon." She tucked him into bed and gave him Jeff, and then she snuggled down next to him with the book she had chosen earlier. "Do you think you'll be able to stay in bed tonight?"

"I think so." He raised his head so he could see the walkie-talkie in its charging cradle on his nightstand. "You'll answer me if I call you?"

"Absolutely. I have mine in the studio. Now are you going to read to me or what?" She handed him the picture book, entitled *I'm the Biggest Thing in the Ocean!*

"Ma, this book is for babies. Can't I read from my encyclopedia?"

"I like stories. Read me a story."

They had read this story probably a thousand times. It used to be Louis's favorite, back when she was the one who read to him, and before he discovered nonfiction books filled with facts about the ocean. It probably wouldn't be long until she'd have to start buying marine biology textbooks for him, but for now, he indulged her request and read the story that both of them had practically memorized at this point. Another plus— it was a very short read.

Louis's voice droned quietly and Anna fought her fatigue. She couldn't allow herself to fall asleep in his bed. She had too much to do. After he finished reading, she cuddled with him for a bit, and then left the room, making sure his nightlight was on and his door was cracked about five inches, just the way he wanted.

❖

Davy and Tally had just finished cleaning up the kitchen after some post-dinner ice cream.

"You want to stay over?" Davy asked her. "Your mom already said it was okay. But I can bring you home if you don't want to."

"I didn't bring any stuff."

"You can borrow from me. Pajamas, toothbrush, whatever."

Tally grimaced. "I don't want to use your toothbrush."

Davy laughed. "I'll give you a new one. Never been used—promise."

"Where will I sleep?"

"You can sleep in my bed. I'll take the couch. Or you can sleep on the couch and I'll take the bed. We'll have to do up one of the spare bedrooms for you, so you can come over whenever you want."

"Whenever I want?"

"If you do want." She tried to keep the uncertainty from her voice.

The walkie-talkie crackled and Davy's and Tally's heads turned toward it on the kitchen counter.

"Ma?" Louis's tinny voice came through the small speaker.

"Let me get down the stairs, why don't you?" Anna muttered as she bustled into the kitchen and lunged for the handset. "I'm here," she said to Louis.

"Just checking." His relief was evident even over radio waves.

"Give yourself a chance to fall asleep, buddy. Good night. Love you."

"Love you."

Anna put the walkie-talkie down. "What are you two doing?"

"Waiting to see how *Operation: Keep Louie in his bed* unfolds," Tally said.

"Tally was just deciding if she wants to stay the night."

Anna said, "You should. We're going swimming tomorrow. We can stop by Mom's and get your suit if you want to come."

The walkie-talkie crackled again. "Ma?"

The three of them chuckled.

Anna clicked the button. "Yo."

"Hi."

"Were you just checking again?" Anna asked with a grin. To Davy she said, "I can't tell yet whether these were a really good idea or a really bad one."

"Yeah," Louis said.

"Still here. Try and go to sleep."

"I was hoping they'd help," Davy said. "I don't want them to become a pain in the ass."

Tally shot Davy a look. "You cursed."

"Whoops."

"You have any paper? I'm going to make a chart so we can keep track and put it on the fridge."

"Tally's making a tally sheet," Anna said to Davy and hiked a thumb at Tally, who sucked her teeth.

"Shut up, Anna."

"Add your name to the tally sheet." Anna turned to Davy. "Is shut up an offensive word?"

"I think we can let it slide this time," Davy said, wanting to keep the peace.

"Let's go to the studio. I've got craft paper," Anna said.

The three of them were soon seated around the worktable while Tally made a chart with everyone's name on it and columns for counting up their swear words. Davy was happy to sit and watch Tally work, but Anna couldn't seem to keep still.

"What's wrong?" Davy asked her.

"It's nothing. As soon as I walk in here, all the items on my to-do list start screaming for attention." She reached out and grasped Davy's forearm. "Thank you for the walkie-talkies. If they work, I'm finally going to be able to get back on track work-wise. And just in time too. I need to build up some stock for the Red Bank Street Fair next Saturday."

"If they help, I'm glad." A bottle rocket of pride burst inside her, and she hoped her face wasn't too red. And she would be content if Anna's hand remained curled around her arm for the rest of the evening.

"Oh, that's that big one I went to with you last summer," Tally said. "Too bad I can't come this year. I have rehearsal."

"Oh, shit," Anna said.

Tally raised her eyebrows and put a slash mark in Anna's column.

"What?" Davy asked.

"You have a part," Anna said to Tally. "You start rehearsing earlier than the chorus. I forgot."

"Just get Mom to go with you. She won't mind helping."

"I need her to watch Louis."

"I can watch Louis," Davy said. "Or do you need help at your fair? I could do either of those things." She pulled out her phone.

"The fair is easy," Tally said. "You and Anna will stand around and answer questions people have about the art. Usually it's how much it costs. And Anna will pay you in fair food—even stuff Mom would kill her for buying."

"You had me at fair food." Helping Anna had become Davy's number one priority. She didn't care what questionable food she would have to eat.

"I couldn't ask you. It's a super-long day. And it's Saturday. You'll be at work. I can handle it by myself."

"I'm putting it in my calendar. I'll make myself free. Which is it? Art fair or babysitting?" *Please say art fair.* Davy liked Louis, but the idea of spending the day alone with Anna was making her heart do these little leaps like it was a dog looking for a treat.

The walkie-talkie squawked. "Ma?"

Tally snatched it before anyone else could. "Louie? This is your aunt Tally speaking. Please go to sleep. It's late. In the morning you can come wake me up. I'll be in Davy's bed."

"I can?"

"Yeah, but only if you go to sleep now."

"Okay." Louis sounded like he was on the verge of dropping off anyway. "G'night."

Davy held her phone a little too tightly while she waited for Anna to answer.

"I can't ask you to do this. I really can manage on my own."

Tally scoffed. "It took both of us to put up that tenty thing in Hoboken, remember? And you're gonna need breaks. It'll probably be a hundred and twenty degrees that day."

"I'm sure you can handle it, but why should you have to?" Davy said. "I'd like to help."

Anna seemed to give in. "How are you with direct sales?"

Davy knew her grin had just turned shit-eating, but she couldn't help it. "I'll have you know that my assistant recently told me I could talk the leaves down from the trees. You're going to have a banner day." She gazed at her phone to hide her dorky expression.

"I hope you know what you're getting into." Anna gave her a rueful smile.

Davy stood and pushed her stool under the table, thinking she should probably go before Anna had a chance to change her mind. "Are you finished, Tally? Why don't we hang that up on the fridge and then watch a movie or something? We can get out of Anna's way and let her get some work done."

"Okay." Tally picked up her chart and followed Davy to the door. "What snacks will we be enjoying during the movie?"

Davy needed to improve her snack game. "I don't think I have any."

"Like you didn't have any ice cream?"

"I didn't know I had that. Anna must have gone shopping."

"There's microwave popcorn in the pantry," Anna called after them.

Davy almost had the door closed when she heard Anna say her name. She turned back and Anna was gazing at her with an inscrutable look on her face.

"Thank you, for everything."

Davy nodded, and reluctantly left Anna alone.

CHAPTER NINETEEN

Anna could hardly believe it. It wasn't even two o'clock and today was on track to be her best sales day ever. Davy was so good at upselling, Anna was worried she wouldn't have enough stock to last until the end of the day.

Setting up at the crack of dawn had been a piece of cake. Davy's analytical brain made erecting the canopy painless, for once, and Anna's stall was ready to go just as the sun started to beat down and early-risers began strolling through. Davy, with her big smile and caffeined-up energy, had behaved almost like a carnival barker, drawing people in and converting them to buyers.

Right now, she stood with a punky, blue-haired woman in her mid-twenties as they studied a smallish still life done in oils on fiberboard. This piece was among the oldest in Anna's inventory, mainly because the proportions were wonky and the colors were a little unconventional.

The woman was obviously interested in Davy, her eyes glued to Davy's face as she unspooled her sales pitch. Davy had no idea how winning she was with her bright smile, her hair hastily done up in two damp, crazy little buns, and her black T-shirt knotted at the waist in an effort to keep cool. She was so earnest and enthusiastic about this mediocre image of some fruit in a bowl with this woman, when all she wanted was Davy's phone number.

Feeling slightly territorial, Anna approached and handed Davy an icy bottle of water.

Davy pressed it to the back of her neck and said, "This is Anna. She's Resnick Studio. She did this." She beheld the piece in Blue-hair's hands like it was a long-lost Vermeer.

"An early work," Anna said. "I was still in art school. Still climbing up that learning curve."

"That's interesting." Blue-hair didn't sound that interested, but Davy did.

"Really? You did this that long ago?" She tried to take it from Blue-hair. "If you don't want it, I do."

Blue-hair kept a hold of it, and her eyes stayed on Davy. "No, I like it." She turned to Anna. "Where did you go to school?"

"Rutgers," Anna replied. "Only three semesters."

"Oh." Blue-hair sounded almost as disappointed as Anna's mother had when she told her she was dropping out.

"I want to buy this one," Davy said to Blue-hair, her eyes intense. "Will you give it to me?"

Blue-hair laughed. "No, you've convinced me. You're a great salesperson. I'll take it." She handed the piece to Anna and gazed coyly at Davy. "Do you want to get a drink later?"

Davy gave her a cold look and held up her bottle of water. "No, thanks. I already have a drink." She walked to the rear of the stall and disappeared behind the mesh screen.

"Um...cash or credit?" Anna asked.

Blue-hair handed her card over. The rest of the transaction was completed in silence. Davy only reappeared, carrying a stack of pre-matted watercolors to refill the bins, after the woman had gone.

Anna didn't quite know what had just happened, but Davy currently looked like she wanted to tear someone's face off. Anna sidled up next to her and stood close enough to feel the heat Davy's body was throwing off. "I like how you used reverse psychology to make that sale. You acting like you wanted it made her want to buy it."

"I did want it," Davy practically snarled. "I was this close to ripping it out of her hands."

"Why? It's a not-very-good rendering of some grapes and pears—pedestrian and amateurish. A Cézanne, it's not. I don't even do anything like that anymore."

Davy wouldn't look at her. She unknotted her T-shirt and fiddled with the hem. "I'm going to get something to eat. You want anything?"

"Sure." Anna wasn't going to get to the bottom of this right now.

"What do you want?" Davy bent and wiped her face with her T-shirt. Anna gawped at her pale stomach for the moment it was exposed.

"Something cold," Anna spluttered. "Whatever you want. I don't care."

Davy left without a backward glance.

❖

Davy's mood seemed to have improved slightly when she came back about twenty minutes later. Her return coincided with an afternoon lull, and they took a break to have lunch. Davy ate quickly and gazed at the fair-goers passing by. She slurped at her lemonade and plucked at her T-shirt. "Why didn't you tell me not to wear black today? If this day were a hot pepper, I bet it would have about three trillion Scovilles." She heaved herself out of her chair and strolled out beyond the shade of the canopy to begin her carnival barker routine again.

Anna let out a long breath as she covertly ogled Davy's lean figure in the sunlight. Her outfit was admittedly not the best option for a day in the heat, but Anna sure enjoyed looking. Davy now stood on the midway and rolled her shirtsleeves up to the shoulder before she approached an elderly couple who brushed right by her. Anna couldn't deny the attraction that had sparked since she had moved into Darling Drive and had been growing with every moment she spent in Davy's company.

Starting with that first teenage crush on Winnie Bowerchuck, Anna's track record with women featured wrongheaded and short-lived entanglements that were mostly about sex. She couldn't say she had ever been in love, but she knew attraction when she felt it. And she was feeling it now. She could accept that she was powerfully drawn to Davy in a way she hadn't felt about anyone in a long time, and she wanted to give in to it, despite the contract and the fabrication of their current relationship. What she was feeling was not fabricated. And the jabs of jealousy when that woman had approached Davy today—they were real. As was her desire to be close to her, to know what she was thinking, to touch her—pretty much anywhere.

She gazed at Davy, who now looked like she had become the cruise director for the entire festival. She was pointing a family with a doublewide stroller toward the toilets, gesturing with an outstretched arm that might be turning pink with exposure to the sun. Anna reached in her tote for sunscreen. She couldn't let that happen.

❖

Davy turned in surprise but went willingly when Anna grasped her by the arm and led her back under the shelter of the canopy. Anna got right into her personal space and unscrewed the cap on a tube of sunscreen. *What the hell is happening right now?*

"Your skin is getting pink. We can't have that, can we?" Anna murmured, and proceeded to slather each arm with SPF. The way she carefully and sensually massaged Davy's skin, focusing so completely on her task...it doubled Davy's heart rate and shallowed her breathing.

When Anna looked up as she squeezed more white cream into her palm, Davy struggled to interpret her expression. It sent signals of ambivalence, but also possession and hunger, and it robbed Davy of the power of speech. Anna's fingers touched her again, and the warmth of Davy's skin intensified, and her legs became a little wobbly.

Anna was thorough. She slid her hand beneath the fabric of Davy's sleeves to extend the coverage right up to her bra strap, which made Davy's nipples perk right the hell up. Then Anna devoted slow and loving attention to each finger to ensure it was protected from the sun.

The whole sensual exchange took less than five minutes, and when Anna stepped away to attend to someone who had wandered in to browse, Davy stood there, dazed, for several long moments. She tried to commit to memory the lingering effects of Anna's light caresses, and she couldn't help imagining her touch on other places on her body. These were not the actions of someone who was concerned with her sun exposure. What had come over Anna?

It was hard to get back into marketing mode. She made far fewer sales after that. Far fewer.

❖

Hours later, at the end of the day, Davy was weary. The satisfaction she derived at how much less stuff they had to pack back into Anna's minivan at the close of the fair made her feel a little giddy. Of course, Anna's work was so good that it practically sold itself, but she had helped with that.

Anna seemed pleased with their numbers as the day descended to twilight and she put away her laptop and cashbox. She had asked Davy to fetch the car so they could begin packing up, but before Davy did that, she approached Anna with three pieces that had gone unsold. Two were small watercolors of dense, green forest landscapes and the third was a mid-sized oil done on canvas. It depicted a beach scene of calm waters at sunset—or just after—when low-lying clouds had refracted the waning sunlight into a million shades, from the pale orange of a ripe cantaloupe to the deep violet of impending night. The colors were laid onto the canvas thickly and in angular planes with a palette knife, suggesting weight and dimension. It was more abstract than figurative—a landscape reduced to its most elemental components—color and light. Anna had nailed that transition from day to night, and Davy wanted to own it.

Anna barely looked up from what she was doing. "You can put those with the rest. I was hoping that oil would sell today, but it is one of the pricier ones. Maybe next time."

"I want to buy it. And these." Davy gestured at the watercolors, suddenly self-conscious. "I've had my eye on them, hoping nobody would grab them. It was kind of like holding my breath for a really long time. Sending the don't-buy-that-buy-this-instead vibes all day long was pretty exhausting. It had to be my vibes that kept people away from them. Yes, it most definitely was. I have very strong vibes sometimes."

One side of Anna's mouth lifted in amusement. "Only sometimes?"

"Yeah." Running her mouth in this mortifying way—what was wrong with her? "And since the day is over and they're still here, they're fair game. Now I get to buy them."

Anna came from behind the table and took the works from her. "They're yours. Thank you for all your help today."

"No, Anna. I insist on paying for them. I know creating art is not cheap. The materials alone—"

"Do you want me to wrap them?" Anna interrupted.

"No! Forget it. I refuse to take them if you won't let me buy them."

"I'm actually kind of relieved."

"You are? Why?"

"I thought you had terrible taste." Anna's eyes held a hint of mischief. "You were so pissed when that woman bought my truly bad still life from art school."

"Ugh. I don't want to talk about that. I'll just go get the car." Davy turned on her heel and fled.

It was almost nine p.m. by the time the minivan was repacked, and they were back on the road, headed toward the Parkway. An industrious quiet had settled between them when Davy returned with the car and they dismantled Anna's stall. The pieces she wanted were nowhere to be seen.

The knowledge that someone else was going to get them—that beach landscape especially—robbed her of the peace she should be feeling from a day well spent. It was going to nag at her for some time to come, she was sure. She fiddled with the AC vents on the dash to distract herself.

"I'm going to have to input today's receipts into my accounting program, but I'm pretty sure this was my best sales day ever." Anna said, her eyes focused on the road in front of her.

"I'm glad I was here to witness it."

"Witness it? You're pretty much the cause of it. Tally is great and all, but when she comes to help, stuff isn't flying out of here like it did today. You were spectacular."

"Really?" Davy felt her face warm at the lavish praise.

"Yep. I can't thank you enough. It was a great day."

"How much of your income comes from events like today's?"

"I used to do probably eighty percent of business through fairs and festivals, but in the past couple of years, my socials have really picked up, so it's a lot less now. These days, I can post an image on Instagram and it'll sell really quickly. And I can charge higher prices in my Etsy store than I do at fairs like today."

Wait, what? "Why don't you charge the same price across the board? And why sell at a fair when you make more from Etsy?" Was Davy being too pushy? Maybe she should just shut up.

But Anna seemed happy to elaborate. "Well, there's the volume I can do in one day. Internet sales come in drips and drabs." She was silent, tapping on the steering wheel for a moment. "I probably should stop selling at fairs. It might help build an air of exclusivity around my work, if that's even a thing, if I started limiting access to it. Then I could charge even higher prices." She paused to change lanes. "The plain truth is that I like coming to events like this. Sure, they're a ton of work, but I get to meet the people who buy my stuff. And they're impulse buying in many cases. They see it—they want it—they buy it. I love it when that happens. When I can watch someone fall in love with something I created—there is no better feeling than that."

"I totally get that," Davy said, even though there was nothing in her own work that remotely compared to it. "And I would be honored to own any example of your work, even if it's a still life where the pears look kind of furry and blue, and the grapes are the size of baseballs."

Anna burst out laughing. "All right, it was an experiment in color and proportion. A failed one, obviously. I was young and trying all these new techniques I was learning about. I know it's terrible." She glanced over at Davy. "I'd really like to know why you wanted it so badly."

This was the third time Anna had asked. Davy couldn't see a way of avoiding talking about it now, since she had brought it up. She simply had to trust Anna and make herself vulnerable. "I wanted it because of what you just said—you were young."

"Ha. You mean you wanted something incompetent and sloppy?"

"No, I wanted it because you painted it only a couple of years after we met." How was Davy going to explain this? "I don't know any details about your life between that summer fifteen years ago and now, but when you said you painted that when you were at school, only like, what, two years after we met? I kind of felt like I could reconnect to the Anna I used to know—the one who welcomed me into her world with a smile and a punch on the arm. The one I never once got bored with even when we were making props for a really bad musical. The one who drove me crazy talking about her dumb crush when I was massively crushing on her. The Anna who painted that still life maybe wasn't so changed from the Anna I used to know, unlike the one I know now. The one who hates me."

Davy could feel Anna sneaking glances at her while she drove, but after she finished talking, Anna stared at her for longer than Davy felt was safe.

"You may want to keep your eyes—"

"I don't hate you," Anna interrupted, gazing straight ahead again. "Of course I don't. You have to know that."

"Maybe not now, but you did."

"I admit, you provoked some really strong feelings by your absence. I didn't understand it. I do now, or I'm trying to. But it was never hatred."

"I thought about you so often back then, wondering where you ended up for school. Now I know—Rutgers. Only a few hours away from Penn." The could-have-beens were killing Davy right now.

"Well, I wasn't there very long. It was kind of a blip on my way to where I am now."

"Why did you leave?" Davy felt desperate for any crumbs Anna was willing to share.

Anna was silent. "It doesn't matter," she finally mumbled.

"Oh. Okay." Davy turned away and looked out the window.

"What?"

"Nothing. I understand. I'm sorry for prying."

"You're not prying. I just don't want you—" Anna exhaled violently. "I dropped out so I could help take care of Tally."

"Oh." Davy had nothing to say after that. Guilt had taken all her words.

"She had some serious sleep issues the first couple of years, and my mom was really struggling, and I had already missed a bunch of class time that last semester, so it made sense to drop because I wouldn't have earned any credits anyway." Anna's words came out in a rush.

"Oh."

Anna twisted her hands on the steering wheel. "And I was selling my stuff at flea markets on the weekends by this time, so I could work at home and take care of Tally while my mom did her Monday through Friday thing. It worked for us. Then a while after Tally started school, I was able to move out. When Louis came along, I just went right back into that routine."

"Oh."

Anna reached out and grabbed her forearm. "Will you stop saying *oh*? I didn't want you to feel bad, but you asked, and that's what happened."

"I should have been there." Davy had to say it. "I should've helped. She's my sister too."

"How could you have? Gregory would've cut you off, right? And if he wasn't telling me about what was going on in your life right up until the day he left, I'm guessing he wasn't telling you what was happening with us."

"I barely heard from him once I started college. It was years before he took an interest in me again."

"See? You shouldn't blame yourself." Anna let out a bark of a laugh that sounded low on the amusement scale. "And if you needed proof that I don't hate you, look no further than me defending you right now. The old me would've dropped dead in disbelief, but I'm seeing the bigger picture now."

Davy didn't say anything. She was morosely imagining a younger Anna, baby Tally on her shoulder, standing at an easel with her paintbrush outstretched. Anna's hand was still on her forearm, but now she slid it down to Davy's hand and took a firm hold of it.

"Listen." Anna darted her eyes to her. "I decided when we signed that contract that I was going to give us a clean slate. I should've told you that. We're starting new. You and Tally, and you and me. Whatever happened in the past, let it stay there."

"Thank you." Davy squeezed Anna's hand. "I feel like I don't deserve that kindness."

"Everyone deserves kindness. Just be kind in return."

Davy tried to let go but Anna wouldn't let her. They traveled in compatible silence for several long moments that way, holding hands, and Davy wanted to know more. She wanted to know anything Anna would tell her.

"How old was Tally when you got your own place?"

"She was seven, I think. In the second grade. And then my mom decided the house was too big for the two of them and downsized to a condo."

"And you stayed in Southfield?"

"Yeah, I didn't want to be too far away. I still spent a lot of time with Tally, although she rarely came to my place."

"Why not?"

"I moved into this big old house near the community college and had anywhere from three to seven roommates at any given time. It was located at the intersection of irresponsible and slovenly and so not child-friendly, but I snagged a room on the top floor and had enough space to work with good light."

"Sounds like the college experience without the hassle of classes."

"Yeah, sort of."

"Did you like living with a lot of people?"

"Yeah, I think it was good for me. I got a little crazy during those years, but then Lou came along, and things changed again."

Davy noticed how Anna zipped right by her self-described crazy years, and really wanted to ask what had made them crazy, but she was more curious about how Louis had entered Anna's life. She took a risk. "Do you mind if I ask about Louis?"

"I don't mind. What do you want to know?"

"Well, he's not your biological son, right?"

"You want to know the whole story? How he and I became a family?"

"Yes, if it's okay."

Anna's nod was slow, and she kept her eyes on the road. "Don't think I didn't hear what you said before, about my dumb crush interfering with your crush on me."

Davy's skin heated up several degrees. "Yeah, I thought that became pretty obvious on our last night together." She didn't know what this had to do with Louis.

"Actually, I had no idea you had a crush on me. We'll have to talk about that sometime. But it's connected. My teenage dumb crush is Lou's mother."

Davy didn't say anything. What Anna said didn't compute.

"Winnie. Remember her? Grizabella from *Cats*? She's Louis's mother."

Davy's mouth dropped open. "She is?"

Anna's lips compressed into a straight line as she nodded again.

What the actual fucking fuck? Davy realized she would have to exercise some tact here. "Were you two in a relationship?" She hoped she didn't sound accusatory.

"We were. Briefly. She was still doing the occasional show with SSCT, and she lived in the house I moved into. She's the one who told me there was a room available."

Davy had about a million questions, but she didn't want this to turn into a cross-examination. Still, she needed a few answers. "So you had a brief relationship and decided to have a child together?"

"Oh my God, no. Winnie had brief relationships with lots of people. I was just one of them." Anna glanced at her. "She was a terrible person to have a crush on. She was a terrible person to have a fling with. She was a terrible person who shouldn't have even considered parenthood. If there was an Olympic event for best all-around terrible person, Winnie would win the gold medal."

"But Louis is so wonderful."

Anna gripped her hand harder. "Thank you for saying that. He is, isn't he?"

"A real case of nurture overcoming nature."

"Well, the jury's still out. He's only five—six in September. I have high hopes that his paternal genes are dominant."

"About that…who is the father?"

"I don't know. That space on his birth certificate is blank."

Davy was quiet, and the only sound to be heard was the ambient highway traffic. How could Anna be with that woman, even for a little while? It had taken a youthful, inexperienced Davy all of about two minutes to diagnose Winnie's rudeness, her carelessness, her narcissism. Davy was so lost in her disbelief she inadvertently sucked her teeth in a loud and ill-mannered way.

Anna looked over at her. "What?"

"Nothing."

"Come on. Just say it."

Davy wanted to say it. She didn't understand at all. "I know I don't have the moral high ground here, and I don't want to disparage your taste in women, but, Anna, she was so awful."

"Yeah, I know that. Believe me. I knew when I was seventeen. I just sort of…forgot for a while."

"How did—I mean, what happened?"

"I was lonely," Anna said. "We're in the suburbs. Homes filled with straight families as far as the eye could see. There wasn't exactly a cornucopia of choice for a single chick like me looking to get busy with other single chicks. Winnie was convenient. I only had to go down one flight of stairs when I was horny." Anna shrugged. "It didn't last long."

Davy forced the idea of a horny Anna out of her mind. "Where does Louis come in?"

"She got pregnant a good while after we ended, and she had already stopped seeing whoever the dad was. I don't think she even told him. For some reason the idea of having a kid really appealed to her. And then everyone in the house helped her out while she was pregnant. Whatever she needed. She was getting a ton of attention, which of course, she loved. And still more attention after the delivery, which was a little complicated—I was there. I was her birthing partner."

"Why you?" Davy thought her question might have sounded a little belligerent and told herself to tone it down, but Anna didn't seem to notice.

"Even though we weren't sleeping together anymore, we were still friends, I thought. And she wasn't really doing much research, so I read some books and articles and would talk to her about it. When it was time to go to birthing class, she asked me to come, and I said yes. I guess I was pretty invested."

"And you had experience with babies from Tally."

"Yeah, I did." Anna sounded almost melancholy. "Anyway, new babies get lots of attention, moms less so. Our housemates' interest flatlined, and then they got annoyed whenever Lou cried. Winnie depended on me, and I let her. But she was so fucking flighty, I worried about him from the day he was born. Sorry about my language."

"Please, I love hearing it. It's like secondhand smoke. I feel like an addict who craves one well-placed fuck." Davy cringed. "In a sentence, I mean. Anyway, go on."

Anna gave a little laugh but then she sobered and it looked like she was trying to figure out how to continue the story. "It got a little weird after that."

"Weird, how?"

"It almost seemed like Winnie was competing with Louis for my attention. She became obsessed with getting her body back in shape, and resentful of Lou for making her that way. She only breastfed for about two months, and didn't seem to form any kind of attachment to him. And even though I knew she didn't really care about me, she was suddenly trying to initiate some…sexy times when I was trying to take care of him. I mean, what new mom wants sex? I think she was feeling totally insecure."

"She sounds psycho."

Anna shook her head, but Davy didn't know if it was in disagreement or about something else.

"Things settled for a while," she continued. "Winnie went out for every audition she could, desperate for some kind of job that I think was supposed to validate who she saw herself to be. I worked and took care of Louis, but that house was not a great place for a kid. There were a million stairs for one thing. I was always worried I would fall while I carried him. Then she told me her doctor wanted her to have a colonoscopy because of some digestive issue and she would have to be under anesthesia."

Davy frowned. *The fuck?*

"She asked me to become Lou's legal guardian in case anything happened to her during the procedure. And I said sure, of course. I didn't really think anything of it. I signed some papers, and she gave me some other papers and that was it."

Something wasn't right about that woman. Davy's stomach churned.

"A few months later, Winnie announced she had booked a chorus role for the national tour of *Aladdin* and she just…left. I was Lou's legal guardian. I am responsible for him. That's the last time I saw her."

"She fucking left? Did she even ask you to look after him?"

"She didn't have to. I already loved him with my whole heart. She knew I would."

"Did she even have the colonoscopy? You're not supposed to need one of those until you're forty-fucking-five. And establishing guardianship for something like a medical procedure would normally be strictly temporary."

Anna looked over at her in surprise, as if it was the first time she had considered it. "You think she planned it all out in advance?"

"From all that you've said, I wouldn't put it past her."

Anna didn't speak, and Davy couldn't tell what she was thinking. She withdrew her hand so both were on the wheel as she took their exit. Davy's palm felt bereft.

"It wouldn't have mattered," Anna finally said. "The worry I have now is what I'll do if she ever comes back for him. She could take him away and I couldn't do a thing to stop her."

Davy could help here. She wanted—no, she *needed* to help Anna. "You could adopt Louis, and I can help you arrange it."

"How can I do that? I have no idea where she is. That tour of *Aladdin* is long over, and she is completely MIA. And what if I do find her and she thinks *oh yeah, I have a kid. I want him back.* Believe me when I say it would absolutely wreck me to give him up."

"But this has to be weighing on you all the time. Don't you want to resolve it?"

"If I could be sure it would be resolved the way I want, then yes, I would. But I can't be sure, can I?"

"Say the word and my firm's investigator will track her down. We can make it worth her while to give up her rights."

"How?" Anna scoffed. "Money? I don't have the kind of money I'm sure she'd want."

Davy was very good at presenting legal options to unwilling people. She didn't believe it would come to that. "Chances are, she would welcome the freedom. My investigator is the best in the business. She'll at least be able to tell us what's what."

"Let me think about it."

CHAPTER TWENTY

Anna stepped back and placed her roller in its tray.

Louis, from where he sat against the wall on his bed, his book open on his lap, looked up when the regular swoosh of interior paint application stopped. "That doesn't look like the Great Barrier Reef."

"Is that where Jeff lives? I didn't know you had a specific location in mind." It would have been great to know that before she started painting. Still, she surveyed the deep cobalt color of Louis's feature wall and liked what she saw. It was dark and moody enough to suggest the undersea setting she was going for, but now she thought she might apply a wash that would add the lightness and texture needed to suggest a shallower reef habitat.

Apropos of absolutely nothing, Anna wondered what Davy would think of it. Over the last week, she found her thoughts returning to Davy and the day they shared at the art fair and how easy and fun it had been. But she had hardly seen Davy since. Her workdays had lasted far into the night all week, and Anna missed the moments in the evenings when Davy would come to the studio, and they would talk about their days. But it was Friday, and they were entertaining tonight. Davy promised to be home early and mentioned she had given her assistant all the Saturdays in August off as well. Maybe that meant Davy could take a few more weekends off too.

Louis was engrossed again in his book. She sat next to him on the bed. "You'll have to show me some pictures of where he lives, so I can get it right. This is the first step in the process. Give it time."

Louis gave her a suspicious nod.

"Have a little faith, Lou." Anna laughed. "This needs time to dry and possibly a second coat. Let's take a break. Want to go check the mail?"

It had become a highlight of Louis's day to go down to where Davy's driveway met the curb and play with the mailbox's little flag after they collected the mail. The mailbox must have been installed by the previous owner. It was a custom wooden affair designed as a mini replica of Davy's home, clad in the same gray shingles and covered with boards that mimicked the style of its roofline. Anna didn't bother to put shoes on or change out of her speckled painting gear before they ambled down the drive.

"I like that the mail gets to live in a house," Louis said. He reached up to pull the door down and collected the fliers and envelopes inside. He handed all of it over to Anna and called *hello* into the now empty box.

"What do you mean?" An envelope from Elmdale Elementary distracted Anna.

"Our mail used to live in a closet at our old place, but now we live in a house, so the mail gets to live in a house too." He slid the red flag into its upright position, then lowered it again.

Closet? Louis must mean the aluminum compartment at the bottom of their stairwell, right next to the entrance of Hunan Lee's. She guessed it did kind of resemble a closet. Anna opened the letter and saw there were some documents she needed to produce before Louis started in September.

"Hi, there!"

Anna and Louis turned to see Leanne Spar walking toward them, her pace brisk and her arm raised in a wave. She looked like a page torn from the Lululemon catalog come to life. "Hi, Leanne. Fancy meeting you here."

Leanne looked pleased as punch to see them. "My goodness, I should've gotten my steps in earlier. August has been ungodly so far. Please forgive this glow I've already attained three minutes after leaving the house." She fanned herself for a moment before directing her attention to Louis. She squatted in front of him with a broad smile on her face. "And who might this strapping young man be?"

Instead of retreating with trepidation as usual, Louis grinned right back at her. "I'm Louis."

Leanne's easy, open manner could make anyone comfortable. "Louis! I've been anxiously waiting to make your acquaintance. I tried some very delicious cookies you made, and Davy talks about you all the time." She put out her hand and Lou shook it willingly, giggling a little. "She told me you might be able to help me out. Did you know that I have a brand-new ice cream-making machine, and I need someone who really likes ice cream to try some that I made, to make sure that I'm doing it right. Do you have any ice cream tasting experience?"

"Yes, I do!" Louis was beyond excited. "I taste ice cream all the time. I'm very good at it."

Leanne laughed. "I'm lucky I ran into you. I'm going to need you to try some real soon."

"How about tonight?" Anna asked. "We're having the Kleinmans over for dinner and trampolining. Would you and Roland like to join us? The outdoor furniture Davy ordered has arrived and we can finally start having guests."

"We would absolutely love it. Consider dessert handled."

"Terrific." Anna made a mental note to text Davy about this development. She hoped she wouldn't mind. "Now this is super casual, Leanne, not casual by your standards. Strictly burgers and dogs, maybe some store-bought potato salad."

"Exactly what I'm in the mood for on a hot August night." Leanne really knew how to turn on the charm. "We'll see you later!" And she was off, pumping her arms and striding away like she was about to conquer all of Elmdale.

Anna turned to Louis. "She's nice, right?"

Louis nodded. "I hope she wants me to taste chocolate. Do you think I'll need a special spoon?"

"Probably not, but we can check. Let's go look at some pictures of the Great Barrier Reef. I have a feeling the whale shark will be a little out of place there. Maybe we'll have to replace him with some other sea creatures."

❖

Davy had missed the 5:19 by one minute and was annoyed she had to wait for the 5:39 now. The later train would definitely be more crowded, and it seemed like everyone and their cousin was in Penn Station right now trying to leave the city on this steamy August Friday evening. She groped for her phone to text Anna her new arrival time while she stood in front of the monitor with about a hundred other people and waited for the track to be announced.

"Hey there, Davy."

Davy swung around to see Roland right behind her, his jacket hooked with one finger over his shoulder and briefcase in hand. She frowned. It was Friday. If she ever got on this train, she wanted it to serve as the airlock between her job and her home life. She deserved to decompress, dammit, and that wasn't going to happen if Roland decided to accompany her all the way home. This week had been brutal. She hadn't been home before ten p.m. all week. She knew other people lived in her home, but damn if she'd seen them in the past few days.

"Whoa. Who pissed in your lemonade?"

"Nobody. I'm just trying to get home and start the weekend, that's all."

"Right. And dinner with the Kleinmans and the Spars."

The Spars? Shit. Anna had texted her about that earlier and she hadn't replied—had immediately forgotten about it in the continuing deluge of work. "Yeah, great." She couldn't keep the weariness out of her voice.

Roland set his briefcase down and retrieved a crisp white handkerchief from his pocket. He regarded her as he blotted his forehead. "You and Joel Kleinman? Getting close?"

"As neighbors. We don't discuss business."

He looked taken aback. "Why not?"

"Because he expressed to me that he wasn't interested. Tonight is purely a social engagement. He has kids around Louis's age, and Anna and I thought it would be nice to get to know them better. That's all. No ulterior motive. No scheming."

Roland's expression revealed how foreign a concept this seemed to him.

"And please don't try to strong-arm Joel anymore. If he wants us, he knows where to find us."

"I have to believe you have some kind of play going, so I'm not going to interfere. I'm going to get a beer. Want one? We can hide them in little brown paper bags and drink them on the train. Won't that be fun?"

Davy sighed. Roland could believe what he wanted as long as he behaved in her home. "Sure."

❖

Davy and Roland parted ways at his house, and Roland said he'd be along after he'd showered and changed. Davy trudged up her driveway and entered the kitchen by the side door. Through the glass panels that looked out on the backyard, she saw Anna sitting out on the patio at their new outdoor sectional sofa with Leanne Spar and Becca Kleinman, each with a glass of rosé in hand. Their heads were turned toward the trampoline, where Louis, Joel, and his daughters romped, their shrieks audible to her inside. She was surprised to see Tally and her friend Su-Jin splayed across the new double lounger that was parked on the lawn, both engrossed in their phones.

She took the stairs two at a time up to her bedroom, planning on a quick change of clothes, and halted in the doorway at the sight before her. She turned on her heel, descended the stairs, returned to the kitchen, and slid the glass panel open. "Hi, everyone."

The three of them turned and welcomed her, but she had eyes only for Anna, who smiled at her in that delighted way that was becoming familiar, and that also made her knees a little bit weak.

"Sorry you missed your train. I'm glad you're home." Anna put her glass down on the teak coffee table.

"I'm glad to be home. Can I talk to you for a second?" Davy gestured for her to come into the kitchen.

"Oh, I know what that's about. To be young and in love." Leanne elbowed Becca. "She wants a private welcome, right?"

"Enjoy it while it lasts, Anna," Becca said.

Anna's face visibly pinked, and she got up without a word and entered the house. Davy turned and retraced her steps through the foyer and up the stairs, certain that Anna was right behind her. She entered her room and moved to the wall where the oil painting of the beach sunset now hung, framed in a weathered wood that complemented the scene perfectly.

"I figured if you ever buy a dresser it could go here, so I positioned it with that in mind. Do you like it?" Anna hung back, while Davy stood close to the painting, finding it hard to take her eyes from it.

"I love it. I really do. Thank you so much."

"And I won't hear of you paying for them, so don't insult me by suggesting it. I had to wait for the wood for the frame, but it arrived yesterday, so I was able to finish them off today. I think it goes well with this, and then I cut it down into narrower strips for the watercolors."

"The watercolors?"

Anna grinned. "Check your bathroom."

Davy poked her head in her bathroom and saw the two forest scenes, now matted and framed with the same wood, hanging one over the other behind the commode. They looked perfect. She returned to Anna, now standing close to her. "I really wanted these. Thank you."

"You're welcome."

Anna took a step and opened her arms and Davy became swaddled in sensation. For a moment, her brain short-circuited and she had no idea how to return a hug. Davy's limbs hung loosely at her sides while Anna pressed herself against her, her arms stealing around her and her hands smoothing across her back. The delicate brush of Anna's eyelashes fluttered against Davy's neck, the minty, herbal scent of her shampoo invaded Davy's nostrils, and the press of her breasts against Davy's chest meant her unconditional surrender. And then, overwhelming all of those stimuli was the heat that combusted deep in her belly, and lower. Davy finally moved her arms, clutching at Anna, pulling her even closer, not wanting to let go but also wanting to do other things, all the things. Everywhere. All at once. Now. Most of all, she was dying to kiss Anna, to tell her without words just how much she was coming to mean to her.

And then it was over, and Anna backed away, bumping into the bed and nearly losing her balance in her haste to put distance between them. "You probably want to freshen up. Come down whenever you're ready."

Davy was alone moments later. Freshen up? She looked down at her rumpled, limp work clothes and pulled her collar up to her nose, taking a sniff. Ugh. She needed a shower. No wonder Anna couldn't get away fast enough.

❖

At the bottom of the stairs, Anna took five seconds to calm herself down. She was okay. Everything was going to be okay. It was only because she hadn't seen Davy in a few days. But she hadn't been prepared for her own reaction to Davy's nearness. If she had stayed any longer in Davy's arms, she probably would've thrown her down on her very conveniently located bed and kissed her senseless. She pressed a hand to her chest, where her heart was attempting to take the Guinness World Record in greatest number of beats per minute. Several deep breaths later, she felt ready to rejoin her guests.

She grabbed the open bottle of rosé from the fridge and pressed it against her forehead for a moment before returning to the patio.

"Well, that was too quick for a quickie," Leanne said, her voice tinged with faux disappointment.

Anna knew she was probably as red as a tomato. She didn't reply to Leanne as she refilled their glasses. "Davy will be down in a minute."

"Hello, all." Roland came through the gate, carrying a bottle of bourbon and a bag of ice. He placed them ceremoniously on the dining table. "My contribution to the festivities. One can never have too much ice."

Tally and Su-Jin had wandered over to the trampoline and were now organizing a game of duck, duck, goose with the younger children. Joel returned to the patio, carrying his shoes, sweat staining his shirt.

"Joel, what can I get you to drink, besides a vat of ice water?" Anna asked.

He fell into the nearest chair and let out an exaggerated sigh. "That tramp is so much fun."

"I haven't uttered those words since college." Roland hooted at his own joke.

Joel laughed too. "Yes to water, and maybe some of Roland's bourbon."

"Coming right up," Roland said, and prepared three drinks. "I know Davy will want one too."

"Want one what?" Davy asked as she slid the glass panel closed behind her. She appeared refreshed in her white skinny jeans and a navy and white striped Breton shirt. Anna tried not to stare, but Davy looked like she was about to step onto a yacht in the south of France, and Anna just wanted to sail away with her. Alone. Why were there so many people around?

"Bourbon and soda. Lots of ice." Roland glanced at Davy. "Yes?"

"Yes." Davy met Anna's eyes and gave her a private smile. "I'm just going to say a quick hi to Tally and Lou and the other kids. Be right back."

Anna placed a large glass of water in front of Joel and paused to watch Davy as she crossed the lawn toward the trampoline. She honestly could watch her all night, but tore her gaze away and rejoined the women.

Becca said, "Fridays, right? It's like the weekend is a bucket that you want to fill up with fun family stuff, and then it ends up only about a quarter full by Sunday night."

"You've got that right. Weekends seem to go by in the blink of an eye. Louis insists that I put the work away for the whole weekend."

"Does that apply to Davy too?" Leanne asked.

"Well, it's harder for her, but she tries."

"You're more understanding than I am," Becca huffed out a laugh. "How is Davy with your son? Do they get along?"

"Louis loves spending time with Davy, and I think Davy is surprised by how much she enjoys his company. It's gone well so far, knock wood."

"And one of the older girls is your sister?" Becca looked toward the trampoline, and Leanne followed her gaze.

Anna nodded. "Tally, in the green T-shirt. Su-Jin is her friend. Tally is my half-sister, and she's also Davy's half-sister."

Neither woman said anything for a moment as Anna's words sank in, and she gave them a little more information. For an instant, she wondered if she should've kept this revelation to herself, but Davy had never said not to disclose it.

"My mother and Davy's father were together briefly, and they had Tally. She grew up with my mom and me. Davy reentered the picture relatively recently."

"That's fascinating. There are all kinds of families in this world." Becca smiled at her.

Leanne nodded. "And you and Davy found love through your shared sister? That's wonderful."

Anna nodded again, relieved that both women seemed to understand, but troubled by the deception.

"How do your mom and her dad feel about you two being together?" Becca asked.

"My mother loves Davy, sometimes more than she loves me, probably." Anna laughed. "But I don't know if Davy's dad even knows about us."

"So it's not a complete Brady Bunch situation." Leanne seemed sympathetic.

"No, but it doesn't have to be. It's the Resnick-Dugan bunch."

Becca smiled at her. "Has a nice ring to it."

Anna smiled back, and she tried to keep her pensiveness out of her expression. Playacting this complicated family was so easy, and she and Davy were doing it well. She didn't want to think about when Davy got her partnership and their ersatz family fell apart, but she had to. Believing in the lie would only make it harder in the end.

❖

The adults lingered after eating, and empty bowls of Leanne's homemade ice cream littered the table.

With all the children, space had been tight around the table, and Davy brought out a few chairs from the kitchen and dragged a small bench over for her and Anna to sit on. As hosts, it was only right for them to take the least comfortable seating, but Davy immediately saw the benefit of sharing her tiny perch with Anna. They had spent the meal bumping elbows and brushing shoulders, their bodies pressed together from hip to knee. A distracting low-level thrum of arousal coursed through Davy's veins. Several times over the course of the meal her concentration had wavered, and Anna had covertly prodded her with a finger or elbow, and all that stealth touching only increased Davy's lax inattention. Now, the children had decamped to the living room to watch a movie, and there was plenty of room, but Davy was content to sit where she was, fused to Anna's side, half-listening to the conversations around her.

There was an expectant silence at their end of the table and Davy snapped out of it. She had obviously missed something—again. "I'm sorry, what?"

"I was telling Leanne about your helping me out at the art fair last weekend," Anna prompted. "She asked if you would ever fill in for Tally again."

Davy overcompensated with a blustery reply. "Oh, sure. Any time. I'd love to."

"I also told her how great a salesperson you were," Anna added.

"You're a woman of many talents," Leanne said to Davy.

"Anna's work is fantastic. It practically sells itself." Davy slapped both hands on the table for emphasis.

"As my fiancée, she's contractually obligated to say that," Anna said to Leanne and directed an indulgent smile toward Davy.

Becca asked Davy, "When did you two realize there was more there besides your connection through Tally?"

"I beg your pardon?"

"Anna told us your history, and about your parents and Tally. I'm really curious. I like to hear couples' origin stories," Becca explained.

"Well, I had been letting my work get in the way of my relationship with Tally and I wanted to change that," Davy said before realizing an accurate telling of this tale would make their lightning-fast engagement seem nonsensical.

Anna jumped in to continue the story. "Davy came to all five performances of *Guys and Dolls* last summer even though Tally was hardly on stage in her small chorus role. We had time to talk during all those intermissions, and while we waited for Tally after the show."

Davy sent Anna a grateful look—then hoped it wasn't so grateful that it spoiled the story. "I made spending time with Tally and the

Resnicks a priority, and I found myself trekking out here whenever I wasn't working."

"Yes, and while Davy saw us as often as she could, it started to not be enough for me."

"Me neither." Davy did a double take at the smolder in Anna's eyes, but kept talking. "And when Roland told me about this house for sale on Darling Drive, it seemed like a sign that I should ask if Anna would consider making the branches of our family trees a little more entwined than they already are."

"And how could I refuse a request like that?" Anna reached across the tabletop and grasped Davy's right hand with her left.

Leanne gazed at their hands. "Neither of you are wearing an engagement ring. Is there a reason for it? A political stance of some sort?"

Davy's mind blanked. She wracked her brain for an appropriate response.

"Forget I asked," Leanne said. "None of my business."

"Not at all, Leanne." Anna's words were smooth. "Davy proposed with a beautiful ring, but with my work I'm constantly taking it off. It's sitting in a little dish in the studio right now. Wouldn't want it covered in paint." She gave Davy a rueful look. "I'm sorry I forgot again, honey." Anna turned back to Leanne. "I think Davy gets a little annoyed with me about it."

"Never, babe." Davy hoped her eyes expressed her thanks to Anna for rescuing her yet again.

"And Davy said she didn't want an engagement ring, but I'm still hoping to change her mind."

"Whyever not, Davy?" Leanne asked.

"She's pretty discreet at work. She wouldn't want to call attention to herself with a big old rock on her finger. Davy's brain commands the attention," Anna answered for Davy.

"It's true. I'm not a big jewelry person." Davy was relieved. She had never even thought about the ring issue. Anna's reasoning was pretty spot-on too. Davy surprised herself—and Anna—by saying, "But I can't wait to wear a wedding band."

"You can't?" Becca and Leanne said in unison.

"That's the real symbol, isn't it? It represents to the world our commitment, respect, and love for each other. I'd wear that with pride." She hazarded a glance at Anna, whose eyes were locked on her. "And a wedding band is less valuable than an engagement ring, so it won't be that big a deal if it gets a few flecks of paint on it."

"Hear that, Leanne? Forgetting to wear my wedding band is not an option, and I won't be able to use paint as an excuse." Anna laughed and looped her arm around Davy's and squeezed. "Don't worry. Once it goes on, it's not coming off."

Davy felt her heart rate shoot up and she couldn't have replied if she wanted to. She felt almost woozy with Anna's proximity. She put her hand on Anna's arm and gave it an awkward pat. Then, from her peripheral vision, she saw Anna's head coming closer to her own. If Davy turned her head, their lips would be within kissing distance, but she sat there, frozen, face forward.

Anna didn't kiss her, not her lips, not her cheek, not anywhere. But she did press her own cheek against Davy's neck and nuzzle against her. Then her lips were millimeters from Davy's ear and she murmured, "That was great. We're really selling it."

It was like ice water thrown over her. Her body was reacting like this was real, like she and Anna had something real, but this was the furthest thing from real. She stood abruptly and grabbed her wine glass. "I need a refill. Who needs another drink? Leanne? Becca? Some more wine? Anna?"

"Over here, Davy," Roland called from the other end of the table, his empty tumbler raised high.

Davy refilled everyone's glasses and took a seat at the other end of the table between Roland and Joel.

"You deserve to relax." Roland patted her on the back. "Davy's been busy this week," Roland said to Joel. "She's been hammering out a contract with Bionational. Our newest client."

Joel looked impressed. "That's gotta be a pretty large chunk of business. Congrats."

Roland continued. "Bionational's priority is staying out of court, which is fine by us. But it looks like Teltech won't be able to avoid it with your privacy situation."

"Yes," was Joel's grim reply. "You're probably aware that we've exhausted all our motions to dismiss, and a trial date has been set for next year. Our legal team has everything in hand."

"Roland, do you want a go on the trampoline?" Davy wanted to avoid talking business. She didn't want Joel to think she hadn't listened to his request.

Roland ignored her. "Your team should've tried harder to settle, but I guess that ship has sailed. You're lucky—in a class action, the onus is on them to come up with the goods. All you have to do is bat away all their assertions. I suppose you're going with no alleged injury-in-fact."

"Yeah, how did you know?"

"It's what we would do."

"No we wouldn't," Davy said.

Both men turned to look at her. "We wouldn't?" Roland said.

"We would not. No alleged injury-in-fact is a good start, but it has to be augmented with additional defense. You can't rely on just that anymore. Remember *In re Nickelodeon*?" This was exactly what Davy didn't want to happen. "But let's not talk about work."

"What other strategies would you use?" Joel asked.

"Oh no, Joel." Roland wagged a finger at him. "You're not getting any free legal advice."

"Of course he is, Roland," Davy said. "He's our friend and neighbor. Give me your email, Joel. I'll send you some info you can pass along to your team. Now, Roland, you're not leaving until you've tried the trampoline. Let's go."

❖

Anna brought in the last of the dirty dishes and piled them up next to the sink. Davy came in from covering the patio furniture just as the walkie-talkie sitting on the counter crackled.

"Ma?" Louis sounded very awake. Anna had put him to bed right after their guests left.

Davy scooped up the handset. "She's a little busy right now. It's Davy. Can I help?"

"Davy?"

"Yeah, little dude. What's up?"

"Davy? How many times did you say a bad word this week?"

Anna turned and leaned against the sink, curious about where this conversation was headed.

"Let's check. I'm walking to the fridge." Davy's smile looked gleeful, but her voice was filled with faux concern. "Oh, shit. Shit, shit, shit. I only cursed one time, Lou. That is a damn, shitty-ass shame. We only get to play for ten minutes. I'm so damn sorry."

"Davy!"

"Yes, Lou?" She looked over at Anna and covered her mouth to stifle her laughter.

"You just cursed a bunch more times!"

"I did?"

"Yeah, like, ten more times!"

"I guess you'll have to spend more time with me, then. Think about what you want to do while you're trying to go to sleep, okay?"

"Can we go to the pet store to look at the fish?"

Davy glanced at Anna, and she nodded her approval. "You got it. Now get some sleep."

"Okay. Love you."

Davy stared at the walkie-talkie for a moment before answering, "Love you too."

Anna quickly turned toward the sink, afraid Davy would see how their exchange had affected her. How her insides were now just a load of goo that her skin was just barely able to contain.

Davy appeared at her side. "You did all the preparation. I'll do the dishes."

Anna gave her a quick glance, taking note of her exhausted smile. "It'll go faster if we do them together." She allowed Davy to nudge her away from the sink, but she stayed close. While sitting side by side at dinner, it was as if a combustion engine deep inside Anna roared to life when her body touched Davy's, and it had idled, purring with longing, all throughout the meal. And now, their forearms pressed together at the sink, she felt that engine kick-start all over again, now with the added appreciation of Davy's tenderness toward Louis.

"It was a really nice night. Thanks for all the work you did to make it happen. And thanks again for my paintings." Davy took the squeeze bottle of dish soap in hand. "Oh, and—I seem to have a lot to thank you for tonight—you were great with Leanne and Becca and our origin story and the rings and everything. Thanks for handling that so smoothly."

All the thank-yous were making Anna feel bashful. Not to mention, she was being thanked for lying her ass off. It had surprised her how easily she had spun the fibs into being, and now that she thought about it, that was kind of distressing. "It was nothing."

Tally bounded into the kitchen. "Can me and Su-Jin make popcorn?"

Anna stepped back and ceded the sink to Davy. She turned to Tally and answered her with the slightest hint of exasperation. "After all that food tonight? Are you really hungry?"

Tally leaned on the counter. "Davy, thanks for the bed."

"Sure," Davy said. "We'll go shopping for some furniture too. And maybe Anna can help you pick out some colors or whatever. However you want to decorate it is fine with me."

"Even black walls?" Tally asked.

"I guess, if you want." Davy sagged against the sink. "Do you really want to paint your room black?"

"Nah. I was just checking. Green maybe. Su-Jin can stay over tonight, right?"

"Yes. Mom called her mom earlier." Anna flicked a dishtowel at Tally. "Why don't you save the popcorn for tomorrow."

"For breakfast?"

"You're maddening. Get the hell out of here," Anna said.

"You cursed. I'm marking it down." Tally didn't mark it down. She scampered back to the living room instead.

Davy loaded the dishwasher and started hand-washing the stuff that didn't fit. Anna took drying duty beside her. The silence between them was comfortable, but Anna wanted more. She had missed Davy this week and even though she knew Davy was tired, she couldn't help initiating more talk.

"I heard Roland talking about you," Anna said. "You signed a big client this week?"

"Yeah, there was a lot of back and forth over the contract. That's why you barely saw me." Davy tried to stifle a yawn. "It should ease up now for a while."

"That's great. It should help with getting your promotion, right?"

"Everything helps."

"And Leanne told me about the Summit. I saw it on the calendar but didn't know what it meant. That's kind of a big deal, or so Leanne said."

"I haven't been in a few years, but yeah, I guess it is kind of a big deal. Mel Archer, one of the name partners, comes from big money. He has a gigantic estate in East Hampton, and he likes to throw this event every August that's part business, part pleasure, part intimidation. The partners will be there, and my competition will be there too." Their hands brushed as Davy handed her a platter. "It's the best chance I have to show them the side of me that they don't see in the office every day."

"The upstanding citizen? The co-matriarch of the Resnick-Dugan clan? The face of the modern American queer family?"

Davy shot her a tired grin. "Yeah, all that."

"Piece of cake," Anna said with more confidence than she felt. "You look exhausted. Let me take over."

"No, I'm almost done. I'm not going in to work tomorrow. Do you have anything planned?"

Anna warmed at the thought of having Davy around, but then tried to ignore it. "Tally's going to rehearsal. Lou and I are tagging along to get those tree flats finished. You should stay home and sleep late. Lounge around the house in your pj's all day."

"Maybe I will sleep late. But then I'll come over and help out with the play. I told Tally I would." Davy turned off the tap and reached for a dishtowel.

"I'm sure she'd love that." Anna rested a hand on Davy's shoulder. "I'm giving Tally and Su-Jin thirty minutes before they have to turn in. Why don't you call it a night?"

"Thank you again, Anna." Davy turned to her, her eyes on the dishtowel in her hands. "Do you think you could arrange to come into the city on Monday or Tuesday next week? Just for a couple of hours?"

Was this something to do with her faux-fiancée duties? Whatever it was, Anna would make it happen. The thought of some guaranteed time with Davy after hoping to see her show up in the studio all week was also a pretty big draw. She'd find a babysitter for Lou, or maybe she could get Tally to watch him. Davy wanted her there. How could she say no to that?

CHAPTER TWENTY-ONE

Anna gave her name to the receptionist in the lobby of Davy's firm and took a seat. She rummaged in her bag for something to wipe the perspiration from her brow. Walking from Penn Station to Davy's office was a mistake. It was approaching midday and it felt like the concrete canyons of Manhattan had absorbed twice the intensity of the summer sun. In an effort to look nice for her visit to the city, she had worn a lemon-yellow linen suit that, while crisp when she put it on, had wilted into what could generously be described as a balled-up paper napkin.

A short, cherubic young woman, exuding purpose and vim, breezed into reception and made a beeline for her. "Hi. Anna?"

She nodded and tried to discreetly shove her damp tissues back into her bag.

The fireplug of a woman extended a hand. "I'm Halima, Davy's assistant." She didn't give Anna a chance to speak as she glanced over her shoulder and said, "Before I take you back, I just wanted a moment of your time."

"Oh. Okay." *What is going on?* She followed Halima halfway down the corridor that Anna remembered led to windowed offices like Davy's.

"Why don't we step into this conference room?" Halima gestured with one hand. "Can I get you some coffee? Sparkling or still water?"

"Water would be fantastic, thanks."

Halima practically sprinted out the door and was back in seconds with a tall glass of cool water for her. She took the seat opposite Anna and scooched the wheeled chair closer to the table. "Now, we don't have a lot of time. Davy will probably kill me for this, but I have to confess—I'm so curious about you."

"You are?"

"She told me everything."

"She did?"

"Yes, and I want you to know that I'm committed to helping Davy accomplish her goal of making name partner in any way that I can. I consider the three of us a team."

"You do?"

"Yes, and I would never betray the trust Davy—and by extension, you—have placed in me. Davy is the best boss, and now she's kind of revealed herself as this badass queer woman who's battling the ACS patriarchy. I find it utterly ridiculous that she has to go to these lengths to be considered for the role. This place needs her leadership, and if it takes a little subterfuge to make it happen, well then, let's shatter that glass ceiling from the side instead of the bottom."

Anna didn't quite follow the metaphor, but she liked Halima's energy. Her protectiveness of Davy immediately made Anna relax, and it spoke volumes that Davy inspired such loyalty in her subordinate. "I'm glad she has you. I know Davy is really busy with a lot of responsibility on her plate, but tell me, is it absolutely necessary for her to work the long hours she does? She comes home so late most nights, looking completely wrung out. I'm a little worried about her health."

"You and me both." Halima gave her look of commiseration. "And she gets really prickly when I try to remind her to eat or take a break. She usually lets me go around six, and earlier on nights when I have class, but I know she stays later—"

"Most nights she doesn't come home until ten or eleven." Anna tried to keep the indignation out of her voice.

"Really?" Halima sat back in her chair, her expression sober. "She sends emails at all hours, but I thought she was sending them from home. You're right, that's totally excessive." Then her features lightened, and she practically beamed at Anna. "But she's given me all the Saturdays in July and August off, which means she must be taking that time off as well. I think I have you to thank for that."

"Shouldn't you have them off anyway?"

"When I was hired, it was with the understanding that I would be working five and a half days a week, and my pay is commensurate with the additional time. Also, one of my benefits is full tuition reimbursement. I'm working toward a master's in psychology." Halima's enthusiasm shone through in her wide grin.

"Wow. That is a nice perk."

"And Davy made sure it was in my contract. She knew I wanted it, and she wanted to keep me, so she made it happen. Like I said, she's a good boss. A fair boss."

"She must trust you if she told you about our arrangement."

"Oh, she didn't at first and I was super pissed. But I got it out of her." Halima's naughty smile was infectious. She slid her card across the table. "Anyway, I wanted you to have my direct line in case you ever need me for anything, or you can't get a hold of Davy."

Anna picked up the card and rummaged in her bag to find her wallet. She wanted it safely tucked away. "Thank you. I appreciate this. I feel like I have an ally now."

"That you do." Halima craned her neck and surveyed the hallway through the glass wall. "I have to bring you back. I didn't tell Davy you're here yet. Oh! How did Louis like those walkie-talkies?" At Anna's look of surprise, she added, "I did a little research for Davy about them. Did they work? Is he sleeping in his bed?"

"Yes, he is. They worked like a charm. Was that your idea?"

"No, it was Davy's. I think sometimes she doesn't realize how much she's been sharing with me. Once she starts talking about Louis and Tally—and you, of course—I can't get her to shut up. Not that I'd want her to. I love hearing about you all, and I think you've all made Davy really happy."

"That's nice to hear."

"Would you happen to have any pictures of him? And of Tally? I would love to see what they look like."

Anna reached for her phone.

❖

Davy couldn't seem to get one single thing done. All morning she had been anticipating Anna's arrival, and now she was ten minutes past due, and Halima was MIA. She thought about texting Anna but decided to give her a few more minutes. Maybe her train was late.

She got up and began to pace. Their weekend had been wonderful. The only fly in the chardonnay had been Saturday afternoon when she was getting ready to join them at play rehearsal. A client called with an emergency that had to be dealt with. By the time it was sorted, Anna and Louis were back and Tally had gone home.

But she reveled in her time with Anna. Every moment she spent in Anna's presence felt like a valuable gift. She was in too deep. After the Bionational deal went through, Davy had told Anna that things would ease up, but there she was, staying at the office until ten p.m. last night. If she was honest with herself, she was a little scared about the strength of her feelings. Avoidance was easier; staying at the office was easier when confronted with the knowledge that Anna was simply fulfilling her end of the bargain, while Davy couldn't get enough of her. But now, Anna was late, and Davy wasn't getting anything done and almost all of her brain was taken up with thoughts of Anna.

Maybe she should go out to the lobby to see if Anna had arrived and was waiting, since Halima wasn't at her desk to receive reception's call. As she passed Conference Room B, she stopped in her tracks when she heard Anna's laughter. She backed up two steps and stood in the doorway. Halima and Anna sat huddled in front of Anna's phone, giggling like idiots.

"This is the best part," Anna pointed at her phone. "Tally tries to do a flip, but she overextends and belly flops. It looks like she lands right on her chin but then she bounces right up again."

Halima snorted and then put her hand over her mouth. "Wait. Back that up. Let's watch it again."

Davy stepped into the room and both Halima's and Anna's heads snapped up.

"Davy!" Halima leaped to her feet. She sounded embarrassed, as well she should.

"Hey, Day." Anna's amused smile didn't lessen when she looked at Davy. In fact, if Davy was interpreting it right, it might have broadened a couple of degrees past delighted right into radiant territory. No, that couldn't be.

Anna stood and leaned toward her, and suddenly Davy didn't know what was happening, because Anna's face was getting closer to her face. Then Anna's lips made contact with Davy's cheek—quickly, chastely— and Davy felt her blood pulsating against her skull. It was the closest thing to a real kiss since the first time fifteen years ago, and Davy just barely resisted placing a reverent, protective hand against her own cheek.

"I was just getting to know your assistant. She's terrific." Anna reestablished the distance between them and threw an arm around Halima's shoulder.

"Yes, well, Halima seems to have gotten lost on her way back from greeting you in reception." Davy's recovery was as quick as she could manage.

"I'm sorry. We got to talking." Anna removed her arm and Halima backed away and skirted around them, exiting without a word. She took Davy's hand and extended it outward, surveying her from head to toe. "You look nice today."

"I look the way I always look," Davy said. "You, on the other hand—I've never seen you in anything like this." She gestured to Anna's yellow suit—cool and carefree summer in the city, albeit a little crumpled.

Anna ran her hands down the jacket self-consciously. "Forgive the wrinkles. I wanted to look smart when visiting my fiancée's place of business, but it's about one hundred and eighty-seven degrees out there and the effort I spent ironing this outfit was totally wasted."

"You do look smart. And beautiful." Davy felt the heat return to her cheeks. She raised her eyes to Anna's and found them brimming with fondness. It was almost too much.

"Thank you. You have a little something…" Anna reached out and brushed her thumb over Davy's cheek, right where her lips had been. "My gloss left a sheen. Sorry. I hope you didn't mind that little improvisation. I thought a tiny public display of affection would be appropriate from your *fiancée*." Anna's emphasis of that last word conveyed its falseness. "I hope that doesn't put me in breach of contract," she added, sotto voce.

"No, it's fine. You're doing a great job." Davy deflated a little bit. Anna *was* doing a great job, so why did that make Davy feel like she was being pricked with about seventeen little darts of disappointment? "Well. We have an appointment about ten blocks away in twenty minutes. Are you up for a short walk?"

Anna blew out a wry little chuckle. "Ready when you are."

A journey up Fifth Avenue in August was akin to a stroll on the surface of the sun. The heavy humidity made it feel like they were plodding through atmospheric vanilla pudding. Their pace was slow, but they still walked faster than many of the tourists clogging the sidewalks. "I'm sorry," Davy said. "We should've taken a cab."

"For ten blocks? Pfft. It's nothing." Anna squinted at her in the midday glare.

"That's it up ahead."

"Is it that department store? Bergdorf Goodman's? I've never been in there. It looks so fancy." She turned to Davy and waggled her eyebrows.

Davy didn't smile even though she loved Anna's playfulness. She was starting to think she should have briefed Anna about their destination. "No, not Bergdorf's, but it's part of it. Maybe. I'm not sure. It's on the corner here, anyway. Let's go in."

Anna read the sign. "Van Cleef & Arpels. Wait, jewelry?" She halted in the middle of the sidewalk. "Hang on a second. What are we doing here?"

Davy drew her out of the flow of traffic and they stood beside the sandy limestone of the building's facade. She gently took Anna's left hand in both of hers. "You need a ring."

Anna shook her head. "No, I don't."

"We're pretty much going to be under a microscope this weekend at the Summit. You can't say you left your engagement ring at home."

Anna took a step back, her agitation clear. She withdrew her hand from Davy's and held it against her chest. "I've never even thought about this part of the whole marriage deal—fake or real. What does it even mean? Do I even want a ring? What does it symbolize? That you own me? And why don't I own you? Why don't you have to get one?"

"Even if we were real, I would never presume to own you. I hope you know that. I would feel tremendously lucky that you decided to share your life with me. And I would wear a ring if you wanted me to, but you told Leanne I didn't want one. That's the only reason."

"I don't want this." Anna folded her arms across her chest and gazed at the display of jewels in the window. The intractable set of her jaw suggested Davy might have some major convincing to do.

She understood. She didn't want to do this either. Their false relationship shouldn't have to include one of the most significant rites of courtship. Anna deserved better than this. She should be entering this shop with her one true love, and instead she got Davy. It didn't matter that Davy's feelings for Anna were getting dangerously close to bursting out of her in an uncontrolled explosion. Anna didn't feel the same. She didn't want to force Anna to wear her ring, but it couldn't be helped. "I'm sorry. You told Leanne you had one. Now you need one."

"How was I supposed to know my words would come back to bite me in the rear end?" Anna showed no sign of accepting the situation. She just stared harder at the fugly necklaces in front of her.

Droplets of sweat gathered on Davy's forehead, a result of the heat but also her brain working overtime to come up with something that might convince Anna to follow her into this stupid fucking jewelry store. "It's not real, okay? It's just part of the act. There will be an endpoint to this, I promise." Davy would do well to remember this too, no matter how much she didn't want it to be true.

Something shifted in Anna's expression, and her shoulders sagged. Davy silently waited while Anna made up her mind. When she turned, her eyes were unreadable. "Let's get this over with."

The chilled air inside the boutique felt arctic. Davy approached the first sales associate she saw. "I have an appointment with Hendrik. Could you please tell him Davina Dugan is here?"

The bi-level space reeked of luxury, with a floor of polished beige marble and vitrines filled with ostentatious jewels. Davy gazed at a glass-domed cloche that held an elaborate emerald necklace, blinking as sweat overran her eyebrows and invaded her eyes. And it was sweat that was making her eyes sting with tears, nothing else. When Anna touched her arm, she turned, and Anna was very close. Only a few inches separated them.

"Here, let me do this," Anna said. She held what looked like a folded Starbucks napkin and daubed it against Davy's eyes and forehead.

Anna's touch was tender, and the regret Davy felt in that moment— for Anna's distress before, for the kindness of her gesture now, for the entire shitty situation—threatened to upset her equilibrium. She grasped Anna's elbows, keeping her close. "I'm so sorry."

Anna scrunched the napkin in her fist, and caressed Davy's cheek with her knuckles. "It's all right. I freaked out a little bit, but I'm okay now. I'm on board."

"Ah, this must be the lovely couple." A slight, balding man, his attire natty and his goatee meticulously groomed, approached with his hand outstretched. "Ms. Dugan?"

"Hendrik?" Davy shook it.

"Yes, indeed. Please follow me. May I offer you some champagne?" He led them up a glamorous, winding, golden staircase to the mezzanine level, where he sat them at a golden table that afforded some privacy from the casual shoppers below.

Flutes of champagne in hand, she and Anna waited in silence until Hendrik returned with a black velvet tray with several styles of rings on it. Anna reached for the one with the smallest stone and held it gingerly between her thumb and forefinger. "I know this might sound unorthodox, Hendrik, but would it be possible to rent this ring for a month or two?"

Hendrik opened his mouth and closed it again. He darted a glance at Davy.

Davy plucked the ring from Anna's fingers and placed it back on the tray. "Don't worry about the cost, dearest. Your happiness is my only concern. Hendrik and I discussed a range of options earlier on the phone." She said to Hendrik, "I thought you were going to show us nothing smaller than one carat."

Anna's eyes bugged momentarily, and her expression reverted back to the obstinacy Davy saw out on the sidewalk. "That's big, right? I really don't want anything that big. And, Hendrik, what is your return policy?"

Davy handed Anna her flute. "Have another sip of champagne, dearest. Hendrik, could you give us a moment? And maybe you could use the time to find a few more appropriate options."

Anna turned on her as soon as Hendrik was out of earshot, clearly heading back toward freak-out territory. "What's wrong with you? Why are you being so patronizing—*dearest*? Our relationship might be bogus, but you don't have to be so…artificial."

Davy ignored that, incensed that they were back at square one again. "The return policy? Really, Anna? For a fucking engagement ring?"

"Is anyone going to get close enough to this ring that we need to buy it from Jeff Bezos's personal jeweler? Why can't we go down to Macy's and find a cubic zirconia? Jesus, I'm so uncomfortable right now." Anna chugged the rest of her champagne.

Davy rested her elbows on the fancy gold desk and pressed her palms into her eyes, utterly weary. "I know it's supremely fucked up for you to be here looking at engagement rings with someone you have zero interest in, but I truly believe it's necessary for this weekend. And we're here now. Let's just get it over with and I'll take you to lunch. We'll get a big fucking steak and an assload of martinis and forget this ever happened." She kept her head lowered and waited for Anna's response, but none came. Had Anna left? Davy didn't want to open her eyes to find out.

"This must be stressing you out too." Anna's reply was quiet, calmer. "You seem to have fallen off the wagon—the no swearing wagon."

"Put it on my tab." Davy didn't give a shit right now about her language. "Make sure you keep track so you can add them to the refrigerator when we get home."

"It doesn't matter. It'll be our secret." Anna's tone softened a little more.

"One of the hundreds we're currently keeping between us." She thought for a moment of this past Sunday afternoon, when Louis—with Tally tagging along—had redeemed her cursing penalties at the pet store where they looked at the dozens of aquariums populated with freshwater fish. They had been gone hours, but Davy didn't mind. Time spent with Tally and Louis was becoming a highlight in her godforsaken life. She would have willingly taken out her credit card and bought Louis all the fish he wanted, but she resisted, telling him she would talk to Anna for him. Then as soon as they got home, she had taken a work call and forgotten all about her promise. But now was not the time to bring it up.

She removed her elbows from the table and put her hands in her lap. If they could just get through this task without any more turmoil, Davy would consider it a win. She raised her head and saw Hendrik returning with his velvet tray.

Anna must have seen him too. She grabbed Davy's wrist and spoke fast. "Will you pick one out? I just can't do it. But don't worry, I'll wear it this weekend."

In some alternate timeline when their relationship was real, Davy might have chosen a ring herself in order to surprise Anna when she proposed. And, she belatedly realized, that's what she should have done in this timeline too. It was just as well they weren't really together, because Davy hated to think how badly she would have bungled a proposal if they were. "Yes, I'll choose for you."

"Great. I'm going to wait downstairs. Maybe pick up a sapphire encrusted tiara or two." She gave Davy a half-smile and slipped away. Davy didn't turn her attention to Hendrik until Anna had completely disappeared from sight.

❖

Anna waited on the sidewalk while Davy paid the cabdriver. The ride to the restaurant was only a few minutes in duration, and Anna would've preferred to walk, even if she would again be drenched in perspiration by the time they arrived. Perhaps walking with Davy would have given her the time to explain why the idea of the ring bothered her so much, although honestly, she couldn't articulate a reasonable explanation. She did know that accepting a ring from Davy when the intention behind it was false had filled her with an emotion she couldn't possibly name, but anguish came close.

When Davy had walked into the conference room earlier that day, it was as if Anna's body lit up with fluorescent levels of dopamine. She hadn't meant to kiss Davy on the cheek, or kiss her at all, but her body hadn't been taking directives from her brain in that moment. It had felt good. It left her wanting more. Things were getting out of hand. And now there was tension between them because of a stupid ring.

At least she had found a compromise that attempted to satisfy her duty to Davy while allowing her to live with herself. But it hadn't mattered anyway, because Davy had marched out of the store and flagged down a taxi, and they had sat in silence the whole way.

The restaurant was called the Grill and it was a stylish, bustling room filled with tuxedoed wait staff and tables dressed in white linens. Two sides of the high-ceilinged space were clad in sleek mahogany paneling and the other two featured floor to ceiling windows that let the summer light in through swooping micro-beaded curtains that shimmered like falling water.

No sooner had they sat down than Davy swore under her breath and stood up again. "Hello, Mel. Do you have a meeting here?"

Anna stood as well and turned to see a bulky older man, an unlit cigar in his hand, who had paused at their table.

"I thought I did. If you're here for the Wax Corp lunch, you can forget it. My assistant just texted. It's canceled. So much for arriving early."

"I'm not, sir. I'm here with my fiancée. Melvin Archer, may I introduce Anna Resnick."

Anna knew he was a name partner. One of the men she was supposed to impress.

He didn't look at her but gave her hand a perfunctory shake. "Delighted. Do you know what's going on over there, Davy? Why would they cancel at this late stage?"

"I have no idea. Wax Corp is Keeley's client."

"I know that," Archer said. "He was supposed to be here too, but turns out he had some flimsy excuse for not coming, some conflict or another. I don't like it. It smacks of unprofessionalism. And now I haven't even had my lunch." He looked longingly at a beef roast about the size of a park bench that rolled by on a wheeled cart.

Anna saw her chance to make a good impression. It could be a way for her to show Davy she was trying, and maybe do a little damage control from the disastrous trip to the jeweler's. "Have lunch with us, Mr. Archer."

He swung his head toward her, his unruly caterpillar eyebrows cantilevered over his eyes like awnings of bewilderment. Beyond him, Davy was giving her a death stare. *Whoops. Too late to take it back.*

Davy seemed to quickly make peace with the situation and composed her expression into one of bland helpfulness by the time he turned back. "Of course, Mel. Join us. I know how much you like the prime rib here."

"They carve it tableside, you know." He slid his cigar into his inside jacket pocket, his mind made up.

"Please sit." Anna offered her chair to him. "Davy's told me a little about your long and storied career at the firm. I'd love to hear more." She stepped back so she could sit beside Davy on the velvet banquette.

He took her seat and craned his neck around the room. "We'll have to make it quick, only three courses. Where's that sommelier?"

While Archer consulted the sommelier and a wine list as thick as the Old Testament, Davy found Anna's hand under the table. Anna grasped it, pleasure and relief surging from deep within her, as Davy's fingers twined with her own. Then she felt the hard planes and edges of the ring as Davy pressed it into her palm.

Right. She had to begin showing it off immediately, in front of one of the men for whom she was performing this pantomime of pre-wedded bliss, a man she was compelled to impress. Anna held it until the cool metal warmed in her hand and reconciled herself to wearing it—this emblem of love and commitment which for them had mutated into a symbol of deception. Her feelings for Davy seemed more real than any relationship she'd had before, but now she was forced to wear a glaring reminder of its dishonesty. She took a breath, slid it on her fourth finger, and reached for her water glass with her left hand.

Davy glanced at it for a second before looking away.

Anna almost couldn't stop looking at it and how it caught and refracted the light on practically every surface. It fit perfectly. The design was simple—a platinum band with a plain setting, in which sat a simple but enormous emerald cut stone. It annoyed her that she was so captivated by it. She kept her hand on the table throughout the whole meal, waiting for Davy's boss to notice it, but he never did. Instead, Anna prompted him to talk about himself, which he happily did while scarfing a dozen oysters, a thick slab of prime rib, a baked Alaska, and most of a bottle of wine.

It was close to three o'clock by the time they finished. The three of them stood on the sidewalk, and Davy hailed a cab for him. Before he got in, he said, "You've got a lovely fiancée, Davy. I look forward to welcoming you to the Summit this weekend, Anna."

Anna waved as his cab entered the dense flow of midtown traffic. "Will that be you once you get the job you want?" she asked Davy.

"What do you mean?"

Anna didn't know what she meant. From what she could see, Melvin Archer was an entitled, self-absorbed, gluttonous, old man. Perhaps he was good at his job, but Anna wouldn't know anything about that. Why would Davy even want to ascend to his level of privilege? "Three-hour lunches on the expense account? Will you invite me again when you're a fatter cat?"

"I eat lunch at my desk most days, you know. This was supposed to be a thank you for coming to the jeweler." Davy raised her arm to flag down another cab. "I was hoping we could smooth over the rough spots from today."

"No need. Consider them smoothed. And didn't I advance you one or two squares on the chessboard by hanging on your boss's every word? I did get in one or two comments about how important my family is to me, and how my greatest wish is to see you become a great leader in our community." Anna fished the ring box out of Davy's jacket pocket and inserted the ring into it. She handed it to Davy as the cab pulled up. "I'll let you hang onto this. I'll wear it whenever you want."

Davy shoved the box back into her pocket. She opened the car door and stood aside. Anna got in, but Davy didn't follow her. Anna lowered the window and Davy leaned down and braced her arms on the door.

Anna gripped her forearm. "The day's almost over. Get in. Come with me."

"Too much to do." Davy gazed at her, and Anna felt like they were truly looking at each other for the first time that day. Davy's deep brown eyes seemed solemn, a little sad.

"Please come home."

Davy shook her head. "Today didn't go the way I pictured it in my head, but I want you to know that I appreciate you being here. I know it's hard. You're amazing." She moved to the front window and handed the driver a twenty. "Penn Station," she told him.

Anna sat back as the cab pulled away from the curb. She looked out the window so if the cabdriver chanced a look in the rearview mirror, he wouldn't see the tears welling in her eyes. Despite what Davy had said, she didn't feel amazing.

CHAPTER TWENTY-TWO

Davy drove down the long driveway that led to Mel Archer's East Hampton Estate. "Are you ready to go in there and win over everyone with our kickass pre-wedding lesbian wholesomeness?" she asked.

"We're going to knock them dead," Anna replied.

With the exception of the snarled midtown tunnel on their way out of Manhattan, their journey out to the eastern edge of Long Island had been pleasant and conflict-free. Both of them seemed to be trying mightily to keep things light and easy, and Davy for one was intent on backing away from the raw emotions running rampant when Anna visited the city earlier in the week.

"Here's what I remember about the Summit," Davy said. "The guest list includes senior associates and above—no juniors or support staff. Things will kick off with lunch, then there'll be a menu of afternoon activities, and dinner. Tomorrow there will be a town hall type meeting with the assembled employees and brunch before everyone fights the traffic all the way back to the city and beyond—unless you commute by helicopter."

"Darn," Anna snarked. "Why didn't I reserve the helicopter this weekend?"

A platoon of valets stood at the top of the drive, and one came forward to whisk Davy's car away, and a headset-wearing event planner checked off their names and explained that they would be staying in the main house with other partners and higher-level colleagues. Their bags would be delivered to their room, which they would be directed to after lunch. She then ushered them through an enormous room that was devoid of all furniture, except for one white sofa, to the rear meadow, which simply looked like a very large backyard to Davy. A good portion of the firm's employees had already gathered, seated or standing in small groups scattered across the lush lawn, and running the bartenders ragged at two bars set up on either side of the pool.

Davy knew this was a work event, but she was resolute that Anna would not feel deserted or uncared for. "We're going to have a good time. There'll be lots of good food and drink, and the beach is close by if we want to escape."

Anna nodded with her chin at the body of water that met the edge of the lawn about a football field's length away. "That's not the beach. Is it a lake?"

"That's Georgica Pond. I've never seen anyone swim in it, but there are boats, I think—of the rowing and sailing varieties."

"This is Mr. Archer's shindig, right?"

"Yes, he usually gets the ball rolling with a speech before lunch."

Anna nodded. "Will the outgoing partner be here? What's his name?"

"Leonard Conant." Davy frowned. "I'm not sure. I haven't seen him around for a while."

"I'm guessing filling his vacancy will be a big topic of conversation?"

"Definitely. It's on everyone's mind."

She pulled Davy closer and spoke in her ear. "We should use this occasion to figure out where you are in the running. I'm good at getting people talking—just ask Mel Archer. I know I impressed him at lunch that day. So put me in, Coach. It's time to assess the competition and start making moves."

"Making moves?" Davy couldn't help it. She was sure her amusement was written all over her face. She wanted to douse herself in Anna's spirit like it was cheap cologne and she was a teenage boy on his way to the prom.

"You think I'm kidding? We've got to lock this down. We've got to carpe all the diem."

Davy knew this weekend was a big deal. It could do a lot to demonstrate to the partners she was what they were looking for, but now that she was here with Anna, after abstaining from her company all week, she simply wanted to enjoy her. Would it be so wrong to act like the crazy-in-love couple they were pretending to be and spend the whole weekend wrapped up in each other?

She spotted Mel Archer glad-handing his way through the crowd, his petite wife following like a tugboat in the wake of a cruise ship. The festivities were about to begin. She grasped Anna's hand in hers. "Okay. Let the move-making commence."

"Welcome, everyone." Mel stood on an ottoman and raised his voice. "Renata and I are so pleased you could all join us for the tenth annual ACS Summer Summit. Since it's an anniversary year, we have a few special surprises in store for you. But we'll get to that. There's plenty to do this afternoon, whether you want to work up a sweat with some athletic activity, or just relax here at the pool or on the beach. And if you've brought your sticks, we have a few tee times over at the Maidstone Club for this afternoon. See Roland and he'll sort you out. But for now, let's all have lunch and appreciate this gorgeous weather." He gestured to the buffet.

People migrated toward the food, except for a handful of men that crowded Roland for the coveted golf spots. Leanne waved at Davy and seemed happy to break away from the pack that had formed around her husband.

"Well, look at you two!" Leanne gave them both air kisses and then a head-to-toe inspection each. "Don't you both look fabulous."

Davy had to agree with her when she looked at Anna. The flowing maxi dress with a subtle print of blush lilies was perfect for the occasion. For herself, Davy had chosen a suit of cool, blue seersucker, and Anna's nod of approval when they left that morning had given her a little lift.

"Ready to conquer the Summit!" Leanne said with a little fist punch into the air.

"You look amazing, as well, Leanne. I'm so glad you're here," Anna said. "This is all a little intimidating. Having a friend here boosts my confidence a little."

"What am I, chopped liver?" Davy asked.

"Of course not, honey." Anna looped her arm through Davy's. "But I don't rely on you for a boost. You're my skyscraper. You take up so much room in my life it's like you almost blot out the sun."

Davy gave her a sidelong glance. *Okay, maybe Anna was overdoing it slightly.*

"Isn't that sweet? And also a little bit twisted," Leanne said.

"And if it wasn't for Leanne, I wouldn't have known how to dress this weekend. She gave me the lowdown on everything I would need."

"You could've asked me." Davy tried not to feel hurt.

"You're busy. And Leanne was happy to help. Right, Leanne?"

"Absolutely. Let's grab some lunch. The lobster rolls are to die for." She charged ahead to the buffet line.

Anna pulled her in close again. Every time she did it, Davy's heart beat a little faster. "Don't get distracted and lose sight of why we're here. I only wanted to put my best foot forward—for you."

Those last words gave Davy a thrill. She tried to tamp it down. "And I probably wouldn't have given you as good advice as Leanne did."

"How many suits did you pack?" Anna's adorable knowing smile would be the death of Davy.

She steered them toward Leanne, now chatting with the people in front of her in the buffet line. "Only three."

"For a weekend at the beach." Anna rolled her eyes, and then added, a bit louder, "That's one of the things I love about you."

Leanne and a few others looked back at Anna.

"What's that?"

"You always put your family first."

It made no sense in the context of their conversation, but it was as if someone had yelled *Action*, and Anna had hit her mark and delivered lines that put Davy in a good light. It was too bad Leanne was talking to a couple of associates who had absolutely no power to choose the next name partner.

Roland joined them at the table once he had dispatched all the golfing hopefuls and dug into the plate Leanne had made for him.

"If you're organizing the tee times, I guess you automatically get a spot, huh, Roland?" Davy asked.

"I wish. I love that course. But Mel and I have to take care of a few things this afternoon, so we'll be working while everyone else is having fun. But if we finish early, we'll use the pond as a driving range, like we started doing two years ago." He leaned toward Anna. "We had this contest to see who could drive their golf ball the farthest, but someone almost got hit at the next house over. Now, we smack the balls into the water, but it's a lot harder to judge who wins."

"I think that's the year I decided my time was better spent working," Davy said, and felt Anna's wedge sandal whack her in the shin. *Shit. Not the best attitude for a future name partner.* She cleared her throat. "But now I understand the value of these weekends. It's such a boon to morale, a real team-building bonanza. Is there anything I can do to help you and Mel this afternoon?"

Roland patted her on the shoulder. "You just relax and have fun. We're glad you decided to come this year. It's never the same without our little superstar."

Leanne picked up the agenda that was left at each place. "It says there will be a live band and dancing tonight. Is that one of the surprises Mel was talking about?"

"Yes. And fireworks." Roland put his finger to his lips. "But you didn't hear that from me."

"Lovely! You picked a good year to come back, Davy. And, Anna, you two can practice for your wedding on the dance floor tonight."

"They're excellent dancers," Roland said.

Leanne glanced at him. "How would you know?"

Roland pressed his lips together as if he wished he could've stopped those words from coming out.

Davy tried not to laugh. Roland wasn't supposed to be at Tally's party. He couldn't keep up with his own lies, not when Leanne was sharp as a whip.

"I think I mentioned to Roland the other night that Davy and I have been practicing, but Davy is the excellent dancer," Anna said. "She makes my flailing look good." She took a sip of her wine. "Where will you be working, Roland? Somewhere out in the fresh air, I hope? The day is too lovely to be inside."

"Not sure," Roland replied. "We have a call right after lunch, but then we could spend the rest of the afternoon outside if we can insure privacy. Maybe the gazebo?" He gazed at the octagonal structure on the right side of the lawn, half hidden in a shroud of beautifully landscaped bushes and trees, about midway between the house and the pond.

Anna gave Roland an amiable smile, but when she turned to Davy her expression turned shrewd and sharp. Davy grinned, loving her adept information gathering. She was glad Anna was on her side.

❖

Most of Davy's colleagues had finished lunch and drifted off to their rooms if they were staying on the estate, or to check in at various inns and hotels if they weren't. Anna wanted a little more time to get the lay of the land and suggested they move to the terrace near the pool. She chose seats where they could see both the house and the endlessly unfurling lawn all the way down to the pond. It was wonderfully picturesque. She hoped to get a few shots with her camera at some point, but only if her primary duties were fulfilled first.

Anna was determined to prove her worth this weekend. This was what their whole agreement was about. It was show time, and paradoxically, Anna was looking forward to exhibiting her genuine feelings for Davy. It would be a relief to gaze at her with unguarded admiration, and gush about her good qualities, and freely cling to her with warmth and affection. Not only did she plan on being the perfect partner, but she also wanted to gather as much intel as she could so Davy could use the situation to her advantage.

After Anna's trip into New York and their lunch with Mel Archer, she understood a little better what Davy needed from her. She also accepted that Davy probably saw all those hours spent at her desk as an investment in her future, but she was still arriving home far too late to actually participate in their lives. Anna had to admit that there were peaks and valleys to their relationship. When Davy was present, things were wonderful, but sometimes her absence made the limited time they spent together a little more fraught. But they had made an agreement, and Anna's growing wild attraction to Davy was not a part of it. Even now, Davy seemed too far away as she stood at the bar waiting for their drinks.

"I'm glad we have a room here. Skulking around and performing covert operations would be much harder if we were staying offsite," Anna said, as Davy handed her a glass of white wine and sat down next to her.

"Slow down, GI Jane. Covert operations?" Davy smiled at her. She seemed to be smiling a lot today, and Anna wanted to be her primary smile inducer.

"What do you think the partners are meeting about today?"

"I have a few ideas, but I'm not really sure." Davy blew out a breath. "Believe me, it's killing me, not knowing."

"You want to go hide in those bushes by the gazebo? If we do it now, we'll be in position when the partners get there later."

Davy rolled her eyes. "We are really not doing that. I draw the line at stakeouts in the shrubbery."

"Suit yourself." Anna put her drink down. "I think there are two ways we can go about this weekend. The first is to spend as much time as we can with the partners to demonstrate your values and ideals. Show them how you meet all the criteria they're looking for. The second is to spend time with your competition and suss out their weaknesses."

"Sounds good. Kevin Keeley is the only person campaigning, besides me, as far as I know. But that doesn't mean the partners won't entertain options from outside the firm."

"Is he here? What does he look like?"

"I haven't seen him, but I'm sure he'll be here. He'll probably golf this afternoon."

"What about his wife?"

"Haven't a clue." Davy's expression changed—it became more alert, but like she was trying to hide her alertness. She tilted her head slightly toward the french doors. "There he is. I think we summoned him through our conversation."

Anna saw a tall man with a golf bag over his shoulder descend the patio steps with a willowy blonde at his side. "I hope he didn't hear us with those gigantic jug ears. They would sound like Big Ben if they were ringing."

"You think he has big ears?"

"Don't you think Dumbo when you look at him? Shh. He's coming this way, but he probably already heard us with those massive wing nuts attached to his head."

Kevin Keeley and his wife looked as if they had stepped from the privileged, preppy pages of *Town and Country* magazine. He wore bright yellow pants with some small, repeated motif embroidered onto them—possibly sailboats. His wife wore a white sweater knotted at her shoulders. Anna thought people only did that in the movies. She expected them to speak through gritted, frighteningly white teeth.

But no, there was no teeth gritting, although they both revealed bright white smiles as they approached. And those were golf clubs of some description plastered all over his pants. "Davy! So great to see a familiar face." He propped his clubs against a nearby table.

Anna and Davy stood. These were his co-workers. Weren't all the faces familiar?

Keeley approached with his hand extended. "Have you met my wife? This is Ainsley."

"Nice to meet you," Davy said and slid her arm around Anna's waist. "This is my fiancée, Anna."

After a round of hellos and how-are-yous, they all sat, and Keeley said, "Thought we'd take the ferry at Bridgeport. What a mistake that was. It took forever. Where is everyone?"

"I'm sorry to say you've missed lunch. Everyone's scattered until this evening." Davy gestured to the bar. "But you can still have a cocktail."

"Right. You must be parched, lovebug," Keeley said to his wife. "What would you like?"

"Just some sparkling water," Ainsley said and patted her flat belly as he walked away. "Have to be careful now that I'm drinking for two again. Oh, let me see your ring." She held out her hand and Anna moved hers closer, but Ainsley grabbed it and inspected it for longer than was comfortable.

"It's beautiful," she finally said, and let go of Anna's hand. "Someone has exquisite taste."

"Thank you. And congratulations on the baby." Anna wanted to move the conversation along. She still wasn't comfortable with this new addition to her wardrobe. "You said again. Do you have children?"

"Yes, two girls, three and six. Kevin doesn't say it, but I know he's hoping for a boy this time. Do you want children?"

Davy said, "We have one already. Louis. He's almost six." She whipped out her phone and showed Ainsley a photo of Louis from their trip to the pet store, which Louis hadn't stopped talking about all week. "He's Anna's, but I can't wait to officially claim him as family."

Warmth spread through Anna at Davy's words. If only they were true.

"Oh, isn't he adorable?" Ainsley smiled as she inspected the picture. "Will you try for any more?"

"I'd love to have another with Davy," Anna said.

"You would?" Davy seemed shocked.

"Absolutely." More improv, but Davy didn't have to know Anna was speaking the God's honest truth. How different it would be to have a child with a responsible, committed partner by her side, sharing the joys and woes of childcare. "Davy would be great at changing diapers and three a.m. feedings, don't you think?" Anna asked the question to Ainsley while she gripped Davy's hand.

"I think she would, but it looks like you took her by surprise. You two should probably talk about it a little more," Ainsley said with kindness.

"Once she makes an honest woman of me, we'll have the rest of our lives." Anna glanced at Davy. Her dumbstruck expression made it seem like she was considering it for the first time. Anna hadn't meant to drop a bomb on her. This was just part of the act, wasn't it? The confounding thing about it all was that Anna wished it could be her life. It was easy to slip into the role of Davy's devoted partner. For her, the line between fiction and reality was becoming so porous it was almost transparent. She moved the conversation away from the prospect of additional family members. "Do you have any pictures of your girls, Ainsley?"

Keeley came back with more drinks for them all, and Anna and Ainsley talked about their children while he and Davy talked about the firm. Anna tried to listen to their conversation while still holding up her end with Ainsley, and it sounded like they were discussing Wax Corp, a company Anna had heard about during their lunch with Mel Archer. Keeley was obviously troubled about something and seemed to unburden himself to her. Davy listened, and offered words of support but no solutions.

A little while later, Roland and Mel stepped onto the terrace from inside the house and wandered toward their little group. Davy immediately stood, and the rest of them followed.

Mel called out, "Keeley, I thought you wanted a crack at Maidstone."

"I do, if it's not too late." The worry that had bathed his face instantly altered to cool confidence.

Roland looked at his watch. "You'd better get over there. The last tee time starts in twenty minutes, and they don't have a fourth yet."

Keeley deferred to his wife. "Is that all right, lovebug?"

"Of course. While you do that I think I'll take the opportunity for a little nap." Ainsley turned to them. "It was lovely meeting you both. I'm sure we'll see each other again tonight."

Anna watched them go. They were sweet in a sickeningly sugary way; it was too bad they were the enemy.

"Miss Anna," Mel Archer advanced and took her hand. For a second Anna thought he was going to kiss it, but he just patted it with his other hand, an unlit cigar wedged between his chubby fingers. "Lovely to see you again. Thank you for joining us this weekend."

"It's my pleasure. I want to support Davy any way I can." *Here we go.* Time to start earning some brownie points.

"Well, make sure she has a good time this weekend. She works hard. She deserves to relax."

"I agree. She works extremely hard. And—"

Mel cut her off. "Enjoy your afternoon, ladies. Please excuse us."

Anna watched the men saunter off toward the gazebo. "So much for the charm offensive. I knew we should've hid in the bushes."

"Don't feel bad. Mel must have business on his mind." Davy gazed at her. "To tell you the truth, I don't know how we're going to convey that I'm the solid, respectable, safe choice for name partner. How do we demonstrate that?"

"We can at least try to eavesdrop on what they'll be talking about over there." Anna nodded at the gazebo.

"How? We can't get close without them seeing us coming."

Anna could see that. There was no way to get near enough. She exhaled in frustration.

Davy patted her leg. "Come on. Let's get changed and do something fun. We can't do anything about it right now."

Anna reluctantly followed Davy into the main house, where they were led up a grand staircase and down a hushed hallway to the room where they would stay. The room was large and spacious, decorated in nautical whites and light blues. Their bags were sitting on a bench at the foot of the bed—and that's where Anna saw the potential problem. It wasn't that the queen-sized bed didn't look comfortable. It looked fantastic, with a cozy-looking quilt and about ten comfy pillows, both for sleeping and for throwing. It was that there was only one bed. Anna didn't know what might happen if she and Davy were to share that bed tonight.

Davy must have had a similar thought. "I'll sleep in the chair." She pointed to an uncomfortable looking wingback chair upholstered in a blue floral chintz.

"Come on. That would be torture."

"Then on the floor. You won't have to share the bed. That's not part of our agreement."

Davy sleeping on the floor was ridiculous. "We're both adults. I'm sure we can manage to share a bed for one night." Just thinking about it made Anna's pulse shift into overdrive.

❖

"Want to dance?" Davy asked, now that they had finished eating their entrees. She had endured cocktail hour chitchat and speeches from anyone who wanted the microphone, the slow procession of courses, and inane conversations with her tablemates. But now the band had picked their instruments back up and she had waited a respectable interval while the dance floor slowly filled. Instead of sitting beside Anna, only seeing her in her peripheral vision, she wanted her face-to-face, and in her arms.

She waited for Anna's nod before she led her to the dance floor, and tried not to drag her in her haste to touch her in a way that was permissible by their agreement. Because dancing was expressly permissible.

The band was playing dinner music, no vocals, a slow, torchy version of "Can't Take My Eyes Off You." She took Anna's right hand in her left, slid her right palm up her side to rest against her back, and tried to keep her breathing steady as she eased them into a simple box step. It felt like she had finally earned a reward for good behavior. Anna gazed up at her through her lashes and Davy stared back, her heart starting to pound. She wanted this too much.

Despite Anna's vigilance with the sunscreen today, her nose and cheeks hadn't escaped the rosy touch of the sun. Davy thought it made her look younger and more beautiful. Her limbs had taken on a bronze cast after the easy afternoon they had spent outside, drifting in a rowboat out on the pond, and then strolling the beach. Anna had brought her camera and taken probably a thousand pictures.

"Feels strange without a hoop skirt between us." Anna's grin was affectionate.

"Tally's party feels like such a long time ago."

"I never asked—how did you become such a great dancer?"

"At boarding school, ballroom dancing counted as a phys ed credit. Since I was terrible at any sport that required a ball, I danced as much as I could. Dancing, swimming, and yoga saved my GPA—and me from a world of sports-based embarrassment."

Anna gave her a thoughtful look. "You went to a girls' school, right?"

"Yes."

"I bet they were lining up for a chance to dance with you."

"A few were. Some said they were practicing for when a guy would ask them to dance. They liked dancing with someone tall, and I was a towering, gawky, beanpole with no boobs. I think some of them figured *close enough*." She cleared her throat. She had absolutely no game. "I know I'm leading, which I always did at school too, but let me know if you want to trade off and move forward for a while."

Anna shook her head. "This feels very natural to me. You're good. It's never been this easy for me before. And I don't know how anybody could mistake you for a guy."

Davy's ears felt hot as Anna gave her a blatant once-over, her eyes lingering on her chest.

"And I wholeheartedly approve of this no-shirt-under-your-suit situation you're doing tonight." Anna's smile was wolfish when it eventually returned to Davy's face.

She squeezed Anna's hand. "I am wearing a shirt. It's just kind of low cut and you can't see it." An obvious fashion fail. "Trust me, it's there."

Anna ogled her, making a show of peeking down her front. "If you say so."

Davy squeezed her hand again, and Anna squeezed back. For a moment they engaged in a silent contest, each exerting more pressure, until Anna broke out in laughter. Davy drew their joined hands close and rested them against her collarbone. The space between them had gradually decreased and now they were only about an inch apart. They could have been the only people on the dance floor, for all the attention she was devoting to her surroundings. Anna was so beautiful, and Davy didn't want to look away. If this song lasted all night, that would be fine with her.

But Anna seemed to be paying attention. "We are the only same-sex couple dancing, you know. Do you feel like you're in the spotlight?"

"Maybe a little. And we're the only same-sex couple here. There are a few juniors and a handful of support staff who are out, but none of them are here tonight. If I get the job, that's something I'll lobby for."

"More queer people?"

"Well, of course, I'd like a ton more inclusivity, but I meant I would lobby for *all* employees to attend any celebrations or team-building events the firm organizes. Everyone works hard. Everyone contributes to the bottom line. They should all be here, even if it means scaling it back to something more cost effective." The band transitioned into another slow jam, and Davy was happy they could continue dancing at the same tempo.

"Playing devil's advocate for a second. You've told me you've brought in a bunch of business. You work harder and longer than anyone I've ever met. Don't you deserve a greater reward than someone who does less?"

"I'm rewarded by my compensation. The firm offers bonuses based on the number of hours billed, plus I negotiate a bonus for every client I bring in based on the projected amount of business we'll do with them." Davy stumbled as another couple bumped her from behind. Anna gripped her shoulder to steady her, and their bodies smushed against each other. Davy could feel Anna's lungs expand as she took in a surprised breath.

Searing heat radiated outward from Davy's core and she fought to keep her arms in position instead of pulling Anna even closer. She could see the muscles in Anna's jaw working as she gazed up at her, their relaxed conversation gone. Anna took a step back but held on, and Davy found the downbeat and got them back into a rhythm again. In a moment she had them gliding effortlessly around the floor again, but now couldn't think what to say, and thought her face was probably beet red.

"Mind if I cut in?" Kevin Keeley had picked the worst possible moment to appear with Ainsley in his arms, his grin large and fatuous. The abruptness of the intrusion made Davy let go of Anna, but she didn't move otherwise. How was this supposed to work? Was he cutting in on her or Anna?

Keeley deftly took her by the arm, leaving Ainsley and Anna to work things out for themselves. It took her a moment to adjust to following Keeley's lead, and she ground her teeth at his blithe arrogance. A glance over her shoulder revealed a giggling Anna and Ainsley, gamely attempting the steps as if they were at their first dance in middle school—about as far apart as they could be while still touching.

Keeley whirled her around and they were across the floor in just a few moves. Sunburn tinted his features everywhere except where his sunglasses left a pale outline. "I thought we should take a moment to talk."

"What about?" She looked over his shoulder but couldn't see Anna any longer. "I can think of two topics—Wax Corp or your golf game, but I don't think I can help with either."

"About Conant's spot. I know you want it, but I want it too. I'm not backing away from it." His smile was mild, but his words were resolute. "They have to make a decision soon."

"You have to know that numbers-wise—I've got you beat."

He nodded. "Yeah, your billable hours are unreachable—at least for me. And you attract business like you're the Pied Piper and all the corporate rats can't help following you."

She raised her eyebrows. "What a way to define our client base."

"Look. We both know you're the better lawyer. If this were only about numbers it wouldn't even be a contest. But I've got other things going for me."

"Besides daddy's senate seat, what do you have?"

He bent his head in acknowledgment. "This probably isn't the best climate to own up to it, but I'm just a younger version of those guys.

They're comfortable with someone like me in the room. Plus, how many decisions do you think they're discussing and making on the golf course? Can't exactly join them there if you don't play, right?"

She didn't want to admit that he had a point. But could that really be a factor in their decision-making?

"Bottom line? Change isn't a word that's in their vocabulary, and that's exactly what you represent."

Davy finally found her voice. "If they want the firm to thrive, they'll have to include it in their calculus. They'd be foolish not to."

"I agree. And should another seat become available, I'd absolutely want you to fill it. But even if you're the better person, I'm still going to fight like hell for this one. My family deserves this."

Anger shot through her. "And mine doesn't?" She got even hotter when he shrugged and looked away. "The belief that *old white men have always done it this way* is not a good enough reason to do anything anymore. Have you been paying attention at all the last few years?" She shifted her stance and guided him back toward where they left Anna and Ainsley. Her taking the lead had thrown him off balance and he stepped on her toes repeatedly.

"Just wanted you to know. May the best man win," he added before she backed away from him.

"She will," she shot back, and added under her breath, "so fuck all the way off." She reached for Anna as if she were a life preserver.

"I guess that didn't go well." Anna dug her fingers into the tense muscles of Davy's shoulder.

She relaxed into Anna's touch, relieved beyond sense to be close to her again. "Typical dick-swinging bullshit. It was a warning shot and an attempt to throw me off my game at the same time."

Anna threw back her head and laughed, loud and long. Then she pressed her lips against Davy's hair, right by her ear. "Don't let him see it bother you. He's nothing."

She wanted so much to turn her head and capture Anna's lips with her own, but Anna was already withdrawing from her space. So many emotions were coming at her right now; she had to shake them off. "How'd it go with Ainsley?"

Anna shrugged. "She babbled about enjoying a strong lead and the first time she and Kev danced, detailing what he wore down to the cufflinks. Asserting her heteronormativity, I guess. As for the dancing? We fumbled through it. She's not you, Ms. Frederica Astaire."

Giddiness raced through her. Anna seemed to always know how to talk her down, redirect her, say the absolute right thing. Davy pulled her close and twirled them in a circle, faster and faster, and then stopped, gazing deep into her eyes as she held her securely around her middle. It would've been a perfect moment to kiss her, except she wasn't allowed to. Davy cast about for something to say. "I like dancing with you." Weak sauce, she thought to herself as the band finished their song.

A commotion could be heard up by the house although the crowd around them made it difficult for Davy to see what was happening. Someone strode across the lawn toward the arrangement of tables and the dance floor, two women in slinky dresses trailing behind him. The man in front of her moved and Davy could see the object of everyone's curiosity clearly. He was wearing a suit, but his shirt was untucked and half-buttoned. He planted his feet not far from the crowd on the dance floor.

"Greetings, people. Sorry I'm late," he shouted, a bottle of liquor in each outstretched hand. The women caught up and he put an arm around each of them. "Now the party can really start."

"Who is that?" Anna asked.

Davy pressed her lips together. "That's Leonard Conant."

"The partner who's retiring?"

"Yup. A real fucking agent of chaos." She watched as Roland and Mel moved swiftly toward him.

"He looks like he probably smells like cigarettes, stale beer, and Aqua Velva."

The partners hustled him back toward the house while his companions drifted toward the bar. The band struck up a livelier tune and more people made their way onto the dance floor, but Anna pulled Davy away from it.

"Come on, let's go find out what's going on with him."

Davy resisted. "Wait. We can't just barge in to wherever they are."

"We'll be sneaky about it." Anna yanked her hand, and they walked toward the house. She gave an exaggerated yawn and said loudly to no one in particular, "I'm so tired. That sun really took it out of me today."

All was quiet in the house. They bypassed the gargantuan sitting room with its single white sofa and heard muffled voices. Anna immediately pulled her toward them. Beyond a curving staircase was a short, unlit hallway, the floor covered in a thick Persian runner, at the end of which was a door left open about three inches. Anna started down the hallway, but Davy pulled her back. "This is a bad idea. We have no cover. If anyone opens the door, they'll see us immediately."

"Let's just see if they're talking about the partnership. If they're not, we'll go back to the party. And if someone comes, we'll just say we got turned around, lost in this giant house." She crept down the hall and Davy had no choice but to follow.

As they got closer, Davy could tell it was Mel speaking. "...putting your package in jeopardy by showing up here." The sound of ice cubes landing in glasses could be heard.

"You said I couldn't come to the office. No one said anything about the Summit." Conant's voice was petulant. "I love coming here every year."

"Probably because no one expects you to do any work. The pressure's off." That was Roland. He sounded both weary and pissed off at the same time.

"Come on, I never felt any pressure."

"Of course you didn't, and your productivity over the last ten years certainly reflects that." Mel again, his voice dripping with sarcasm.

"Relax. I just came to enjoy the party and have fun. And to find out how the search for my replacement is going."

"Why do you even care?"

"I imagine it will be one of my last official duties—to cast a vote at my final partner meeting. So who's on the ballot?"

Davy hadn't been aware Conant would vote. She'd done her best to steer clear of him once she learned of his lousy work ethic and caddish reputation.

"We can discuss this once we have a few concessions from you." Roland's voice.

"Such as?"

"Your exit date, for one. You've avoided signing the paperwork, and like Mel said, you're endangering your severance package."

"Fine. I'll sign. Why does this have to be so adversarial? Lighten up, gents. So tell me, who's on the short list? Keeley's on it, right?"

"He's under consideration," Mel said. "He has certainly let his interest be known, but he's not our front-runner."

"Who's that?"

"Davy Dugan. She's head of litigation now, and attracts business like flies to honey," Roland said.

Anna grabbed Davy's arm and shook it, her teeth flashing a smile in the murky light.

"Honey? Sure, I guess. If you're into skinny dykes." Conant's voice was dismissive. There was at least one mutter of protest, maybe, but he talked over it. "Who'd she fuck to make partner already? You, Roland, right? You've always had a sweet spot for the girl wonder. What'd you do? Coat your dick in pussy juice?"

"Shut your revolting mouth, Len." Roland's voice was low and harsh.

Davy shut her eyes. Anna put her arm around her waist in a gesture of support.

"And this is why you're out," Mel said. "You can't even keep up the appearance of civility anymore."

"Why should I? Might as well light the world on fire on our way down. Women, fags, Blacks—they're all coming for us. Fuck, she checks two of those boxes."

"She's worked harder and brought in more business in her eight years at ACS than you have in your whole career," Roland said. "A departure from our typical choice may be what the firm needs. And her ability to bring in business is indisputable. She just signed Bionational. That'll be at least fifteen million in billing per year."

Conant's voice turned smug. "She's not getting that business on her own. Greg Dugan told me he tipped her on Bionational. I got the impression daddy does it often for her. It goes to prove women can't get the job done. They need a man to do it for them."

Rage ripped through Davy, that her own father would make that fallacious insinuation. She didn't realize she had made a move toward the door until Anna pulled her back.

The anger in Roland's voice seemed to dissipate. "Greg Dugan is a snitch and a crook. He wouldn't piss on his grandmother if she were on fire. But what does that matter if the firm gets the benefit of it?"

"It may not matter to the firm's bottom line," Mel said. His voice was much closer to the door now. "But it does speak to Davy's character."

Roland again, all business. "The bottom line *is* all that matters, so who cares if it's Davy or her asshole father who brings in Bionational or any other client. There's no conflict of interest, and it's win-win for us." The fact that he didn't even question whether or not the allegation was true was like a spear to Davy's heart.

Mel's grave voice sounded like it was inches away. "It reminds me of how her father left the profession. In disgrace. Is she headed down a similar morally corrupt path? Is it a case of the apple not falling far from the tree?"

A pregnant silence lengthened. The recoil from her father's shady profiteering was a long-delayed punch to the face. But did they honestly think that? Did her track record from the last eight years suggest that? Her rage mutated into a thick, insoluble despair. All her efforts to forge a path separate from her father and his many sins had come to nothing. She only registered Mel's next words because they seemed to be poured directly into her ear.

"Our choice should reflect our attempt to distance ourselves from the improprieties Dugan and this odious fellow represent."

"Hey—I'm right here," Conant protested. "And *I'm* not a felon."

"Maybe not. You're a different sort of liability. And you weren't always this bad, but these days…if the proverbial shoe fits," Mel replied. "Much as I like Davy, perhaps we should take a step back and reconsider. But before we do that, I'm going outside to have my cigar like I was going to before Len's bombastic arrival."

"Quick! He's coming." Anna spun around and dragged Davy down the hallway and into the vast empty sitting room. She pushed Davy down into the soft cushions of the solitary white sofa.

Remnants of phrases cycled through her brain—*distance ourselves, Davy's character, a snitch and a crook*—but when Anna threw a leg over Davy and straddled her lap, it pushed every last thought out of her head. Anna loomed over her like a wild, predatory goddess. Her nearness overwhelmed Davy and drowned her in sensory overload—the scent of Anna, orange blossoms combined with salt and SPF, her fierce eyes pinning Davy to the couch cushions, and the silky feel of Anna's bare thighs bracketing her hips, holding her down.

Then Anna grabbed her face with both hands. "Sorry," she whispered, and kissed her, tendrils of her hair falling around them and forming a curtain of privacy.

For a moment, Davy didn't respond. The entire world went quiet as Anna's lips—hot, soft, insistent—lingered over hers. When she finally understood what was happening, she surged against Anna and kissed her back. She slid her hands over Anna's hips and around her back, pulling her body closer. She'd had Anna in her arms all night on the dance floor, but this was different. In about a thousand ways.

Adrenaline gushed through her and her response became desperate, urgent. Her lips clung to Anna's, and when her teeth bit at Anna's lower lip, Anna's gasp allowed her to enter, and Anna's tongue roughly brushed against Davy's.

When Anna drew back slightly, Davy gripped her shoulders and brought her close again. Anna's hot breath against her mouth heated every inch of her skin. Then the sweet, intense pressure of Anna's lips was back and Davy sank into it. Nothing mattered except for the feel of Anna, the smell and the taste of her. Davy wanted to suffocate in her.

There was a sound that wasn't connected to breath, or skin, or fabric, but Davy's brain was still laboring a few beats behind, and it wasn't until Anna broke off their kiss that she realized it had been a door closing. Anna raised her head and surveyed their surroundings. She slid off Davy's lap but stayed close, her legs tucked under her. "He's gone."

Davy felt the loss of her warmth and weight keenly and struggled to concentrate. It was going to take her a minute. "Who?"

"Your boss. Mel." Anna's smile was fond. "You didn't notice? He walked right by—tiptoed, more like. He either wanted to give us our privacy or was mortified on our behalf. I don't think he even knew it was us."

"Oh."

"And I know we violated the contract, but I didn't think you'd mind."

Davy just stared at her. It almost felt like she was outside of her body with all that had transpired over the last fifteen minutes. The swirling aria of Anna's kiss crashing into the fury and rage of the moments preceding it left her unable to process the whipsaw of stimuli that was still coursing through her.

Anna gazed at her with concern. "Are you okay, Day?"

"I don't think I am," she said, and burst into tears.

CHAPTER TWENTY-THREE

Anna had left an emotionally spent Davy sitting on the bed in their shared room while she went searching for water. The sight of her, eyes vacant and shoulders sagging in defeat, made Anna's heart ache for her.

When she returned, Davy had changed into a T-shirt and some shorts. She lay on the Persian rug-covered floor in front of the bathroom, a throw pillow from the bed under her head.

She set two glasses of ice water on the night table. "You're not sleeping on the floor. Get up."

Davy turned on her side, away from Anna.

Let her be for a minute. She changed into pajamas, packed her dress away into her suitcase, washed her face, and brushed her teeth. When she came out of the bathroom, she got another pillow from the bed and lay down on the floor beside Davy. They were quiet. Davy's eyes were dry, but the skin around them was puffy and pink. Every few seconds, she scratched at her neck.

"What are you doing? Why do you keep scratching?"

"I don't know," Davy grumped. "It itches."

"Stop that. Let me see." Anna batted her hand away. Three large mosquito bites had arisen where her shoulder met her neck. Connecting the points would have made a textbook isosceles triangle. Anna got up and reached for her tote bag. "I have something for that." She rummaged for a clean napkin and the bottle of calamine lotion she knew was in there, and dabbed at the spots on Davy's neck. "Better?"

"Sweet relief." Davy exhaled. "Thanks. That bag is magical, I think."

"Just a typical, in-case-of-emergencies, mom bag." Anna lay back down so they were facing each other.

Davy's eyes were bright for a moment, like she was about to make a joke, but then must have thought better of it, and her expression turned solemn again. "I think we should talk about the kiss."

Anna took a moment to weigh how she would respond. She wasn't ready for that yet. She needed some time to wrap her head around her feelings. The potential for them to be unwieldy and maybe messy was real, but she could put them to the side until she had a quiet moment to process on her own. There was no way that explosion of emotion would be going back in the bottle, but it would keep until Davy's crisis was dealt with. "I don't regret it or anything, but I don't think we should talk about it right now. I think we should talk about you."

If Davy's eyes could register temperature, they had just dropped a couple of degrees. The whistle and bang of a firework exploded somewhere outside, and through the window a flash of rosy light dappled Davy's features for a moment. It was followed by the report of several more rockets, in a variety of shades. She rolled onto her back and stared at the ceiling. "Go watch the fireworks if you want. I'm in for the night."

"Not interested." Anna propped her head on her hand and saw Davy's closed expression. She might not want to talk about the kiss, but that didn't mean she wasn't going to be there for Davy right now. "Not when there are so many things to chat about."

Davy frowned. "Such as?"

Anna kept her voice light. "How you're feeling after listening to those jerks talk about you like you weren't even there."

One side of Davy's mouth lifted in what Anna hoped was grudging amusement.

"Or was that ex-parte communication? Listen to me with the lawyer talk. Way too much *Law & Order*." She waggled her eyebrows. When Davy still didn't say anything, she said, "Seriously, are you all right?"

"I'm fine." The way Davy bit off the words suggested otherwise. "I'm just sorry that I dragged you into this farce of a situation when it was totally unnecessary. Pretending to be in a committed relationship to show them what a fine, upstanding idiot I am—unnecessary. The clients I signed, the bazillion hours I work, the cleaning up after other people's messes I do—all of it, a giant motherfucking waste."

"You know that's not true."

"It is, if all it takes is the mention of my fucking father and his scandalous exit from the law for them to *take a step back and reconsider*. Never mind the years of scrupulously considering the ethical implications of every fucking decision I make, knowing that his dirty shadow loomed over me. Not only was I scarred from his god-awful parenting, but I have to carry the stain of his reputation with me like a fucking scarlet letter albatross hair shirt for the rest of my life. He made me become a lawyer, and then scuttled any chance I had of ever succeeding. He was the reason I couldn't get a clerkship. He's the reason none of the white shoe firms wanted me. All because of his fucking greed."

Anna reached out to where Davy's hands were resting on her stomach. She interlaced her fingers with Davy's. "I'm really sorry to ask you this—"

"You want to know what he did."

"If you want to tell me."

Davy tightened her grip on Anna's hand. "He was arrested at the beginning of my last year in law school. At that point, he had only one client—a hedge fund known for operating on the shadier side of the street. I guess after being privy to way too many deals where millions upon millions were being made through inside information, he gave in to temptation and started cashing in himself."

"And the cops found out?"

"The SEC, and then the US Attorney. But I'm sure by the time they caught him he had socked away a ton in offshore accounts. Anything that wasn't privileged, he disclosed to the authorities. Then he pleaded out and got disbarred as part of the deal."

"It's not fair that you were painted with the same brush."

"No." Her voice was cold. "But that was the reality."

"I didn't know any of this."

"Your mom knew. I'm not surprised she didn't tell you about it. It was definitely in the financial press, and it was the juiciest story in the legal community. And he made me promise not to tell Tally." She snorted. "Who was six years old at the time."

"But your firm hired you. They must have known about your father."

"I have Roland to thank for my job. He saw something in me, thank God, and gave me a chance."

"I think the entire firm owes him—and you—their thanks." Anna gazed down at Davy, who was still staring at the ceiling. She wondered if she should ask her next question.

Davy cut her eyes over to her. "What? I can feel your hesitation. Just say it."

"Okay." She didn't want to sound insensitive. "Why do you even want to be a name partner?"

Davy rolled onto her side, presumably to look Anna in the eye. "What do you mean, why?"

"I mean, sure, they took a chance on you, and maybe you want to pay that back. And it's the pinnacle of achievement at your firm, but is it the pinnacle of achievement everywhere? Or for you personally? Does it really reflect what you want in life?"

Davy stared at her for a moment, speechless, then looked away. Her eyes filled with tears again. "You're assuming I know what that is."

"Oh, Day. I didn't mean to make you cry."

Anna took Davy into her open arms and tried to soothe a wound that must've been open and bleeding for years.

CHAPTER TWENTY-FOUR

Anna took the exit off the Parkway that would have them home in about ten minutes. Davy's car was a lot nicer than her minivan, and a pleasure to drive, which was good because Davy was completely out. Her head was tilted back against the window, eyes closed and mouth wide open. Every once in a while, her breathing would get heavy enough to be defined as snoring, but then she would unconsciously shake herself out of it with a loud snuffle that made Anna giggle. She guessed Davy would hate this undignified capitulation to deep slumber, but it was so endearing, and if anyone needed sleep after her weekend of emotional upheaval, it was Davy.

Anna had awakened in the middle of the night flat on her back on the floor with Davy's head resting heavily on the center of her chest and an arm thrown across Anna's body. She had been breathing heavily, down for the count, like she was now in the car. One side of Anna had been freezing cold, but the other was deliciously warm from the heat of Davy's body pressed against her. She hadn't dared move, deciding half a chilled body was infinitely bearable.

When she woke again, morning had broken and Davy had been in the shower. Her back protested when she got up, but her own hot shower eased most of her aches. When she came out of the bathroom, Davy was dressed and ready for the day. Anna gave her a long hug, but she hadn't seemed inclined to talk.

At the pre-brunch town hall meeting, where they had taken a position at the rear of the gathering, Davy stood with crossed arms and a furrowed brow. Roland and Mel traded off speaking about their agenda items from a raised platform by the pool. Kevin Keeley stood near them with a self-satisfied grin on his stupid face. Conant was nowhere to be seen. The only item that interested Anna was the news that Conant's retirement banquet would be held in two weeks, on the Friday of Labor Day Weekend, and that's when the new name partner would be announced. She glanced at Davy when Roland reported this, but she looked utterly impassive.

That was the weekend of Tally's play, but if Anna could still attend the Thursday, Saturday, and Sunday performances, she didn't think Tally would mind her missing Friday's. The announcement of the new partner, whether it went Davy's way or not, meant that Davy's side of their agreement now had an end date. The banquet would probably be the last time Anna had to pretend to be Davy's fiancée, but she didn't want to dwell on that for the moment.

Davy paying back her sleep debt in the car had allowed Anna time to ponder everything that happened last night. And she had replayed their kiss in her head probably more times than was healthy. It still had the power to make her face feel like it was inches from an inferno—twelve hours later. She couldn't have jettisoned it from her mind if she tried.

Maybe it was the excitement of their sneaky shenanigans, or the thrill of almost getting caught in those same shenanigans. Or maybe it was the simple fact that it had been a while since the last time she had been so thoroughly kissed, and she had forgotten what a kiss could do. Whatever the reason, this particular kiss affected her like she'd been hit by lightning, a tsunami, and a cyclone all at the same time. And she was dying to know if the feeling would be the same if they did it again.

She was the one who insisted on the no kiss clause in their contract, and here she was desperate to change the terms. If the opportunity to kiss Davy arose again at any point during what remained of their agreement, Anna would not refuse it. And that was a problem since Davy was operating under the assumption that all parties were satisfied with their current arrangement. But this so wasn't the case anymore. At least not for Anna. Would it be possible to alter the terms of their contract? Maybe even chuck it away completely? Her feelings for Davy were stronger than anything she had ever felt before. For the first time in her life, Anna wondered if it might be love. Whatever it was, its inexorable pull was becoming something beyond her control. And with the end of their fake betrothal drawing near, she needed to know how Davy felt.

When she made a left turn onto Darling Drive, Davy woke. She scrubbed at her face and looked around with confused eyes. "We're almost home. God, I was terrible company. You should've woken me up."

"You needed the rest." She pulled into the driveway. "We made good time. My mom is bringing pizza when she drops off Louis later. Tally will come too if rehearsal ends on time."

Davy gave her a groggy nod. She pulled her phone out but then just as quickly shoved it back in her pocket. Without a word, she took both suitcases out of the trunk and wheeled them inside, leaving Anna's at the top of the stairs. Then she went into her room and shut the door.

❖

Davy stood in front of Anna's sunset painting, at a loss for what to do with herself. It was Sunday afternoon, and in her new normal since she had invited Anna and everyone that came with her into her life, this stretch of time was usually when she took a break. Gazed at fish with Louis. Shot the poo with Tally. Focused on someone other than herself or those associated with the bullshit of her job. But Tally and Louis weren't here right now.

It had also become the increasingly precious part of her week when she spent luxurious hours reveling in Anna's presence, covertly watching her watch over those closest to her, watching her subtly influence their happiness, watching her impart love to them.

Anna's life wasn't all golden sunlight-tinged perfection, though. It was also washing endless dishes, nagging Louis to put the seat down, engaging in battles of will with Tally, and seeing to everyone else's needs before her own. It seemed effortless, how Anna kept the individual worlds of her family spinning, but Davy now knew it took a lot of work. And she had loved witnessing it, loved being part of it, wished she could be around for more of it. For the first time in her life, Davy felt like a member of a family. Like she belonged with Anna and Tally and Louis and Pam. But what the hell did she know about families?

An image of her father flew into her brain and the shame she felt at what she and Anna had overheard pressed on her like an anvil come down from the sky. And then the way Davy had broken down and wept all over Anna—twice—all messy and needy and clingy. She shut her eyes in utter embarrassment. Davy had never done that, had never needed another person like that for support. There had never been anyone to fill that role before. It made her feel exposed. Deficient.

A quiet knock interrupted her thoughts. The top half of Anna's body appeared from behind the door. "May I come in?"

"Sure."

"I'm putting a load of laundry in if you have anything you want washed." Anna's posture was tentative, her hands hidden behind her back.

The offer was new. It was nice, but maybe slightly too intimate at the moment. "No, I'm all right, thanks."

Instead of leaving, Anna came further into the room and sat on the bed. She held the diamond ring out to Davy. "I wanted to give this back to you. Maybe you could put it in your safe?"

Davy took it without comment. If there was a clearer indication that Anna wanted nothing more to do with her, Davy didn't know what it was. It didn't matter anyway. The reason for Anna to wear it no longer existed.

"I guess the last time I'll have to put that ring on will be at the retirement dinner."

"Probably not. I think your duties are already complete."

"What do you mean?"

"It's over. Roland'll still back me, but Archer and Conant will go against him. Two against one. It would be a waste of time for you to go."

"You don't know that for sure, though."

Davy shrugged and studied the ring in her hand. "You were there. You heard them." When she looked up, Anna's blue gaze was pinned to her—thoughtful, somber, worried maybe. Davy couldn't begin to guess what was going through her mind, but then a thought occurred to her. "You and Louis are still welcome here, you know. You've been great. Even if my chances of getting the name partnership have been reduced to zero, you don't have to worry. Louis will have a terrific school year."

"I'm not worried. I know you'll keep your promise." Her voice was soft and sure, her expression affectionate.

Davy looked away as she remembered a time when she hadn't kept her promise to Anna.

"And I'm not counting you out just yet," Anna added. "Not only am I going to that jerk's retirement dinner with you, I will still be your fiancée for the next two weeks. Don't we have plans with the Kleinmans? It's easier to keep the pretense going."

Easier for whom? Davy watched as Anna plucked at the quilt in a preoccupied way. She didn't seem to be in a hurry to leave.

She looked up at Davy and said, "I was wondering if we could talk a little more about—"

Davy's phone rang. She pulled it out of her pocket and, after refusing the call, tossed it on the bed next to Anna. "Sorry about that. What were you saying?" The phone began to buzz again.

Anna glanced at it. "Well, I know we have this contract, but—do you want to get that?"

"No, ignore it." Davy reached for it and paused when she saw it was the CEO of Bionational. She stabbed the decline button again. "Okay, what—" The phone buzzed again almost instantly. "Fuck!"

"Get it. It's fine. They obviously need to talk to you." Anna picked up Davy's phone, connected the call, and handed it to her. "I'm going to start that laundry."

❖

After forty-five minutes of putting Bionational's matter to rest, Davy was exhausted. The bruising her ego had suffered after the weekend's eavesdropping session had been a blow, but at least she was still good at her job. The efficiency with which she had just handled this so-called crisis told her that much.

She could hear the agitation of the washing machine down the hall in the laundry room, but that didn't mean Anna was still in there. And even if she was, Davy couldn't be sure Anna would want to resume their interrupted conversation. Things felt unsettled between them, but Davy was hesitant to go back and settle them. She didn't want to think about how hard it would be when they reverted to roommates-only status, and she lost the privileges her faux engagement with Anna had afforded her. Expressing admiration or affection or intimacy toward Anna wouldn't be allowed, even if those emotions were now powerful and genuine. For the moment, Davy was okay with allowing the uncertainty to linger if it meant she could wallow in this contractual ambiguity a little longer.

But there was one thing Davy needed to resolve. It would help her regain some semblance of self—keep her from feeling like she was lying on the battlefield, armor-less and wounded and vulnerable to whomever came along with the flimsiest of weapons. And it was best dealt with immediately. She dialed her father's number, expecting and willing to say what she needed to say to his voice mail. But to her mild surprise, he picked up the phone.

"Hello, Davina. I'm afraid I can't talk. Can we resched—"

"It's come to my attention that you've been telling tales. Listen carefully. Do not ever insert your sorry self into my life again, or lie about your involvement in business dealings I may or may not be pursuing. You had nothing to do with my Bionational deal. If I ever hear your name connected with mine in any way, I will not hesitate to sue you for slander."

His condescension oozed down the phone line. "Even a first year law student knows how hard it is to prove slander. And I don't—"

"Defamation, then, *Dad*," Davy snarled. "Stay out of my life. Don't ever call me again. You did plenty of harm as a father, but you will not harm my career anymore."

"What happened?" His tense delivery meant she had gotten his attention.

"I've finally had enough is what happened." She ended the call.

❖

Anna stood in the doorway of the laundry room, looking toward Davy's closed door. Even with the washing machine churning through its spin cycle, she could hear Davy's voice raised in anger. After a moment or two of quiet, Davy emerged, and appeared surprised to see Anna standing there.

"Hey." She ran a hand through her hair. "I guess you heard that."

"A bit. Everything okay?"

Davy shrugged and said, "It's whatever. You're still doing laundry? Can I help?" She followed Anna as she retreated back into the laundry room.

"I was just wrestling with this fitted sheet," Anna said and let her frustration come out as she took it in her hands again. "Why are these so impossible to fold? This is my third attempt."

Davy grabbed at one side. "Let's do it together."

Anna gave her a dubious look, but gamely stood back until the sheet was completely unfurled between them in the tiny room. As if they were dancing the steps to some powdered-wig, old-timey tune, they bisected its width by meeting in the middle. When their two ends came together, Davy gripped Anna's raised hands and wouldn't let go. They stood there, arms outstretched, the half-folded fabric between them, and Davy said in a voice devoid of emotion, "I just told my father to stay out of my life."

Anna threw the sheet aside. "Davy, I'm sorry." She wrapped her arms around her and tried to convey all the support and love and strength Davy deserved right now. When Davy first tried to pull away, Anna wouldn't let her. It felt good to be close to Davy, to say without words how she felt. She tried to suffuse that hug with all the things Davy should know to be true: *you're courageous; you're strong and compassionate; you're worthy of unconditional love; you're so valuable to me.* But Davy's body was tense, and when she again tried to pull away, Anna released her.

Davy settled against the dryer and wiped a hand over her face. "I seem to be leaning on you for emotional support a lot this weekend."

"You can lean on me any time."

"But this isn't what you signed up for." Davy gazed at the floor.

"That doesn't matter. We're more than just two people who signed a contract, aren't we?" Anna wanted Davy to look at her, to be honest with her about what she felt.

She crossed her arms. "The last thing you need is another person using your strength to help them be strong."

Anna could feel Davy shutting down, but she couldn't see a way to prevent it. She took a breath. "Shouldn't I have a say in what I need? Love doesn't have limits. There's always room for more. It's like that big ol' in-case-of-emergencies bag I carry around everywhere. There's always space to throw something else in."

Davy's head shot up when Anna said the word love, and she looked like she was struggling to find words. Finally, she said, "I don't want to make your bag heavier than it already is." And she turned and left.

CHAPTER TWENTY-FIVE

Anna put the finishing touches on the coral reef that now teemed with life on Louis's bedroom wall. The main attraction was Jeff the octopus, serenely overseeing the many reef dwellers that poked out from the various nooks of his domain. Even though whale sharks preferred open water, she managed to sneak one up near the top of the wall, telling Louis he was off in the distance.

"What do you think?" She put her brush down on her palette with an air of ceremonial finality. "It's done."

"I love it, Ma. I want to look at it forever." Louis leaned against her side.

Anna squeezed his shoulder but didn't say anything. She would've liked for Louis to have forever in his new room, but she honestly didn't know if they would finish out the month, much less the year. Things were strained at 14 Darling Drive, at least between Davy and her.

Their charged conversation that Sunday afternoon had led Anna to believe that Davy would resume her late nights at the office, but the opposite had been true. She left the house impossibly early, changing her routine to make the 5:00 a.m. train, but now she'd been home before six every night this week, bringing home takeout for dinner, helping with the dishes, stretching out on the sofa to watch TV with Louis, and inviting Tally and Pam over every chance she could. The one thing she wasn't doing was talking much to Anna, except for inconsequential things like adding toilet paper to the shopping list and passing the potatoes, please.

Maybe she was coming home early as part of some post-Summit work strategy, but Anna couldn't understand how coming home *early* would help her get the partnership. She was glad to have Davy around, contributing to their family, but it hurt that she had withdrawn emotionally from Anna. She honestly didn't know what to do about it. And tonight they were supposed to meet at the country club with Becca Kleinman and her girls, but despite what she had told Davy, Anna didn't think she had it in her to playact this false relationship anymore. At least this part of their contract was ending soon.

"Okay, Lou. Get your bathing suit on."

His eyes got huge. "We're going to the pool?"

"Yes. You have a lesson, and then we can swim for a while before dinner. But before that we have to swing by your new school with some papers."

"Papers?" He was already rooting through his drawer for trunks. "For Ms. Mobley?"

"Yeah, I guess. Indirectly." She was impressed he remembered his new teacher's name. "But we probably won't see her, bud. We're only going to the office."

"Okay. Hurry up! Why aren't you ready yet, Ma?"

❖

The hallway leading to the admin office of Elmdale Elementary was filled with at least two classrooms' worth of child-sized desks pushed against one wall, and their accompanying chairs had been stacked into leaning columns so high they looked as if they belonged in Pisa. The whine of an industrial floor polisher could be heard somewhere deeper within the building. In the office, a woman made photocopies while she talked on a landline that had an extra-long cord.

When she finished, she greeted Louis with a smile. "Hello, there. School doesn't start for another week and a half. You don't have to be here yet."

Louis took a step back and gazed at her warily.

"This is Louis. And I'm Anna Resnick. I called earlier. He's starting first grade."

"Great. Welcome, Louis." She stepped to a computer and clicked a few times, and then clicked a few more. "I'm afraid I don't see a Louis Resnick. How do you spell it?"

"Oh, sorry. His last name is Bowerchuck, not Resnick."

"Ah. Here he is. Did you bring the documents listed on the paperwork?"

Anna handed them over and received two items in return.

"While I make copies of these, you can fill out his emergency contact card and his lunch form. Have a seat over there, if you like."

She sat at a small round table in front of the assistant principal's office and rummaged for a pen in her tote bag. As she started filling in the forms, Louis stood next to her, scuffing the toe of his Croc against the carpet.

"Ma?"

"Yeah, Lou."

"Why is my name different than yours?"

Her pen stopped moving. Louis had been three the last time they talked about this, and of course, he hadn't really understood. She turned to face him.

"We're a family, and families should have the same name," he said.

"That's sometimes true, but not always. Tally and I are sisters, and we don't have the same last name. We're still family. Families are more about the people you love, not what their last name is."

"But why don't I have the same name as you?"

Anna tried to think of a way he might understand. "Remember that video of the baby dolphin being born? How he came out of his mommy's tummy?"

"Yeah, we watched it a bunch of times." He smiled. "You cried."

"I did, but they were happy tears because it was really nice to see that. It's kind of a miracle. And it's the same for people. A baby comes from a mommy's belly, but you didn't come from mine. You came from another woman's belly, and she wanted me to take care of you. You have her last name because you came out of her belly."

He pressed his lips together. This explanation didn't seem to work for him. "But I should've come out of your belly. I want you to be my mommy."

"I am your mommy, Lou. I'll always be your mom, no matter what happens."

Now he looked distressed. "What could happen?"

"Nothing." Regretting her slip of the tongue, she pulled him onto her lap and kissed the top of his head. "Nothing's going to happen." Her deeply submerged fears had edged closer to the surface, and she had never felt more helpless. Which god did she need to pray to in order to make her words true?

"I want your name," he murmured into her shirt.

❖

Davy hesitated after she passed through the cool shelter of the Elmdale Country Club's lobby and tried to recall which direction she should go to find the pool and Anna and Louis.

"Davy."

Joel Kleinman walked toward her, having just exited the men's locker room with his racquet under his arm.

"Joel, I didn't know you'd be here. Nice to see you." She shook his hand. "On your way to the tennis court, I see."

"Yeah, I booked some time with the pro. Did you get a racquet yet? When are we going to play?"

"You're going to have to give me a lot of time to prepare for that. This body may look like a temple, but it's really a poorly managed Dunkin' Donuts."

He laughed. "Okay. Let me know. Hey, let's set up a lunch next week. I have something I want to run by you."

"Sure, I'll call you." Davy watched him walk away, wondering what that was about. When she reached the pool complex, she saw Louis first. He wore his orange goggles and splashed around the shallow end of the medium-sized pool with Joel's girls. His squeal of delight at evading being tagged in their game made Davy giggle.

Then she saw Anna, who stood in waist high water against the edge of the pool, a short distance from the children, deep in conversation with Joel's wife Becca. Maybe Anna could sense her watching, because she looked up almost instantly and gave her a hesitant wave. As Davy made her way past the chatter and activity of families splayed on chairs and loungers around the pool deck, Anna waded over and climbed the wide steps out of the shallow end. Davy involuntarily slowed as she allowed herself to gaze at Anna in her bright blue bikini. Anna—in all of her jaw-dropping, eyeball-drying hotness—was coming toward her, and it was all Davy could do to keep her shit together and not fall to her knees in supplication.

"Hey." Anna greeted her while shaking her arms and flicking water from her fingertips. "I just got out."

"I noticed." Davy tried not to let her eyes linger over Anna's body too blatantly before raising them to her face. *I really, really noticed.*

Anna leaned in slightly and gave her an air kiss. "I didn't drip on your nice outfit, did I?"

Davy looked down at herself. She'd left her briefcase and suit jacket in the car, but she still looked incredibly out of place. "Don't worry about it."

"I brought you a change of clothes." Anna squinted at her. "And your new bathing suit."

"Why are we doing this, again?"

Anna shifted her weight, her discomfort becoming clearer. "I have no idea. It's my fault. We could've canceled. But we're here now, and Louis is having fun. Let's make the best of it." She pointed to a group of chairs. "We're sitting over there and your stuff is in the yellow bag. Get changed, and don't forget sunscreen."

Given her marching orders, Davy did what she was told. Seeing Anna unhappy opened up a hollow feeling in her. Davy was obviously failing. She had been trying—really trying—to finish out the final days of their false engagement honorably. It was what Anna said she wanted. All Davy's effort had gone into being a good housemate, to pulling her weight as a functioning member of their household unit, in preparation for their transition to post-fiancée living. But cracks had appeared in the space between them anyway, and Davy didn't know how to get them to a place of casual friendship. Plus, seeing Anna in a bathing suit was really doing a number on her peace of mind.

The following hour was an excruciating test of her will and sanity as she desperately tried not to get caught staring at Anna's breasts while she and Anna and Becca stood in the water and talked about amusing television shows on Netflix. She had absolutely nothing to contribute to the conversation. Then one of Becca's daughters scraped her foot pretty badly and she herded them from the pool and toward the changing rooms. Anna got out to order some food at the snack bar while Davy stayed to spend some time with Louis.

"Let's play remora." Louis splashed to the top step and leapt at her, and she barely had time to lift her arms before she was inundated by him and about a tidal wave's worth of water. He was adorable, with his long eyelashes that had fused into damp clumps, and his hair that had molded into improbable swoops.

"How do you play?"

He swung around to her back like a monkey and wrapped his arms around her neck, his legs clamped around her waist. "You're the shark and I'm the remora. I have to stick to you and you have to keep moving, because that's what sharks do. They never stop."

"Why don't we call this game what it really is—a free ride for Louis." She towed him around the perimeter of the pool while he complained that she wasn't *sharky* enough.

"Okay," he finally said. "We're done. You can stop being the shark." The way he said it clearly conveyed his disappointment with her predatory swimming skill. Davy couldn't seem to make anybody happy right now.

Anna called them out of the pool, but Louis refused to come. "Five more minutes."

She dried herself off and took the lounger next to Anna, who had blessedly—or confoundingly, Davy couldn't decide—donned a cover-up. Louis lingered near the pool steps, and played with a little toy submarine someone had left behind.

"You got suckered into shark and remora, huh?" Anna gave her a tiny smile. "The food will be ready in a little while."

It was dinnertime, and families were leaving the pool area in droves. The sun was hanging low on the horizon, and the cool breeze made it a perfect August evening. The silence between them was fraught, but it was a different kind of fraught than Davy had come to know lately.

"I know we're in a weird place right now," Anna said. "And this probably isn't the best time for me to be asking for a favor, when you're trying to figure out how to share your home with us for the next ten months."

"I'm fine with sharing our home—"

"I need your help."

She went on high alert. "Anything. What is it?"

Anna paused before speaking, and it looked like she was in pain. "Today, Lou asked me why we don't have the same last name."

"Oh, boy. He did?"

Anna nodded and relayed what had happened in the school office that day. "I need to find her. I have to settle this. It's not fair to Louis."

"Do you remember me telling you about our investigator, Sophie? She's excellent. I'll talk to her right away if that's what you want."

"It is." Anna gripped her hand tightly. "Thank you. Putting this in motion scares me to death."

Davy wanted to pull Anna into her arms and keep her safe—keep them all safe. "I understand, but I think you're doing the right thing." She didn't want to make promises about what finding Winnie Bowerchuck might mean for Louis, but this holding pattern wasn't working for anyone.

She reached for her phone. "Let me take some notes. Give me all the details you can about her." She looked down to unlock it. "Oh shit."

"What?"

"It's Tally. She sent a text ten minutes ago. She needs a ride."

Anna frowned. "But she's at rehearsal. At this stage they usually go until late."

Davy shot off a quick text back to say she was coming. "I'll go get her." She sat up and looked at Anna and then her phone again. "But wait—"

"Go. It'll keep. We'll talk later. I'll see you at home."

Davy paused only to put on the shorts and shirt Anna had brought over her wet bathing suit and then left as quickly as she could.

❖

Tally was sitting on the steps of the theater by herself when Davy pulled up. She got in the car and mumbled her thanks.

"It's no problem. Are they finished rehearsing for the day?" Davy suspected they were not. There were still a bunch of cars in the parking lot.

"No, but I am. I told them I was sick." She crossed her arms over her chest and looked out the window.

"Are you?"

Tally shook her head.

"Want to talk about it?" Davy pulled away.

Tally grunted a negative response.

"Do you want to go home?"

"No, your house." She was quiet for a minute. "Do you have anything to eat there?"

"I'm not sure. If we don't, we'll get Chinese or something."

Tally perked up slightly at that. "Awesome."

Duh. Here was her bargaining chip. "But only if you tell me what's wrong."

Tally hissed in frustration and was silent the rest of the way home.

Maybe Davy shouldn't be bargaining here. Was it bad parenting? Scratch that; she wasn't a parent. Was it bad sister-ing? She had absolutely no idea, but she couldn't help if she didn't know what was wrong. Once they arrived home, Davy said, "I'm going to change. Be right back."

"You might want to brush your hair too. It's a mess."

Fucking rude. Davy tried to have sympathy for Tally, but she still had to bite back telling her where to go. When she came back downstairs, Tally was lying on the sofa, her phone resting on her stomach. Davy sat on the other end of the sectional and opened the food delivery app on her own phone. "What do you want?"

Tally sat up. "Where are you ordering from?"

"The place across from the train station. It's the only one I know."

"Is it any good?"

"I don't know. I've never been there before."

Tally sniffed. "Crab rangoon and soup dumplings. They shouldn't be able to screw that up."

"Okay, Ms. Food Snob of the World." Not even a please or thank you. "What do Louis and Anna like?" She knew they were eating at the club, but she didn't want to exclude them in case they were still hungry.

"Just get some fried rice for Lou. Anna doesn't like Chinese."

"She doesn't?" There was still so much she didn't know about Anna. It made her heart hurt a little.

"I think it's because she lived above Hunan Lee's for so long. She got sick of the smell. Maybe she's over it now. She used to like Moo Shu Chicken. With brown rice—not pancakes."

Davy scrolled through the app and added the dishes.

"What do you like to get?" Tally asked her.

Whatever Halima ordered for her? "I'll eat whatever, but beef with broccoli, usually."

Tally sneered. "You're so basic."

Davy paused, then tossed her phone onto the coffee table without adding her basic beef with broccoli to the order.

"Wait, I want a soda."

"Doesn't matter. I'm not placing the order."

She flopped against the cushions with a huff.

"You think I should reward your shitty behavior right now with delicious Chinese food?"

"You cursed."

"Fucking sue me." Davy's voice sounded hard and angry to her own ears. She immediately wished she could take it back, especially when she saw Tally's spooked expression. "Sorry. You were really pushing my buttons, though."

"Anna says I'm really good at that."

"She's right."

"And Su-Jin says that too sometimes."

Davy watched as Tally dropped her head and fat tears rolled silently down her face. "Problems with Su-Jin?"

Tally brushed at her tears with the back of her hand like they were annoying gnats. "I told her she was being unsupportive. She called me a jerk. Then I called her a bitch. Now she's not talking to me."

Davy moved closer to Tally. "I really want to help if I can. Will you tell me more?" To her surprise, Tally butted her face against Davy's shoulder and began to sob. She put her arm around Tally and let her cry. No questions, no platitudes, no shushing or there-theres, just a solid, warm body to cry against. It was what Tally needed right now.

They were still huddled up on the couch when Anna and Louis came in. Louis started to speak but closed his mouth when he saw Tally crying. He looked back at Anna and pointed, but she pulled him away and headed upstairs, and Davy heard Anna say something about a smelly little boy. The bath water started to run a minute later.

After a while, Tally was cried out, and she pulled herself together a bit. "Su-Jin is on stage crew even though I know she doesn't like it that much. She does it so we can hang out together."

"That's nice of her." It sounded familiar. Why else had Davy done stage crew with Anna all those years ago?

"Yeah. When I was in the chorus last summer, there was lots of down time while the director worked with the featured players, so we spent a lot of time together. I would help with painting and scenery and whatever she was doing because it was fun and I was with my best friend."

Davy felt a flash of guilt. She had told Tally she would help but she never had.

"But now, I'm a featured player and even if I'm not doing anything, I have to sit with them and pay attention. And I thought I was making friends with them, but some of them are assholes who roll their eyes and whisper about the stepsisters when we do our parts."

God, actors were the absolute worst. "I'm sorry about that. People can be mean."

"So now, whenever me and Su-Jin are together, she says I talk too much about them, but it's only because they're stressing me out! I don't know what to do. We open next week. I want to be great, but I don't know if I'm really doing a bad job or if it's just these people trying to mess with me."

"It sounds like you have two separate issues here, and we'll talk about the quality of your performance in a minute. I think you need to make time for Su-Jin and talk about everything you told me. But concentrate on her side of it and how she's feeling. And probably apologize. Do you want to invite her over?"

Tally looked excited for a moment. Then her face fell. "She's still doing play stuff. Their deadline for finishing the set is tomorrow."

"Why don't you text her and ask if she wants to sleep over here when she's done. You and I can pick her up."

"It's gonna be late, like eleven o'clock or something."

"It's okay. Make sure she gets permission from her parents. And I'm going to text your mom and tell her you're here."

"Thanks, Davy." Tally chewed on her lip as she held her phone. It looked like she was contemplating what to say. Then her thumbs were a blur as she composed a long message, and she grinned with relief when she got a near instant reply, and then another one about a minute later. "Her mom said she could come."

"Good, and your mom said you can stay."

"She'll never say no to me staying here. She thinks it's awesome you're around now."

Davy couldn't not ask. "And how do you feel about it?"

"About what?" Tally didn't look up from her phone.

Really Tally? Focus. Jesus. "About me being around more?"

"I like it," Tally said without hesitation. "You're great."

The relief that flowed through her was not surprising. "I'm glad I could change your mind."

Tally looked confused. "What do you mean?"

"Dad told me you didn't want to see him or me anymore. I'm glad you let me back into your life."

"I never said that. I like you." She seemed to think about it for a second. "I told my mom that I didn't want to go for tea at that hotel in the city anymore. I hated that place. And Dad was never that nice to me, but you always were."

"I really liked being with you at those birthday tea dates, but I can see how they got old for you. And I should have made an effort to see you more often. I'm really glad we're closer now. I don't ever want to lose you."

"You won't, especially if you order that Chinese food you promised." Tally nudged her with her elbow. "And can I get a Mountain Dew? No, make it two, one for Su-Jin too. And she likes spring rolls. Can we get some of those? I'm going to wait to eat until she gets here."

"Yeah, yeah." Davy picked up her phone and placed the order.

"So what are we going to do until we go pick her up?" Tally seemed to be bouncing back nicely from her emotional break.

"I know exactly what we're going to do. You're going to perform your part for me, and I will give you my unbiased opinion. I have a lot of experience in judging the authenticity of a performance."

"You do?" Tally looked dubious.

"Of course. I'm a lawyer. What do you think court is but legal theater? I think of defendants and witnesses as characters in a play." She didn't really, but Tally didn't need to know that.

"Are you sure?" Tally gripped the couch cushion in what appeared to be anticipation.

"Yeah. Do you have music or anything?"

"I recorded the rehearsal pianist. I have the whole first act and part of the second." Tally connected her phone to the wireless speaker. "This is gonna be so great. I'll have to do some of the other parts too so it'll make sense. And you'll tell me if it's good—or bad? Honestly? And maybe help me figure out how to be better?"

"I can't think of anything else I'd rather do." Davy sat back and prepared to watch. "Now, be the evil stepsister you wish to see in the world."

❖

It was around one a.m. when Davy finally trudged upstairs. She allowed the girls to bunk down on the sectional sofa so they could giggle and chat to their hearts' content without disrupting Louis or Anna. After Tally's one-woman rehearsal—she was good, no doubt about it—they picked up Su-Jin. It had only been a mild case of hurt feelings and out of proportion teenage angst, and they were fast friends again before the last crab rangoon was devoured.

Now instead of turning right into her own room, she found herself moving down the darkened hallway toward Anna's. Her door was open, as it usually was in case Louis needed her. The moon shone through the curtainless windows and Anna's outline was clear on her small twin mattress, which was pushed up against the wall. She didn't really think Anna would still be up and wanting to talk about Winnie, but now that she was there, ogling Anna like a creeper, she couldn't force herself to walk away.

"Did you have a nightmare?" Louis whispered.

She turned and there he was in his stretchy pajamas, cradling his walkie-talkie to his chest. He shuffled past her into the room and stood next to Anna's bed.

"Ma." He jiggled her arm. "Ma, wake up. The batteries are dead and I had a bad dream."

Anna reached out to him, her voice gravelly with sleep. "You did? Get in here and tell me about it."

He climbed into her bed and crawled across her. It seemed to be a practiced thing, and his spot was in the cocoon formed by the wall and his mother's body. "Davy's here. I think she had a nightmare too."

Anna lifted her head. "She is?"

"Sorry."

"No, come in, Davy."

She came closer. There was no room in the bed, so she sat on the floor. "Sorry."

Anna yawned. "Stop saying that. I'm glad you're here. I miss you."

Davy turned her head toward her. Had Anna just said that?

"Ma, can I tell you and Davy about my dream?" Louis whispered.

"Yes. Remember what we do? We're going to pretend to write your dream on the ceiling."

"And then we're going to erase it and it'll be all gone," he said, secure in the knowledge that his mother could take all the bad things away.

"Right."

Davy shifted so her back rested against Anna's mattress and prepared to listen.

Louis struggled to articulate his dream. "I was in this giant bowl of spaghetti and meatballs. It was so giant it was as big as a pool. And it wasn't yummy like real spaghetti. It was yucky. And I called for help so many times, but nobody came to help me. Not even you."

"Oh, honey, I'm sorry. That does sound scary. I'll always come to help you."

Louis kept relaying his dream, but his words came slower and less urgently. Sometime during the telling, Davy felt Anna's hand on her head. Her fingers dug into Davy's hair and sifted through the strands. It was the most comforting feeling in the world, and she almost purred with contentment when Anna's hand massaged her scalp and then rested there—a gentle weight that made her heart feel light but kept her grounded. Long after Louis's story had halted and the breathing of both people in the bed had evened out and became regular with slumber, Davy stayed where she was on that hard, unyielding floor. She had no idea how she was going to avoid falling in love with Anna over the coming year. She was already more than halfway there.

CHAPTER TWENTY-SIX

Davy arrived back in her office after lunch to a scene she very much wished she had seen from the beginning. Halima had Roland backed into a corner behind her desk, and she had her finger in his face. His hands and eyebrows were raised so high, he must have thought either that her finger was a gun and she was holding him up, or that it was a ruler and she wanted to measure the width of his eyelids.

"Hey, you two. What's going on?"

"Davy, of course, I appreciate your privacy," Roland started to say.

"He was snooping at your calendar," Halima said at the same time.

"You only need to ask, Roland." Davy spread her arms wide. "I'm an open book. Halima, thank you so much, my beloved little pit bull. Take an extra-long lunch. I'm sorry I was so long at mine."

"I never realized how supremely loyal Halima is." Roland followed her into her office. "And scary," he added, under his breath.

"She is loyal. Loyalty is a highly valuable quality, in my opinion." Davy couldn't say how hurt she had been by what she perceived as Roland's disloyalty—his nonexistent defense of her character—at the Summit, because she wasn't supposed to have heard it. "And I'm loyal right back. Can't function without her. What do you need?"

"Lunch with Joel Kleinman today, I see? Are there developments?"

"Possibly. I'll know more later." Maybe she was less than an open book. Not closed, exactly, but definitely face down at the moment. She didn't want to share what was spoken of at her lunch with Joel just yet. She guessed she'd have to be more direct. "What's up? Why were you looking at my calendar?"

"Two items we need to discuss. First, things are going tits-up at Wax Corp."

"Oh, shit. What happened?" She had a sneaking suspicion she already knew.

Roland shook his head. "Keeley made an absolute hash of things. We're wining and dining them tonight in the hopes of salvaging the relationship. We need you to come. Seven o'clock at Ai Fiori."

"I can't. It's my sister's opening night. She's in a play."

"Cancel it. This is im—" Roland furrowed his brows. "You don't have a sister."

"Yes, I do. Tally. You met her."

"I never did. When?"

"Well, you didn't meet her at her party, the one you crashed in June, when you were shitfaced. It was in July, when we had you and Leanne over for dinner with the Kleinmans. Remember the trampoline? Tally showed you her side flip? And Leanne said if you tried it she wasn't taking care of your injured ass."

Roland thought for a second. "That's not your sister. That's Anna's sister."

"Yes, she is. She's my half-sister and Anna's half-sister."

"I'm so confused." He put a hand to his chin.

"My dad and her mom fucked about fifteen years ago and had Tally as a result."

"Davy," he tsked. "So crass."

"I have another meeting, Roland. I don't have time to draw you a diagram."

"And you and Anna are getting married?"

Davy hesitated. It had rolled off her tongue without a thought before. Now the lie stuck in her throat. "What do you think?" It was an evasion that wouldn't hold up in court.

"How do your father and her mother feel about it?"

"Roland, I don't have time for this and it's really none of your business. I told you, I have a meeting."

"I know, with Sophie. Why are you meeting with our investigator? Which of our clients needs her?"

Davy wasn't about to tell him Sophie was looking into a personal matter regarding Anna's son. She pointed toward the door. "Can we talk about this later? There she is and I don't want to waste her valuable time." Thank Christ for Sophie's punctuality.

"Okay, okay. I'm leaving. Oh, my second thing." He paused in the doorway.

"What is it?" she asked, beyond exasperated at this point.

"The senior partners need to meet with you tomorrow morning."

Davy stilled. "Why?" Conant's retirement dinner was tomorrow night. It had to be about the partnership.

"We'll discuss it tomorrow. You have an opening at ten."

❖

Anna had saved an aisle seat for Davy. The auditorium was filling up and there was still no sign of her. She had texted that she had to take a later train than she had planned, and she had also, strangely, asked if Anna had a valid passport.

Finally, she appeared and rushed down the aisle, her suit jacket flapping and a bouquet of flowers in each hand. She plonked herself down beside her. "Sorry I'm late. She handed Anna one of the bouquets—irises again, just like the first flowers she gave her. "Here, these are for you. For painting the best tree flats I've ever seen."

"You haven't even seen them yet. They're still behind the curtain." Anna buried her nose in the flowers. It was such a sweet gesture. There had been a slight thaw between them over the last few days, but these flowers were like a sirocco gently warming her from the inside out. "Thank you. They're gorgeous."

"And roses for Tally. Do you think that's a good choice?"

"It's perfect. She'll love them."

"How is she doing? Is it too late for me to go back and wish her luck?"

"Yes, but she probably still has her phone on. You could text her, but don't say good luck."

"Right, right. Break a leg." Davy wiped the sweat from her brow and quickly shot off a text. "Look at this crowd. Is it sold out?"

Anna surveyed the nearly full theater. "Looks like it. That's *Into the Woods* and Sondheim for you. Everyone loves it."

Davy fanned herself with her hand. "It's so hot in here."

"Here, have some water." Anna hoisted her giant tote onto her lap and retrieved a bottle for her.

Davy eyed the bag like it was a respected adversary, but she accepted the water and gulped it down quickly. When she sat back in her chair, it looked like she was finally giving herself a moment to relax. "It's just us? Your mom and Louis aren't here?"

"Mom was only too happy to babysit. They'll come on Sunday to the closing performance. Once is enough for her." Anna reached out to brush away a nonexistent speck of dirt from Davy's shoulder. She couldn't help touching her. The conversation she wanted to have about dissolving the contract had never happened, and Anna was beginning to accept that Davy didn't see her the way Anna wanted her to. But her desire for Davy was like a pot at a continuous roiling boil and sitting close to her now was a test of her self-control.

"I have some news."

The careful delivery of those words plus Davy's serious demeanor told her something was up. Anna suffered some minor mental whiplash as she yanked her thoughts out of the gutter. "Is it about...?"

"Yes. Sophie found her. It took so long because she changed her name."

"She's not Winnie Bowerchuck anymore? What's her name now?"

"Winsome Bowers." Davy's voice dripped disdain.

"Where is she?"

"She's an entertainer on a cruise ship that sails in the Caribbean. But her contract is ending after the voyage that leaves tomorrow and Sophie has no idea where she's going after this. Maybe *Winsome* doesn't know either."

"So if we don't get her now—"

"Who knows when we'll find her again. So you and I are flying down to Miami tomorrow and we're getting on that boat." Just then the lights dimmed and the curtain came up. "Don't worry. It's all arranged," Davy whispered. "We'll talk more at intermission."

Anna tried to concentrate on the show but all she could think about were the obstacles preventing them from leaving tomorrow. Davy didn't seem to have the same problem—she laughed and clapped at all the right moments, and stomped her feet and whooped like she was at a Knicks game when Tally and her fellow evil stepsister had their big moment in Act I. But then, Davy'd had time to wrap her head around a spontaneous trip to find Louis's birth mother.

As soon as the lights came up at intermission, Anna turned to Davy. "We can't go. The retirement dinner is tomorrow. You have to be there."

"We are absolutely going. Why do I need to attend a dinner for a guy I don't even respect? And especially now that it's turned into Davy's diabolical defeat, there's no point. This is way more important."

"But—" Anna didn't know what to say. She had been planning on pulling out all the stops for her last performance as Davy's fiancée. She was torn by her disappointment over that and anxiety over the Winnie situation.

"Look, it's fine. There's supposed to be a meeting between the partners and me tomorrow, probably so they could let me down gently in private, but we'll be on the plane. I didn't bother canceling. Halima will tell them what's what. If they can't deal with it—fuck 'em. It's their own damn fault for waiting so long to make a decision."

"Are you sure?"

"God's honest truth? I don't even know if I'd take it if they offered it to me. What I do know is that you and Louis and Tally and your mom mean a whole lot to me. And you all are more important than anything else."

Anna had the urge to grab her by her jacket and kiss her senseless. It was probably the hottest thing Davy had ever said to her. She turned away and buried her face in Davy's flowers, using them as a proxy for what she really wanted to do. When she was able to think a little more clearly, a million thoughts about the situation flew into her head. "But we haven't had time to figure out what we're going to do when we meet her."

"I started working on this when you allowed me to get Sophie involved," Davy said. "I've consulted with an old law school buddy of mine who does family law in Trenton. She made sure all my i's were crossed and my t's dotted according to New Jersey law, and I've already retained her for the adoption. We're ready."

"Louis doesn't have to go, does he?"

"No, he shouldn't go."

"I need to talk to my mom. How long will we be gone?"

"Our first opportunity to get off the ship will be Sunday morning. We'll be back Sunday afternoon." She fished her buzzing phone from her pocket. "That's Halima. I'll take it out in the lobby. You call your mom. We don't have much time until the next act starts."

❖

Davy connected the call as she dashed up the aisle. "Halima. What's up?"

"Davy! I was going to leave you a voice mail. You're not missing the show, are you?"

"It's intermission."

"Oh, good. How is it? How's Tally?"

Davy smiled. "Terrific. She's phenomenal."

"Just wanted to give you a quick update. I've confirmed your flight. Your return flight tickets are booked for Sunday, but you can change them to another day if you want without a fee—you know, just in case you and Anna want to stay for all five days."

"We won't, but thanks." Davy's response was wry. Halima thought she knew everything.

"I've also booked a couple of surprises for the cruise. I hope you enjoy them."

"This is not a pleasure trip. We're going down there to take care of something very specific." She rubbed her forehead. Halima knew all this.

"Davy, you've changed. You've started delegating. You've become super-efficient at your job—and it's unbelievable to me that you have the capacity for even more efficiency. All the while, you're counting the seconds until you can leave the office at five o'clock on the dot every day. We both know the reason for that. I'm so happy for you and Anna. If you can, take a little time to enjoy each other away from real life."

"Lord save me from psychologists in training," Davy muttered. "That's not what this is, and you know it. You know what the contract says. Now that the partnership nonsense is over, we are simply two people sharing a house for the sake of Louis's education."

"And what does the contract say about you rushing down to the Caribbean to be Anna's hero?"

"Ugh. Leave it, Halima." Davy changed topics. There was no advantage to sticking with this one. "Sorry to make you the messenger of my absence to Roland and Mel tomorrow."

"No problem, boss. I hope to subtly heap a ton of scorn on them for the way they handled this whole situation. My God, can you imagine Keeley running things? Right off a cliff, just like Wax Corp."

Davy laughed. "You are the absolute best. I'm getting you a raise no matter what happens tomorrow."

"Don't say it unless you mean it."

"Oh, I mean it. Good night."

"Enjoy the rest of the show! And the cruise!"

CHAPTER TWENTY-SEVEN

Anna was feeling superstitious. Everything was going so smoothly, she couldn't help wondering when the other shoe was going to drop. She followed Davy down the passageway to their stateroom after an easy flight and an even easier boarding process. She had never seen anything like this ship. It was a floating town—no, city. It was so large, Davy called it the eighth continent.

Davy marched ahead and said over shoulder, "Just a word of warning—I doubt there was much available cabin wise at the last minute. We'll probably be in some broom closet with bunk beds and a tiny little porthole—if we're lucky."

It seemed like they walked for miles, from the middle of the ship to somewhere toward the bow, but they finally found their stateroom number, and Davy opened the door with her key card.

"Whoa." Davy halted in the doorway.

Anna nearly bumped into her. "What? Don't stop. Keep moving. Or is it so small there's not room for both of us?"

"No, there's definitely room." Davy moved aside and Anna stepped into their stateroom. It was enormous, and featured a dining table for four, a sitting room with a big, comfy-looking couch and a couple of easy chairs, and sliding glass doors opposite that led to a balcony. The sun streamed in and brightened their view of the port, where they would still be docked for another hour or two.

The suite also had a spacious bathroom and a separate bedroom with a king-sized bed. Anna took a breath in and held it for a few seconds when she saw it. Only one bed. Again.

Davy was still in the sitting room. "Want an obscenely large chocolate-covered strawberry?"

Anna joined her at a counter area that had an ice bucket and coffee station, and several gifts wrapped in cellophane: the aforementioned strawberries, a cheese tray, a bottle of champagne, and two white baseball caps with the cruise line's logo embroidered on them. "What in the world?"

"Halima. She told me there would be surprises. I think she went a little nuts."

"She got us this suite? And all this stuff? With a day's notice?"

Davy nodded. "A few *hours'* notice."

"I think she needs a raise."

Davy nodded again. "I'll make it retroactive to yesterday." She rolled their carry-ons into the bedroom. "I'm going to take a quick shower, okay? Traveling makes me feel gross."

Anna sank into one of the easy chairs. The whirlwind packing last night, the few hours of sleep, the trip to the airport, the flight, the transfer to the cruise terminal, the embarkation process—it was a relief to just stop for a moment. She hadn't had time to think about what was actually at stake here, or how their encounter with Winnie could play out. But now that she did, the nerves were starting to kick in. Was this even a good idea? Why couldn't she just allow things to stay the way they were? She knew that was dumb, but it was easy. Here she was going to be confronting Winnie in a very short time and she didn't even want to think about all the ways this could go badly.

The water stopped running and she heard Davy moving around in the bathroom. Seconds later she appeared, steam surrounding her as the door opened, in one of the cruise line's branded bathrobes.

Davy took one look at her and sat on the couch near her chair. "You look positively green and we haven't even left the dock."

"It's not seasickness."

"I know." Davy leaned in. "Anyone would be struggling with this. You are legally Louis's parent right now—why mess with that? But asking Winnie to give up her parental rights so you can adopt him is the safer thing, the better thing for him." She retrieved her phone. "Sophie gave me a rundown of Winnie's schedule."

"How did she get that?"

Davy shrugged. "I told you. She's really good at her job." She scrolled and then started reading on her phone. "Winnie may be at the Sail Away party that happens while we—"

"Let me guess—sail away."

"Right. Apparently, Sophie couldn't get confirmation on that, but Winnie will definitely be performing in a revue called *Golden Age of Broadway* tonight, and then she's in—oh, Jesus."

"What?"

"*Cats*. Tomorrow."

The look of absolute disgust on Davy's face made Anna giggle. She couldn't help it. A sort of rapprochement had been reached since they had begun traveling, and Anna wanted to embrace it, enjoy it, make it permanent. She guessed Davy was trying to make a hard situation easier for her. Anna wouldn't want to be here with anyone but her.

Now Davy's expression changed to one of determination as she switched to another app and began clicking away. A moment later she smiled, but it was not a happy one. "Halima has already gotten us seats for both shows. Her raise is now pending."

Anna gave Davy a playful shove and left her hand on her shoulder. "You can't punish her just because you may have to sit through one of the most popular musicals of the 1980s."

"I like that you said *may*. Want to check out the Sail Away party? Maybe we can decrease the odds of having to watch a bunch of humans embarrass themselves by prancing around pretending to be cats and get this done really fast. Then we can relax for the rest of our time."

Anna headed for the bathroom. What Davy said made perfect sense, and she had to meet her fears head on. "Give me twenty minutes to shower and get ready."

❖

Anna kept her eyes peeled as she returned from the bar with two lurid red cocktails in tall, curvy glasses, both laden with skewered tropical fruit and a stripey paper straw. The Sail Away party on the lido deck was a mass of happy people, all of them excited to get their vacation started with drinks and dancing. There were lots of crewmembers around wearing uniform navy blue polos, hyping the crowd and leading line dances, but she had yet to see Winnie.

Davy was ending a call when Anna sidled up to the spot they had staked out by the railing, ideal for surveying the party while viewing their departure from Miami.

"Everything okay?" Anna handed her a drink.

"Yup. All good. Any sign of her?"

Just then the ship's horn sounded—a deep, basso profundo that rattled Anna to the core. A cheer went up from the assembled partygoers, and the band struck up Kool and the Gang's "Celebration." When the vocalist started singing, Anna turned around.

"That's her, isn't it?" Davy said from behind her.

"Yes." It had been over four years since Anna had seen Winnie, and she looked much the same, from this distance. Apprehension and anger sat low in her chest as she watched this careless, callous woman singing up on the stage. She wanted Winnie out of Louis's life forever, and that was only going to happen if she initiated contact. There was a crowd up by the band, dancing and cheering for Winnie, and Anna moved to join it without a backward glance.

❖

The ship chugged along, the wind lifting their hair as they sat at a cocktail table near where the Sail Away party had been. It was over now, and the sun was setting on the starboard side of the ship, but Davy couldn't appreciate it.

Anna had stood in front of the bandstand and watched Winnie sing, and Davy could tell the exact moment Winnie saw her. She stuttered over her lyric but then recovered and hadn't glanced Anna's way again. When the set was over, Anna hustled over to the steps where Winnie descended, had a few words with her, and then returned to where Davy had been standing by the railing, watching the drama unfold.

Winnie had instructed Anna to wait at the lido bar, and that she would join her shortly. That was over two hours ago.

"I don't think she's going to show."

"Let's give her another ten minutes," Anna's gaze swung wildly, as it had every few minutes the whole time they had sat there.

"Her revue starts in an hour. She's not coming. We've tipped our hand."

"What are we going to do?" Anna asked.

"Let's gird our loins for the golden age of Broadway."

❖

Davy walked into the Crown and Anchor pub at around midnight. It was one of the quieter bars, now that the nightclubs were running full throttle. She approached the bartender. "Do you know Winsome Bowers? One of the performers in the Broadway Revue?"

The young Filipino man shook his head. "Sorry."

"I do," a pretty, red-headed server said as she used the drink gun to fill several glasses.

"Can you get in touch with her?" Davy put her hand on the bar, a hundred-dollar bill poking out from under it.

"Why?" The server eyed the money.

"I thought she was amazing," Davy simpered. "I just became a fan. Do you think she would meet with me?"

"You're definitely her type. I think I know exactly where she is."

"The crew bar?" the bartender asked with a smirk.

"Of course, isn't everyone who's off duty?" The server picked up the phone on the wall and made a call. After a few moments on hold, she was talking to Winnie. "Yeah, there's someone here at the Crown and Anchor. She wants to meet." The server casually inspected Davy, who wore the tightest jeans she'd brought and a sleeveless blouse of Anna's that showed off her arms and had the top four buttons undone. "No, not blond. She's tall, dark, and sexy. Says she's a fan. And I think she *really* wants to meet you." Another glance at the hundy on the bar. A moment later she hung up. "She'll be here, but you'll have to keep it on the down low. She could get fired for fraternizing with a passenger."

"Got it." Davy handed her the money and then pointed to a quiet table across the room. "I'll be sitting over there. Can you point me out to her when she arrives?"

About twenty minutes later, Winnie breezed into the bar. There was the tiniest sliver of a chance that Winnie would recognize Davy from that summer years ago, but she was willing to risk it. No way someone as narcissistic as Winnie would remember Davy, who had gone out of her way to *not* kiss Winnie's ass. Davy did her best to look both alluring and fannish.

"Hey, there. You were at the show tonight?" Winnie sat extremely close to her on the same side of the table for four.

"I sure was." Davy had seethed all the way through it. She had thought there might have been a chance of catching Winnie after the show, at the ship's equivalent of the stage door, but no such luck. An hour and forty-five minutes she would never get back. Anna had sat silent and stone-faced throughout. Davy doubted any of the numbers had even registered for her. At least the time had allowed Davy to come up with this alternate plan.

She ran a finger down Davy's arm. "I hear you're a fan of my work?"

"Yes, I can't believe I'm meeting you in person. May I buy you a drink?"

"Sure, Long Island iced tea."

Davy gestured for the server and ordered a white wine for herself, which she had no intention of touching, and Winnie's drink. "You were really something tonight. Where'd you learn to sing like that?"

"Oh, I'm just naturally talented. Which number was your favorite?"

"It's so hard to pick one."

"Most people like 'I Dreamed a Dream' from *Les Mis*. It's so sad. I'm told that I squeeze a lot of emotion out of it. What did you think of that one?"

"Yeah, there wasn't a wet eye in the house. So, have you been working on this ship for long?"

The server brought their drinks and Winnie took a long drag from the straw of her Long Island iced tea. "Seven months. This is my last sailing before my vacation. I have a month off and then I'll come back for another seven months."

"Right. Seven months is a long time. You deserve a break."

"Yeah. I'll probably stick around Miami. Where are you from?"

"New Jersey. I'm a lawyer."

"Oh, wow. Like, trials and stuff?"

"No. Family law. I help kids, mostly. Did you know that when a child is abandoned, the parent is on the hook for child support until that child is adopted? And did you also know that a guardian could sue the parent for the arrears of nonpayment? That means over the course of, say, four years, it could easily add up to thirty thousand dollars or more, plus legal fees, court costs, etc." Davy looked over at the bar and nodded, and Anna slid from her barstool and approached the table.

Winnie started to get up, but Davy clamped a hand on her arm. "Please don't. We just want to talk. And anyway, not to point out the obvious, but we're on a ship at sea. You're stuck until we get to Jamaica, so you might as well hear us out. You wouldn't want your employer to find out about your *potential* legal troubles, would you?"

"Hi, Winnie." Anna sat down. "I didn't want to do it this way, but you didn't show up at the lido bar before."

"Yeah, because I knew you would try to pull something like this," she sneered. "He's not here is he? You're not going to dump him on me. I don't have any money either, so don't think you can get any out of me."

Anna sat back in her chair, exuding a glacial calm. "I guess it's a good thing I don't want your money, then."

Davy placed a manila folder on the table, along with a pen. "Today is actually your lucky day, Ms. Bowers. Anna has no intention of collecting the child support she could rightfully claim, nor does she want recompense for the fraudulent way you obtained her signature on Louis's guardianship papers. All she wants is the freedom to adopt Louis, and you are standing in her way. Now, you are well within your rights to retain legal representation and discuss your options, but any attorney would basically tell you the same thing I will tell you now. Sign." She opened the folder and placed the documents in front of Winnie.

"What are these?" she muttered.

"The first is an affidavit that summarizes your contact—or lack thereof—with Louis since his birth. You may read it over, make any changes, initial them, and sign. I believe it's accurate. The second is a petition for the termination of your parental rights in a voluntary surrender that identifies Anna as the prospective adoptive parent. There are two copies of each. One for Anna and one for your records. Sign here and here." Davy indicated with the point of her pen before placing it in front of Winnie.

"And if I don't?"

"We'll start legal proceedings immediately."

Winnie's eyes took on a shifty cast. "How much is my signature worth to you?" she asked Anna.

Anna was about to say something, but Davy swept the papers back into the folder. "Anna gave you a chance, Ms. Bowers. Now we get to do it my way. I suggest you find an excellent attorney, because there is no one better than me, and I intend to make you pay. Dearly."

Winnie slapped her hand on the folder. "All right. I'll sign."

They sat in silence as Winnie read and signed the documents. Then she sucked all the liquid from her Long Island iced tea, her cheeks hollowing with the effort.

Davy tidied the papers and stowed them in the folder. The slurping sound Winnie's straw made as she finished her beverage grated on her absolute last nerve. "I wish you a pleasant month of vacation, Ms. Bowers, but in no way guarantee it. I'm also pleased to inform you that I will not be seeing *Cats* while onboard this ship. Good-bye." She glared at Winnie until she got up and left.

"Oh my God, that was so stressful," Anna gasped. "I can't believe her. She didn't want to know one thing about him."

Davy's posture sagged now that they were alone at the table. "I'd call her a cunt, but she lacks both warmth and depth."

"If she only knew how amazing her little boy is."

Davy took a sip from her glass of wine and then handed it to Anna, who gulped at it. "He was never hers, Anna. He's yours. He always was, and now you're one step closer to making it legal."

"I truly don't know how to thank you." Anna reached across the table and grasped Davy's hand.

Did Anna really not know that Davy would do anything and everything for her?

"You were so bold. So forceful. So competent. I can see now how good you must be at your job."

Now she was starting to get embarrassed. "It was nothing. What do you want to do now? We can't get off this tub for another thirty-six hours."

Anna didn't say anything. Her eyes ensnared Davy's and held them as if in a vise grip. She hadn't let go of Davy's hand, and now she brushed her thumb over Davy's palm. It felt simultaneously like Davy's skin was melting from her body and every nerve ending was standing at attention. When she felt herself bending toward Anna like a time-lapsed flower toward the sun, Davy removed her hand from Anna's grip and sat up straight. "We could, um, take a stroll on the promenade deck? Find a nightclub and go dancing?"

Anna studied Davy for a second longer, and then it looked like she had come to some kind of decision. She nodded and stood. "Okay, a stroll. Let's go." They walked together in silence out onto the open-air deck.

The deck was shrouded in shadows and the turbulence of the waves many decks below was a constant cushion of sound. There weren't many people about, which suited Davy just fine.

She had thought Anna would be happier now that Louis's situation had been resolved with almost no fuss, but she seemed lost in thought as she walked beside Davy, her head down and arms folded across her chest to ward off the chill. A bit detached, in her own head.

"What would happen if I wanted to change something in the contract?" Anna asked suddenly. "Is that possible?"

Why would she want to change things now? Davy retreated behind lawyer speak, afraid to ask. "If one or more parties wishes to deviate from a signed contract, it is acceptable to renegotiate and amend it as currently written as long as they are able to reach a new agreement."

Anna nodded but didn't say anything else. Davy waited. Although she was bristling with nerves, she refused to ask Anna what she wanted to change.

She stopped walking and faced Davy. "I don't want to be dishonest anymore."

Davy frowned. *What did that mean?* "You're no longer required to pretend to be my fiancée. And there's nothing dishonest about living in Elmdale for its school district."

"I know, but it's really easy for me to behave like I have genuine, deep, abiding feelings for you—that's the dishonest part."

Davy was listening to the words, but they weren't making sense to her. "I'm sorry. I don't understand."

"I want it to be real." Anna's eyes were intense. "I want to know what it's like to be with you in an honest way, and I'm hoping you want that too. I don't want there to be clauses that tell me I can't kiss you, or touch you, because all I think about is kissing you, and loving you. And I don't want there to be any misunderstanding that what I feel for you is real."

"It is?" Davy didn't think she could hide her astonishment.

"It really is." Anna's smile was full of affection. "This reaction—this surprise that you could be worth it, that you can't see how incredible you are—is one of the thousand reasons why I care so much for you." She took a step closer. "And now that I've said all that, I'm wondering how you feel about it."

Davy didn't know what to say. Part of her was filled with wonder that Anna could be saying these things—to her! But would she even know how to do this? And Anna didn't realize the burden Davy might place on her if she accepted what Anna was offering. "You're the best person I know, Anna. And if I could have anyone, there's not a doubt that I would choose you, but..."

That little line that creased Anna's brows was painful to see. "But what?"

"But I'm afraid I would need you too much."

The crease disappeared as her eyebrows lifted in surprise, and her smile almost took Davy's breath away. "Well, good." Anna moved closer still and put a hand on Davy's waist. "That's what love is. You'll need me too much, and I'll need you too much, and all of our needs will be satisfied somehow."

"That's what love is?" Davy knew her father's definition of love was wrong, but was this one right? Did need equal love?

"Part of it. I needed a really big something today, and you came through and got it for me like you were born to do it. Did it bother you that I asked?"

"No! Of course not."

"Were you mad that you had to come down here for me and Louis?"

"No, but it's different. Doing this for you will make your life better. I would do it a million times."

"So maybe I need *you* too much."

Davy shook her head. "Never."

"Why doesn't it work both ways, Day?" Anna came closer. Her voice was soft as velvet. "You make my life better. I love you, so anything you need, I want to provide it for you."

"Love?" Davy needed to be sure she had heard right.

Anna encircled her arms around Davy's waist, fitting their bodies snugly together. The only sane place for Davy's hands was on her shoulders. "Love," Anna repeated. "I absolutely love you."

"I love you too." Davy gazed at her in wonder. Could it be this easy? Just saying the words and knowing they were true? Because Davy knew they were true. She loved Anna with her entire being. A feeling of certainty, and of faith, stole over her. This was the exact right thing, and she felt all her muscles relax except the ones in her hands, which gripped Anna's shoulders more securely so she would stay just as close as she was now.

"I'm glad that's settled." Anna heaved a sigh, and her grin was playful. "So the contract is null and void?"

Davy nodded and grinned back at her. "The prohibition on kissing is hereby lifted." It was like the pilot light deep within her ignited something flammable in her veins and her body went whoosh. There wasn't a force on earth that could stop her from kissing Anna. She bent her head. Anna lifted her face to meet her. The touch of her lips on Anna's was powerful. It was profound. It was a promise.

Before she got too lost in it, she pulled back slightly, mesmerized by Anna's closed eyes, her lips curved upward in a joyous smile. Now that Davy could see it, had it within her grasp, she wanted it for the rest of her life. Should she make that clearer? Was it too much too soon? Maybe she'd start with one thing. "I hope we'll be kissing all the time now. On a near constant basis, in fact."

"Near constant, huh?" Anna's eyes opened and the light in them seemed to lift Davy off the ground.

She lowered her gaze from Anna's eyes to her lips. "Do I have your permission to do that again?"

Anna laughed, and her voice descended into a low, sexy register that had Davy forgetting to breathe. "Should I sign something that covers all future kisses? A blanket kiss consent form? Some kind of release?"

"If you're looking for release we'll have to go a bit further than kissing." Davy tried to be her equal in voice-sexiness but knew she probably failed utterly.

Still, Anna clutched at her arm and began moving them down the deck. "Then I think you'd better take me back to our room right now."

CHAPTER TWENTY-EIGHT

As soon as they were inside their stateroom, Anna pushed Davy up against the wall just inside the cabin door. Davy gripped her waist, and then her fingers drifted, splaying out over the flare of Anna's hips and lower, until Davy was grasping greedily at her ass.

"Why is this ship so big? That was the longest walk of my life." Anna crushed her lips against Davy's before she could answer. Now that the air was clear, and there were no obstacles in the way, she intended to satisfy every last scintilla of her curiosity about Davy.

She pressed her whole body into Davy, prolonging the contact between their lips in slow, deliberate caresses that elicited a moan from Davy. Anna smiled against her mouth. She loved hearing that. It sent a bolt of lust right through her. Davy broke away from her mouth and kissed her way across Anna's jaw and down her throat. Anna's pulse thundered under Davy's lips, and she could hear the huskiness of her own breathing.

Anna wanted it fast, hot, immediate—a sprint toward their mutual climaxes. But there was also the desire to luxuriate in the anticipation of getting to the finish line. This was their first time. Wouldn't it be better to go slow, to take her time exploring every exquisite inch of Davy? They weren't at home. No one was going to interrupt them. She dragged her hands through Davy's hair and tugged gently. Davy raised her head and her hazy, unfocused gaze met Anna's. "We have so much time," Anna said. "Let's go slow. We haven't even started."

It took Davy a moment to reply. "It feels like we have." Her voice sounded ragged.

"Well, yeah." Despite what she said, it was taking all Anna's self-control to not unbutton Davy's blouse and rake her eyes over more of Davy's skin. She focused on Davy's neck instead, planting a light kiss right where she saw Davy's muscles working as she swallowed convulsively.

Anna let her tongue absorb a hint of salt from Davy's skin and willed herself to go slow. "It's the precursor. It's the overture."

"The overture?" Davy's chest heaved. "How are you finding these words in your brain? I can't even string two..." Her hands clutched at the fabric of Anna's pants at her hips.

"The show hasn't even started yet. And we have so much uninterrupted time. We have German opera amounts of time." Anna yielded to the temptation of pushing Davy's blouse off her shoulder and laying kisses along her clavicle.

"I've never...Is that a lot?" Davy's hands slid upward and snuck under her shirt. The touch of her fingertips on Anna's bare skin was electric. A slower pace might become torturous, but Anna had a feeling it was going to be the really good kind of torture.

"Hours and hours and hours. And that's just Act I."

"If you say so, but my legs are starting to fail me so can we move to the bed? And maybe be naked relatively soon?"

Anna took Davy by the hand and led her into the darkened bedroom. The only source of light was the moon from behind the sheer curtains at the window. She removed her clothes while Davy sat on the edge of the bed and watched, her mouth slack. It felt good to be the object of Davy's intense gaze. Once she was naked, she sat beside Davy and began to unbutton her blouse.

"For going slow, this is happening faster than advertised." Davy took her eyes from Anna's breasts with what appeared to be a major effort and looked down at Anna's busy fingers, which were now pushing Davy's shirt from her shoulders. "Not that I'm complaining."

"There's going slow, and then there's masochism," Anna said. "You made requests. I'm not going to deny you. I'm going to give you everything you ask for." Her fingers stilled at the front clasp of Davy's bra. "May I take this off?"

"Yes." Her voice rasped, but she unbuckled her belt and shucked her jeans and underwear down her legs before Anna could remove it. A puddle of fabric pooled around her ankles, and Anna stifled a laugh and took a moment to remove Davy's shoes and to fling her jeans across the room. Now Davy was naked but for her bra, and the outline of her erect nipples was plain to see beneath it. Anna couldn't help touching them, and Davy drew in a dramatic breath as Anna brushed her thumbs over the satin-covered points just once. She undid the clasp and smoothed her hands up Davy's chest and across her shoulders to shed the straps from her body. Davy's skin felt hot and soft and smooth, and Anna had to restrain herself from cupping Davy's breasts in her hands, from tasting them with her tongue. But she wanted something else even more. "Will you give me everything I ask for?"

"Yes, as long as it includes you asking for an orgasm sometime before we're supposed to get off this boat."

"We'll get there." Anna batted away the pillows and stretched out on the bed completely flat, her arms outstretched and her legs together. "I want you to lie down on top of me."

"Oh God, yes. I can do that." Davy threw a leg over Anna's hips and cast her hungry gaze over Anna's body, suspended over her on her knees and hands. Anna pulled her down so their torsos were connected. "You feel unbelievably good," Davy groaned.

But it wasn't enough for Anna. She reached up and cupped Davy's face in her hands and gazed into eyes she was sure reflected the desire to please her. "Take your knees off the mattress and rest your legs on top of mine. I want all your body weight on me. I want you to be my blanket."

Davy awkwardly did as Anna asked, but now her palms rested on either side of Anna's head as she looked down at the way their bodies were fused from their stomachs to their toes.

Anna swept her arms upward and took Davy's arms with her.

Davy fell all the way on top of her with an *oof*, and her head was now next to Anna's. She turned so that her mouth was close to Anna's ear. "I can't see your face," she whispered.

Anna reveled in having the entirety of Davy's delicious weight on top of her. She grasped Davy's hands in her own and held them above both of their heads, making it difficult for her to move. "What do you feel?" Her words were pushed out with the last of her breath and she took all the air she could back into her lungs.

"I can feel your voice. I hear it, but I can feel it too, the vibrations. It's unreal, but I also felt your lungs expanding when you took a breath. Can you breathe?"

"Yes." Anna gripped her hands tightly. Davy was right. The hum of her words had a presence, and each syllable dissolved into her like drops of honey into hot tea. "This is what I want. To be as close as possible to you with nothing separating us." Safety, protection, love—those were the emotions surging through her with Davy's body draped over her. She loosened her grip and stared at the ceiling, cataloguing the sensations that came from having absolutely nothing between them. Davy's breaths came short and sharp, and then Anna felt her suddenly relax. It was as if Davy's muscles had finally received the message that this was where they were going to be for a while and the tension left her body. Her breathing slowed. Her raised arms made her ribs press into Anna's belly, and she could feel Davy's nipples, still hard right above her own. It was the sexiest, most intimate sensation Anna had ever felt, and it was arousing almost to the point of delicious pain. "I love your skin—so soft and hot wherever we're touching," Anna said. "I can feel your thigh muscles on top of mine, and your bony toes."

Davy's laugh was a tremor against Anna's body. She pressed her lips against Anna's neck, just below her ear. Her tongue, hot and wet, sent molten heat rocketing to the junction between Anna's thighs. She exhaled through her teeth slowly and tried to keep her breathing steady. All her attention was now focused on where their centers met, which seemed several degrees warmer than any other place where their skin touched. Could she feel a brush of hair against her mound or was she imagining it? It didn't matter. She would know the answer at some point during the night and she was fine with living within ambiguity right now. She felt Davy's mouth smile against her neck, could envision her white teeth flashing in the dark.

"What is it?" she whispered, and turned her face toward Davy's, breathing in the scent of her sweet-smelling shampoo.

"Even your breathing is sexy as hell—rhythmic—like a boat. But we're on a boat, and I haven't once felt that rocking motion of being on the water. Just your breathing is doing that."

Anna tuned into it. Davy was minutely rising and falling in time with her breaths. She squeezed Davy's hands. "Keep them where they are." Then she drew her arms downward, dragging her fingertips lightly over Davy's skin, skimming her triceps, skirting the swell of her breasts, until she held her lightly at the waist.

Davy's breath was warm against her neck. "Ticklish."

Slowly, Anna began to clench and unclench her inner thigh muscles and her buttocks, letting her hips rise gently against Davy's. She created her own undulating, rocking motion, and while the regular rhythm of it teased her own pussy, she wondered what it was doing to Davy's. She kept doing it, and Davy's harsh breaths sounded loud in her ear. Davy's lips and tongue pressed against her neck again and Anna shivered as she continued to roll her pelvis up against Davy's.

After a minute, Davy drew in a breath and held it for a few seconds, then expelled it against Anna's neck so violently it threatened to throw

Anna off her rhythm. "Anna, I'm more turned on than I have ever been in my entire life."

"So am I."

"Are you going to come?"

Anna gave a wheezy laugh. "I sure hope so. Eventually. Are you?" Before Davy could answer, Anna opened her legs and wrapped them around Davy's narrow hips. Davy cried out, and her urgency drowned out the sound of Anna's gasp. Their bodies slotted together in this even more intimate way felt true, and absolutely perfect. Davy pushed up on her hands and ground against her now, and there was just enough light for Anna to see the wildness in her eyes before she bent and fused her mouth to Anna's. Davy's tongue pushed past her lips, rasping against Anna's in languorous strokes.

Their slow buildup had served its purpose, but now Anna was ready to apply fast, sharp, vibrant satisfaction, like when something she created coalesced in those few, final, culminating strokes. But they were creating this together, and she needed Davy's help. She tore her mouth from Davy's. "What do you like?"

"What?"

Anna took advantage of Davy's distraction. She threw her arms around Davy and rolled them over. Suddenly Davy was under her, uncomprehending. "Oh, God. How did you do that?"

Anna grinned and slid down Davy's body. "Do you like this?" She took a nipple in her mouth while her fingers gently pinched the other one.

Davy's fingers dug into her shoulders. "Yes, yes."

"What else? Do you want me inside you? Do you want my mouth on your clit?"

"Yes!" Davy's voice was breathless. "I want all of that. Please, Anna. I need it all."

Satiating Davy had become the narrow focus of Anna's entire world. She slid farther down and encouraged Davy's thighs to open wider with the tips of her fingers. She dropped kisses along Davy's thigh, preparing her for her presence, and then inhaled deeply. She dipped her head down and drew her tongue down one hot, wet, swollen lip of her labia and up the other. Davy gasped and touched her hair, and Anna reached up and held her hand. Davy moved their hands so they rested on her breast, and Anna squeezed her nipple at the same moment her tongue touched her clit.

"Anna!" Davy cried out.

She took that as positive feedback and tenderly painted Davy's clit with her tongue, pouring all the love she had for her into the task. Davy strained her hips toward her and Anna concentrated on making Davy feel good. She gave her actions shape and shading to bring Davy harmony, and unity, and resolution. And in another moment, all of Davy's muscles went rigid for several long seconds and then became pliant and soft again.

"Anna." Davy's voice was hushed with awe. "I just saw a million colors, but my eyes are closed."

❖

Davy felt Anna move up beside her. She turned on her side and took Anna's face in her hands and kissed her quickly before she had to pause to catch her breath. "Do you know how much I love you?" she demanded.

"How much?" She could hear triumph and exhilaration in Anna's voice. It lifted Davy up past her current wonder and contentment, straight into whirling, blissful elation.

"So much that I'm going to try like hell to make you feel as good as I do right now, but you set the bar pretty damn high."

"How good do you feel?"

"Good times a million. You are absolutely incredible. I probably shouldn't say this, but it's been a few years since I've had an orgasm that wasn't from my own hand, or toy. You're astounding. That was astounding."

"It's been a few years since I've…" Anna seemed to think about how to say it. "…bestowed an orgasm on anyone else. I love feeling you come apart like that."

"How do *you* feel?" Davy straddled Anna's waist and gazed into her eyes. "You have to be about ready to burst. My turn for bestowing an orgasm. Are you ready?" She dragged her fingertips down the middle of Anna's chest before coming to rest above her belly button.

"So ready. Get to bestowing, girl." Anna grabbed Davy's hands and placed them on her breasts. Her breathing hitched as Davy caught her erect nipples between her pointer and middle fingers, and squeezed so that just the tiniest top of the tit was revealed between them. Then she quickly swiped her tongue over one and then the other.

"What do you like?" Davy asked as she loosened her grip. She didn't let go, though. Anna was more endowed than Davy was, and she couldn't seem to stop touching her lush, irresistible flesh. It was as if her fingers had minds of their own as they gently kneaded and soothed Anna's nipples. She wanted to please Anna immediately, but also for the rest of her life. She was going to commit to memory everything and anything that got Anna worked up, as this appeared to be doing.

"They're so sensitive." Anna drew a breath in between her teeth. "Just keep playing with them. But put your mouth on them too."

Davy squeezed Anna's breasts together to close the distance between her nipples. This way Davy's mouth didn't have to travel that far from one to the other. Anna clamped her hands onto Davy's forearms, keeping them in place. After lavishing one nipple with all of her teeth, tongue, and lips' attention, she did the same to the other. And the sounds Anna made—little, breathy moans—were adorable, and hot, and they made Davy's clit twitch.

But then she heard Anna's voice, plaintive and fitful. "No, no, no."

She looked up to see Anna with her eyes closed, shaking her head in agitation. She sat up, appalled. "I'll stop. What's wrong?"

"Don't stop!" Anna pulled her back down. "It's not enough. I need more. I need you inside me."

Relief flooded her. She gazed into Anna's flushed, tense face as she pushed two fingers into her drenched pussy. Anna whimpered and gripped her shoulders. Her distress seemed to lessen slightly.

Anna's eyes opened and it was as if she were looking directly into Davy's soul. "Fuck me, Davy."

Those words set Davy on fire. She hovered over Anna as she plunged into her again, setting a rhythm that Anna's pelvis instantly caught. Anna threw her head back and her breasts shimmied in time with each thrust, and Davy had never seen anything as gorgeously seductive and wanton. She eased down beside her, not wanting to miss one second of how Anna's emotions rippled across her face as she came closer to the edge.

Anna's breathing became labored, and Davy brushed damp tendrils from Anna's forehead. Anna's eyes locked onto hers, and her hand snaked down to cover Davy's. She pressed Davy's fingers deeper within as her climax began to blossom, and Davy felt every throb of Anna's orgasm. She had never felt closer to another human than she did right then with Anna.

Anna reached around Davy's neck and pulled her down. After the storm of emotion, Anna's kiss felt like something delicate and tentative, and its uncertainty made Davy's eyes well with moisture. She kissed Anna back and tried to infuse into it not only her willingness to give Anna whatever she needed, but also the constancy of her love through whatever life might throw at them, as long as Davy could accompany her on wherever that ride took them.

It was a lot to say with only her lips and tongue.

"I love you too," Anna said. She pushed Davy onto her back and curled into her, her leg thrown across Davy's torso and her head resting on her chest.

Davy wrapped her arms around Anna and let the happiness that sat so lightly on her skin seep down into every pore. This was her life now, and she deserved this chance with Anna, and she was going to do everything she could to hold onto it.

❖

Hours later, Anna woke. She could see it was still dark through the sheer curtains covering the bedroom window, and the bed was empty. She donned a robe she found in the wardrobe and spied Davy through the open sliding glass door in the sitting room, where she leaned against the railing of their balcony in a matching white robe. She grabbed the white cruise line ball caps from Halima and stood on the threshold between the sitting room and the balcony for a moment. The sound of the churning waves masked her arrival. It also gave her a moment to savor the view.

"Peaceful out here," Anna said.

Davy turned, clutching her chest. "Jesus fuck you scared me."

"Whatcha doing?" She took a position next to Davy, put on a hat, and then fitted the other one onto Davy's head.

Davy gave Anna's hat an appraising look. Then she took hers off and switched it with Anna's. "I think this one goes better with your outfit." She carefully tucked the stray strands of blond hair behind her ears.

Anna pushed Davy's brim up a half inch. "You're cute."

"I've thought you were cute since I was seventeen years old."

Anna smiled. She opened the lapel of her robe and looked down at her chest. "Stop fluttering in there," she said to the organ beneath her skin.

"It's true. Stomping around in your Doc Martens like a badass, you've had a tiny studio apartment in my heart for a long time. Rent controlled."

"Then why were you out here while I was in there?"

"I'm just watching the water. It's kind of mesmerizing." Davy pulled the hat lower on her forehead. "I didn't want to wake you. I couldn't sleep."

Anna gripped Davy around the waist and pulled her closer. "After the day we've had? All the travel and excitement and dealing with Winnie, not to mention the physical activity of the previous few hours, and you can't sleep?"

Davy's expression might be described as preoccupied, perhaps a bit pensive. "I am tired, but my mind is racing."

Anna didn't feel the same, and it made her feel a little guilty. By sorting out the Winnie situation, Davy had removed one of the largest obstacles to her peace of mind, and Anna only felt serenity and gratitude—and enormous, encompassing love for Davy. Whatever was bothering Davy, it was now Anna's job to remedy it, and she would do anything to remove the tension from Davy's face.

"You really got my heart racing earlier. And it's picking up speed right now too." She placed her fingertips on Davy's cheek and gave her a short, sweet, soulful kiss. "But we can't have my heart and your brain competing against each other. Tell me why your mind is racing, Day."

"I'm sorry. It's ridiculous. I have everything I could possibly want right here, and still, my stupid brain won't turn off. I want to be in the moment with you, but…" Davy shook her head.

Anna took her hand. "Come back to bed. Let's talk about it." Once they were back under the covers, and Anna was holding Davy securely in her arms, she said, "What's on your mind?"

"The partnership is mine if I want it."

"Davy!"

"I got the call this afternoon while we were at the Sail Away party. The two of them on a conference call wanting my answer so they could announce it at Conant's retirement dinner. I haven't given them one yet."

"Congratulations." Anna took off her cap and pressed a kiss on Davy's temple. "There's no one more deserving."

"Well, Keeley mismanaged a really big client right into the arms of another firm. They couldn't give it to him. I was the last person standing."

Anna pushed the brim of Davy's cap up and tried to look her in the eye. "Don't do that. Don't belittle your achievement."

Davy nodded and took the hat off. When she raised her eyes to Anna's, the conflict residing in them was clear to see.

"You don't seem very happy." Anna smoothed a hand over Davy's mussed hair.

"I had lunch with Joel Kleinman a few days ago. He wants to give ACS a piece of Teltech's litigation business."

"Roland will be so pleased. How did you manage that?"

"It didn't take much. I gave Joel some legal advice a while ago. Now he's giving me the impression that he's lost faith in his current team. If we do well, we could end up with all their business."

"And of course you'll do well. All of this seems like good news."

"It is." Davy's tone was ambivalent. She didn't sound excited.

"But?"

"I like my job. I like sniffing out potential clients and beating out everyone else for them—when I get to do that. And I admit, I like solving the problems of large, usually soulless, companies. I know corporate law isn't the noblest of professions, but I'm good at it."

Anna pressed her lips against Davy's neck. "You are. My corporate warrior."

"But my current workload is unsustainable. We both know that. I'm doing the work of three people. If they want me, there will have to be some changes. I can still produce and add value on a work schedule that allows me a life too."

"You seem to have a large enough supply of bargaining chips to make that happen. So what's the plan?"

Davy shifted so she was practically on top of Anna, her torso nestled between Anna's legs. "The plan is to go in and negotiate for what I want. But that's very far away and I suddenly don't want to think about it anymore."

"Has your mind stopped racing?"

"It's passed the baton to my heart." She parted the edges of the bathrobe Anna still wore and kissed her right between her breasts. "Why did we get back in bed with these stupid robes on?"

"A problem with an easy solution." Anna undid the knots on both their robes and spent five seconds moving fabric around so the only thing that separated them was skin. She thought she could feel Davy's heart beating—strong and sure. She slid her hand over so it rested on Davy's breast, and the reassuring thump filled her with something that felt a lot like joy. "Before this intermission between the acts of our sexy German opera is over, and we leap back into the action, I want you to know that I support you, no matter what. I love you, and I want every corner of your life to be lit up with happiness, even the irritating, time-consuming, worky ones."

Davy slid up her body and kissed her soundly. "You make me happy. Now turn off your phone and unwrap your candies because Act II is starting."

CHAPTER TWENTY-NINE

When their taxi pulled up at 14 Darling Drive, Davy saw Pam's car in the driveway. "Did you know your mom was going to be here?"

Anna looked up. "No. I texted her from the plane but just to say we landed. She doesn't have a key. What's she doing here?"

"She should have a key." Davy heard shrieks coming from the backyard. "And I think I can guess."

They left their bags by the side door and strolled hand-in-hand over the lawn to the trampoline. Pam sat in a patio chair she had dragged over while Tally and Louis romped on the trampoline

"Ma! Davy!" Louis cried. He boinged to the edge and did a little flipping move that had him on the ground in a moment. How did he learn to do that, Davy wondered. To her surprise, he crashed into her legs and hugged her first, then did the same to Anna. "I missed you. You were gone so long."

"I missed you too, Lou. I really did." Anna dropped to her knees and held him for so long he began to squirm.

"I'm going to see Tally's play tonight," he announced.

"I think you're going to like it," Davy said.

He pulled away and ran back to the trampoline. "Ma! Come jump!"

Anna gave her a look and then went to jump. Soon her shrieks were the loudest.

Davy sat on the ground next to Pam's chair. "Busy weekend for you, I'm sure. With Louis to take care of and ferrying Tally back and forth."

"It was fine. Keeps me young. I'm guessing things went well from all the height Anna's getting. Look at that smile on her. You'll have to remind her of that someday when she's not as happy."

Davy watched her, couldn't take her eyes from her.

"And look at the smile on you. It's a little bit goofy if you'll allow me to say so."

"I can admit to a goofy smile." It didn't dim one bit when she tore it away from Anna to look at her mom. "And yeah, things went well. Anna can proceed with the adoption. Should be six months max before it's official."

Pam let her hand drop over the side of her chair and reached out. "You are a blessing, Davy. Anna would never have been able to do this without you. You're a credit to your people."

She took Pam's hand. Her people? She had no people. Certainly not her father.

"He's still your people," Pam said, as if she could hear Davy's thoughts. "And the fact that you have become the generous, compassionate, honorable woman you have with that kind of example—it's extraordinary. You're extraordinary."

Pam gave her hand a little shake, and Davy looked over and saw tears in Pam's eyes.

Davy said, "You're my people. You and Tally and Louis and Anna. And you always will be."

"Aren't we lucky for that?" Pam withdrew her hand, signaling the end of their moment of high emotion. "Now, something you should probably know is that Anna kicks. In her sleep. She has since she was a child. I hope you have a big bed because you'll need a lot of space."

She felt her cheeks get hot. "How the hell did you know…?"

Pam grinned at her. "I'm happy for you both. Someday you and Anna are going to have to tell me the real reason you decided to move in together, but that's a story for another time, isn't it. Why don't you go jump around with them up there? Work out the kinks from sitting on the plane."

Davy joined them on the trampoline and couldn't remember ever feeling so light and free. It didn't take long until all four of them were a giggling dog pile in the middle of the mat.

Pam called to Tally and Louis that it was time to go. "Tally needs a shower before her call time, and Louis and I have to get spiffed up for our closing night theater date, right, Lou?"

"Right, Grammy." Louis gave Davy and Anna a hug and left the trampoline without complaint.

"How were the last two shows, Tal?" Anna asked.

"Good." She scooched over to the ladder. "You're coming tonight, right?" She didn't bother waiting to hear their reply as she hurried to catch up with Pam and Louis. "Hey, Ma, we're striking the set tomorrow. Can Su-Jin sleep over? Then we can just go over together..."

Davy balanced her knees on the wobbly surface and watched the three of them leave the yard. She knew she'd be seeing them soon, but their visit had been so quick. Then she gazed at Anna, who was lying in the middle of the mesh on her back with her hands beneath her head. There were definite benefits to a quick visit, though. She crawled over and lay down next to her. She copied Anna's pose and looked at what she was looking at—a cornflower blue late summer sky with fluffy clouds slowly drifting across their field of vision. "Look." Davy pointed to a cloud. "What do you see?"

"Um, a duck."

"A duck?" Davy couldn't keep the dubiousness from her voice. "How is that a duck? Where's its beak? Where's the duck head?"

"Under the water," Anna's tone suggested Davy was the crazy one. "That's its ass in the air while it dunks for a fish."

Davy tilted her head. "Nope. Don't see it. And you cursed."

"Well, shit. What do you see?"

"It was a trick question. I see a cloud." She grinned. "And that's two marks on the refrigerator for you."

Anna nodded, accepting her fate.

Davy turned on her side and propped her head in her hand, loving the view of that captivating, contented smile of Anna's. "I just realized something. I'm the only one who gets punished for cursing in this house."

"Is hanging out with Louis really a punishment?"

"Of course not, but it's the principle of the thing. You should have to do something for ten minutes every time you curse, just like I do."

"What do you suggest?"

"Why don't you spend that time with me?" She trailed a finger along the soft skin of Anna's inner arm. "I'm sure I can think of something for us to do together."

Anna closed her eyes. The silence stretched between them, and Davy began to feel uneasy. "What? You don't want to spend your cursing penalty time with me?"

"Hang on, I'm not finished doing the math in my head."

"What math?"

"I'm trying to calculate how many swear words I'd have to say to spend the rest of my life with you."

Davy felt her breath leave her. It was exactly the right thing to say. She rolled toward Anna, then threw her leg over her. The trampoline swayed slightly. Davy braced her arms on either side of Anna's head. "That was really good."

Anna's smug grin told her she already knew that. Only one way to erase it from her face. She kissed Anna, long and purposeful and sweet.

Davy settled down so they were lying next to each other again. When she moved her body, she felt the bounce. She wiggled her body again and tested that springiness. Maybe they could—

"We're not having sex on this," Anna said.

"How did you know—"

"How do you think?"

"I bet it would be fun."

"I bet you're right, but what about the neighbors? Maybe on a moonless night sometime…"

"Checking the phases of the moon just got added to my to-do list. Fall's coming. We should do it sooner rather than later." As if it were already chillier, Davy pressed into Anna's body and rested her head on Anna's shoulder. Anna wrapped an arm around her.

"Louis starts school on Thursday," Anna said.

"Damn. Summer went in a blink."

"It always does, doesn't it?"

"Actually, I haven't noticed lately. I let the seasons pass me by, like almost everything else in life that wasn't work."

Anna squeezed her tighter. It made her feel safe.

She shifted so she could look Anna in the eye. "No matter what happens, I'll never go back to the way it was before. Those crazy hours, they're a thing of the past. You have to believe me. I want to be an equal partner in our life together."

"And I was dead serious when I said I want to spend the rest of my life with you. And when we're ready, not right now, but soon, I'll propose to you, with a wedding band, because I know how you feel about diamond engagement rings. And I hope with all my heart you'll say yes."

"I won't keep you in suspense. My answer's going to be yes."

Anna's sigh of relief seemed heavy and real, as if Davy would ever say no to her. She wasn't a fool.

"I'll return the engagement ring. If it makes you unhappy, I don't want it in the house."

"Well…" Anna looked uncertain.

"What?"

"It's so pretty." Now her expression turned sheepish.

Davy sat up. "Do you want to keep it?"

"Maybe? Is it weird that I want it now?"

"No, it makes complete sense. Now that it's real. Now that we're real." She lay back down. "Tell you what. I'll keep it for our real moment. You can ask me however you want, and I'll get a second chance to not fuck everything up in the worst way. This is great. I'm going to make it all perfect."

"You didn't fuck anything up. If it wasn't for your psycho idea, we wouldn't be here right now." Anna reached over and took her hand. "It doesn't have to be perfect. It only has to be us."

They lay there on their giant trampoline for a while, and Davy decided she was a big fan of psycho ideas. She couldn't believe this was her life now.

"Do you mind going to Tally's show again?"

"Not at all. Tally is talented, so it's no hardship. And I never got around to helping out, so it's the least I can do. Anyway, I kind of liked that show."

"Look at you. We'll make a theater-lover out of you yet."

Davy wouldn't admit to that yet, but she could envision a life where she and Anna sat side-by-side and watched amateur theater until they were old and gray. She would sit through endless musicals if it meant her life could stay as excellent as it was right now.

Anna turned on her side, her eyes lively. "You know, we have a few hours before we need to head over there."

Davy looked at Anna. "Oh?"

"Yeah. And there was something I needed to show you in your bedroom."

"Well, what are we waiting for?" She couldn't flail herself off that trampoline fast enough.

❖

Davy rose to her feet at the curtain call and clapped with all her might for Tally—and for everyone standing on the stage with her. It was even better the second time around, such an amazing exploration of what happens after the happily-ever-afters of those classic fairy tales. It really made her think—about Tally, and of course, Anna, but mostly about her father. She was still angry, but in a while she would get in touch and try to work things out. He was her father, after all.

Pam and a sleepy Louis left after Act I, and now she and Anna waited in the lobby for Tally to finish chatting with her friends. Anna—who seemed to know everyone—was pulled into a conversation with some theater-y types. As Davy watched her laugh and talk, she realized there was something missing. She leaned in and whispered in Anna's ear. "Hey, where's your tote bag?"

Anna blinked. "I must have left it under my seat." She made a move.

"No, stay here. I'll get it." Davy was happy to excuse herself from the humid lobby for a moment. She wandered halfway down the left aisle and watched a stagehand roll the ghost light into position before he exited into the wings. The stage was mostly bare now. The scrim at the rear of the stage that depicted greenery and a distant forest had been pulled aside about halfway, exposing the bare back wall. She got a little shock when she saw the graffiti there, inscribed by hundreds of former stage crew and thespians, recording their participation in all the shows this theater had hosted over the years.

Davy was pulled toward it like she had no control over her limbs. In an instant she had climbed the steps. She examined the scrim. Instead of hand-painted canvas like Anna's long-ago creation for *Cats*, this was a silky material and the image appeared to be screen-printed. She flicked the scrim back further to reveal the wall of tribute. It all came rushing back. As sharp in her mind as if it had happened yesterday—the scissor lift, their first, sweet, youthful kiss, and Anna commemorating their summer together on the back wall of this theater.

And there it was. It had been high above all the other scrawled messages fifteen years ago, but now it was surrounded by other more recent scribbles, and it didn't stand out so much. But it was there. *A and Day: Now and Forever.* Emotion rose in her at this testament to their younger selves.

A floorboard creaked downstage. Davy turned and Anna was there, the person she most wanted to see. The person she would always want to see. "I didn't get your bag yet. I got distracted reliving some very old and very precious memories." She gazed upward at Anna's handiwork.

"Memories, huh?"

"Don't you dare start singing."

Anna grinned. "That is some excellently rendered graffiti if I do say so myself." She wrapped her arms around Davy's waist.

Davy pressed herself even closer. She took in a breath and tried to reconcile who she had been that summer with who she was now—and the fact that Anna was still beside her. "Now and forever—could it be prophetic? Did the guy who wrote it somehow know? That you and I would find our way back here, and I would be hoping with everything in my heart that I could have forever with you?"

Davy felt helpless against the urge to kiss her. She grabbed the edge of the scrim and twirled them in a circle, executing the maneuver as if it were the most important dance move of her life. They were wrapped in a loose envelope of fabric that gave them just enough privacy for Davy to angle her head and—

"Anna? Davy? Is that you guys? I know it is. I can see your feet." Tally's voice was loud, perplexed, and still a little distance from the stage, if Davy had it right. And she hoped she had it right. She needed a minute. Twenty seconds at least.

"Her timing is impeccable." Anna rested her forehead on Davy's shoulder.

Davy elbowed the scrim away from them. "I guess now's a good a time as any to tell her. I hope she's okay with it." She took Anna's hand and they descended from the stage and met Tally in the aisle.

"You two were sucking face." Instead of bothered, Tally appeared downright gleeful. Her garish stage makeup made her face look surreal.

"Incorrect," Davy said. "We were *about* to suck face."

Anna pulled Tally into one of the rows and sat her down. Davy went into the row below and leaned on a seat back.

"This must be a surprise for you," Anna said to Tally. "And a little strange, that your sisters are embarking on a romantic relationship."

Tally said, "Is this where I'm supposed to ask what are your intentions toward my sister—*to both of you*? Haw haw." Her guffaw made it seem like she thought it was the funniest thing in the world.

"How do you even know about that? It's so old-fashioned." Davy was bewildered.

"TikTok." Tally said it like it should have been obvious.

"You're making light of it. But are you okay?" Anna remained dogged.

"Why shouldn't I be? I love you both. Makes sense that you should love each other. Wait. It's love right? You're not just hooking up?"

"You're fourteen. How do you even know about that? Please tell me you're not hooking up." The disapproval in Anna's voice was so thick it could've frosted a cake.

Tally's neck recoiled. "I'm not six. And I don't have to be doing it to know about it."

Anna wagged a finger at Tally. "I want you to come talk to me if you're even thinking about—"

Tally rolled her eyes. "Oh my God, Anna, I already know—"

Davy interrupted her. "To answer your question, no, we are not just hooking up. I love Anna. I love you. I love Louis and your mom. This is a forever-type situation." She gazed at Anna, proud that she was able to say that.

"Ooh, Hallmark Channel, look out. She said forever, Anna. You two are in looooove!" It was nice to see Tally was not yet the adult she pretended to be, and that she could, in fact, still behave as if she were six silly years old.

"Okay!" Anna turned to Davy. "Shall we go home? Tally, you're going home too. To your home. We'll drop you off."

Tally skipped ahead of them up the aisle, a bouquet from Pam held out in front of her like a drum major's baton. "Uh-huh. Okay. Just want to get me out of the way so you can make with the smoochies." Then she came back and linked her arms with both of them, and her flowers whapped Davy in the stomach. "Hey, can we move my bed into your room, Anna? Cuz you're obviously going to move into Davy's room right? And your room's bigger. So can we, please?"

"Look at this crazy girl." Anna gestured to Tally. "You sure you don't want to take it back? This family is crazy."

Davy grinned at her over Tally's head. "Not a chance. And I think my type of crazy is going to fit right in with yours."

And as the three of them walked out into the late summer night, Davy knew she had finally found her family.

About the Author

Want a little more of Davy and Anna's story?
Go to Nan's website for a free epilogue to *The No Kiss Contract*!
http://www.nancampbellwrites.com

Nan Campbell grew up on the Jersey Shore, where she first discovered her love of romance novels as a kid, spending her summers at the beach reading stories that were wholly inappropriate for her age. She was, and continues to be, a sucker for a happy ending.

She is a seasoned traveler, having visited many countries across six continents, and hopes to make it to the seventh someday. She hates to cook but loves to practice her cocktail-making skills. She also loves karaoke, which is unfortunate for anyone within range of her singing voice.

Nan and her wife live in New York City, where they struggle to balance their natural homebody tendencies with all the amazing things the city has to offer.

Books Available from Bold Strokes Books

Curse of the Gorgon by Tanai Walker. Cass will do anything to ensure Elle's safety, but is she willing to embrace the curse of the Gorgon? (978-1-63679-395-5)

Dance with Me by Georgia Beers. Scottie Templeton mixes it up on and off the dance floor with sexy salsa instructor Marisa Reyes. But can Scottie get past Marisa's connection to her ex? (978-1-63679-359-7)

Gin and Bear It by Joy Argento. Opposites really can attract, and as Kelly and Logan work together to create a loving home for rescue cat Bear, they just might find one for themselves as well. (978-1-63679-351-1)

Harvest Dreams by Jacqueline Fein-Zachary. Planting the vineyard of their dreams, Kate Bauer and Sydney Barrett must resist their attraction while battling nature and their families, who oppose both the venture and their relationship. (978-1-63679-380-1)

Outside the Lines by Melissa Sky. If you had the chance to live forever, would you take it? Amara Rodriguez did and it sets her on a journey to find her missing mother and unravel the mystery of her own heart. (978-1-63679-403-7)

The No Kiss Contract by Nan Campbell. Workaholic Davy believes she can get the top spot at her firm if the senior partners think she's settling down and about to start a family, but she needs the delightful yet dubious Anna's help by pretending to be her fiancée. (978-1-63679-372-6)

The Value of Sylver and Gold by Michelle Larkin. When word gets out that former Boston homicide detective Reid Sylver can talk to the dead, the FBI solicits her help on a serial murder case, prompting Reid to assemble forces once again with Detective London Gold. (978-1-63679-093-0)

When It Feels Right by Tagan Shepard. Freshly out of the closet Marlene hasn't been lucky in love, but when it comes to her quirky new roommate Abby, everything just feels right. (978-1-63679-367-2)

Lucky in Lace by Melissa Brayden. Straitlaced stationery store owner Juliette Jennings's predictable life unravels when a sexy lingerie shop and its alluring owner move in next door. (978-1-63679-434-1)

Made for Her by Carsen Taite. Neal Walsh is a newly made member of the Mancuso crime family, but will her undeniable attraction to Anastasia Petrov, the wife of her boss's sworn enemy, be the ultimate test of her loyalty? (978-1-63679-265-1)

Off the Menu by Alaina Erdell. Reality TV sensation *Restaurant Redo* and its gorgeous host Erin Rasmussen will arrive to film in chef Taylor Mobley's kitchen. As the cameras roll, will they make the jump from enemies to lovers? (978-1-63679-295-8)

Pack of Her Own by Elena Abbott. When things heat up in a small town, steamy secrets are revealed between Alpha werewolf Wren Carne and her human mate, Natalie Donovan. (978-1-63679-370-2)

Return to McCall by Patricia Evans. Lily isn't looking for romance—not until she meets Alex, the gorgeous Cuban dance instructor at La Haven, a newly opened lesbian retreat. (978-1-63679-386-3)

So It Went Like This by C. Spencer. A candid and deeply personal exploration of fate, chosen family, and the vulnerability intrinsic in life's uncertainties. (978-1-63555-971-2)

Stolen Kiss by Spencer Greene. Anna and Louise share a stolen kiss, only to discover that Louise is dating Anna's brother. Surely, one kiss can't change everything…Can it? (978-1-63679-364-1)

The Fall Line by Kelly Wacker. When Jordan Burroughs arrives in the Deep South to paint a local endangered aquatic flower, she doesn't expect to become friends with a mischievous gin-drinking ghost who complicates her budding romance and leads her to an awful discovery and danger. (978-1-63679-205-7)

To Meet Again by Kadyan. When the stark reality of WW II separates cabaret singer Evelyn and Australian doctor Joan in Singapore, they must overcome all odds to find one another again. (978-1-63679-398-6)

Before She Was Mine by Emma L McGeown. When Dani and Lucy are thrust together to sort out their children's playground squabble, sparks fly leaving both of them willing to risk it all for each other. 978-1-63679-315-3)

Chasing Cypress by Ana Hartnett Reichardt. Maggie Hyde wants to find a partner to settle down with and help her run the family farm, but instead she ends up chasing Cypress. Olivia Cypress. 978-1-63679-323-8)

Dark Truths by Sandra Barret. When Jade's ex-girlfriend and vampire maker barges back into her life, can Jade satisfy her ex's demands, keep Beth safe, and keep everyone's secrets…secret? 978-1-63679-369-6)

Desires Unleashed by Renee Roman. Kell Murphy and Taylor Simpson didn't go looking for love, but as they explore their desires unleashed, their hearts lead them on an unexpected journey. 978-1-63679-327-6)

Maybe, Probably by Amanda Radley. Set against the backdrop of a viral pandemic, Gina and Eleanor are about to discover that loving another person is complicated when you're desperately searching for yourself. 978-1-63679-284-2)

The One by C.A. Popovich. Jody Acosta doesn't know what makes her more furious, that the wealthy Bergeron family refuses to be held accountable for her father's wrongful death, or that she can't ignore her knee-weakening attraction to Nicole Bergeron. 978-1-63679-318-4)

The Speed of Slow Changes by Sander Santiago. As Al and Lucas navigate the ups and downs of their polyamorous relationship, only one thing is certain: romance has never been so crowded. 978-1-63679-329-0)

Tides of Love by Kimberly Cooper Griffin. Falling in love is the last thing on either of their minds, but when Mikayla and Gem meet, sparks of possibility begin to shine, revealing a future neither expected. 978-1-63679-319-1)

Catch by Kris Bryant. Convincing the wife of the star quarterback to walk away from her family was never in offensive coordinator Sutton McCoy's game plan. But standing on the sidelines when a second chance at true love comes her way proves all but impossible. (978-1-63679-276-7)

Hearts in the Wind by MJ Williamz. Beth and Evelyn seem destined to remain mortal enemies but are about to discover that in matters of the heart, sometimes you must cast your fortunes to the wind. (978-1-63679-288-0)

Hero Complex by Jesse J. Thoma. Bronte, Athena, and their unlikely friends must work together to defeat Bronte's arch nemesis. The fate of love, humanity, and the world might depend on it. No pressure. (978-1-63679-280-4)

Hotel Fantasy by Piper Jordan. Molly Taylor has a fantasy in mind that only Lexi can fulfill. However, convincing her to participate could prove challenging. (978-1-63679-207-1)

Last New Beginning by Krystina Rivers. Can commercial broker Skye Kohl and contractor Bailey Kaczmarek overcome their pride and work together while the tension between them boils over into a love that could soothe both of their hearts? (978-1-63679-261-3)

Love and Lattes by Karis Walsh. Cat café owner Bonnie and wedding planner Taryn join forces to get rescue cats into forever homes—discovering their own forever along the way. (978-1-63679-290-3)

Repatriate by Jaime Maddox. Ally Hamilton's new job as a home health aide takes an unexpected twist when she discovers a fortune in stolen artwork and must repatriate the masterpieces and avoid the wrath of the violent man who stole them. (978-1-63679-303-0)

The Hues of Me and You by Morgan Lee Miller. Arlette Adair and Brooke Dawson almost fell in love in college. Years later, they unexpectedly run into each other and come face-to-face with their unresolved past. (978-1-63679-229-3)

A Haven for the Wanderer by Jenny Frame. When Griffin Harris comes to Rosebrook village, the love she finds with Bronte de Lacey creates a safe haven and she finally finds her place in the world. But will she run again when their love is tested? (978-1-63679-291-0)

A Spark in the Air by Dena Blake. Internet executive Crystal Tucker is sure Wi-Fi could really help small-town residents, even if it means putting an internet café out of business, but her instant attraction to the owner's daughter, Janie Elliott, makes moving ahead with her plans complicated. (978-1-63679-293-4)

Between Takes by CJ Birch. Simone Lavoie is convinced her new job as an intimacy coordinator will give her a fresh perspective. Instead, problems on set and her growing attraction to actress Evelyn Harper only add to her worries. (978-1-63679-309-2)

Camp Lost and Found by Georgia Beers. Nobody knows better than Cassidy and Frankie that life doesn't always give you what you want. But sometimes, if you're lucky, life gives you exactly what you need. (978-1-63679-263-7)

Felix Navidad by 'Nathan Burgoine. After the wedding of a good friend, instead of Felix's Hawaii Christmas treat to himself, ice rain strands him in Ontario with fellow wedding-guest—and handsome ex of said friend—Kevin in a small cabin for the holiday Felix definitely didn't plan on. (978-1-63679-411-2)

Fire, Water, and Rock by Alaina Erdell. As Jess and Clare reveal more about themselves, and their hot summer fling tips over into true love, they must confront their pasts before they can contemplate a future together. (978-1-63679-274-3)

Lines of Love by Brey Willows. When even the Muse of Love doesn't believe in forever, we're all in trouble. (978-1-63555-458-8)

Manny Porter and The Yuletide Murder by D.C. Robeline. Manny only has the holiday season to discover who killed prominent research scientist Phillip Nikolaidis before the judicial system condemns an innocent man to lethal injection. (978-1-63679-313-9)

Only This Summer by Radclyffe. A fling with Lily promises to be exactly what Chase is looking for—short-term, hot as a forest fire, and one Chase can extinguish whenever she wants. After all, it's only one summer. (978-1-63679-390-0)

Picture-Perfect Christmas by Charlotte Greene. Two former rivals compete to capture the essence of their small mountain town at Christmas, all the while fighting old and new feelings. (978-1-63679-311-5)

Playing Love's Refrain by Lesley Davis. Drew Dawes had shied away from the world of music until Wren Banderas gave her a reason to play their love's refrain. (978-1-63679-286-6)

Profile by Jackie D. The scales of justice are weighted against FBI agents Cassidy Wolf and Alex Derby. Loyalty and love may be the only advantage they have. (978-1-63679-282-8)